EVERYONE IN MY FAMILY HAS KILLED SOMEONE

ALSO BY BENJAMIN STEVENSON

Greenlight
Either Side of Midnight
Find Us

EVERYONE IN MY FAMILY HAS KILLED SOMEONE

BENJAMIN STEVENSON

MARINER BOOKS
New York Boston

HarperCollins books may be purchased for educational, business, or sales promotional use. For information, please email the Special Markets Department at SPsales@harpercollins.com.

Originally published in Australia in 2022 by Michael Joseph, an imprint of Penguin Random House Australia.

FIRST US EDITION 2023

Library of Congress Cataloging-in-Publication Data has been applied for.

ISBN 978-0-06-327902-5
ISBN 978-0-06-330772-8 (international edition)

22 23 24 25 26 LBC 5 4 3 2 1

Aleesha Paz.
At last this one's yours.
Though they always have been, and always will be.

Do you promise that your detectives shall well and truly detect the crimes presented to them using those wits which it may please you to bestow upon them and not placing reliance on nor making use of Divine Revelation, Feminine Intuition, Mumbo Jumbo, Jiggery-Pokery, Coincidence, or Act of God?

—*Membership oath of the Detection Club, 1930, a secret society of mystery writers including Agatha Christie, G. K. Chesterton, Ronald Knox, and Dorothy L. Sayers*

Fold here

1. The criminal must be someone mentioned in the early part of the story, but must not be anyone whose thoughts the reader has been allowed to follow.
2. All supernatural or preternatural agencies are ruled out as a matter of course.
3. Not more than one secret room or passage is allowable.
4. No hitherto undiscovered poisons may be used, nor any appliance which will need a long scientific explanation at the end.
5. *Author's note: Culturally outdated historical wording redacted.*
6. No accident must ever help the detective, nor must he ever have an unaccountable intuition which proves to be right.
7. The detective must not himself commit the crime.
8. The detective must not light on any clues which are not instantly produced for the inspection of the reader.
9. The stupid friend of the detective, the Watson, must not conceal any thoughts which pass through his mind; his intelligence must be slightly, but very slightly, below that of the average reader.
10. Twin brothers, and doubles generally, must not appear unless we have been duly prepared for them.

—*Ronald Knox's "10 Commandments of Detective Fiction," 1929*

EVERYONE IN MY FAMILY HAS KILLED SOMEONE

PROLOGUE

Everyone in my family has killed someone. Some of us, the high achievers, have killed more than once.

I'm not trying to be dramatic, but it is the truth, and when I was faced with writing this down, difficult as it is with one hand, I realized that telling the truth was the only way to do it. It sounds obvious, but modern mystery novels forget that sometimes. They've become more about the tricks the author can deploy: what's up their sleeve instead of what's in their hand. Honesty is what sets apart what we call "Golden Age" mysteries: the Christies, the Chestertons. I know this because I write books about how to write books. There are rules, is the thing. A bloke named Ronald Knox was part of the gang and wrote down a set once, though he called them his "commandments." They're in the first part of this book in the epigraph that everyone always skips but, trust me, it's worth going back to. Actually, you should dog-ear it. I won't bore you with the details here but it boils down to this: the Golden Rule of the Golden Age is *play fair.*

Of course, this isn't a novel. All of this happened to me. But I do, after all, wind up with a murder to solve. Several, actually. Though I'm getting ahead of myself.

The point is, I read a lot of crime novels. And I know most of these types of books have what's known as an "unreliable narrator" these days, where the person telling you the story is, in fact, lying most of the time. I also know that in recounting these events I may be typecast similarly. So I'll strive to do the opposite. Call me a *reliable* narrator. Everything I tell you will be the truth, or, at least, the truth as I knew it to be at the time that I thought I knew it. Hold me to that.

This is all in keeping with Knox's commandments 8 and 9, for I am both Watson *and* Detective in this book, where I play both writer and sleuth, and so am obligated to both light upon clues *and* not conceal my thoughts. In short: play fair.

Actually, I'll prove it. If you're just here for the gory details, deaths in this book either happen or are reported to have happened on page 14, page 46, page 65, a twofer on page 75, and a hat trick on page 81. Then there's a bit of a stretch but it picks up again on page 174, page 208(ish), page 218, page 227, page 249, somewhere between page 243 and page 250 (it's hard to tell), page 262, and page 355. I promise that's the truth, unless the typesetter mucks with the pages. There is only one plot hole you could drive a truck through. I tend to spoil things. There are no sex scenes.

What else?

My name would be useful, I suppose. I'm Ernest Cunningham. It's a bit old-fashioned, so people call me Ern or Ernie. I should have started with that, but I promised to be reliable, not competent.

Considering what I've told you, it is tricky to know where to start. When I say "everyone," let's draw the line for that statement at my branch of the family tree. Although my cousin Amy did bring a prohibited peanut-butter sandwich to a corporate picnic once and her HR rep almost carked it, but I won't put her on the bingo card.

Look, we're not a family of psychopaths. Some of us are good, others are bad, and some just unfortunate. Which one am I?

I haven't figured that out yet. Of course, there's also the little matter of a serial killer known as the Black Tongue who gets mixed up in all this, and $267,000 in cash, but we'll get to that. I know you're probably wondering something else right now. I did say "everyone." And I promised no tricks.

Have I killed someone? Yes. I have.

Who was it?

Let's get started.

MY BROTHER

CHAPTER 1

A single beam of light rotating through the curtains told me my brother had just pulled into my driveway. When I walked outside, the first thing I noticed was that Michael's left headlight was out. The second was the blood.

The moon had gone, the sun yet to rise, but even in the dark I knew exactly what the dark spots were, flecked on the shattered headlight and smeared alongside a hefty dent in the wheel arch.

I'm not normally a night owl, but Michael had called me half an hour before. It was one of those phone calls that, as you blearily read the time, you know is not to tell you about winning the lottery. I have a few friends who occasionally call me from their Uber home with a roaring tale of a good night out. Michael is not one of them.

That's a lie, actually. I wouldn't be friends with people who called after midnight.

"I need to see you. Now."

He was breathing heavily. No call ID, from a pay phone. Or a bar. I spent the next half hour shivering, even in a heavy jacket, wiping circles in the condensation on my front window to better see his approach. I'd given up sentry duty and retired to the couch when his headlight flicked the back of my eyelids red.

I heard a growl as he brought the car to a stop, then killed the engine but not the electrics. I opened my eyes, savored the ceiling for a moment, as if I knew that once I stood up my life would change, and went outside. Michael was sitting in the car, head on the wheel. I cut the lonely spotlight in half as I walked in front of the bonnet to knock on the driver's window. Michael got out of the car. His face was ash gray.

"You're lucky," I said, nodding to his busted headlight. "Roos'll mess you up."

"I hit someone."

"Uh-huh." I was half asleep, so only barely registered he'd said some*one* and not some*thing*. I didn't know what people said in these situations, so I thought agreeing with him was probably a good idea.

"A guy. I hit him. He's in the back."

I was awake now. *In the back?*

"What the hell do you mean *in the back*?" I said.

"He's dead."

"Is he in the back seat or the boot?"

"Why's it matter?"

"Have you been drinking?"

"Not much." He hesitated. "Maybe. A bit."

"Back seat?" I took a step and reached out for the door, but Michael put an arm out. I stopped moving, said, "We need to take him to the hospital."

"He's dead."

"I can't believe we're arguing about this." I ran a hand through my hair. "Michael, come on. You're sure?"

"No hospital. His neck turned like a pipe. Half his skull is inside out."

"I'd rather hear it from a doctor. We can call Sof—"

"Lucy will know," Michael cut me off. His mention of her name, said so desperately, made the subtext clear: *Lucy will leave me*.

"It'll be all right."

"I've been drinking."

"Just a bit," I reminded him.

"Yeah." The pause lingered. "Just a bit."

"I'm sure the police will under—" I started, but we both knew the name Cunningham said aloud in a police station practically shook the walls with the spirits it summoned. The last time either of us had been in a room full of cops was at the funeral, among a sea of blue uniforms. I'd been tall enough to coil myself around my mother's forearm, but young enough to stay glued there all day. I briefly imagined what Audrey would think of us now, huddled in the freezing morning arguing over someone's life, but pushed the thought away.

"He's not dead because I hit him. Someone shot him, *then* I hit him."

"Uh-huh." I tried to sound like I believed him, but there's a reason my dramatic résumé consisted mostly of nonspeaking roles in school plays: farm animals; murder victims; shrubbery. I went for the door handle again, but Michael kept it blocked.

"I just grabbed him. I thought—I don't know, it was better than leaving him in the street. And then I couldn't think what to do next, and I wound up here."

I didn't say anything, just nodded. Family is gravity.

Michael rubbed his hands across his mouth and spoke through them. The steering wheel had left a small red dent on his forehead. "It's not going to matter where we take him," he said at last.

"Okay."

"We should bury him."

"Okay."

"Stop saying that."

"All right."

"I meant stop agreeing with me."

"We should take him to the hospital then."

"Are you on my side or not?" Michael glanced towards the back seat, got back in the car, and turned the engine on. "I'll fix things. Get in."

I already knew I'd get in the car. I don't really know why. Part of me figured that if I was in the car I could talk some sense into him, I guess. But all I really knew was that my older brother was standing in front of me, telling me it would all be all right, and it doesn't matter how old you get—five or thirty-five—if your older brother tells you he's going to fix things, you believe him. Gravity.

Just quickly: I'm actually thirty-eight in this bit, forty-one when we catch up to the present day, but I thought if I shaved a couple of years off it might help my publisher pitch this to a big-name actor.

I got in. There was a Nike sports bag, unzipped, in the footwell of the passenger seat. It was stuffed with cash, not tied together with neat little elastic bands or paper belts like in the movies, but jumbled up, vomiting onto the floor. It felt strange to simply rest my feet on it, because there was so much of it and, assumedly, the man in the back seat had died for it. I didn't look in the rearview mirror. Okay, I shot a few glances, but I only saw a black lump of a shadow that looked more like a hole in the world than an actual body, and I wussed out every time it threatened to come into focus.

Michael backed out of the drive. A shot glass or something rattled across the dash, fell, and rolled under the seat. There was a faint waft of whiskey. For once, I was glad my brother was into hotboxing, because the weed smoke lingering in the upholstery masked the smell of death. The boot clanged, latch broken, as we bounced over the curb.

A horrible thought shot through me. He had a shattered headlight *and* a busted trunk: like he'd hit something twice.

"Where are we going?" I asked.

"Huh?"

"Do you know where you're going?"

"Oh. The national park. Forest." Michael looked across at me, but couldn't hold my gaze, so he threw a furtive look to the back seat, apparently regretted it, and settled on staring forwards. He'd started to shake. "I don't really know. I've never buried a body before."

We'd driven for over two hours by the time Michael decided he'd taken enough dirt roads and pulled his rumbling cyclops of a car into a clearing. We'd hopped off a fire trail a few kilometers back and wound our way off road since. The sun was threatening to rise. The ground was covered in glittering, soft snow.

"Here'll do," said Michael. "You okay?"

I nodded. Or at least I thought I did. I mustn't have moved at all, because Michael snapped his fingers in front of my face, forcing me to focus. I summoned the weakest nod in human history, as if my vertebrae were rusted shackles. It was enough for Michael.

"Don't get out," he said.

I stared straight ahead. I heard him open the back passenger door and shuffle around, dragging the man—a hole in the world—out of the car. My brain was screaming at me to do something, but my body was a traitor. I couldn't move.

After a few minutes Michael came back, sweating, dirt on his forehead, and leaned in over the steering wheel. "Come help me dig."

My limbs unlocked at his bidding. I expected the ground to be cold, to hear the crunch of morning ice, but my foot instead went straight through the white cover, up to my ankle. I looked closely. The ground wasn't snow coated, it was blanketed in spiderwebs. The webs were strung between high stiff grass, maybe a foot off the ground, crossing over each other in such a thickness and with such a pure white, it looked solid. What I had thought was glittering ice was the twinkle of fine threads in the light. Michael's footsteps had punched through the net like holes in powder. The webs covered the entire clearing. It was majestic, serene. I tried to ignore the lumpy shape in the middle of the webbed clearing, where Michael's footprints ended. I followed Michael, and it was like wading through a levitating fog. He led me away from the body, presumably so I wouldn't have a breakdown.

Michael had a small trowel but he made me use my hands. I don't know why I agreed to dig. The whole drive, I'd thought that Michael's fear, that small dose of shakes he'd shown when we'd left, would settle in. There was supposed to be a moment when he would realize what he was up to his neck in and turn the car around. But instead he went the other way. Driving out of the city, into the dawn, he'd become calmer, stoic.

Michael had laid an old towel over most of the body, but I could see a white elbow, sticking out like a fallen branch above the webs.

"Don't look," Michael would say whenever I glanced over.

We kept going for another fifteen minutes in silence until I stopped.

"Keep digging," Michael said.

"He's moving."

"What?"

"*He's moving!* Look. Wait."

Sure enough, the webbed surface was twitching. More significant than wind through the clearing. The impression had changed from solid snow to a rippling white ocean. I could almost feel it through the threads, like I was the spider that spun it, the central nerve.

Michael stopped digging and looked up. "Go back to the car."

"No."

Michael walked over and peeled off the towel. I followed, and saw the body in full for the first time. There was a dark glistening stain above one hip. *Someone shot him, then I hit him*, Michael had said. I wasn't sure; I'd only seen gunshots in the movies. The man's neck had a lump in it as if he'd swallowed a golf ball. He was wearing a black balaclava, but it wasn't quite the right shape. The fabric was bulbous in the wrong places. When I was a kid, a bully at my school used to put two cricket balls in a sock and swing it at me. That's what the balaclava looked like. I got the feeling the fabric was the only thing holding his head together. It had three holes, two for the eyes, which were closed, and one for the mouth. There were small red bubbles pooled on his lips, pulsing. The froth of bubbles was growing, spilling onto his chin. I couldn't see any of his features, but I could tell from his mottled, sun-damaged arms and the engorged veins across the backs of his hands that he was at least twenty years older than Michael.

I knelt, interlocked my hands, and gave a couple of rudimentary compressions. The man's chest caved in a way I knew it shouldn't, right down the sternum, and for a moment all I could think of was that his chest was like the bag of money, unzipped down the middle.

"You're hurting him," Michael said, putting his hand under my arm and pulling me up, before guiding me away.

"We have to take him to the hospital." I made one last, pleading stand.

"He won't make it."

"He might."

"He won't."

"We have to try."

"I can't go to the hospital."

"Lucy will understand."

"No."

"You must have sobered up by now."

"Maybe."

"You didn't kill him—you said he was shot. Is the money his?"

Michael grunted.

"He clearly stole it. This makes sense. You'll be okay."

"It's two hundred and sixty grand."

Reader, you and I already know it's actually two hundred and sixty-seven grand, but it still struck me that while he hadn't had time to call an ambulance, he'd had time to roughly count the cash. Otherwise he'd have said two-fifty, a round figure, if he was guessing. He'd also said it like an appeal. I couldn't tell from his tone if he was offering me any, or if he was just stating a fact that he thought was important to the decision.

"Listen, Ern, it's our money . . ." he started to beg. So he *was* offering.

"We can't just leave him here like this." And then as firmly as I'd ever spoken to him in my life, "I won't."

Michael thought for a minute. Nodded. "I'll go check on him," he said.

He walked over and crouched by the body. He was there a couple of minutes. I was glad I'd come; I still believe it was a good thing to do. An older brother doesn't listen too easily to his younger brother, but he'd needed me here. And I'd made it okay. The man had been alive the whole time, and we'd get him to the hospital. I couldn't see much, Michael being tall, but I could see his squatted back and his arms, stretched out towards the man's head because he knew to cradle the neck in case of a spinal injury. Michael's thin shoulders moved up and down. CPR, kick-starting the man like a lawnmower. I could see the man's legs. I noticed one of his shoes was missing. Michael had been there a long time now. Something was wrong. We're on page 14.

Michael stood and walked back over to me. "We can bury him now."

That wasn't what he was supposed to say. No. No. That was all wrong. I stumbled back and thumped onto my arse. Sticky threads snaked my arms. "What happened?"

"He just stopped breathing."

"He just stopped breathing?"

"He just stopped."

"He's dead?"

"Yes."

"You're sure?"

"Yes."

"How?"

"He just stopped breathing. Go wait in the car."

MY STEPSISTER

CHAPTER 2

We'll get to my story, I have to tell you about some others first, but I wish *I'd* killed whoever decided our family reunion should be at a ski resort.

I am normally resolute in declining any invitation that comes with an Excel spreadsheet attached. But overpreparation is a specialty of my aunt Katherine's, and the email invite for the Cunningham/Garcia Family Reunion, complete with animated pixel snowflake, listed attendance as mandatory. I'm well known in family circles for being ready with an excuse—not that people have really minded my absence for the last three years—be it a sick animal, a busted car, or a time-sensitive manuscript.

Katherine was taking no chances this time. The invitation promised a fun and secluded weekend where all of us could catch up. She'd bolded the words "all of us," as well as the word "mandatory." Evasive as I am, even I can't argue with bold type. And while "all of us" didn't mean me specifically, I knew who it did mean, and that meant I was going. Besides, in between filling out the spreadsheet with my allergies, shoe size, how I like my steak cooked, and my car license plate, I'd allowed myself the fantasy of a snowcapped village and a weekend filled with crackling fires and log cabins.

Instead, I had cold knees and was an hour late for lunch.

I hadn't realized the road would be unplowed. It was a clear day with a weak sun breaking up the pack snow just enough to slide the tires of my Honda Civic around, so I'd had to double back and rent chains for an exorbitant price at the bottom of the mountain, and then kneel in muddy slush on the shoulder to wrestle them on, snot forming stalactites out of my nose. I'd still be there if a woman with a snorkel on her Land Rover hadn't pulled over and given me a mildly judgmental hand. Moving again, I watched the clock creep forward as I alternated between heating the car and using the air-conditioning to defog the windows, but, with the chains on, I couldn't go above forty. I knew exactly how late I was—thanks to the Excel schedule Katherine had emailed around.

At last I saw the turn, a pyramid of loose rocks with a sign for SKY LODGE MOUNTAIN RETREAT! pointing to my right. I imagined the sign had a comma, so it instead read, SKY LODGE MOUNTAIN, RETREAT!, which I thought was good advice ahead of a Cunningham get-together. I had no one in the car to tell my joke to, but it's the type of thing Erin would have found funny once, so she laughed in my head and I took credit for it anyway. I'm aware that it's cute that our names, Ernie and Erin, are practically anagrams. When people used to ask us how we met, we'd say, "Alphabetically." I know, it's sickening.

The truth is much more mundane; we'd bonded over being brought up in single-parent households. When we met, she told me her mother had died of cancer when she was young, and she was raised by her father. I'll tell you about my father later. But she already knew about him when we met; infamy is easy to google.

At the turnoff was a squat building that looked like a pub, based on the sign that just said BEER! in housepaint. There were stacks of skis leaning against the wall. It was the type of place where you could lick the windows instead of buying a drink and the sous chef was a microwave. I filed it away as a potential refuge. The weekend was a family reunion, after all; I expected it to be a series of meals scheduled around tactical retreats to private rooms. It would pay to have other options.

Oh. Erin's not dead, by the way. I realize in making an oblique reference to an old flame, it sounds like I'll reveal later on that she's been dead the whole time, because that's what happens in *these* kinds of books, but that's not the case. She was driving up the next day. We were even still technically married. Besides, the page numbers don't line up.

Not long after the turn I realized I was no longer climbing, but going downhill, and soon I broke through the trees to find myself on the ridge of a spectacular valley, at the base of which lay Sky Lodge. Advertised as the highest drive-in accommodation in Australia, which, to be fair, is like bragging about being the world's tallest jockey, it included a nine-hole golf course carved into the mountainside, a lake, brimming with trout, to fish from or row across, whatever "fireside comfort and rejuvenation" meant, access to the neighboring ski resort (lift pass not included with stay, of course), and even a private helipad. I'm quoting from the brochure, because it had snowed heavily overnight and everything, from the road in front of me, to the now par-400 golf course, to the flattened-out tundra a couple of hundred meters downhill from the guesthouse that I assumed was the lake, lay under the same fresh powder. The valley looked flat, steep, small, and endless at the same time.

I gently rolled down the hill, taking it easy. Pure white has a habit of messing with depth perception, and without the small collection of half-buried buildings at the bottom for reference I might not have even noticed the steepness of the incline until braking would have been futile, locking me into a rapid skid to the bottom: where I would have wound up both very dead and very on time for lunch.

The center of the retreat was a multistory guesthouse, painted bright yellow to stand out from the mountain, with a pillared entryway. It puffed smoke from a brick chimney that braced a side wall like a rod, and it had an advertiser's dream amount of snow dappled on the roof. Within the five rows of windows, several glowed with soft yellow light, like an advent calendar. The guesthouse was preceded by a gauntlet of a dozen chalets, built in two rows of six, with corrugated iron roofs that reached all the way to the ground, matching the slope of the mountain, allowing floor-to-ceiling windows on the front face, for unimpeded views of the rocky peak. I would be staying in one of these shark's teeth, but I wasn't sure which one was number 6, my designation on Katherine's itinerary, so I rolled through to where several cars were parked to the side of the guesthouse.

I recognized a few of them: my stepfather's Mercedes SUV, which had a dishonest BABY ON BOARD sign in the back window, because he thought cops pulled him over less frequently with it; Aunt Katherine's Volvo station wagon, snow-bogged already because she'd driven up a day earlier; Lucy's [REDACTED CAR TYPE], blending in with the snow, the car so often Instagrammed and gloated about as her "business reward." My rescuer's Land Rover was also there—of course it was; in a book like this it may as well have had the license plate "M33T-QT." I recognized it by the large plastic snorkel.

Katherine was steaming across the lot before I'd gotten out of the car, leaning into a slight limp caused by a car accident in her midtwenties. She was the dictionary definition of Baby Sister to my father, the age gap so significant that when my mother pumped out us Cunningham Boys in her thirties, I was closer in age to my aunt than my mother was to her sister-in-law. So, growing up, I remember Katherine as youthful, energetic, and fun. She'd bring us presents and regale us with fantastic stories. I thought she was popular, too, because people would talk about her at family barbecues when she wasn't there. But age gives perspective, and now I know the difference between being popular and being talked about. Intervention came in the form of a wet road and a bus stop. The accident broke a lot of her bones and crumpled her leg, but it also straightened her out. Now, the only thing you really need to know about Katherine is that her two favorite sentences are "What time do you call this?" and "re: my previous email."

She wore a bright-blue thermal top under a puffy North Face vest, some type of rustling waterproof pants, and hiking boots that looked stiff as stale bread. All pristine and straight off the rack. She looked like she'd walked into an adventure store, pointed at a mannequin, and said, "That one." Her husband, Andrew Millot (but we all call him Andy), who had followed her out but kept his distance, was woefully underdressed in jeans and a leather jacket, looking as if he'd spent his time in the same adventure store checking his watch. Without grabbing my bags or my coat, deciding that it was better to be lashed by cold air than Katherine's tongue, I hurried to intercept her.

"We've eaten," was all she said, which I think was supposed to be both criticism and punishment.

"Katherine, I'm sorry. I had trouble on the mountain past Jindabyne. Fresh snow." I pointed back at the chains on my tires. "Luckily someone helped me put these on."

"You didn't check the forecast before you left?" She sounded incredulous that anyone would commit such treason to punctuality as to not account for the weather.

I admitted that I hadn't.

"You should have factored that in."

I admitted that I should have.

She ground her jaw. I knew Katherine well enough to know that she just wanted to have her say, so I stayed silent. "All right then," she said eventually, then leaned in and planted an icy kiss on my cheek. I have never known how to reciprocate a cheek-to-cheek greeting, but I decided to take her advice and factor in the weather—her stormy demeanor—and settled on a *mwah* sound in the air beside her face. She pressed a set of keys into my hand and said, "Our room wasn't ready yesterday so you're in Four now. Everyone's in the dining room. Good to see you."

She took off back towards the guesthouse before I could make small talk, but Andy waited and walked with me, offering me a casual shoulder lean of *hello* rather than taking his hands from his pockets to shake my hand. The cold was bracing, but I was committed to socializing now so my jacket had to languish in the car. The wind was cruel; it found every crevasse in my clothes, invaded and patted me down like I owed it money.

"Sorry about that," Andy offered. "You should go easy on her." That was Andy in a nutshell, wanting both a blokey alliance and to stick up for his wife: the type of guy who says, "Yes, honey," at a dinner party but then wobbles his head and goes, "*Pfft*, women, right?" when she's in the loo. His nose was red, but it was hard to tell if the cause was alcohol or temperature, and his glasses were slightly fogged up. His short, jet-black goatee sat on his face like it had been taken hostage from a younger man; he was in his early fifties.

"I didn't do a rain dance last night just to piss her off," I said.

"I know, mate. It's just a tricky weekend for everyone. So, you know, you don't have to make fun of her for trying to make it a little easier." He paused. "Not a big deal, hey—don't let it get in the way of us sinking a few beers this trip."

"I didn't make fun of her. I'm just late." I could see my stepsister, Sofia, having a cigarette on the porch as we approached. She raised her eyebrows as if to say, *It's worse inside*.

Andy took a few steps in silence, and though I inwardly begged him not to, drew a breath and said, "Yeah, but," and I decided there's nothing sadder than a man trying to stick up for a woman who can stick up for herself, "she put a lot of work into those invites, and you didn't have to make fun of her spreadsheets."

"I didn't say anything."

"Not now. When you sent it back. Under allergies you wrote 'spreadsheets.'"

"Oh," I said. Sofia overheard and scoffed, ejecting a plume of smoke out her nose. Erin, who's not dead, would have liked that one too. Andy didn't need to say aloud what I'd written under "Next of kin"—*It's a family reunion, so anyone here, unless Avalanche*—for me to feel a right arse. I conceded. "I'll go easy."

Andy smiled, pleased that his husbandly virtues, if not affectionate, were at least box-ticking.

He headed inside, miming a drink as he left to imply that he'd order me one, affirming our laddish allegiance, while I stopped to say hello to Sofia. Being Ecuadorian, from steamy Guayaquil, she hated the cold, and I saw at least three collars around her neck beneath the coat on top. Her head looked like the bud of a flower, poking out from a ring of collared petals. Even rugged up, one arm was wrapped across her waist to hug herself warm. I knew I was better accustomed to cold than she was, having plunged myself into various ice baths over the years (fun fact: apparently low temperatures increase male fertility), but I didn't wish to linger in conversation, the cold was burrowing into me.

She offered her cigarette to me, though she knew I didn't smoke; it's just something she always liked to do. I waved away the smoke.

"Good start," she said, mocking.

"Make friends early, I always say."

"Glad you're finally here. I was waiting for you to rescue me—I knew you'd distract everyone. Here." She handed me a small, square piece of cardboard, which had a grid printed on it. Inside each box was a short phrase, relating to different family members:

Marcelo shouts at a Waiter; Lucy tries to SELL you anything. I spotted my name—*Ernest ruins something*—in the middle left column.

"Bingo?" I asked, reading the heading: *Reunion Bingo.*

"Thought it would be fun. Just made them for you and me. Everyone else is too sour." She wrinkled her nose and held her card up; I could see it had a cross already on it.

I snatched the card from her. It had different statements than mine, as well as a couple of generic events. The grammar was all over the place, random caps for emphasis, absurd parentheses, no full stops. Some were more tongue-in-cheek than others. I could be relied on to be tardy, just as Marcelo could be relied on to chew out hospitality staff, but the bottom right square said: *Avalanche.* I looked back at mine; the same spot said: *Broken Bone (OR Someone Dies)* with an incongruous smiley face. The square that Sofia had already crossed through read: *Ernest is late.*

"Not fair." I gave it back to her.

"You better catch up. Shall we?"

I nodded. Sofia finished her smoke and flicked the butt off the porch into the snow. But against the sparse, fresh white, it was glaringly out of place. She gave me a forlorn look and then trudged off the porch, bent down, and picked it up, pocketing it.

"You know," she said, leading me inside, "you'll have to play nice if you want to make it out of this weekend alive."

I swear to God she actually said that. And she even winked at me. As if she's the one telling the damn story.

CHAPTER 3

The guesthouse itself was a hunting lodge masquerading as the Ritz: every surface, banister, and door handle had ornate polished-wood accents; there was soft lighting from wall-mounted electric lamps made of frosted glass molded into flowers, and the foyer even had a red carpet, complete with a chandelier hanging low from the roof, glittering beside the second-floor walkway. In fact, everything from the waist up was almost elegant enough to make up for the snow-damaged lower half: the hotel equivalent of taking a pantsless video call in a collared shirt. The carpets, well-worn from stomped snow-caked shoes, sat atop a swollen wooden floor that creaked like it wasn't quite nailed down, and the patchwork rugs and hastily plastered mouse holes evidenced a building maintained by the motto that it was easier to find quick fixes than to get a tradie up the mountain. Not to mention the damp. The whole place smelled like my car after I'd left my sunroof open during a thunderstorm. Altitude adds several stars to a hotel rating, and while this was a two scraping by as a four, it had a cozy charm.

Conversation evaporated upon my entry to the dining room, where everyone was midway through dessert, and I was greeted by the symphony of spoons clinking down on plates. My mother, Audrey, who was at the head of the table, sized me up. She had fishing-wire silver hair tied in a bun, and a scar above her right eye. She hesitated—she may have been deciding whether or not I was my brother (it had been a while since either of us had seen her)—and then pushed her chair back from the table, dropping her cutlery with a clatter. This was an argument-stopping technique I remembered from my childhood.

Marcelo, my stepfather, was sitting to her left. Marcelo is a heavyset bald man with one of those folds above the back of his neck that I've always assumed he has to floss in case mold builds up. He put a heavy hand on Audrey's wrist. Not in a controlling way; I don't want to misrepresent my mother's relationship or invoke any predisposed judgment of stepfathers. You see, my stepfather always wore a late-1980s platinum Presidential Rolex—which, when I'd curiously googled the eye-watering price, I learned weighed just shy of half a kilogram—meaning that everything he did with his right hand was, literally, heavy-handed. The advertisement for the watch, I recalled, was quite ridiculous: *An Heirloom Should Be Heavy Enough for History*. Marcelo had worn it for as long as I could remember. I assumed I wasn't in the running to inherit it. Stupid as the slogan was, it was better than some of the others I'd seen—like *Three Hundred Meters Depth, Bulletproof Glass: Safe as a Bank Vault*—which pretended all millionaires were part-time scuba instructors.

"I've finished," Audrey said, shaking off Marcelo's hand with a clunk. Her plate was still half full.

"Oh, grow up," Sofia grunted, taking a seat next to Lucy (my sister-in-law, who you might remember Michael mentioning in Chapter 1), who was opposite Marcelo. Lucy had clearly preened for this weekend: her blonde hair was freshly cut in a bob and the tag was jutting out of the collar of her newly purchased knitted cardigan. I don't know if Sofia was emboldened by having Lucy as a shield or if she just hadn't noticed my mother's proximity to sharp cutlery, but such backtalk would have been suicidal for a blood relative. Instead, the only thing that died was my mother's resolve to leave the table, and she creaked back into her seat.

Andy and Katherine rounded out the punctual members of the family. I took my place quietly next to Sofia, in front of a covered plate. It turned out someone had saved my main, beef cooked to spreadsheet specification, and Katherine must have spent some time glowering at the cloche because it was still lukewarm. Lucy had an extra plate in front of her, which meant she'd pinched my entrée, and I wondered if she was just hungry or if it was a deliberate gesture.

Something you should know about me is that I like to look at everything two ways. I'm always trying to see both sides of the coin.

"Well," Andy said, clapping his hands together in an attempt to break the ice, which only someone who'd married into the family would be stupid enough to try. "How about this place, huh? Anyone checked out the rooftop yet? I heard they have a jacuzzi. You can tee off from the roof too. Concierge told me if you hit the weather station, they give you a hundred bucks. Who's up for it?" He hunted enthusiasm by peering over at Marcelo, who looked like he was dressed for a golf trip rather than the snow, with a checkered sweater-vest that even I knew was made of cotton, not wool, and therefore was a real death wish in the wet and cold. Judged as I'd felt by the woman with the snorkeled four-wheel drive, at least I'd brought a polar fleece.

"Ern?" Andy continued looking around the table. Katherine, who was between him and Marcelo, nudged him quiet. Talking to the enemy was forbidden.

We all ate in silence, but I knew everyone at the table was thinking the same thing I was: that whoever's idea it was to kick off this weekend a day early, when we all knew the reason we were here wouldn't arrive until tomorrow, deserved to be strapped to a toboggan and given a shortcut down the mountain.

You can tell a lot about someone from whether they can handle an uncomfortable silence. If they ride it out or snap it off. Patience seemed to be a trait lacking in those who had married in, as Lucy was the next one to attempt conversation.

I'll tell you a little bit about Lucy. Lucy runs an independent online business, by which I mean she loses money on the internet periodically. She is a Small Business Owner in the same way Andy is a Feminist, in that she declares it loudly, often, and she's the only one who believes it.

I won't name the company because I don't want to get sued, but I recall her being promoted to Vice Executive Regional President (or something) a while back, along with about ten thousand others. An arbitrary title, unless of course it was referring to her own vice of badgering friends into buying shit they didn't need, in which case she was certainly presidential. That was also why she'd got the car I'd seen out front, which according to her post on Instagram was a freebie reward from the program. I knew that it was actually just a lease, and the gifted component was merely a monthly contribution, with incredibly strict conditions that, if breached, revoked the "free" part and left the owner with a very expensive loan. That is, the car was free until it wasn't.

I was sure Lucy no longer fulfilled the conditions and was paying for it out of her own pocket. But that was key to the whole thing: to never let the reality outweigh the image of success. A friend who is a car salesman told me that he'd had to ban a certain type of woman from taking photos with cars on the lot, pretending to have just earned one to post about online. They'd leave infuriated, clanking away in their smoke-belching hatchback with some giant novelty red bow unused in the back. This was why, you'll understand,

I redacted the model of Lucy's car, because they are very specifically linked to a certain company.

Lucy commits to the rhetoric; she describes it as a business and tenses up whenever anyone says *that* specific word. So out of respect, I won't use it. I'll just say the Egyptians built them.

In an attempt to fit in with the family, Erin used to dutifully attend Lucy's parties, buying the cheapest of whatever product she was shilling that month. Once home, she'd type up an invoice with a restaurant name and a value as a multiple of how boring or arduous the party had been, and leave it on my pillow: *In-law Tax Invoice: Eyelash curler $15; rate x 3 (makeup tutorial rate); >1 hour, overtime x 1.5 = $52.50: Bella's Italian.*

"Everyone get up here all right? I got stung by the speed trap—two hundred and twenty dollars for going maybe seven over. It's ridiculous," Lucy said. And the relief that it wasn't a sales pitch was almost palpable, though it did my bingo card (*Lucy tries to SELL you anything*) no favors.

"Revenue raising," Marcelo chipped in. "They bring out the extra patrols to catch the tourists, let the locals go. That's also why it's a forty speed limit. Road like this should be seventy, but they want to make you impatient."

"You think there's a case in it?" Lucy asked hopefully.

"Not in the slightest." I don't think Marcelo meant for his disinterest, while honest, to be so cold, but it iced the table.

"Has everyone been to their chalet yet? They're lovely." Katherine was the next one to try. "We stayed last night and the morning views are just . . ." She trailed off like there was no word in the world that could do justice to both the beauty of the sunrise and her skill in picking competitively priced mountain views.

"I didn't realize," said Marcelo slowly, "that we would have to *walk* between the hotel and our accommodation."

"Trust me, it's much nicer than the rooms upstairs here,"

Katherine defended, like she had stock in the resort. "Besides, I wanted him to have some space. You know? To spread out in. A nice view. Not some stuffy room that's not much bigger than . . ."

"I don't think he'll give a shit, provided there's fresh linen and cold beer," Lucy said.

"Doesn't mean *we* can't stay here," Marcelo grumbled.

"We got a discount for booking six chalets, remember?"

"Might pay for your speeding fine." I couldn't resist needling Lucy, but aside from a flicker of a smile from Sofia, I was ignored.

Marcelo dug in his pocket and pulled out his wallet. "How much do you want for me to switch rooms?"

"You'll manage the walk, Dad," Sofia said. "I'll piggyback you if you want."

That finally got a wry smile out of him. "I'm injured," he moped theatrically, clutching at his right shoulder. Sofia, a surgeon, had done Marcelo's shoulder reconstruction herself, just over three years ago, and it had long healed. It was obvious he was putting it on. For what it's worth, he seems pretty well healed when he swings a punch at me in Chapter 32.

Normally, a surgeon wouldn't be allowed to operate on family. But Marcelo is accustomed to getting what he wants, and he'd insisted he'd only trust his daughter's hands. The hospital's nose for a wealthy potential benefactor ironically turned enough blind eyes for the Garcia Wing of the ophthalmology center to be built.

"Settle down, old man," Sofia joked, spearing some beef. "I hear you had a top-class surgeon."

Marcelo's indignation was similarly overacted. Clutching his heart like he'd been sniped with an arrow, he may as well have put her on his shoulders and carted her around. He might have, had his shoulder, of course, not been so badly "injured." The affection between them was almost tangible. Marcelo was father to only a daughter, and while he was kind to Michael and me (when he'd married my mother it was obvious he'd relished having boys to raise), Sofia would always be his little girl. Even his stony, lawyerly façade broke down in front of her, as he aped about to get a giggle the way fathers do.

"Or we could nick a snowmobile," Andy said, excited by the oasis of conversation. "I saw a couple of them parked outside and asked if they rented them out. Groundskeeper said they're for maintenance only. Maybe we could grease his wheels." He rubbed his thumb and two fingers together.

"What are you, twelve?" Katherine said.

"Honey, I just thought it would be fun."

"Fun is the views and the atmosphere and the company, not the spa and golf balls off the roof and zooming around on a death trap."

"I think it sounds fun," I offered. Katherine reheated my meal again with another glare.

"Thank you, Ern—" Andy started, but Audrey interrupted with a loud cough. He turned to her. "What? Are we just all going to pretend like he isn't here?" he said, pretending I wasn't there.

"Andrew . . ." Katherine warned.

"Come on! When was the last time you all saw each other?"

Big mistake, Andy. We all knew the answer to that one.

My mother was the one to say it out loud. "The trial."

Suddenly I'm back in the witness box, listening to a lawyer who keeps one hand in his pocket and the other darting a laser pointer around the room as if the jury were feline, postulating over giant cardboard pictures of a webbed clearing that I still sometimes dream about, with arrows and lines and colored boxes superimposed over the top. And I'm in the middle of answering a question when my mother stands and walks out, and all I can think of is why they insist on courtrooms having the tallest, heaviest, *loudest* wooden doors possible. Because surely something discreet is better suited to the environment, but the architect must have moonlighted as a Hollywood screenwriter and wanted dramatic entrances and exits, and really I'm only thinking about those damn noisy doors because it means I don't have to look over at my brother in the dock.

You're a savvy reader, so you probably already noticed there are a couple of empty seats at the family lunch table. I already told you Erin is driving in tomorrow. Katherine's only child isn't coming—this is Amy of the peanut-butter sandwich incident—because she lives in Italy and the importance of this reunion was about a five-to-seven-hour drive and no more. But it should be no surprise that Michael's not in this scene either. I might, sort of, be responsible for that.

So now you know a few things: why my mother refuses to speak to me; why my brother isn't there yet; why he's looking forward to fresh sheets and a cold beer; why I couldn't conjure up my usual excuse to get out of the weekend; why Lucy is dolled up; why Katherine bolded "all of us" on the invitation.

It had been three and a half years since I knelt in spiderwebs and watched my brother murder a dying man. Three years since my mother walked out of a courtroom while I was explaining to a jury how he did it. And in less than twenty-four hours, he would arrive at Sky Lodge a free man.

CHAPTER 4

Ever since the funeral, with its folded flag perched ominously on top of the coffin and pews filled with white-gloved, polished-gold-buttoned officers, I've known what it feels like to be an outcast. A policeman's funeral shows the best and worst sides of brotherhood. How it can provide place and pride for many—I saw an officer, hexagon cap cradled in his elbow, flick open a Swiss Army knife and carve an infinity symbol into the coffin's wood, an eternal bind—but clamp shut to others. I remember an argument in the foyer with the dead man's two families—one of blood and marriage, and one of blue uniforms—each insisting that they knew what was best: cremation or burial. It was a futile fight, won by blood in the end and the body buried. Legally it made sense, but I also assume cops sit in patrol cars and have "if I die" conversations, like soldiers folding friends' letters into breast pockets, so who knows?

It was a busy funeral, more like a film set buzzing with activity than a reverential chapel. All the attention—the photographers out in front of the church, the swiveled heads and sideways glances, the shocked whispers: *My God, those are* his *kids*—taught me that there's a difference between being watched and being seen.

That much one-sided voyeurism—"*his* kids"—forms a bubble around you, keeps you locked off. I remember looking at the whipped cream dripping off Mum's otherwise pristine black dress as we walked out of that church and suddenly knowing two things, as sure as a child knows anything. Dad was gone. And we were in that bubble together.

Being a mother to fatherless boys is no small feat. Audrey had to be amorphous: the prison warden, the snitchy inmate, the bribe-taking guard, and the compassionate parole officer all rolled into one. Marcelo had been my father's lawyer before he started his corporate firm and had taken to hanging around after Dad's death, I assumed because he felt sorry for my mum. He and Dad must have been friends. Don't get the wrong idea of a man turning up in a white singlet with a power tool (Marcelo hung bookshelves once at such a slope my mother complained they made her seasick); he just brought the checkbook to pay for one. And soon giving us a hand turned into asking for one. When Marcelo proposed, with his young daughter in tow, my mother took us out for burgers and asked if we wanted them to be part of our bubble. The fact she'd thought to ask had been enough to convince me. Michael only wanted to know if he was rich, before attacking his cheeseburger.

Growing up, there were days when it was us against her, as it often is with teenage boys; sometimes rebellion over five minutes of video games trumps fifteen years of care. But no matter how many slammed doors or shouting matches, it was always—always—the three of us against the outside world. Even Aunt Katherine only ever got one foot inside—maybe because she was Dad's sister. My mother was there for us, and she expected us to be there for one another, above all else.

Even the law, apparently.

Part of me understood why she'd walked out of that courtroom, because I had stepped outside our bubble and was siding with the others.

I know you're probably thinking that three years isn't much for a murder sentence, and you'd be right. The guy—his name was Alan Holton, if you're interested—*had* been shot, and it was difficult to prove whether the bullet or Michael had more to do with his death. Yes, Michael had hit Alan with his car when he stumbled onto the road after being shot, and, yes, he'd made a terrible mistake not taking him directly to a hospital, but he'd had an impeccable defense in Marcelo Garcia (famous both for his corporate law firm Garcia & Broadbridge, now one of the largest in the country, and for refusing to walk forty meters in the snow), who had leaned heavily on Alan's notoriety as a career criminal, the ambiguity of an unaccounted-for gunman, and a gun they never found.

Even Marcelo's presence at a murder trial was, in itself, staggering, and I think put laser-pointer guy off his game, but that wouldn't be giving enough credit to Marcelo's defense. He'd argued that Michael couldn't have been expected to make rational decisions given the circumstances. While Michael had failed his duty of care towards Alan (this is important, because in Australia your legal responsibility to help someone only materializes once you *begin* to help someone, which I learned during the trial) by putting him into his car but not driving him to medical help, he'd also feared for his life, your honor, as he didn't know if the shooter was still out there or if he was likely to be attacked or followed. So the rub, without getting all technical, was three years in jail.

Testifying cost me a lot, and by the time the final bargain was accepted—the prison sentence was negotiated behind closed doors in the judge's chambers—it hadn't even mattered. I've made a lot of bad choices in my life, not least accepting Andy's invitation for a drink at the bar after lunch, and I still haven't decided if testifying was one of them. Sure, I'd have had to learn to live with staying silent, but I've had to learn to live with speaking out too, and I'm not sure which is worse. I'd love to tell you I did it because it was the right thing to do. But the truth is, in my brother's low growl—"He just stopped breathing"—there was something different. And I could say something clichéd here like, "He didn't feel like my brother anymore," but it was, in fact, the opposite. He felt like a Cunningham. I saw him without the layers. And if there was something in him like that growl, like his shoulders, his forearms flexed as he strangled the life out of someone, then was it in me too? I wanted to banish that part. So I'd turned to the police. I hoped there was some part of my mother that understood why I'd done it. And when tomorrow came, I was hoping there'd still be some part of me that did too.

I'll admit to being a little wobbly as I crunched my way across the snow to my chalet. Andy had been excited enough by the promise of a drinking buddy that he'd been willing to swap allegiances and I'd humored him as long as he was buying. Andy is a horticulturist. He grows the grass on cricket pitches and football fields to the right length and specifications. He is a terrifically boring man in a terrifically boring marriage, which, I have always found, makes for a generous shout.

I'd brought a wheelie bag with an extendable handle that is convenient in airports but not so much on mountainsides, which I managed to move in a bunny-hop, lift-and-drop movement, as well as a sports bag, which I hung over my shoulder. Though it was only mid-afternoon, the mountain was starting to darken as the peak blocked the sun, and, despite the warmth of a few beers in me, I could feel the immediate change. It was like what I'd heard happens on Mars; it snap-freezes come dark. Andy thought he'd go check out the jacuzzi after our drinks and I hoped he'd changed his mind, otherwise they'd have to chisel him out of it.

Despite the temperature, by the time I'd struggled my bags to my half-buried chalet, I'd worked up quite a sweat. The snow was hip high but the staff had shoveled a canyon to my door, which my bag pinballed off as I dragged it. The windowed face of the hut had a protruding awning, so the views remained unimpeded by snowdrifts.

As I fumbled with the keys, I spied a torn piece of paper staked with a twig into a mound of snow by the door. I picked it up. Someone had written a message in thick black marker, and the words had started to bleed as the paper got soggy, so it had a creepy feel.

It read: *The fridge sucks. Dig.*

There was a large S on the bottom right: Sofia. I leaned over and dusted the mound with my hand, revealing the silver tops of the six cans of beer she'd buried for me. Since Michael's trial, Sofia had been the only one who kept in touch. I'd known my banishment was severe when even Lucy didn't email me anymore to invite me to her Free Seminars. But Sofia had reached out. Perhaps because she was, like me, an outsider. She'd been inserted into a new family, in a new country, by her father. I say "inserted," but no one climbs the ladder of corporate law by paying enough attention to their children, doting as Marcelo was when he was around, so I really mean "dumped." And while she could never argue that she was unwelcome in our home, I think she could always feel our invisible bubble. After the trial leveled the field, we'd turned from cordial stepsiblings into genuine friends. It was why she'd invited me, and me alone, into her bingo game.

I packed the snow back over the drinks, pleased that there was at least some warmth left on the mountain, and headed inside. The chalet was a single room that had a strange, tilted feeling—like being off-balance on a ship—due to the incline of the roof. This uneasy feeling was compensated for by the panoramic view: it was the first part of the trip that had been "as advertised." I'm not too proud to pat my aunt on the back here and say it was breathtaking. Especially with the last fingers of sunlight curling over the ridge, and the long shadow of the peak stretching across the slope.

The roof was over three meters high on the window side, framed with a wooden-beam ribcage, before gradually tapering across the chalet, over a lounge, television, an abundance of rugs, and a cast-iron fireplace. The roof must have only reached snow level and not the ground, because I was surprised to discover a back wall; it was lined with cupboards stocked with hotel kitchen appliances, and a cubic alcove for a bathroom where practicality had again bit the bullet: stooped showers were another concession for the views. A third of the way across the room, a ladder led to a bedroom loft. The staff had pre-set the heating—the fireplace must have been ornamental as it wasn't on—and my skin prickled as I adjusted from the outdoor temperature. The damp odor of the main hotel was replaced by an oaky, ashen smell, likely from a candle labeled *rustic fireplace*.

I left my wheelie bag in the middle of the floor and was tucking the sports bag into one of the cupboards when the phone next to the television rang. My phone had a little number 4 on it. There was no keypad for outside numbers, just a column of speed-dial buttons and mini lights, labeled with the chalet numbers, as well as one labeled *Concierge*. Currently number 5 was lit up. It was Marcelo.

"Audrey's not feeling well." He said "Audrey," not "your mother." "We'll get room service tonight and see you in the morning."

Skipping a family dinner suited me fine; lunch had already used up most of the tolerance I'd budgeted for the whole weekend. I got a lukewarm bottle of water from the fridge—which did suck, Sofia was right—and necked it, because I'd read somewhere that spending a day in the snow can dehydrate you more than one at the beach. Then I foraged for one of the buried beer cans, reclined on the couch, and before I knew it, I'd dozed off.

*

I woke to a hammering at my door. Of course I did. You've read these kinds of books before.

I had a moment of panic because sometimes I have these dreams—well, memories—about choking, and as I was wrenched from sleep the giant window and the feeling of space made me think, momentarily, that I'd fallen asleep outdoors. The ridge met the deep black sky under the spectacular brightness of stars unblemished by city fog or clouds. The wind outside sounded like it was groaning, and puffs of snow kept spitting off the ridge and swirling into the sky. Closer to me, the mountain was dimly lit from the spill of a halogen spotlight for the night skiers in the neighboring valley, and the slope was dappled with bone-finger shadows of leaf-stripped trees. The temperature had continued to drop, trying to snake its way into the room; I could almost feel the breath of the glass pulsing against the indoor heating.

I rubbed my eyes and hauled myself upright, lumbering to the door. I opened it.

Sofia stood on the threshold, hands folded into her elbows, flakes of ice in her wind-tousled black hair. "Well?" she said. "Did you bring the money?"

CHAPTER 5

Okay, look. Here's the thing. I didn't lie. Michael asked me to hold on to the money.

When he drove me back home that morning—I was silent in the passenger seat, still pulling sticky spiderweb tendrils from my forearms—he'd said it was probably safer if I kept it for now. I could see the thinking: that Alan either took it or was supposed to give it to someone, and something had gone wrong along the way. Whether Michael had anything to do with the "going wrong" part, I wasn't sure, but if someone was a few hundred grand light, they probably wanted it back. I was another layer—the security blanket—in case the gunman had seen Michael's car. If there was a gunman at all, of course.

I'd taken the bag with silent understanding. Michael had maybe implied he'd pay me for looking after it, but I was struggling to hear anything, just an underwater-style echo in my head that accompanied his moving lips. In a daze, I'd walked into my house, thrown the bag on the bed, vomited, and called the police.

Twenty minutes later I was cuffed, in the back of a wagon, guiding two yawning detectives to the clearing. I know they didn't take me seriously at first, because they went through a drive-through Macca's on the way, and I've never heard of someone witnessing a murder and having to wait for a McMuffin. That was before everything kicked off. Before there were sirens and ambulances and news vans and even a helicopter landing in the middle of the field. Before there were think pieces on the murder and, even more popular, editorials on the webbed field (the natural oddity had been produced by spiders relocating from a nearby flood). Before I was locked in an interview room, and they were in my face with photos and hot McDonald's breath, telling me that Michael had given me up and I should just confess.

When they let me go, after what I assumed was the maximum time they could hold me, I learned that Michael hadn't said anything at all. They were just trying to see if I was lying to save my own skin. They dropped me home. I asked if they wanted to get KFC on the way, because I wasn't in a rush. Turned out they were a tough crowd.

It was only when I got home and saw the black bag sitting on my bed where I'd left it that I realized I'd forgotten to tell them about the money.

I swear, I just assumed they'd search the house. At the start I was more focused on Alan and trying to remember which turn was which and exactly what time it had been when my brother picked me up, when he dropped me off, and when he asked me to wait in the car. And then I thought that they already had the money, and they'd ask about it eventually, but they didn't. And then suddenly it's the next day and I'm signing a piece of paper as true and accurate, and I still haven't mentioned the money. And neither has Michael—who may not even know that I'm the one who turned him in yet, and so, I figure, maybe he thinks I'm still on his side and protecting it for him. And then I'm on the stand, and still no one's mentioned it, and neither Michael nor Marcelo bring it up to screw me during the trial, like I'm half expecting them to, and I know I'm well past the point of mentioning it without really putting a spanner in things, and so it sits, unspoken. And the judge reads the verdict and I go home and the bag is still in my house but the world is different. My brother's in jail and I have a bag with $267,000 in it. I know the amount for sure myself now, because I've had time to count it.

That was another reason I couldn't miss this weekend. I'd told Sofia my plan a few weeks ago. I planned on giving Michael the bag tomorrow. I wasn't thinking of it as an apology, because I didn't do anything wrong, but maybe it was some kind of offering. It wasn't an olive branch, but it was certainly green (metaphorically, at least, because it wasn't all hundreds). And almost all of it was still there, too. What a good brother I am.

"Is all of it there?" Sofia asked, looking at the disemboweled bag in front of her on the couch. She hovered instead of sitting down, nervous about touching it.

"Most of it," I confessed.

"Most of it?"

"Well . . . there were some emergencies. It's been three years. I don't know if he even counted it."

"You *said* he counted it."

"He probably counted it," I conceded. "I'm hoping he might not remember exactly."

"You know what I'd do if I was in prison for three years thinking my brother stole a bag of cash off me? I'd think about it every single day. To the cent."

"I figure he thinks I've spent it all, and so he'll be pleased to get it—"

"—most of it—"

"—most of it back."

Sofia gave an exaggerated exhale, complete with fluttering lips, and wandered over to the window. She tapped a finger against the glass and watched the mountain for a moment. "Why'd you take it?" she asked softly, serious now.

She'd seen through all the bullshit I spouted to myself about hanging on to the money because I kept missing my chance to turn it in. Because I was too embarrassed; because I thought it would be too complicated. She could see that there was something else there. Was it as simple as greed? I wasn't sure. I wasn't expecting Michael to pull me into a hug and split the cash tomorrow, but I'd be lying (and I promised not to) if I didn't say I'd felt some peace at having this bag in the back of my closet for the last three years, especially with everything that had happened with Erin. It was pack-up-and-leave money. It was everything-goes-south money. It was start-afresh money. I didn't want it, but I was glad it was there.

"I didn't take it." I repeated my usual line. "I got stuck with it."

Sofia frowned, disappointed. She knew my excuses were rehearsed.

The truth was: I'd taken two wads of cash and put them in my underwear drawer before I'd left that morning. The truth was: right up until Marcelo had turned the tides of the trial, I'd thought Michael was going away for a much longer time, and so the money wouldn't matter. The truth was: one of the only reasons I hadn't spent more of it was I didn't know where it was from or whether it was traceable; otherwise, I would have at least put it in an account and spent the interest. The truth was: I still hadn't decided whether I *was* going to give Michael the money tomorrow.

I'd brought it in case he asked about it. I'd told Sofia I planned on handing it over for accountability, to try to keep myself from backing out.

There's a look people have when they make up their mind about something. It's nothing physical, more a sixth sense, like the prickly necked feeling when someone's looking at you. That happened then. The atoms in the air changed. Sofia had made up her mind about something.

"What if I told you I needed some of it?" she said.

The phone rang, startling us. Of course it did. You've read these kinds of books before. The little number 2 lit up. It stopped after two rings, before I could move to answer it. I checked the time. A quarter past eleven. If you're keeping track of the page numbers, you'll know someone just died. I just haven't found out about it yet.

"Think about it," she said, and I realized she'd been waiting for me to say something.

"How much do you need?"

"Maybe fifty." She chewed her lip. She picked up a handful from the bag, held it as if weighing it. "Grand," she added, as if it were possible I'd have thought she'd be visiting me in the middle of the night for fifty dollars.

"Michael knows I have it."

"He knows he left it with you, not that you have it." She'd practiced this, had her arguments loaded into the chamber just like my excuses. "You could tell him the police took it. You could tell him you donated it. You could tell him you burned it."

I could pretend I hadn't thought through all of these options myself, but I won't. I'm reliable, remember?

"What kind of trouble are you in?" I asked. What I didn't say was that there were richer, more-legal people for her to ask. Her father, for one. And fifty grand was a lot of money, sure, but she was a surgeon who owned property: if she wanted fifty thousand dollars (she'd said "maybe fifty," which to me meant she needed exactly fifty), that was what she needed to patch the gap between what she could obtain on her own and the total. And she wanted cash. Which meant fast, quiet, and off the books. She was in a much bigger hole than she was letting on.

"I don't need help. I just need money."

"It's not my money."

"It's not his either."

"Can we talk about this tomorrow?"

She put the money down, but I could see her rifling through her mental notes to make sure she'd said everything she'd come here to say, as if she were sitting in a job interview and the interviewers had asked the dreaded "So, do you have any questions for us?" She must have decided she'd ticked off all her most convincing points, because she walked to the door and opened it. A swirl of freezing air shot through.

"Just look at how they've treated you. And you still think *you* owe *them*? One day you'll realize family isn't about whose blood runs in your veins, it's who you'd spill it for."

She put her hands in her pockets and trudged into the night.

I went back inside and looked at the money in a kind of stupor, trying to analyze everything that had just happened.

I wondered if Sofia was right. That even though my family had made a deliberate effort to shut me out, I still felt obligated to them. Was that why I was here? It was too big a question after too many beers too close to midnight, so I gave up on self-examination. I picked up the phone and called back Room Two.

"Hello?" To my surprise, Sofia's voice came down the line. "Ern?"

"Oh, hi, Sofia." I checked the lights on the phone, and I'd definitely dialed 2. Maybe I'd misread the blinking light before; Sofia couldn't have called me and been in my chalet at the same time. "Sorry, just checking you made it back all right. Being night and all. Wouldn't want you to wander into a crevasse and miss the family reunion."

"You call this a family reunion? Seven people?" She laughed and the phone crackled. "*Pfft.* White people."

I tried to laugh with her, but I was in my head about how normal we were pretending to be, which stiffened me right up, and so I only managed a strange, strangled grunt.

"Okay, Ern," she said. "Thanks for checking in. Promise me you'll think about it?"

I didn't have to promise—I could think of nothing else—but I did. We said goodnight and I hung up. I finished my beer, left the curtains open for the sunrise, and climbed into the loft. I rolled onto my side and looked out at the sharp ridge peeling into infinite sky and felt very small. I wondered what everyone else was doing right now. Sofia, like me, halfway up a mountain, thinking about a bag of money; Erin, in an itchy-sheet motel somewhere halfway on the drive, thinking about God knows what; and Michael, looking at the same sky through a prison window for the last time, maybe thinking about what he'd like to do to me.

I dozed off, somewhat shortsightedly hoping it would all work itself out tomorrow.

CHAPTER 6

When I woke, there was a steady flow of puffy jackets walking past my window. They seemed to be heading towards a small huddle, a few hundred meters further up the slope on the snowed-over golf course. Maybe thirty people. A snowmobile zipped past the congregation, engine whining. Someone further up the hill waved their arms. I couldn't tell if their meaning was *over here* or *stay back*. A flare snaked a luminescent trail into the sky and popped, the crystal-laden ground reflecting the red glow. Light travels well across snow and, as the flare faded, I noticed the snow was still shimmering: not just red, but mixed with blue. Not shimmering, flashing; reflecting a set of colored lights that must have been by the guesthouse. Police.

I scorched my hands in a fireman's slide down the loft's ladder and started shoving the money back into the bag. Luckily, people's attention appeared to be solely focused up the hill and I was able to get the money packed and back in the cupboard, and some pants on, before anyone saw anything they shouldn't have. I finished dressing as fast as I could, pulled open the door, and spied the only person on the mountain wearing jeans walking past.

"Andy!" I called from the doorway, hopping into my left boot. He stopped and turned, waved, and then waited. I hurried in a snow-handicapped wobble over to him. We were in thin enough air that I was out of breath and puffing when I reached him. My breath misted between us, fogging up his glasses. "What's going on?"

"Some poor bastard." He pointed up the hill and started walking. His look of curiosity instead of fear answered my question before I asked it: *One of us?* I fell into step beside him, thankful that I'd inadvertently dialed Sofia last night and knew she'd made it back to her cabin. Being caught outside overnight would certainly be lethal, even on a calm night like last night. I shivered. It would be an awful way to go.

There was a dead man with frostbite-blackened cheeks lying on his back in the snow. He was all covered—black ski jacket, black gloves, boots—except for his face and for a second my brain flashed to another dark lump in the middle of a white clearing. I shook off the thought, peered over the shoulder of the guy in front of me. There were a couple of dozen gawkers, the promise of drama smoking people out of their hotel rooms like wasps.

In front of us was one male cop, about my age, maybe younger, wearing a beanie with ear flaps and a jacket with a wool collar, trying to keep people away. If I'm honest, he looked flustered, like he had no idea what he was doing. Andy had ambled off to join Katherine, who'd beaten us there, despite this not being on her schedule. Everyone seemed to be in silent agreement that about ten meters was enough distance to preserve the crime scene, and a semicircle had naturally formed. It hadn't snowed heavily overnight, so the corpse and the three prominent sets of footprints leading up the hill towards it were clearly preserved.

Of the footprints, three sets headed up the hill but only one returned. The returning trail became choppy, with occasional smaller holes next to the shoeprints: I assumed it was the person who found the body running back to report it, panicked, lurching down the hill, putting a hand down here and there. The second set of footprints were clear, linear prints. I assumed they belonged to the cop, currently with the body.

The third set of footprints headed up the slope like the others. But then they broke form: moving backwards and forwards, up and down, all inside a few square meters. It was as if someone was trapped inside an invisible box, ricocheting off the walls. That set of footprints ended at the body. There was no return journey.

The people around me were muttering, pulling out their phones, taking photos and videos. But no one seemed distressed. There were no consoling arms or mouths covered with one hand in dainty shock. Everyone appeared to be doing what I was doing: looking at the body out of intellectual curiosity. Maybe it was because he was frozen, and so felt more like part of the mountain than an actual person who had been breathing twelve hours ago. The scene was curious, but not violent. But surely *someone* would be screaming, trying to push past us up the hill to get to their loved one. *Does no one know him?* I wondered.

"Is anyone a doctor?" The policeman had given up trying to disperse the crowd. He repeated himself as he peered into the mob, revealing his observational skills to be at the low end of the scale between Blindfolded and Sherlockian. It was an exclusive alpine resort in peak season—half these bloody people were doctors.

I spied Sofia, opposite me in the semicircle, raising her hand.

Katherine leaned over to Andy and whispered something in his ear, shook her head.

The policeman beckoned Sofia over to him, and then led her in a wide berth around the tracks. At first they stood a few meters from the body, with Sofia gesturing down at the man, and then the policeman nodded and she knelt beside him. She cradled his neck in her hands and tilted it one way, then another. Peeled his lips apart. Unzipped the jacket and placed her hands underneath it. She waved the officer down and he knelt beside her, hesitantly letting her guide his hands over the body in the same way. When Sofia was happy she'd shown the officer enough, she zipped up the jacket and stood. They had a short conversation that was whipped up and into the sky by a blast of wind. I saw a brooding gray cloud pushing over the ridge.

"Ernie, Andy," Sofia called. She was scooping her arms through the air. *Get up here.* I looked at the policeman for approval, and he mimicked her. Andy and I gave the existing trails a wide berth, but the prints up the hill were getting more and more crowded nonetheless. Outside of the huddle of spectators, I could tell the wind was picking up. My cheeks stung. I couldn't bring myself to look down when we arrived; I focused instead on Sofia, but she was lost in thought, gazing at the corpse.

"We need to move the body," the policeman yelled above the howl of the wind. "Get it out of view. I saw a garage on the way in. It will be cold enough for now."

Andy and I both nodded. The policeman pointed across the slope.

"We need to go up"—Sofia waved her arms in an exaggerated circle—"and around! To preserve the scene!"

She wanted to go around the tracks, even though snow was coming, and it likely wouldn't matter. Which meant she was worried about more than just moving the body: she thought it was a crime scene, unlike the policeman. He certainly wasn't canvassing the area, taking photos. He might have to rely on the photos of the stickybeaking guests, in which case he'd be glad he hadn't shooed us off.

It was a silent agreement that Andy and I, who were standing at the corpse's feet, would grab the ankles, and Sofia and the cop would take the wrists. We tried our best to keep him in the air, but as we shuffled down the hill in shin-deep snow, his head occasionally lolled back and gouged a valley in the fresh powder. He wasn't that heavy, but he was hard to wrangle. I hooked my fingers into the side of his boot to help my grip. They were sturdy, steel-capped. Sofia was walking backwards, trying to hold his wrist to her chest, but the cop had turned, head into the wind, his arms behind him at waist height. I could hear Andy grunting beside me. He turned to me halfway down and I saw his jaw was set with grim concentration. Spit fizzed in his beard.

He saw me looking at him. "You good, mate? Need a break?"

I shook my head. I didn't say: *I'm fine. I've done this before.*

CHAPTER 7

A stack of wooden pallets in the maintenance shed subbed in as an autopsy table. Around us were several benches strewn with tools, a snowmobile with half its guts pulled out, a few generators along the far wall beside a stack of tires, and an assortment of tennis-racquetesque ski shoes hanging on nails. There was no heating, and with the tin walls and concrete floor, it was like stepping into a fridge. It would do as a makeshift morgue. The one benefit of the extreme cold was the lack of odor from the body.

We lowered the body onto the stack of pallets, which were slightly too small, and the man's limbs sagged over the sides. We took a moment to recoup, breathing heavily. I tried not to look at his discolored face. I'd read about frostbite, of blackened extremities—noses, fingers—dropping off, but I'd never seen it up close. The policeman finally decided to take a few pictures. Andy rubbed a toe up and down the back of his calf. Sofia shivered, cupped her hands over her mouth and blew into them, then remembered she'd just been handling a corpse and returned them to her sides. The policeman finished with his photos and turned to us.

"Thanks, fellas," he said. Sofia rolled her eyes, reminding the cop that she too had lumbered a corpse down the mountain. He stumbled over his next words but didn't correct himself, just plowed on. "Normally I wouldn't move the body, but with the front coming in, I don't want to have to dig him out later."

The cop was a few inches taller than me, which may have been his thick boots, and a few kilos heavier, which may have been his thick coat, but I'd have to ignore his full cheeks. He didn't have a gun on his hip. I don't know why I noticed that, I just did. He had dark green eyes, and crystals of ice had settled on his eyelashes. It was clear the morning had rattled him, because his gaze darted around the shed before settling on the body, which seemed to suspend his thought process entirely.

"I'm Ernie," I said, to try to snap him out of it. "Ernest Cunningham. This is Andrew Millot. You've met Sofia. Also Cunningham, hyphen, Garcia."

"Garcia, hyphen, Cunningham," Sofia corrected with a smile.

"Let's get, hyphen, the fuck out of here," Andy said, who had spent the whole time immobilized, like the cop, staring at the body. "This is giving me the creeps."

"Oh." The cop returned his attention to us. "Darius. Officer Crawford, I guess, but Darius is okay. Formalities are for sea level." He extended a hand in greeting. I pointed at the inside of his wrist, where the cuff had a dark stain on it. There was a similar mark on his other wrist too; a stain from carrying the body.

"You've got blood on your coat, Officer Crawford," I said, declining the shake. Cunninghams don't believe in a first-name basis for law enforcement.

Crawford went pale. He looked down at his wrists and breathed deeply.

"You all right?" I asked.

"I, um, I haven't dealt with a lot of these."

"Dead bodies?"

"Murders," Sofia cut in.

"Well, perhaps, but let's keep that quiet for now." Crawford gave a feeble grin. He'd seemed gormless out in the snow, but up close he looked worse. Seeing the blood had apparently not only made him queasy, it also made him realize he was in over his head.

Andy mouthed the word "murder?" back at Sofia. Even in mime, I could hear the incredulous pitch of his voice. She nodded solemnly.

"I guess I should ask if you know the guy. Do you recognize him?" Crawford continued.

"Is this an interview?" I asked. I'd spent too many hours sitting behind two-way mirrors to be answering questions without knowing who was asking and what for. "Why don't you question whoever found the body?"

Crawford shook his head. "I'm just trying to find out if you know who he is. I could get here the quickest from Jindy, but there'll be proper detectives on their way who can do the list-of-suspects thing. But I figure I should find out if he was staying here or came over the ridge—maybe a night skier who got turned around."

"He's not wearing skis," Sofia said. I realized she was very pale too, as white as the snow on the ground.

"Yeah, I understand. Do me a favor though—take a closer look." He showed us a close-up photo on his phone of the dead man's face. It was mostly blackened, including his lips. "Ring any bells?"

All three of us shook our heads. Not only did I not recognize him, but on closer inspection, I realized it didn't resemble frostbite at all. Sofia suddenly held up a hand and ran out the door. We watched her go, confused, until the distinct sound of retching was carried over to us on the wind. Andy and I stood, trying to figure out whether it would be more helpful or embarrassing for us to go out with her, and both settled on inaction.

I'll hold it here to mention that *I know* some authors are incapable of having a woman throw up without it being a clue to a pregnancy. These same authors seem to think nausea is the only indication of childbearing, not to mention their belief that vomit shoots out the woman's mouth within hours of plot-convenient fertilization. By some authors, I mean male ones. Far be it from me to tell you which clues to pay close attention to, but Sofia's not pregnant, okay? She's allowed to throw up of her own volition.

"All right," Crawford said to Andy and me. He seemed happy with our response to the photos, his obligation to the investigation complete, and even a touch more comfortable around the body. "I guess that's it for now." He walked over to the benches and rummaged around until he found an open brass padlock with a key hanging from it. We followed him out the front as he screeched the tin door closed and fiddled with the lock. "I'd say don't go anywhere—"

"—but you can't." I finished it for him.

"Ernest's done this before," Sofia added, emerging from the side of the shed, wiping her mouth. "Dead bodies," she said sheepishly, by way of explanation. "It never gets any easier."

Crawford let out a heavy breath. He seemed tired. I pegged him as a country cop who'd spent most of his career with his feet on the desk or giving tourists like Lucy speeding tickets. He seemed more annoyed to have been pulled from his comfortable day than interested in the corpse. "All right. I've called it in. I understand you're waiting on another guest?"

"What's that got to do with anything?" I said.

"Just crossing t's and dotting i's. I'll be in the guesthouse if you need me, but hopefully there'll be some detectives here soon. Depending on snow and traffic." He glanced up at the mottled sky doubtfully and clicked the lock closed.

"Murder?" Andy complained as we walked down the hill. While the mob had dispersed, there were still scattered people dotted across the resort who had watched us put the body in the shed. I was glad the shed had no windows, otherwise there would have been some icy foreheads. "He was clearly outside overnight, froze to death. You're not even a doctor anymore and you're getting involved, telling that cop it was a *murder*?"

I hadn't known Sofia was no longer a surgeon. I wondered if it had something to do with Katherine whispering in Andy's ear when she raised her hand at Officer Crawford's request. I wondered if it had something to do with her needing fifty thousand dollars. I glanced at Sofia. If Andy had meant it as an insult, it had bounced right off her. Her expression didn't change. Gave nothing away.

"Blood?" I thought aloud, trying to figure it out for myself. "Officer Crawford got blood on his sleeves from carrying the body. If the guy died from exposure overnight, why would he be bleeding? You're saying he was attacked?"

"His face is blackened from frostbite," Andy argued. "What the hell did you tell that cop?"

If our family had a motto, it would be: *Non fueris locutus est scriptor vigilum Cunningham*. Which is Latin for: *Cunninghams don't speak to cops*. I don't speak Latin; I'm not ashamed to admit I googled that. Andy was offended by Sofia's cooperation on Katherine's behalf. "On behalf of" was a typical position for Andy to take. His middle name should have been "Proxy."

"The blood's from an injury on his neck. And you were carrying his feet—you didn't get a good-enough look. That's not frostbite on his face," Sofia said. "It's ash."

"Ash? Like charcoal?" I said. "Out here?"

"It's clogged in his windpipes, caked on his tongue. If we cracked him open, we'd find it in his lungs, I'm sure. It doesn't make sense.

If it wasn't for the fact that he doesn't have a single burn mark on him, and he's in a snowfield that has no signs of being melted, I'd say the cause of death was obvious."

"Enlighten us." Andy was clearly unconvinced.

"He died in a fire."

CHAPTER 8

All I can hope for, when I die, is to be a buzzing topic of conversation over breakfast. Our meal was with the masses—Katherine must have booked the private room for yesterday's lunch—and the dining hall was alive with conversation. Snippets jumped out as I threaded my way through the long wooden benches: *Frozen solid!*; *I got stuck in the bunker on Hole Eight last year too, not as bad as this guy though, maybe he needs to work on his chip shot*; *I heard he's not even staying here?*; *I'm not letting Jason and Holly out of my sight.*

I joined the line, shuffling past the bain-maries, and filled my plate. The bacon was untouched, assumedly because people were confronting their own mortality and avoiding saturated fats. I loaded up, then joined my family, sitting next to Lucy and across from Sofia. This was closer to my mother than I preferred, but I thought it too pointed to leave a gap and sit on the other side of Andy and Katherine. While every other table was trading theories about what had happened to the man on the mountain, which I thought would be an opportunity for Sofia to propound her murder theory, she was uncharacteristically quiet, head down, pushing her food around rather than eating it. Instead, I had to listen to

Marcelo gently defend himself against Lucy's latest investment opportunity pitch, some harebrained scheme that was so multilevel it needed an elevator. I used to make fun of her for it, until I'd realized that these companies prey on women by weaponizing certain feminist ideals—namely independence, both financial and in business—to fabricate a sense of self-worth. Lucy, with her husband in prison, was a perfect target to become addicted to this faux success.

Marcelo, to his credit, was weathering her Boss Babe attack calmly, waiting for her to tire herself out. "I'm glad you're enjoying being a part of something, but be careful. Like with that car they've given you." Marcelo couldn't resist just one dig at her. "I hear it's on a pretty rigid contract—you could get stuck with a very expensive lease."

"I know what I'm doing," Lucy huffed. "We actually paid it off in advance." She said the last part proudly, but Marcelo clearly didn't believe her. She was quiet after that.

I looked around the room and saw Officer Crawford sitting on his own by the window, gazing up at the peak. Waiting for the real detectives so he could go home? I'm not sure. All the lights were on inside the dining hall, but with the rumbling sky it could have passed for early evening. Maybe he was watching the entry road, worried about getting stuck up here. I realized that he would be able to see the maintenance shed from his angle; he was keeping an eye on it. I felt chastened for not giving him enough credit. He was probably working through what Sofia had told him. I'd been thinking about it too, remembering the footprints, the way they darted in that small, square area: an invisible box. I now knew I was looking at the last movements of a burning man. A frantic dance back and forth, with no idea of direction, as he was engulfed in flames. And yet: not a drop of melted snow.

"All I'm saying," Andy was enthusing to Katherine, interrupting my thoughts with his volume, "is that we now know from Bitcoin what to watch for. We're not talking doubling or tripling like traditional stocks. It's a real game changer." I noticed Sofia slide a piece of paper from her pocket, dash an X on it with a flourish, and shoot me a wink. I realized I hadn't been keeping track of my own bingo card. I couldn't cross off Lucy's sales pitch because she was talking to Marcelo, not me. I *could* cross off the bottom-right square (*Broken Bone OR Someone Dies*) but decided it was tacky. To do it in front of people at least—I did want to win.

There was a pyramid of croissants in the middle of the table. Andy reached for one, but Katherine slapped his hand.

"I washed my hands," he complained.

"Some things don't wash off." She wrapped a napkin around a pastry and dropped it onto his plate. He picked up his cutlery, sulking.

"Don't worry. He'll get here before the storm," Marcelo said to Audrey, but our table was so starved of conversation that everyone's ears pricked up at the opportunity. Even mine.

"We're staying?" Lucy asked.

"You think they clear the resort every time someone hits a tree on a black diamond run?" Marcelo shook his head, matter-of-fact. "People die in nature. Without the right skills and knowledge . . . If you don't respect the mountain, what do you expect?" He shrugged, with the confidence of someone who believes if you're successful in one thing, you're successful in all things. I'd seen Marcelo scream at a teenager over froth on his latte: if he didn't respect a barista, I doubted he respected a mountain.

"It's nonrefundable," Katherine added, between sips of orange juice. Then she shot a look at Sofia, as if she was most likely to object. "We're staying."

"And what would even be the point of leaving?" Marcelo finished his thought. "We're probably *more* aware of the dangers now."

Andy and I both glanced over at Sofia. Me, out of curiosity, to see if she'd respond; Andy, in more of a challenge. Her fork scraped her plate, but she didn't look up.

"Michael's not going to want to turn up and see the place crawling with cops, asking questions about some dead guy," Lucy said.

"They won't have any cause to ask him questions," Marcelo said. "He was two hundred kilometers away last night."

"I just don't think it's good to remind him of—"

"Michael can decide for himself. When he gets here." Audrey's firm voice cut through. She had a mother's touch for putting an end to arguments. We were staying. All of us. It was nonnegotiable.

"What if it's the Black Tongue?" Sofia finally spoke. Andy blew croissant flakes over the table with a surprised snort. "You know the most common cause of death in a fire is not burning, it's suffocation. The fire pulls too much oxygen from the air."

"Not over breakfast, love," said Marcelo.

"Bit dramatic," choked Andy, thumping his chest to work the pastry through.

"What's a Black Tongue?" Lucy and I asked in unison.

"Bit light on current affairs, are you?" Andy said, making a *Psycho*-esque stabbing motion in the air.

"I'm serious," Sofia said. "Andy, like I told you outside, there's something strange about the—"

"Don't pull me into this," said Andy.

"Ern?"

"I believe you, but I didn't get a very good look."

"I wouldn't rely on Ernest—he's got a bit of form for backstabbing."

"Lucy, honestly." Sofia was begging now. "Listen. From what I've read, I think it fits—"

"Little Miss Wants to Be a Hero has a diagnosis, does she? We're supposed to trust you?" Katherine's tone was so vicious, it caught me by surprise. The way she lingered on the word "trust." "You saw the body for what, a minute, maybe two?"

"I carried the damn thing down a mountain. Trust me. Something's not right. Officer Crawford's going to want to hope his buddies get here soon, because I don't think he realizes what he might have stumbled into."

There are usually two types of cops in these books: Only Hopes and Last Resorts. At this stage, Darius Crawford's only hope was to *be* a Last Resort. I wasn't prepared to count on him any more than I would a bombmaker's fingers. Sofia had clearly made the same assessment.

"Can you even hear yourself?" Katherine was just mocking her now. It was like a school cafeteria. If she had had a chocolate milk, she might have poured it on Sofia's head. "Are you even sober?"

Andy was going to need a Heimlich if he kept choking on his croissant. Marcelo took a sharp breath, shocked by Katherine's remark. I was not so surprised; Katherine had been a teetotaler since her accident, and anything other than total sobriety may have offended her.

"I didn't see you volunteering to help," I waded in, if only so Sofia could see someone was on her side. I wasn't going to ask her at the table, as it would turn into a full-blown argument, but I was curious to hear more about whatever the Black Tongue was.

Katherine talked across me to Sofia. "That's because I assumed he was asking for real doctors, not suspended ones."

I'd only found out half an hour ago, while looking at a body, mind you, that Sofia's surgical career was on the backburner, so I was still getting my head around it. I'd just assumed it was a midlife crisis, a career shake-up. But Katherine was making an accusation. The same one she must have whispered to Andy in the crowd.

Sofia flushed red. She stood up and, for a second, I thought she was about to lunge across the table and Officer Crawford might well have an even busier day, but instead she folded her napkin, tossed it on her plate, and said pointedly before leaving: "I'm still registered."

"Was that really necessary?" I hissed at Katherine after Sofia was out of earshot.

"I'm surprised she hasn't told you. I thought you two were bolted together these days. Figures."

"Told me what?"

"She's getting sued." Katherine smirked. And all I could think of was: *maybe fifty*. "By the family of someone who died on her table." Andy made a *glug-glug* mime behind her. I now recognized the bite in Katherine's words, accusing Sofia of being a drunkard. I thought of the six-pack of beer buried outside my door. She liked a drink, sure, but I'd never known her to overdo it. Had she made a mistake? Why hadn't she told me?

I turned my attention to Marcelo. "If she's getting sued, are you defending her?"

He looked over to Katherine, almost an appeal, but met her hard stare. He shook his head and said bluntly, "Her mess."

I thought this very uncharacteristic of him; I'd always thought Sofia was his little princess. "You'll defend Michael on a murder charge but not your daughter?"

"Michael's served his time," Lucy said. "No thanks to you."

"You're still going to stand by him?" I spat. It was meaner than I intended, because while I *was* getting mad, I wasn't actually mad at Lucy. She and I should have been united, at least, on this, but she'd clearly decided she wanted to bury her head in the sand, outsource her anger to a scapegoat (me), instead of dealing with the actual pain of the breakdown of her marriage.

Audrey pulled one of her standing-from-the-table routines to shut us up. Everyone made to leave. But I wasn't done. I was furious. Crawford was curiously watching our family; we must have been talking more loudly than I'd realized. I wondered if he knew we were Cunninghams: read, automatic suspects. He had known that Michael was expected to join us, so I supposed he did.

"I can't believe I'm the one who has to say this, but are we really going to storm out of every meal? Can't we just stick together for half a minute? This is a reunion. Shouldn't we start, like, reunion-ing, or whatever?" I don't know why I said it. Maybe seeing the dead man had affected me after all, and I was seeing in Sofia's exit the ostracism I'd felt for the last three years. Maybe I'd decided who I'd *spill it* for. Maybe I'd eaten too much bacon.

If a man on fire couldn't melt snow, my mother's fury, as she addressed me directly for the first time that weekend, sure could have.

"The reunion starts when my son arrives."

MY WIFE

CHAPTER 9

I don't want to talk about it.

MY FATHER

CHAPTER 10

I suppose it's time I told you how my dad died.

I was six. We saw it on the news before the station called to tell us. In the movies they always show up at the door and there's a subdued type of knock—you know the one—where you know what kind of bad news is behind the door before you open it, and the policemen aren't wearing their hats. I know it's stupid, but I do remember the phone ringing and thinking it was a solemn ring. It was the same trill I'd heard a thousand times before, but in that moment it felt a millisecond slower, a decibel louder.

Dad was always out at night; it came with the territory. I have affectionate memories of him, I truly do, but what I think of most when I think about him is the spaces he left. It was easier to tell where my dad had been than to see where he was. The empty armchair in the living room. The plate in the oven. Stubble in the bathroom sink. Three empty holsters in a six-pack in the fridge. My father was footprints, residue.

When the phone rang, I was sitting at the kitchen table. My brothers were upstairs.

Yeah, I said "brothers." We'll get to that.

The TV was still on, but Mum had switched the sound off a while ago, saying she just couldn't listen to the reporter anymore. There was a helicopter shining a searchlight on a petrol station—it looked like a police car had run into the big white ice freezer, with split bags of ice scattered across the crumpled bonnet—but I still didn't know anything was wrong. Mum must have had an inkling because even though she was pretending to be uninterested, I noticed too many sideways glances to the TV. And she kept tactically invading my view of the screen by deciding she definitely did need to rummage in that particular cupboard or it was the perfect time to rub this particular spot of the bench raw with Jif cleaner. Then that ring. The phone was wall mounted, next to the door. She picked it up. I remember the *thunk* of my mother's head on the doorframe. Her whispering: "Goddamn it, Robert." I knew she wasn't talking *to* him.

I don't know exactly how it actually happened. If I'm honest, it's something I've never really wanted to dig too deep into, but I've managed to piece it together over the years from news reports, asides from my mother, and memories of the funeral, so I'll tell you that. In my version of events there are necessarily a few assumptions, mixed with some parts I'm pretty confident about, as well as the things I know for sure.

Let's start with the assumptions. I assume the petrol station had one of those silent alarm buttons. I assume the attendant had a pistol in his face, but managed to scrape his quivering fingertips along the underside of the counter until he found that button. I assume that button sent a message to the police station, who wired it to the nearest patrol car.

Now for the stuff I'm pretty confident in. I'm pretty confident the shooting started before the patrol car came to a stop. I'm pretty confident getting shot in the neck is a slow and painful way to die; I've heard it's like drowning. I'm pretty confident the driver was the first one hit. And I'm pretty confident the bullet in his neck was why he crashed into the ice freezer.

Here's what I know for sure. That the passenger-side policeman got out of the car, walked into the service station, and shot my dad three times.

I know that for sure because it was the same officer who came up to my mother at the state funeral with a hefty slice of cake and said, "I'll show you where I shot him," before smearing a finger of cream across her belly and growling, "Here," tracing a lingering sticky spiral on her hip, "here," and then squashing the rest of the cake in the center of her chest: "and here."

My mother didn't flinch, but I remember hearing her let out a long-held breath through her nose, as the cop returned to a circle of his back-slapping friends.

This is one of those tricks writers use, I'm afraid. The state funeral I attended as a child was not my father's. It was for the man he killed. My mother said we had to go because it was the right thing to do. She said there'd be TV cameras, and they'd talk about us if we went but they'd talk about us more if we didn't. And that's when I learned what it was like to be an outcast. I wasn't me anymore. Not just for the funeral, at school too. And later, when I had to tell a girl I was dating about my childhood. And when I didn't want to tell a girl about my childhood but she googled me anyway. (Erin, with her own traumas of a violent father, had been one of the first to understand me on this level.) There was that time a detective from Queensland drove the ten hours to Sydney just to accuse a Cunningham of an unsolved assault on his beat. I was sixteen at the time and had never left the state. I imagine it was a long drive back north for that bloke, sitting with the humiliation of not only his prime suspect being a teenager without a driver's license but also Marcelo's telling him to shove his unreliable hair analysis up himself. My point is, our name pops up on a list, even for something as fallible as hair matching (not permitted in courtrooms since the 90s for a reason), and it may as well be highlighted. Like when Detective McMuffin had me holed up in an interview room a couple of decades later and wouldn't believe anything I was telling him. I wasn't Ernest Cunningham anymore. I was "*his* kid." My mother became "*his* widow." Our family name was an invisible tattoo: we were the family of a cop-killer.

Mum became law. She did not care for police, so neither did we. I think she only liked Marcelo at first because he was a lawyer for small-time crooks like my dad: his approach to the law was not one of respect, but one of loopholes and trickery. Corporate law is just the next evolution of skulduggery: the criminals are the same, they just drive better cars. Even now, Dad's shadow loomed large, and if it had been a city cop and not Officer Last Resort who had to deal with the ash-faced man, I knew we'd all already be in cuffs. Prime suspects.

Now you know how my father died. Hopped up on something (they'd found a syringe by his corpse), trying to knock over a petrol station for a few hundred dollars. I know, I'm a jerk for burying it in Chapter 10. But I'm putting it here because it's about to be important. And I figure you should know how we learned what it meant to be a Cunningham: to close ourselves off and protect each other. That was the door that Sofia had felt closing on her at the breakfast table. And even me, the very definition of an outcast, had only half-heartedly stuck up for her, still trying to keep one foot inside the circle. That was how we did things. Until I saw a sliver of my father in Michael's eyes that night in a spiderweb clearing, and tried to run as far away from it as I could.

Non fueris locutus . . . I forget the rest.

CHAPTER 11

The entrance to the roof was up half a dozen flights of groaning, threadbare carpeted stairs. I peered into the corridors as I passed each level; it seemed there were about eight rooms per floor. I had a few reasons for doing this. One: I wanted to estimate the number of guests. I figured there were about forty rooms, with a couple of empties, so maybe sixty to eighty people. Two: I wanted to see if Officer Crawford was door-knocking. He had seemed a bit squeamish around the body, and I doubted he'd ever run a murder investigation before, but I still thought he'd be able to conjure up a rudimentary line of questioning. A corpse required at least a smidgen of urgency, I thought, but he seemed determined not to give it. Considering the breakfast hall had been energetically gossip-filled instead of morose, I was still wondering if *anyone* here knew who the dead man was, and if anyone even cared. Three: it's always been a habit of mine to try to sneak a peek into hotel rooms that are being made up, just because I like seeing what's inside. I used to come back to a hotel room and tell Erin that the room across the hall had the beds on different sides of the room, the TV mounted on the wall, or different-colored curtains to ours. It sounds like such dull insight (go on, editor, take this bit out, I dare you), but ask yourself if you've ever walked past an open hotel door and *not* looked inside. It's impossible.

Now that I think about it, that was what was bugging me so much about the mood over breakfast. It felt like everyone was walking past a door without looking inside.

Maybe I'm saying something about humanity's innate curiosity. I'm the guy who sat in his brother's car with a body in the back just to see what he'd do. I'm the guy who's walking to the roof for mobile reception just to google "the Black Tongue." I'm the guy who's about to look through way too many doors. Maybe it's important after all.

Little plaques on each level had arrows for the various sets of room numbers or facilities. The Dining Room and Bar were on the ground floor, as well as a Drying Room (important rooms are always proper nouns in mystery novels), while on various upper levels were a Laundry, a Library—which I figured must have the fireplace from the brochure, and I am therefore blaming it for getting me into this mess in the first place, so I decided it had better deliver an almost fairy-tale level of warmth and crackling to make up for my current situation—a Gym and an Activities Room, which had the words POOL/DARTS next to it. I reminded myself to focus less on the dead body and try to enjoy the vacation part of it all, as relaxing as it had been so far. While I very much doubted Michael and I would play a social game of pool, I was sure we could find something brotherly to do together. He might like to throw darts at me.

As I continued up the stairs, the little arrow next to ROOF changed from pointing up to pointing sideways, and I saw a housekeeping cart in the adjoining corridor. Score. I peeked inside: twin room, shit fridge.

There was a woman already on the roof, smoking a post-brekkie cigarette. I knew it wasn't Sofia before she turned around, because Sofia is a lazy smoker; she'll let a dart burn down to her fingertips if she's not paying attention, then she'll say, "Oh," and light another one. Lucy smokes like she's siphoning gas, so I knew it was her from the short, desperate gulps.

The cold was bracing. I nestled my hands in my pockets next to several tiny shampoo bottles I'd nicked from the housekeeping cart (I'm not above it) and walked over to her.

"Hang on," she said, and sucked the soul out of the cigarette. I had a friend at university who used to chew gum, pin it to her headboard overnight, and chew it again in the morning. That was how Lucy treated cigarettes: mileage. I could see that she was telling herself that it was her last. I also could see that she really believed it, as I'm sure she did every time. Turns out, this time, she was almost right. She would only have one more.

"Internet," I said, taking out my phone by way of explanation (battery: 54%).

I had to be standing on the roof to get a single bar of reception, and even then it was hit and miss. Which I'm well aware is, like, *a thing* in these books. You'll just have to get over it. And I know there's a storm front coming in. And I know I glossed over the fact that there's a freaking library with a fireplace in the building (which happens to be where I will solve the damn thing). It's pretty much the whole How-To-Write-A-Mystery checklist at this point. If it's any consolation, no one's phone runs out of battery until page 280. So the reception and the battery thing is a cliché. I don't know what to tell you—we're in the mountains. What do you expect?

"I'm sorry about before," I said. Seeing as we were shoulder to shoulder, I spoke outwards, lobbing my apology into the void of the mountain. It's the only way blokes know how to show humility, by pretending we're at a urinal. "I'm still processing everything, but I shouldn't have snapped at you like that. I just figure, you know, today, we could have each other's back. Shared experience."

"How about you fix your marriage, and I'll fix mine?"

It was a lot of bravado for someone clinging to nicotine for courage. But I didn't want to start another argument so I just said, "Fair."

We stood in silence, watching the mountain. A faint mechanical clanking came from the distant chairlift. It was still early enough for some people to be pulling on their boots, but I figured the most avid had already been up for hours, finding the freshest snow. I could see roads tracing their way through treetops like veins, a river gouging the white plateau below, and all the way downhill to where the ground turned from pure white to mottled and patchy brown. The wind howled across the roof, rippling the clamped umbrellas that were skewered through the centers of a row of wooden tables. Andy was right: there were three artificial grass squares with golf tees on them, lining one side of the roof. At the far end, a spa behind an aluminum fence, its cover half open, mist shrouding the water.

My eyes couldn't resist darting to where the body had been found. It was a long way from anything: the nearest resort's ski slope on the ridge, the tree line up the hill, or even the entrance road. From up high, my perspective was clear enough to form an opinion. There was no way the dead man had stumbled to where he lay unless he was already at Sky Lodge: it was just too far.

"You got a look at him," Lucy said, surprising me. She had seen my gaze settle on that specific patch of snow. I looked at her properly for the first time. She was wearing bright-pink lipstick and had mascara-lined eyes. I'm sure the look she was going for was sultry, but she was so pale from the cold that any splash of color seemed to leap off her face and she looked like a cartoon character. She had on another pristine outfit—a yellow turtleneck that was very form-fitting for snow gear. "When the cop asked you and Andy to carry the body. He kept us all too far back to see. But you got a look?"

I cleared my throat. "I guess. If it was Halloween, I was the donkey's arse though."

"Huh?"

"I took his feet."

"Well?" she said expectantly. "Did he look like Michael?"

"Oh, Lucy." I understood some of the desperation in her voice. She'd probably made the assumption over breakfast, otherwise our family would have had a much more somber conversation, but still, no one had told her directly. "It wasn't Michael."

"It looked nothing like him?"

"I mean, it wasn't him. And I'm probably the only one here that looks like him, and I think I'm still"—I patted myself down theatrically to assert I was still alive—"yep, I'm still standing. Listen, Sofia's just got us scared. Shall we find out what she's on about?" I held up my phone. Lucy had been the only other one at the breakfast table who hadn't known what the Black Tongue was.

She shook her head. "I looked it up already. It's a while ago, but it seems it was big news at the time, plenty of press, and so of course they had to come up with a catchy killer's name. Someone murdered an elderly couple in Brisbane. And another woman in Sydney."

I realized why I hadn't heard about it. For the last couple of years I hadn't been able to stomach the more gruesome news stories, since I became a part of one. "What are their names?" I asked.

"Ah." She scrolled her phone, skim-reading an article. "Alison Humphreys and . . . I dunno. Oh. Williams for the couple—Mark and Janine."

"Sofia said they suffocated? Like . . . torture?"

"It's a slow way to die. I'd probably just"—she made a little gun with her fingers and flicked it against the side of her head—"rather than go through that. People are worried it's a kind of serial killer. They've only done it twice. Well, I guess there was a couple, but does that count as one or two? Like, obviously it's two victims, but in terms of making the killer a *serial* killer, what are the guidelines?"

"It's not my area of expertise."

"Don't you write these things?"

"I write *about* writing these things."

"Maybe it's to do with theatrics. Maybe a couple of spectacular murders is worth more than a string of mundane ones. Certainly for a newspaper, anyway." Before I could ask her if a man burning to death in an unmelted snowfield counted as a spectacular murder or not, she went on. "Sofia's off her rocker. I don't believe a serial killer is hiding out at this retreat. I just wanted to know if you recognized the body, maybe from lunch yesterday, or when you were in the bar with Andy, or just around?"

It sounded like a hurried excuse to me. "Why do you want to know who he is?"

"Because nobody seems to know and it's giving me the creeps. And no one seems to be missing."

"I'm sure they have a guest book. Maybe he was staying by himself."

"Word is, everyone who should be here is accounted for."

"How do you know that?"

"I talk to people. The owner. You should try it sometime."

"I didn't recognize him," I confessed. I know I'm the narrator, but it interested me that I wasn't the only one scratching around the death. Crime novels always look at the motives of a list of suspects, but only from the perspective of the inspired inquirer. Am I really the detective just because it's my voice you have to listen to? I guess this whole story would be different if someone else wrote it. Maybe I'm only the Watson after all.

So what made Lucy especially curious, and up here with me grappling with an intermittent internet for clues? I caught the faintest glimmer of disappointment in the way she set her jaw, and figured something out. "You're digging around because you want to get rid of Crawford," I said. "You know that the longer it takes to identify a John Doe, the more police they'll send. And if Michael's on edge, it will ruin your plan for the weekend."

"I can't have any distractions," she whispered. I didn't have the heart to tell her that, under that policy, her fluorescent lipstick would have to go. "Michael deserves his family back. This is my last chance to give it to him."

I realized there was another reason for her to be on the roof. She was hunting that one bar of reception. Hoping a text would slip through.

"Have you heard from him?" I asked.

"No."

"Her?"

Lucy laughed. "I think she might have deleted my number. I'm the *ex*. You?"

"I wasn't expecting to."

"I guess we are on the same side." She sighed.

"Are you worried about seeing him?"

"I know he'll be different. But I'm scared about how much. I couldn't sleep last night. I kept dreaming that he wouldn't even know who I was. I keep wondering what'll be left of the old version of him, if there'll be anything at all. I'm scared there might not be."

I didn't say my fear was the opposite: that he wouldn't have changed at all.

It occurred to me that Lucy had never asked me about the money. She mustn't have known about it. That's a huge amount to keep hidden in a marriage, I thought.

She surprised me again by putting out a hand. I took it: a truce. Her hand was shaking so much I'd have had to grab her by the elbow to keep it still. "You shouldn't have done that to him," she muttered, before letting go. So low and quiet I almost missed it. I opened my mouth to argue, but she raised a hand. "I'm not saying it's your fault. I'm not that narrow-minded. But none of this would have happened if you hadn't made that choice. He might have ended up in jail, but it would have happened a different way. I hate you for that." She wasn't angry; rather, she was calm and sincere, so I knew it was true. "I just wanted to say it aloud to your face. Just once."

I nodded. I'd had a feeling she wanted to say this to me—Just Once, like she liked having Just One More cigarette, but I understood. I'd been thinking a lot about the same thing the last twenty-four hours. I didn't blame her.

A rumble echoed across the rooftop, the growl of a car's engine really grappling with the terrain, picked up in the wind and ferried to us. I looked to the entry road and saw a pair of headlights emerge from the trees. It wasn't a car though: it was a midsized box-truck. One you'd hire to move house. It was comically impractical for the conditions and started bouncing down the slope. Five, maybe ten, minutes away.

"Here we go," I said.

Lucy took a deep steadying breath and fumbled out what would be her last cigarette.

CHAPTER 12

The gaggle that formed in the parking lot, uphill from the guesthouse entrance, was not unlike the one that had formed earlier on the mountain: it was the same wary semicircle, except that instead of clamoring for a glimpse at a dead man, we were all there to see one resurrected.

Lucy wasn't the only one wondering how much Michael had changed: none of us had visited him in prison. It should be no surprise to you that my invite got lost in the mail, but, maybe out of embarrassment, maybe out of shame, Michael hadn't wanted visits from anyone. He'd decided to treat prison like a cocoon, hiding himself away. There had been some communication with a few members of the family, but never in person. Phone calls. Emails. I'm not sure if serving divorce papers by mail counts as writing letters, but if it does, he wrote some letters too. But contact was sparse. So his arrival was indeed momentous.

There was the crunch of the handbrake being pulled on. Then the engine cut out, the truck sighing onto its suspension, and there was just the whistle of the mountain wind. A crack of thunder would have added to the mood, but I promised not to lie. I noticed Michael's truck had perfectly applied tire chains.

Lucy primped her hair, checked her breath in her palm. My mother folded her arms.

The passenger-side door opened, and Michael got out.

Some of you will have just figured something out. But I'm going to let it sit.

After three years and change, I'll admit I was expecting the desert-island version of my brother: wiry hair hanging down to his shoulders, a forest of a beard, and beady, nervous eyes: *So this is civilization*. Instead, we got the opposite. He had longer hair, sure, but it was styled into a wave, and it was thick and full. Maybe even dyed. He must have had time to spruce up because he was clean-shaven. And while I was expecting extra lines of hardship somewhere in his brow, he had smooth skin, rosy cheeks, and bright eyes. Maybe it was the snap of cold, or maybe prison, away from the elements, was an underrated skincare regime, but I was damned if he didn't look younger than when he went away. The last time I'd seen him he'd been sitting in the dock, hunched, wearing a suit like it was a straitjacket. But here, he seemed refreshed. Resurrected.

In a black North Face down jacket over a button-up collared shirt, he looked like someone who'd paid to climb Everest. He took a deep breath of mountain air, savored it, and let out a wild "*Cooee.*" It echoed back across the valley.

"Wow," he said. "Katherine, you've nailed the spot." He shook his head, hamming up how incredulous he was at the beauty of the place, or maybe he was genuine, I'm not sure. Then he made a beeline for my mother. I suppose I should start calling her "our mother" now. Or maybe I should just call her "his mother," and I should stick with "Audrey."

Michael leaned in and gave our mother a hug, said a few words into her ear. She grabbed him by both shoulders and shook him, as if to check if he was real. Michael laughed and said something else that only reached me as a murmur, then turned to Marcelo, who gave him a firm handshake and a fatherly pat on the upper arm.

Michael worked his way around the semicircle. Katherine got a hug with an air kiss. Andy got a handshake while he said, "Nice truck," and commented that he hoped it had some guts to get back up the hill, in the way that uncomfortable men believe they should talk about cars. My stomach was rolling more with each person Michael greeted, shuffling along the line. Lined up like this, it felt like meeting the Queen. I could feel my heartbeat in my throat. I wrestled with my collar; too many layers. I worried I'd be a foot shorter, having melted through the snow, by the time he got to the end of the line. Sofia gave him a one-armed hug, as if reluctantly paired up at a school dance, with a perfunctory "Welcome back, Mike." That stood out: my brother has had many names in his life—Mickey, Cunners, Ham, The Defendant—but no one calls him Mike. By the time he got to Lucy, she'd gnawed off half her lipstick and she fell into his arms as if she'd broken a heel. She buried her head in his neck, and whispered something. I was the only one close enough to hear his response: "Not here." She gathered herself, pulling back and taking quick, hitching breaths through her nose in an attempt to portray calm. Sofia put a hand on her back. Then Michael was at the end of the line, in front of me.

"Ern." He stuck out his hand. His fingers were prison-filthy, dirt under the nails. His smile was convincingly warm. I couldn't tell if he was glad to see me or if he'd just excelled in the prison's amateur theater society.

I took his hand and choked out, "Welcome home," even though I wasn't sure if he was either.

"I'm sure Katherine's got lots planned, but I'm hoping we can find a quiet beer sometime," he said. In my head, he was asking about the money, but it didn't match his tone. I was aware of Sofia watching us, trying to make out our words, and suspected her comforting Lucy was actually a tactic to be one step closer to our conversation. "I have some things to say that I think I owe you. I hope you'll take me up on it."

If you polish those words differently—words like "owe" and "things to say"—it becomes a threat, but his voice was . . . *humble.* That's the only word I can think of to describe it. Everything I'd thought this encounter would be, it wasn't. I was struggling to reconcile the man in front of me with the man I'd built in my head: one full of anger, pain, and revenge. I thought it might have been a front for everyone else, and the mask could drop when we were alone, but it didn't feel like a trick. Call it brotherhood. Call it blood. I'd brought a bag of cash in the hope that he'd hear me out. He'd brought a handshake and a smile and hoped the same.

I was nodding as quickly as Lucy was breathing. I managed to fish out "Yep" from somewhere between my arse and my tongue.

That was when the driver's-side door of the truck opened. This is the part most of you will have figured out when Michael emerged from the passenger seat.

"That was quite a drive," Erin said, stretching. "How's the coffee here?"

CHAPTER 13

Admittedly, this was not so big a revelation as to warrant a chapter break. We'd all known who was in the driver's seat. Of course we had: Lucy had already arrived, and as if Katherine would leave something as important as picking Michael up to improvisation. It was not a surprise to see Erin, nor to see her with Michael.

Before you accuse me of dragging out the reveal of her exiting the truck, I'd suggest that Erin simply had an innate sense of suspense or, more likely, she hadn't wanted to make Michael's arrival even more awkward, so had hung back in the truck until he'd finished his royal line of greetings.

I'd found out about them six months after Michael went to prison. I think I was first, and then it trickled through the rest of the family. Though I've always pictured Lucy finding out at the same time as me: in her dressing gown, excitedly opening a large yellow envelope, knowing it was prison mail from the fact that it had been torn open, plundered, and taped back up, just as my wife said to me over an otherwise uneventful breakfast that she was *planning to spend more time* with my brother Michael.

Okay, I did drag that out.

If you're wondering about my choice of words, most of my breakfasts are uneventful; I have simply never found meals with that much milk involved to be dramatic. I have only had three *eventful* breakfasts in my life. You know about two of them. The other involves sperm: we have to get to know one another a bit better before we get to that.

People accuse marriages of losing their spark. Like they have a supernatural zap of energy that can be mishandled, misplaced. And perhaps the case could be made that if my wife was able to cultivate a relationship with my convicted brother exclusively by phone and email (because he didn't have visitors) without me noticing, our marriage was already over. And don't allow me to paint her as the bad guy here, because she isn't and it was—over, that is. The night Michael visited, body in the back of his car, we were already in separate rooms. Otherwise she might have seen the money when I threw it on my bed. But it wasn't the spark that was the problem. It was the lighter, the flint, the matches. And they weren't lost, they were taken. It wasn't that we lost our spark, it was that we didn't have the tools to make it anymore.

"I don't want it to be weird," she'd murmured at that breakfast. She'd been spinning her wedding ring on her finger as she said it. Which I took less as a metaphor for an imploding marriage than a realization of how much weight she'd lost. A person's cheeks or hips give a window into short-term ups and downs, but when you see it in their *hands* . . . I had known we were both thinning out, but I used to have to pull that ring off her like I was starting a chainsaw. Seeing it so loose made me think about what I was doing to her. Don't get me wrong, there was nothing cruel between us: no screaming matches or thrown plates. But we'd reached the point where, in even being together, we were doing something to each other. Maybe if she hadn't been spinning it I would have said something different, but she was and so I didn't.

"You can do whatever you want," I said.

She gave me one of those smiles where your eyes glisten in a way that means you're not really smiling, and told me not to tell Lucy yet.

I didn't feel the need to ask her anything else. Breakfast was not the time. And then, well, I just never asked. I've thought about it, sure. Sometimes I wonder if she just liked the danger. I've read that it's a thing, women falling for death row inmates, with some even having multiple wives. Or maybe someone in jail felt like a relief to her. A relationship that had literal boundaries, where she didn't have to worry about the other stuff, the stuff that had torn us apart. Michael was incapable of having my faults, because he didn't intersect with her life at all. I've gone through all the options, believe me. Maybe she'd been drinking the Cunningham Kool-Aid and, ironically, saw it as an act of loyalty. Maybe she believed him over me. Maybe *he* had the flint. When I was feeling spiteful, which I try not to be, I wondered if it was because they had something in common that I couldn't match. This is called foreshadowing.

Michael was easier to figure out. I always thought he just wanted to take something from me.

Erin stepping out of the truck, while not a surprise, was indeed momentous. Because Michael had truly had no visitors in prison, and certainly no conjugal ones. This weekend was not only the first time I was seeing them together, it was the first time they were seeing each other. Their relationship was quite a mystery, and each of us had different ideas of what it actually meant. Call me fatalistic, or maybe just lazy, but I was happy to roll over: I considered them together, but always stopped short of calling them a couple. Lucy, with her tag-riddled wardrobe and emergency-beacon lipstick, clearly felt that it was something she could still weasel between. Everyone else seemed to vary on a scale between Disbelief and Acceptance, most hovering around Skeptical.

Looking back, I can't have been as aloof as I'm writing myself here, because it did occur to me that they hadn't spent the night together yet, with Erin only picking Michael up from the Cooma Correctional Centre, about a two-hour drive away, that morning. She would have stayed in the itchy-sheet motel I imagined her in last night. I don't know why that's important—who cares if they'd spent the night together or not—but I'll admit it popped into my head. I mention that here because, I figure, if I had thought about such things, Lucy was probably clinging to them.

Erin made her way around the circle much more efficiently than Michael, partly because she had fewer people to shake hands with, as Lucy made a big show of tying up her shoelace. When she got to me, I extended my hand.

"Nice things," I said. It's a private joke we have; I was playing for a laugh.

She didn't smile. Instead, she took my hand and brought me into a cold, one-armed hug. Her breath was warm on my ear as she whispered, "It's family money, Ern."

They were urgent, stolen words. Michael had told me the same thing the night he'd buried Alan. *It's our money.* I knew what it meant. He'd earned it. He'd killed for it. He was laying claim to it, and offering me a share for my silence. I can't say what I was expecting to hear from Erin, perhaps something apologetic or, when she leaned in close to my ear, something sultry, or a combination of the two: apologetically sultry. But I hadn't expected her to be Michael's messenger, while he smiled and said he owed me a cold one. *It's family money, Ern.* Was there a hint of what might happen if I didn't play along? I couldn't be sure. The look in her eyes was earnest, not threatening. Maybe just a warning. She was gone before I could decide, and I couldn't ask her in front of everyone anyway.

The group quickly split into factions. Lucy and Sofia closed in on Michael and me. Lucy assumedly didn't want to let Michael out of her sight, and Sofia probably didn't want me to blurt out anything about the money until I'd decided whether to give her any. Erin formed a cluster with my mother and Marcelo. Without seeming too interested, I tried to read my mother's expression. It was unfamiliar to me, so I figured it must have been warm and welcoming. Katherine joined Erin's huddle, and Andy, momentarily stranded in the middle, floated over to our group.

Michael, perhaps realizing it was up to him to set the tone and that if he didn't talk, no one would, was trying to keep things light by telling us how he'd forced Erin to stop at every petrol station on the way up so he could sample a different chocolate bar at each.

"Best one?" I'd made a little deal with myself to be as civil to Michael as he was to me, so I thought I'd try to join in.

"Results are inconclusive." He nodded, then tapped his belly. "I'm going to need a lot more data."

Lucy laughed far too loudly.

"What's with the truck?" Sofia asked. "Did you not get the 'mountain lodge' part of the invite? I'm surprised you made it up here."

"Hire place stuffed the booking—it was supposed to be a van. They only had this one, or else we were taking Erin's hatchback and that just wasn't enough for my stuff, seeing as my storage unit renews tomorrow and they've sucked me dry enough already. So it's basically got my living room in the back of it. We were a bit worried, but it's got grunt."

"You brought an armchair to the snow?" Andy laughed. I was still grappling with his use of the word "we."

"I would have just paid the extra. You brought that whole thing just to save a few dollars?" Sofia asked.

"I think it's very sensible," Lucy muttered. "I thought I still had most of our—"

"It's what they had." Michael talked over her. "Plus, we made sure they gave it to us for a good discount, of course. And I'll have to move my things next week, so might keep it a few days extra. Worth the risk of getting it up here."

"You can keep stuff at mine if you need to," I said, half to fill the air and half because I wasn't entirely listening; I had one ear out for a glimmer of Erin's conversation with Katherine. Here's a tip: don't whisper secrets with too many s's in them—the hiss snaps through the air. I heard Katherine say "separate rooms" but I couldn't tell if she was asking or confirming. I wish it hadn't caught my ear, but it did. I realized Michael and Sofia were both looking at me curiously. It took me a second to realize what I'd said, and once I did, I half expected Michael to say, *I already am*.

"Might take you up on that, bro," he said instead.

"I quit smoking," Lucy cut in.

Michael looked at her like a parent looks at a child who's interrupted their glass of wine to show them a somersault and said, "Well done," in a way that meant "Run along." "So, what do we do for fun here? Trust me, I'm excited by the restaurant and the bar, but I'm not spending my whole weekend cooped up inside."

Andy and I said in unison: "There's a jacuzzi on the roof."

"Everyone!" Marcelo called us over. Lucy did a pass on the inside of Andy worthy of Formula One to wind up next to Michael. Sofia and I trailed behind.

"You're blushing," Sofia needled quietly. "What's the matter, starstruck?"

I shook my head. "I'm all over the place. This isn't what I was expecting."

"Me neither." Sofia wrinkled her nose. "Cuidado." Even though I don't speak it, sometimes Sofia threw Spanish words at me. I knew this one, having heard it a few times: *Be careful*.

As we joined Marcelo's group, Michael drifted over to Erin, who slid her hand into his back pocket. When we were married—sorry, we are still married; technically, I should say, when we were together—Erin hadn't been a fan of public displays of affection. She'd had a difficult, sometimes violent childhood, raised by a single father who hit her in secret and hugged her in public. As a consequence, she struggled to see over-the-top fondness as genuine, as anything more than an act. She didn't trust it. I mention this because we would rarely kiss in public, and certainly never indulged in any back-pocket action. A palm on the small of my back, maybe. Her show of affection towards Michael struck me as very performative. Possessive, even. I wasn't sure if it was for me or for Lucy. Maybe I was jealously overthinking it and my brother just had a better arse.

"We've decided," Marcelo said, loud enough for the group but directed at Michael and Erin, "that we should tell you something together—otherwise you might hear it from others."

"I'm not sure . . ."

"Lucy, please. Michael, the last thing we want is to give you any undue stress this weekend. But we either tell you now, together, or we wait for hearsay and rumor to kick in."

My mother was nodding along, which, as usual, held more weight than Marcelo's words. Michael shot a quick look towards the rest of us, but I could have sworn he was searching out my face. Perhaps he thought it had something to do with the money. Or something to do with him and Erin.

"There's been an incident," said Marcelo. "The body of a man was found this morning. It seems he lost his way overnight and died of exposure." Marcelo's gaze swiveled across the group, but settled on Sofia, as if daring her to speak up. "That's as simple as I can tell it."

"There are police here," Michael surmised. "Patrol SUV by the maintenance shed. I didn't think anything of it, but that makes sense. Okay. Poor guy."

"There's something else you need to know." This time it was Sofia. Lucy spun around and stared daggers at her. Marcelo cleared his throat to talk over her, but Michael raised a hand in his direction, which, I think purely because that had never happened to Marcelo before, stopped him mid-breath. I swear the snap of his mouth closing echoed across the valley. "They don't know who it was. Apparently, it's not someone staying here. No one's really doing anything at the moment, but there are more detectives on their way. They may wish to do some questioning."

Everyone nodded in agreement, impressed by Sofia's newfound tact. I wasn't buying it; I think she was trying to push Michael's buttons. Words like "detectives" and "questioning." She was trying to scare him.

"Detectives for someone who died of exposure?" said Erin, thinking aloud, realizing something was wrong, and giving Michael a worried look. Sofia's smile in reply was a thin line. She'd seeded what she wanted.

"If you don't want to stay, we can go somewhere else," our mother said. "We wanted it to be up to you."

"You've got nothing to worry about," Marcelo said. "In my experience, being in prison is a pretty good alibi. Besides, the officer here, he's not what we'd call *experienced*. The body's got him rattled. So he's waiting on his superiors. They'll come, they'll be here five minutes, and then they'll all be out of here."

"And the accommodation is—" Katherine started, and I knew she was one breath away from the word "nonrefundable."

"Crawford's his name," I cut in.

"Crawford. Sure," Katherine said, with the implication that it didn't matter. "He doesn't have the chip on his shoulder that the city cops do. Seems the name Cunningham doesn't travel like it used to."

"And as for police presence"—Lucy jumped on the reassurances because she clearly thought, if we did disband, she was a hundred dollars and a motel room away from losing Michael for good—"there pretty much is none. He's not asking questions. We've barely seen him around."

"This cop that's supposedly not doing anything," Michael said. "Is that him?" He pointed to the steps of the guesthouse, which Officer Crawford was currently hurrying down. He steamed over to us, sought our faces for the new arrival. Spotted my brother.

"Michael Cunningham?"

Michael raised his hands in jest and said, "Guilty."

"Glad we agree. You're under arrest."

CHAPTER 14

Katherine was right: the name Cunningham didn't travel like it used to. If it had, Officer Crawford may have better considered his personal safety before striding into a circle of us.

"What do you think you're doing?" Lucy was first to erupt. She barged in front of Michael, forming a physical barrier.

"There's been a misunderstanding," Katherine said, firming up the defense beside Lucy and dragging a reluctant Andy with her.

"Everyone just chill out," Andy said, faking a small shaky laugh. He was a married-in Cunningham, remember, so he still held the usual law-abiding citizen's reverence for police.

"Get out of the way." Crawford had handcuffs dangling from his left hand like a lazy whip, I noticed.

"Can't you just leave our"—this was my mother, not sprightly enough to be part of the blockade but the venom in her words was enough of a shield—"*fucking* family alone?"

I suddenly believed every news article I'd read about mothers lifting cars to save children. Well, the ones they liked anyway.

"Audrey," Marcelo soothed her, "that won't help." He stepped forward and introduced his Rolex to Officer Crawford. "I'm his lawyer. Let's go inside, sit down, talk it out."

"Not without the cuffs."

"You and I both know that's not how policing works. He's only just arrived, how could—"

"Dad," Michael said, and it took me a moment to realize he was talking to Marcelo. "It's all right."

But Marcelo was in full flight. "You don't get to call martial law on this resort just because you're the only policeman here. I know you're in an uncomfortable situation and someone out there is missing a father or a brother or a son—and my family and I will be happy to participate in informal interviews to assist in your identification. But to imply there's anything criminal . . . that's . . . well, that's just a staggering accusation. It's profiling based on the family history. We will sue. If you wish to detain him, you'll need cause and a charge, of which you have neither. Now, I'm only working six minutes pro bono, and I think we've just ticked over. Are we done?"

I felt the urge to apologize simply being in the proximity of Marcelo's tirade. But Crawford dug his heels in. "We are not done. I'm allowed to use my discretion, seeing as there's been a murder."

This started a murder-murmur as everyone repeated the word in disbelief. I caught Sofia smiling. Marcelo balled his fists. My mother was not one for gasping, but she covered her mouth with one hand.

"Some *incident*," Michael said pointedly.

"You're finished," Marcelo growled to Crawford. That was legal speak that even I understood. "I've ruined people over less."

"And I've stood up to people over more."

They were interrupted by the slam of the guesthouse doors. A tall woman, my age, with a tanned jaw but a pasty coloration around her eyes—a ski-goggle tan—was standing on the deck. She was bare-armed, in a T-shirt and vest, unbothered by the cold. I recognized her as the woman with the amphibious Land Rover who'd fixed my tire chains.

"Officer, do you need a hand? People are on edge as it is—what's all the yelling?"

"It doesn't concern you," Marcelo said, tiring at the prospect of another argumentative party.

"I own this resort, so I think it does."

"Well, in that case, could you tell this wannabe Poirot to stop harassing your guests? And if you want to quell panic, how about not throwing the word 'murder' around?"

"First time I've heard the word 'murder.'" The owner raised an eyebrow at Crawford. "Really? You mean Green Boots?"

As far as color-based nicknames go, Green Boots was easier to understand than the Black Tongue. It was the colloquial name given to a man who'd died hiking Everest; because it was too dangerous to retrieve the body, it remained just off the path, his neon green boots serving as a landmark for climbers. While this morning's body hadn't been wearing green boots—I'd know, I carried the left foot—they'd clearly settled on the name as shorthand for our frozen mystery guest.

"I have reason to believe his death could be suspicious."

"Why? Because of her?" Katherine's pitch lilted, both in incredulity and possibly the altitude, as she pointed across at Sofia. "You'd get a better medical opinion from a shaman. What did you tell him? How long until the actual detectives get here?"

"I am a doctor," Sofia assured Crawford.

"Are we ignoring the fact that, even if this death *is* suspicious, Michael has an alibi?"

"Dad. Let me—"

"*I'll handle it,* Michael. Are you sure you want to go down this road, Officer? Your suspicions are based on some rap sheet that you dug up, maybe a bit of family history, and your loyalty to your badge, because blood bleeds blue and all that. Your bias is not only showing, it's making you look like an idiot. You tell me how Michael can be involved when he just got out of prison this morning, for heaven's sake?"

Marcelo's outburst sucked the breath out of everyone. Crawford looked among all of us; I assumed he was trying to scope any shred of remaining support. I avoided his gaze. Even Sofia looked at her toes: her belief in Black Tongues and Green Boots aside, she knew when someone was Red Faced.

"Come on," Marcelo said, taking Audrey's hand and starting to move towards the guesthouse.

But Michael didn't move. He swapped a nervous grimace with Erin.

I'm not embellishing to report that there was, at last, a thunderclap.

"I thought so," Crawford said. "Do you want to tell them, or should I?"

"I didn't hurt anyone." Michael put his hands up and took a few steps towards Crawford. "But I'm happy to cooperate to help you find out who did." He was looking at me when he said this.

"Michael! Stop! Officer, he doesn't know his ri—"

"He is not my lawyer."

"What are you doing?" Audrey walked back over and put a hand on his shoulder. "You were in Cooma last night. It's okay, you just tell him."

"It's cold, Mum. Go inside."

"Just say the words. Just say it. Tell him." She started thumping his chest with her spare, balled fist. As if she could force the confession out of him. Then, I think because of a combination of the cold and the exertion, her knees drooped and she gently sagged into the snow. Michael tried to catch her but was too slow to do much except guide her down, where she sat in the snow. Crawford, Sofia, and I all hurried to help her up, but she swatted us away. Katherine and Lucy both started shouting at Officer Crawford for keeping an old lady in the cold.

"Mrs. Cunningham," Crawford said, loud enough to quiet the rabble, "Michael was released *yesterday* afternoon."

Yesterday? I remember the slow dawn of realization. *But that meant—*

Michael's eyes darted to Erin. I think I saw Lucy's face collapse inwards. The first snowflake landed on my eyelash.

"That's not bulletproof. Okay. Okay, so he wasn't in prison. Sure." Marcelo was reeling off his thought process, trying to find the best option, while hauling Audrey up. "But that doesn't mean he was here. You can't stay there, love, you'll get wet. So, just tell us where you were last night, Michael, and that'll be the end of it."

"I'd rather go with you, Officer."

Crawford clicked the handcuffs on and gave Michael a reassuring look. Even without knowing the full subtext of Michael's concealment, Officer Last Resort could see that this was the less harmful option. I noticed he put the handcuffs on very loosely. Maybe not loose enough to slip through, but loose enough to not be threatening. He turned to the owner—look, chronologically I know the owner hasn't told me her name yet, but it's bugging me, so I'm going to start calling her Juliette, because she tells me soon—and said, "I need to keep him on his own, for the safety of the guests."

"He'd get out from wherever you put him. No rooms or chalets lock from the outside only—it's a fire hazard," Juliette replied. (See, I told you it'd be easier.) "We're a hotel, not a prison."

"What about the Drying Room?" Lucy said. Her face was darker than the sky, her voice throaty, tongue thick with anger. I would find out later, but she must have already known the Drying Room was nothing more than a heated closet-sized space filled with wooden benches for boots and clothes racks for coats, which smelled like damp mold and the type of sweat you only get when you're wearing something so waterproof it traps everything inside as well as keeping it out. It was a petty revenge, but it was the best she could do on short notice. Her tone was smug as she added, "I saw it has a slide bolt on the outside."

"Um, the Drying Room is not really for people to stay in," Juliette said.

Crawford looked up, held a flat hand out, and watched a few small flakes land in it and melt. He was keen to wrap this up and get inside. He turned to Michael apologetically. "It'd only be for a few hours."

Michael nodded.

It occurred to me then that this would have been a perfect time for Erin to speak up. If prison wasn't Michael's alibi, then she could be. We all knew they were together anyway, so what was a night between them? When she still didn't say anything, and I realized that whatever they were keeping secret was worth being locked in the Drying Room on suspicion of murder over, my curiosity was piqued.

"Where did you learn to be a police officer?" Marcelo might have hit Crawford if he hadn't had my mother draped across his shoulder. "None of this is legal."

Police officers in these books, while being Last Resorts or Only Hopes, can also have character traits such as By The Book or Screw The Rules. It appeared Crawford had surprised me again.

"I'm happy to cooperate," Michael repeated.

"It'll be all right," Erin said, giving him a hug. Her hands slid down his spine and into his rear pocket, the other one this time. Not that I noticed.

Then they were all walking towards the guesthouse. I followed, swept up in the tide. Marcelo was keeping pace, having handed Audrey off to Sofia, talking Crawford's ear off in language I'll deem colorful, both for the flurry of legal terms and the graphic descriptions of how one could fornicate with their own face.

"I need you to give me some space," Crawford said at the top of the stairs, in a stern voice that belonged to Screw The Rules cops. He was talking to Marcelo, but we all stopped. Being that we were all at different heights on the stairs, it felt like we were in a stage play or posing for a wedding photo. "Get warm. We'll talk soon."

Crawford put his hand on Michael's back and guided him towards the door.

"You will not talk to him without me present." Marcelo got in one last jab.

"That man does not speak for me. He is not my lawyer," Michael said. Then he turned and raised both cuffed wrists, clasping the lower half of his hands in a club shape, both pointer fingers together. He was pointing at me. "*He* is."

CHAPTER 14.5

Right. A lot has happened, so I thought I'd jump in here with a quick recap.

I know: it's a bit weird. But I want us all to be on the same page. If you're confident in your cognitive abilities, you can skip ahead.

Books like this generally tease out the backstory of an ensemble of reprobates, lock them in a singular location, and then present a body that can be linked to parts of each player's backstory as possible motive. I'll try that.

The backstory: Three years ago, my brother Michael arrived on my doorstep, with a man named Alan Holton in the back seat of his car. Alan was dead, then he wasn't, then he was again. Even though I knew it would effectively banish me from the family—mistrustful as we are of police after my father was killed robbing a petrol station—I sided with the law and turned my brother in.

The location: We'd all met up at the Sky Lodge Mountain Retreat! to welcome Michael back from prison. It's Australia's highest drive-in accommodation. There's a storm coming, because of course there is. But please don't think it so clichéd that we're trapped there, because we're not: we're just stingy and indecisive. Although,

I guess we are a bit stuck there now, seeing as Michael's been locked in the Drying Room and we can't just leave him behind—but that's more the focus of the next couple of chapters and this is supposed to be a recap.

The ensemble: There's my mother, Audrey, who blames me for the fragmented state our family is currently in; Marcelo, my stepfather, partner in esteemed legal firm Garcia & Broadbridge, who wears a university tuition on his wrist and represented Michael in his murder trial but won't touch Sofia's negligence case; Sofia, Marcelo's daughter and my stepsister, who needs at least fifty grand for something, perhaps to do with a malpractice suit that may cost her her medical license, is a surgeon who, among other achievements, handled Marcelo's shoulder reconstruction; Katherine, my hyperorganized teetotaler aunt, whose idea the whole weekend was in the first place; Andy, Katherine's husband, who wears his wedding ring like some men wear Purple Hearts; Lucy, Michael's ex-wife, who stuck by him during the trial but whom he divorced while he was in prison because he had formed a special connection with . . . ; Erin, my current wife, though we're separated, who has found solace in my brother's letters (and, apparently, his arms for a night) after, I think it's fairly obvious, some past trauma ripped us apart; Michael, who lied about getting out of prison that morning and previously asked me to look after a bag containing $267,000 cash; the resort owner, Juliette, roadside assist and concierge in one; Officer Darius Crawford, a cop who's so far out of his depth he might have just come out the other side in China and started to float again; and me, shunted from the family and stuck with a bag of blood money. That's the cast. I think we well qualify as the required reprobates.

The body: This morning, a man was found dead in the middle of the snow-covered golf course. Sofia believes it's the work of a serial killer named the Black Tongue, and that the victim didn't die from exposure. According to Lucy, no one is missing from the hotel guest list. If you think that her telling me this is suspicious, I'll remind you that Juliette, who, as the owner, has access to the guest list, coined the anonymous nickname Green Boots, which implies that Lucy's gossip is correct. The problem is none of us could possibly be linked to the dead man by motive, because none of us know who the hell he is.

Here are some important nuggets I'd like to highlight at this point:

1. Someone was in Sofia's chalet when she was in mine; they called my room's phone.
2. Sofia's also the only one with an alibi, because she was with me in my chalet at the exact time Green Boots died, which you're not technically supposed to know, but I've told you anyway.
3. Marcelo called off dinner because my mother was unwell. I had no contact with Andy, Katherine, or Lucy overnight.
4. Sofia, Andy, and I have seen Green Boots' face, but Crawford didn't exactly spend the morning holding an open casket, so we might be the only ones. None of us recognized him.
5. I still don't know where the bag of cash came from. It's about to occur to me that someone may be after it.
6. There were three sets of footprints to Green Boots, only one back, and it didn't snow overnight.
7. Lucy's taste in makeup is second only to Erin's taste in men and Michael's taste in terrain-appropriate vehicles.
8. I haven't forgotten I dangled the plural "brothers" before.
9. Michael would rather be suspected of murder than tell the truth about where he and Erin were the previous night.
10. We are 67 pages away from the next death.

And in the middle of it all is me. Someone who writes books about how to write books, with no legal background, who has just, for reasons I can't yet fathom and with questionable legality, been nominated as legal counsel for a suspected murderer—or maybe serial killer, if I take Lucy's word about the dramatic prerequisites—who is supposed to despise me.

If you're happy that I'm playing fair, we'll move on.

CHAPTER 15

I could have caught Audrey easily, but we had all flocked into the foyer as a group and I wanted to wait until everyone spread out. As Michael was guided away to the Drying Room, he told me he'd send for me—he actually used those words, as if I was a court jester—once he'd had some time to think. Some time to conjure a convincing alibi, I suspected.

Everyone else dispersed to the bar, the restaurant, or their rooms. Michael's arrest had been quite the show for the other guests: there were a lot of greasy-forehead smudges on the front windows. Marcelo guided Audrey upstairs. He had her under his light arm, folded into the wing of his coat, and was talking in a soothing monotone. My mother is not old enough to find stairs an obstacle, but old enough to be good friends with the banister, so they moved slowly. I'd half expected Marcelo to chase after Crawford, raining verbal fire, but he'd given up that fight and instead bashed at his phone (battery: unknown). I imagined he was trying to get a bar of reception to call someone who could fire Crawford.

I waited until they reached the first-floor landing, which I decided was probably spacious enough to corner them into a conversation.

It had been a long time since I'd spoken to my mother face-to-face, after all. She might know something.

As I made to follow them, someone rested their hand on my shoulder from behind. It wasn't aggressive, but there was the slightest tug backwards. I turned to see Katherine wincing apologetically, in the way people do when their face is trying to tell you they're sorry for what they're saying. It's the face Andy often makes behind his wife while she's explaining why they're leaving a party early.

"Is now the best time?" she asked, doing the Katherine thing of being concerned and responsible, but also just a tad condescending. Sure, she was a good dozen years younger than my mother, but she'd started to coo at Audrey. Katherine was by no means mocking or insincere about it, but it was clear: she thought my mother was getting on.

"Oh," I said, nodding in solemn agreement, "I agree. Let's wait for a few more corpses." Then I remembered I'd promised Andy I'd go easy. After all, she was only trying to help. I softened, explaining, "If I'm going to help Michael, I'm going to need to know as much as I can. I'll have to talk to her eventually."

Katherine seemed to begrudgingly accept my reasoning. "Just try not to get her worked up." There it was again, concern for Audrey's frailty rather than her happiness. "That's if she even talks to you, anyway, which she probably won't."

"I have to try."

"So what's your angle?"

"Dunno. Groveling?" I shrugged. "She is my mother after all. I'll just have to get through to her maternal side."

Katherine laughed. It was hard to tell if it was cruel or empathetic, but she let go of my shoulder, not holding me back. "If that's your whole plan, I hope you brought a Ouija board."

*

Audrey was in the library flicking through a novel by Mary Westmacott but not exactly reading it, in a high-backed, studded red leather chair. It would have been the perfect chair to sit in for a denouement. Despite having LIBRARY written on the door, the room was a booklover's nightmare: water-damaged, moldy yellow paperbacks with brittle potato-chip-dry pages ringed the room, mounted on bookshelves crafted out of old-timey wooden skis and snowboards. The pamphlet-adorned stone fireplace in the corner held hungry crackling embers, the architect seemingly quite unaware of the combustibility of books. The fire kept the room too warm, but it smelled less damp than the rest of the hotel. There were no guns on the mantel, certainly none of Chekhov's: I would have been hard-pressed to murder someone with the taxidermy pigeon and framed war medal that were there instead.

On seeing me, my mother closed her book, stood, and turned her back, pretending to be busy picking through the rest of the Ws on the snowboard-shelf.

"Audrey," I said. "You can't ignore me forever."

She slid the book in—it was miscategorized, if you ask me, since Mary Westmacott is a pseudonym for Agatha Christie, but what's in a name?—turned and frowned when she saw I was blocking the doorway.

"Come to gloat?" She folded her arms. "To tell me you were right about him?"

"I wanted to see if you were feeling better, actually."

It took her a second—either to process that I was reaching out, or to remember her alibi for canceling dinner, I wasn't sure—and then she snorted her derision.

"I can look after myself." She was being evasive, betraying her likely frustration at being over–cared for, which she no doubt saw as a threat to her independence. I imagined Katherine had been needling her about her age and faculties recently, and I'd only added to it by checking on her. "If that's all?" She made to step around me.

"Michael hurt somebody, Mum. I did what I thought was right." I deliberately said "I thought" in the middle, even though I *knew* I was in the right. "I'm doing what I think is right now."

"You sound like your father." She shook her head. It was not a compliment.

I was curious; it was rare to hear her talk about Dad. "How?"

"Robert could justify anything. The way every robbery was the big ticket, the last one. He talked himself into absolution, too."

"Absolution?" My father had found no absolution; he'd died in a gunfight with two policemen, killing one of them. Unless she meant that he had talked himself into each crime he committed, believing it was for his family, a necessity, and that he was a good enough man to walk away from the next one. Just like Lucy's cigarettes. "Dad was a bad person. You know that, right?"

"He was an idiot. If he'd just been a bad person, I could have lived with that. But a bad person who thinks they're a good one—now that's what got him into trouble. And now you're forcing me to watch you make the same mistakes he did, and you expect me to smile and pretend it's okay? Just when our family was coming together . . . and now *this* to deal with."

Her words rattled me. The same mistakes my father made? Was she accusing me of being involved with Green Boots' death? I was aghast at the implication. Then, because I was hurt and because I'd never said it to her face, I lashed out. "Michael is a killer."

"He killed someone. But does that make him a *killer*? People kill people and get medals for it. People kill people because it's their job. Michael's not rare or different. You label him a murderer? Do you think the same of Katherine? Of Sofia? If you had to make the same choices he did, for whatever reasons he made them, what would that make you?"

"It's not the same."

"Isn't it?"

"I think there's a body outside who would disagree with you."

"Michael didn't kill him."

"I believe that." I said it so quickly, I realized I did. "But someone did. And it seems all too convenient that this happened *this* weekend, with Michael arriving. It's got something to do with us, I know it."

That seemed to annoy her. There was something else in her agitation, in her glances behind me.

I took a chance and stepped towards her, lowering my voice. "Do you know who the dead man is?"

"I don't." At the risk of spoiling things, she's telling the truth here. "But he's not one of us. That's all that matters."

"What is it you're not telling me?"

"So you want to find a killer, do you? Because it's easier to conjure up someone with a knife or a gun that you can hunt, someone who is objectively *bad* so that you can ignore what you know is true? What happens if you find them? Do they pay the price? It's okay if the villain dies at the end of a novel—in fact, they're *supposed* to. What if that's what Michael did to Alan? And it's just the end of Michael's story you've got confused with the start." She needed a couple of breaths after that tirade. I digested the truth in her words. "We're here because of *you*. Michael is in that room because of *you*. You did this. You're just like your father. He knew what he was leaving us to fight, and he left us to fight alone anyway, and we paid the price. We all did." Her voice was venom. "If only he'd left us a weapon to fight it with. But he didn't. Nothing in the bank. And you did the same thing to Michael."

For a second I thought she was accusing me of keeping Michael's money, and I was about to ask her how she knew about it, when I realized she was simply saying that, by dying, our father had left us poor. In truth, we hadn't grown up *that* poor. But I didn't really know what it had been like to raise us alone. In any case, maybe she meant it as a metaphor.

"Dad was a killer just like Michael." I blocked out her argument and stuck with the black-and-white truth. "The only difference was he was a junkie as well."

"Your father was not a junkie!" Audrey bellowed.

"They found a needle on him, Mum. Stop lying to yourself!"

"Stop panicking your mother." A voice came from behind me: Marcelo, holding a mug of something brown and steaming. He'd said it jokingly, but caught on to the intensity of the room pretty quickly. He slid me out of the doorway with a brush of his forearm. Audrey slunk past, grabbing the drink on the way out and shuffling quickly down the corridor.

Marcelo raised his eyebrows. "Everything all right?"

I nodded, but it was so mechanical he saw right through it.

"I know, everything's upside down. The way I see it, Michael obviously wants to talk to you. This who's-his-lawyer crap won't go any further than the next few hours, but if it helps us get Officer Crawford on our side, so he sees that we're cooperating, we may as well play along." He could see I was wary. "Oh, don't think I'm lying down. I'll destroy him later, promise. There'll be nothing left of him. But I know when to put 'em up and when to let 'em sit. And I think I'm benched for now. You should talk to Michael first, because that's what Michael wants. We're playing his game, not Crawford's."

I found myself wondering if mixing sports metaphors was a universal trait of stepfathers, or if it was just Marcelo.

"But you're the real lawyer. A good one, too. You got him a meager three years on a murder charge—that's a pretty good result. Why doesn't he trust you anymore?" I asked.

"I don't know." He shrugged. "Seems like he doesn't trust anyone much. Maybe he'll tell you why."

"When you meet a client for the first time, how do you know the difference between the heroes and the villains?" I asked. "Like, I know you have to be unbiased, but you must think some people are lost causes, and others have some hope?"

"That's why I got into corporate law—I don't have to worry about that. They're all dirtbags."

"I'm being serious."

"I know, mate." He reached out and squeezed my shoulder. Marcelo always found an alternative word that danced around "son" for me, as if he wasn't entirely comfortable with it, even now. "Mate" was one of the more serious, an upgrade from "buddy." "You're asking about your dad."

"Audrey said he was a bad person who thought he was a good one."

Marcelo considered that for a second. "I couldn't say."

I got the feeling he could, but didn't push it.

"You were friends. What was he like? Were you close?" I surprised myself by asking.

Marcelo scratched the back of his neck. He found the words slowly. "Yes. I knew him well." He made a show of checking his watch. It was not a topic he was comfortable with—I assume because he'd married his dead client's wife. "I'd better catch up to your mother."

I stopped him. "Can you do me a favor?" He nodded. "You have researchers, paralegals, contacts in the police—all that stuff, right? Can you check out the victims of the Black Tongue? Lucy says they were a woman named Alison Humphreys and a couple named Mark and Janine Williams. Anything that might be useful."

He paused. Probably hesitating at encouraging me along this path. "Who was the first one again—Williams and . . . ?"

"Alison Humphreys."

"Got it. Sure thing, champ." He loosened up. Thankfully he

didn't affectionately punch me in the arm, otherwise we would have had to go outside and play catch, and I hadn't brought my baseball glove. "I'll ask around."

I didn't follow him out, choosing to spend a few minutes in the library alone to gather my thoughts. I found myself looking at the medal above the fireplace, thinking about what my mother had said: some people were awarded for killing. The medal was a dark bronze, framed on blue velvet in a glass-faced portrait, with a small rectangular slip of paper, like that inside a fortune cookie, mounted beneath it. The paper had a grid of dots on it, but it wasn't Morse code or anything I recognized. Beneath all of that was an engraved plaque: AWARDED FOR CARRYING A LIFE-SAVING MESSAGE THROUGH HEAVY FIRE, 1944. The medal itself was engraved with the words FOR GALLANTRY and WE ALSO SERVE.

Relax. I didn't just spend eighty words describing a medal because it wasn't important. I realized my mother was looking at things with a biased eye, but she was right. All killing wasn't equal; that's what the medal meant. Audrey was telling me she believed Michael had a good reason for it.

You did this, she'd said. And under her curt words I heard again everything Lucy had told me on the roof: *It would have happened a different way*. I realized I believed her. I'd sent Michael to prison—what if his anger had metastasized, created something worse? I felt ashamed for my guilt—Michael had deserved to go to jail—but felt it anyway. Knowing that none of this was my fault gave little comfort. It was a sliding doors thing. What had I made him into?

And so, right then, I decided to help him. Not because I thought he was innocent, and not because I thought he was guilty. But because of what everyone had been telling me since we arrived.

You did this.

I was the reason it had happened *the way it did*. Call it the shame of testifying against blood in the first place, the emotional banishment from my mother, or the guilt from my indoctrinated Cunningham loyalty, but my conscience couldn't handle it anymore. I made up my mind: I'd do the digging. I would either pave my way back into the family with Michael's absolution, or deliver the final, validating nail in his coffin. Call me a traitor, in league with the coppers, but I also had a feeling one of us was involved. It seemed clear to me: the only way to put my family back together again was to find out which one of them was a killer.

Well, we all are—I've already told you that. I just mean most recently.

MY MOTHER

CHAPTER 16

People—husbands mostly, sent on errands—were running to their cars amid the vicious slanted ice that had just started coming down in sheets. I could barely see the car park through the chaos, but they were all doing the same kind of half-hop, half-lurch that comes with shielding your elbow over your brow. The wind was whipping powder up off the ground too, adding a swirling mist below knee height that looked like sea foam on crashing waves. It was level ground, but all of them fought the wind like they were hiking uphill. I saw occasional flares of orange—cars unlocking—as they made it further into the gray. Like some kind of relay, the next batch to brave it huddled under the awning, blowing into hands while surveying the storm. I can only assume they were discussing among themselves whether what was in the car was really necessary after all, and figuring out how best to frame this icy quest as possibly shag-worthy heroism.

I was sitting in the bar—which could sort you out a coffee—with Sofia. We were perched on high stools, pulled up to the front window, and had been watching the storm increase in ferocity. Marcelo was somewhere deeper inside the building, arguing with Juliette over how to get a room in the guesthouse. My mother would have either been with him, or independently arguing with Crawford. I hadn't quite figured out what it meant to be Michael's lawyer yet, so I was fueling up on caffeine before approaching the Drying Room, which, because Michael wasn't ready to see anyone yet, Crawford had locked before taking up sentry duty in a chair outside. Lucy was sitting on her own across the room. She had a lunchtime pint, but she was simply spinning the glass in its own condensation. Erin wasn't there, having made the move to her chalet before the storm hit. Katherine had a pot of tea and was looking at a plastic-sleeved binder. I wondered how many murders it would take for her to crack and have a pint, too. I suspected at least a couple more. I assumed her binder had her itinerary. I wouldn't be surprised if she'd printed out the weather forecast and was trying to figure out how she'd misread it. I'll give you two guesses where Andy was.

The group of husbands on the porch decided there was a break in the sleet and made a run for it. I tapped the glass and said, "And they're off," as if calling a horse race. "I Should Have Gone Earlier is in the back, just shy of I'd Rather Freeze To Death Than Admit I'm Wrong, who's a few lengths behind I'm Only Out Here Because Of Outdated Relationship Archetypes and out by a nose is Are You Sure You Couldn't Live Without It Babe."

In strode Andy, shaking ice from his beard as he pulled off his coat and hung it on the hooks beside the doorway. He flopped into a seat across from Katherine, put a small purse on the table, and said, "Are you sure you couldn't have got on without this, babe?"

Sofia laughed, too loudly, and, when Katherine snapped her a look, quickly pivoted her attention back to the window in mock fascination at the storm.

"What's with you guys?" I asked. I didn't have to point for Sofia to know who I was talking about, but Sofia still shrugged like she didn't understand me. "Come on. Katherine. She was really on your case this morning. I didn't even know you two were close enough to have those kinds of arguments."

"Was she? I didn't notice," Sofia deflected. I wasn't convinced. Katherine's scorn was like your mother's eye; you knew when it was on you. But she clearly didn't want to talk about it. "So, you're a lawyer now?"

"I guess so."

"Don't you have, like, ten steps for solving crime or whatever? Just do"—she wriggled her hands in the air like she was performing a magic trick—"a bit of all that."

"They're rules, not steps. And they're not mine. Plus," I leaned over and whispered conspiratorially, "I don't even like legal thrillers."

"What are you going to do next, then?"

"Well, I figure if I go to law school, do an internship, and slot in my Honors somewhere, I should have Michael out of that closet in, oh . . . about eight years."

"Can he even do that? Nominate you, I mean." She took a huge gulp from her mug. It rattled as she placed it back on the saucer. "And why you?"

"I don't know," I said, which was the truth to both her questions, but what Michael had said to me outside—*I have some things to say that I think I owe you*—lingered. "A person can represent themselves in court without being qualified, right? Maybe this is just an extension of that. Or it's not legal at all. But Crawford's not really playing by the rules here, either. I'm not sure he even understands them, and maybe Michael's using that to his advantage. If he plays along, he gets what he wants. Marcelo seems to think it's a good idea to get Michael to talk to me, so I'm playing along for now."

"How could being locked up in a sweat box be what he wants?"

"At the moment, I'm guessing it's one of two things: if I'm technically his lawyer, he gets to speak to me as much as he likes, in private, right? Crawford has to let him. He said he wanted to talk to me outside. So maybe Michael wants me there."

"And your second guess?"

"It's the same as the first. If he wants me in the room, then maybe he's trying to keep someone else out of it."

"He's scared?"

I shrugged. Those were all the theories I had. Sofia rubbed her eyes, yawned, and settled her gaze out the window again. Before, I hadn't been able to see uphill to the makeshift mortuary, or downhill to the lake, but now I couldn't even see the car park. Everything was completely grayed out within a few meters. The dance of ice in the air against that blank slate was reminiscent of looking under a microscope—these little gray cells—and for a second I imagined the mountain on a molecular level. After the storm passed, the ground would be a different shape: the snow would be a knee-high mass of pure white cover, as if it had been laid down in one thick blanket. I realized we were watching the mountain rebuild itself, atom by atom.

"You look like you've barely slept," I ventured. Outside, I'd thought her paleness was just the cold, the shock of seeing the dead body, but inside, she looked properly frail. I could see it in her drawn face, and hear it in the rattle of her coffee cup, giving away her shaking hands. I thought of Andy's *glug-glug* gesture, of Katherine's sharp tongue.

"Really?" Sofia raised an eyebrow, onto me immediately. "We're doing it this way?"

"Just talk me through last night. I dunno, for your alibi, or whatever. I don't really know where else to start," I said, trying to sound casual instead of curious.

She sighed, drew her finger across the coffee foam and licked it, not answering.

I resorted to begging. "At least help me practice."

"Here's a timeline: Dad called to tell me dinner was canceled because Audrey wasn't feeling well, so I ate bar snacks in here because I couldn't stomach the dining room and, to be honest, I was building up a bit of liquid courage to come and talk to you. And then, after I saw you, I went back to mine. You want some excuses? It's been a hell of a morning, which is why I look like shit. Thank you, by the way, for the implication that if a woman looks slightly bedraggled, she must be a murderess. Can I remind you that I'm also the only one here, including Officer Crawford, who cried murder in the first place? And, most importantly, you know I went straight back to my room, because you called me pretty much as soon as I walked in the door. You're my alibi, dummy."

"I guess," I said, thinking it over. Unless you skipped the recap, you'll know it was about to occur to me that someone might be after the money, and it just did. "Just tell me who you owe money to?"

She sat bolt upright at that and glanced around the room. "Stop talking so loudly about it," she hissed. "What the hell is that supposed to mean, anyway?"

"The money you asked for. I think you might owe it to someone."

"Ernie, listen, I don't want it anymore. Not if you're going to humiliate me like this. I never should have asked. I'll survive."

"Why do you need fifty thousand dollars if you're not paying someone off?"

"I don't owe it to anybody." Her tone was clear; that was the last time she'd say it. "Can we talk about something else?"

"Someone was in your chalet last night," I said.

She squinted, scrunching her cheeks up like she'd eaten something foul. I'd surprised her. I couldn't tell if she was surprised that someone was in her room, or surprised that I knew about it.

"While you were in mine," I explained. "Remember how my phone rang? It was from your room—I know that because when

I called back, you picked up. I figure someone was looking for something, and they must have knocked the speed dial."

"By someone, you mean Green Boots? You think he was in my room? Looking for money?"

"It's occurred to me."

"That I killed a debt collector to protect myself?"

"Or someone killed him to protect you."

She thought about that for a second. Not being a detective, I had a difficult time distinguishing whether this pause was out of offense or calculation. She tilted her head slightly and said, "Before I respond to that salacious accusation: have *you* decided yet?"

"You mean about the mo—" I remembered her hiss to keep it down. "I haven't really had the—"

"So you haven't decided?"

"I haven't decided."

"Will it help your decision if my life's in danger?" She drummed her fingers on the table.

I reached across and put my hand on hers, stilling her. With as much gravitas as I could manage, which, for me, is not much, I said, "Is it?"

I looked up and noticed she was holding in a grin. She let it split her face. "Come on! Listen to yourself. Debt collectors? What, like for the mob? Do we even have a mafia in Australia? I think you're racially profiling me because I'm South American." She wrinkled her nose comically.

"That's more the cartel than the mob," I said. "It'd be a drug mule, not a debt collector. If we're typecasting you, that is."

"Oh, well, in that case. Chain me up." She held out her wrists in mock compliance.

"I'm sorry. I'm tired. It's no excuse, but it's hard to think straight out here."

"I put you on the spot. I get it—it looks pretty suss that I'm asking you for money one minute and then Green Boots shows up frozen solid the next day. Listen, I asked you for the money because there's a bag full of it, and I don't think Michael deserves it, and, yeah, it would help me out with something. But it's personal. Can we *please* talk about something else?"

"You might not like the other topics of conversation I have in mind." That got a chuckle out of her. Friends again. "So, do you want to pretend to be interested in how I slept or if I enjoyed a podcast I listened to on the way up, to both of which the answer is 'fitfully,' or do you want to choose between the Black Tongue or the Other Thing?"

"Honestly, it's not that big a deal." She tapped her spoon against the side of her mug as she talked; perhaps the rhythm of it was taking her mind off the memory. It seemed more like an action designed to look casual than a natural tic. "I've lost patients before."

So, the Other Thing.

"And don't think that I mean that lightly, because I don't. It sucks. Every single time. But surgery has complications. We've got amazing technology, and even better medicine, but there're still risks in even the smallest procedures. You can get an embolism from a broken arm—you know that?"

"Is that what happened?"

"Look, I'm human. I'm doing a job. Some days are your best days, and some days not so good."

"Are you saying you made a mistake? You're a fantastic surgeon, Sofia. Marcelo trusted you with his shoulder, and he needs that for slamming his fist on the table dramatically in court. That's like operating on Beyoncé's voice box."

"You're overstating it somewhat, I think. And Dad's—well, you know he likes to control things." The spoon tinked again. "I've replayed it in my head enough. I can honestly say that no, I didn't make a mistake. I made the right choices in the moment. If I had to do it again today, I'd do it the same. The review will clear me. It's just that the people involved are, well, a bit more *in* with the hospital administrators, so it's dragging out. And that has set some tongues wagging."

Her eyes darted to Katherine. I couldn't tell if I was imagining it, but Katherine's eyes seemed to flick away from us, as if Sofia's gaze was a white snooker ball, ricocheting into Katherine's black. Katherine wasn't in the medical field, and she certainly could never be described as having influence. I scanned everyone else. Andy had found a deck of cards somewhere (or maybe he just had them on him at all times for amateur magic tricks, I wouldn't put it past him) and was dealing himself a hand of solitaire. Across the room, Lucy perched a cigarette between her lips. Before you call me a liar about her last cigarette, a waiter came over and told her she'd have to go outside. She looked longingly out the snow-battered window, which was groaning in its frame, and pocketed it.

My mind lingered on Katherine. "When they review something like that, is alcohol one of the things they look at?" I asked.

"Why jump to that?"

"Well, you know how Katherine feels about alcohol. And she's called you out a few times. At first, I thought she was annoyed at you ruining the weekend with your murder theories, but now I see she's painting you as some unreliable, swaggering drunk, which we both know you're not. It seems she's taking it personally." Sofia took a breath to answer, but I changed my mind. "No, sorry. Look, I've clearly got to figure out how to interview people without accusing them at every turn. All I'm saying is, you know she's entrenched with AA since the accident—she's well respected, knows it inside out. She'd actually be a good ally. *If* anything like that were the case. We're here for you."

Sofia snorted. "She's high and mighty, isn't she? You don't remember very well if you think that's when she got cleaned up. Oh, sure, for a couple of weeks maybe. She was wild, man. Dad and

Audrey had to cut her off completely for her to turn it around. I'll take my advice elsewhere."

Katherine's accident and the consequences and rehabilitation all rolled together for me. It was a surprise to hear they were spread out. "You didn't answer my question though."

"I had *one* glass of wine," Sofia said, putting the spoon down at last. "Eight hours before, at least. With food. But when something like this happens, they start turning over every stone. And if some intern says they saw you at a bar—which was a restaurant, by the way—the night before, and they can't be sure, but it looked like you were really putting it away, that doesn't help. Maybe the intern didn't see it right, or maybe they've got a grudge, or maybe someone's gently encouraged them"—she rubbed her thumb against her fingertips—"to embellish things . . . People have things to gain from this. It's all political. The lesson is, don't go for dinner at the spot all the med students use as a boozer. Saying you're there for the food, which I was, is the same as saying you read *Playboy* for the articles."

"Ian Fleming's been published in *Playboy*," I said, not sure it helped her point. I thought for a second, plucked something from my memory. "So's Atwood, actually."

"Exactly! Like I said, I had a meal. I wasn't impaired. It wasn't a mistake. And, look, they don't test doctors like they test athletes. So, what are they going to say? An intern saw me having a glass of wine? Any death goes to the coroner within thirty days, sure, but that's standard practice to review it. They're not basing it on anything. They'll find nothing untoward."

That sounded to me like the flurry of justifications a person gives when they've thought about defending themselves, but I let it slide. "Why isn't Marcelo representing you?" I asked. "Sure, the hospital has lawyers. But he's a cut above."

"Like I said: it's political. Besides, you're a lawyer now—you doing anything next week?"

I snorted at that. "Why's Katherine taking it so personally?"

"Katherine's pissed . . . well, because that's her natural state of being, but specifically because she heard the rumors and came to me with the same questions you did. She offered me help, and when I explained what I've just explained to you, she didn't take it well. She probably thinks I'm past saving. I don't want to be her little project anyway."

I nodded. That did sound like Katherine.

"Now, believe it or not, I have some questions for you."

"Only fair."

"Why are you doing this? There's a policeman here; let *him* do the investigating."

"We both know if it's not his first day, it's his second. And"—I rapped the window with my knuckle—"I wouldn't be relying on his backup to make it up here."

"That still doesn't mean it's up to you to solve this."

"Michael's asking for my help. And I think I owe him that."

"Owe, owe, owe. You use that word so much. A family is not a credit card."

Heads up: I know this is basically the "Why Don't You Just Walk Away" scene, perhaps with some healthy lashings of "This Doesn't Concern You." I'm aware, as I was at the time, that this is often a tactic to stop a nosy investigator (me) from uncovering something about the person asking them to back off (in this case, Sofia). This is not to be confused with a "You're Off The Case" scene, which would be Crawford's problem, not mine. But Sofia's motives were clear to me. If I walked away and Michael left this resort in cuffs, the money would stay with me. And I wouldn't hang on to it for another three years, let alone another twenty-five; I'd spend it. Or give it away. I didn't read her attempt as trying to divert attention away from herself, but rather to remove Michael's piece from the board, leaving the money up for grabs. And if she was trying to frame him, she'd be trying harder, goading me instead of warning me off. I was convinced that she had a selfish motive, but not a murderous one.

"Ernest?" A voice came from the doorway. I turned to see Juliette peering into the bar. "Officer Crawford says it's okay now."

I waved my agreement, stood, and said almost apologetically to Sofia, "I should hear him out. Figure out his alibi for last night, at least."

"*Oh*, I get it now." She punched me playfully on the arm. "Ernie, you jealous sod."

"I'm not—"

"But you *are*. You don't care about Green Boots. You just want to find out where Michael and Erin really were last night."

You know what scene we're in now. It's called "Sex Is Always A Motive."

"He lied to me. Us," I admitted. "I'm curious."

"Twice actually."

"Huh?"

"He lied to you twice. Furniture? Storage units? Seriously? That thing's a monstrosity. I bet all his stuff's at Lucy's place anyway, just as he left it. They were still together when he went to jail, remember?" She shook her head like she was stating the obvious.

"I'm not following."

"Ask him what's *really* in the damn truck, Ernie."

CHAPTER 17

Juliette was waiting for me in the corridor. At first I thought maybe she'd taken my lack of mechanical aptitude as a sign that I was too dim to follow the arrows pointing to the Drying Room, until I realized she was leading me against the arrows. I had no idea where we were going. Sometimes books like these have maps behind the front cover, and the resort layout might have come in handy at this point.

"We haven't met properly," I said, as she threaded me through housekeeping carts vomiting fluffy white towels. "People call me Ern."

"As in, cremated?"

"It's short for Ernest."

"Well, that's what people should call you then, isn't it?" she said bluntly.

"You'd get along with my mother." I sidestepped a room service tray with a crime scene of two crumpled energy drink cans and a chocolate bar wrapper on it. "She also finds me tiresome."

She stopped at a door without a number—so, not a guest room, I deduced—at the end of the corridor and slid a key into the lock.

She turned back to me before she opened it. "I know you're anxious to see your brother. This'll be quick." I noticed that her lips were wind-chapped in the way mountaineers' lips often are, peeling and crevassed, like you could stick an icepick in and climb them. "Oh, I'm Juliette, by the way." Finally, an introduction. My editor has just breathed a sigh of relief. "I helped you fix your chains."

She said it like it was new information, so I said, "I remember," to correct her but it came out throatier than I intended. In retrospect, more than a little lecherous. She examined me for a second longer.

"Clearly I've made an impression. You've already invited me to meet your mother. And stop staring at my lips."

I didn't tell her I was thinking of peeling them, not kissing them, but either way, I felt myself blush.

She opened the door, revealing a cluttered office with two desks nudged up against one another in the center. The filing system could only be labeled as cyclonic; mountains and valleys of paper covered the floor. The walls were ringed with bookshelves, which at least had papers filed into bright orange binders, but those binders, the small semblance of organization, were stacked horizontally. I thought it was a bit rich for someone who didn't know how to stack a bookshelf to judge my vehicular ineptitude, but I let it slide because I was still chastened from being called out on the lips thing. In the middle of each desk was a blocky computer you could do weights with, wired to keyboards that were the pasty, discolored white usually reserved for outdated plastic computer accessories or teenagers' bedsheets.

Juliette took a seat on a black leather chair and started clacking the stiff keys with one hand, beckoning me over with the other.

"How long have you been here?" I asked, half to know more about her and half to discover which century her computer was from.

"I grew up between here and boarding school in Jindabyne," she said in a drone, more focused on pulling the grime-fossilized mouse off the desk with a *pop*. "It's a family business. Grandad and some buddies built it after the war—they wanted to be away from people, I think. I moved to Queensland in my twenties, only because I picked the warmest place possible. Mum and Dad took over, and then they died, and, well, there's a certain inevitability around family stuff, because I came back to sell it six years ago and I guess I got snowed in."

"Family is gravity," I said.

"Something like that."

"Which war did your grandfather fight in? I saw his medal in the library."

"Second. And, ha! No. That's Frank's medal."

"Frank?"

"F-287 actually, but Grandad just called him Frank. The bird."

"The stuffed pigeon?" I snorted. "You're shitting me."

"It's called a Dickin Medal. They give it to animals."

I thought of the engraved words—WE ALSO SERVE—and it made sense. The slip of paper was presumably the coded message, flown through enemy lines, wrapped around the bird's leg. It was an adventure ripe for a Disney film.

Juliette continued. "My favorite is the ship's cat who got one for boosting morale and eating a rat infestation. No joke. Pops loved that bird—he trained a whole flock of them, but Frank was special. He carried a map with all of the machine gun locations, lists of troop numbers, names, coordinates, and he saved a lot of lives. Grandad had him stuffed when he came home. It's a bit weird to put on display, but I like it." She tapped the computer screen. "Ah. Here it is."

She was pointing to a green-tinged security camera video playing on screen, which she had paused. I figured the camera must have been somewhere above the front door of the guesthouse, because the angle was tilted up the hill, and the frame included the parking lot, a good chunk of the driveway, and the pyramid shadows of a couple of the chalets on the very edge, just out of focus. It didn't reach far enough to show where the body had been found. There was a time stamp in the bottom left, a few minutes shy of 10 pm. The green tinge was some kind of night-vision filter, I guessed.

"Which rooms are those?" I pointed at the chalets.

"This is the even side: Two, Four, Six, and Eight."

Marcelo and Audrey were in Five, so theirs wasn't on screen. Sofia was in Two, right on the edge of the screen, only a sliver of roof visible. I was supposed to be in Six, but Katherine and Andy had taken it when their room wasn't ready a day early. I didn't know which room Lucy was in. "Four's mine," I said.

"I know, Mr. Cunningham."

"Stalking the guests. That's an invasion of privacy."

"Is it now?" she said. You might think she's flirting, but at this point I'm not so sure. You won't hear about us locking lips for another 89 pages, when I'm naked, if you're wondering.

"Is there anyone else in the chalets?" I asked.

"Just your group booking. Half are empty."

"Okay. And this camera, does it move? It's not a great angle."

She shook her head. "If we didn't bolt it into its case, it'd snap off every time there was a storm. Besides, it's not a security camera, it's a snow cam. It's just meant to show people what the resort's like on any day, so they can plan their drives, you know . . . pack tire chains"—she paused a second to let me digest the insult—". . . and the right clothes, or see if they should book a lift pass or not. It's also not a video feed, see—it's snapshots."

She clicked play, and I saw it was indeed a series of photos playing on a reel, one taken every three minutes, the timer in the bottom left jumping forward with each image. She let it play. Occasionally there was a blob of gray, which was someone walking to their chalet, but it was pretty much useless, because every person was too blurry a shadow to make out any features. The only positive was that it covered part of the driveway, but even then, the timing had to be right to nab a photo of a moving car in the three-minute window. I knew from making the trip a couple of times already that it was a slow-ish walk through the snow from the chalets to the guesthouse, so the one positive was that, unless someone was really hurrying, it would catch most people, unidentifiable as they might be.

Juliette let the tape roll. It must have been on fast-forward, because each photo was held on the screen for about twenty seconds rather than three minutes. Just before 11 pm, a person moved towards Chalet Four, which I knew was Sofia coming to visit me. A dozen or so frames later, she headed out of shot back to Chalet Two. It was hard to tell direction or intent from a loose shadow, but it lined up well enough that I was happy with my summation. I had hoped to catch a glimpse of someone else sniffing around Chalet Two between the two photos of Sofia, but I was out of luck. Whoever it was had completely missed the three-minute window, which was either an amazing fluke or very well planned. The film skipped forward through the night, uneventful, with just the occasional smoker from the guesthouse, and two shadows holding hands and looking at the stars. Noticeably, no one walked up the hill to the golf course.

Just after the clock ticked past 1 am, Juliette started gripping the mouse harder. She was watching for something. A few photos later, she found it and clicked pause. "I thought this was interesting," she said. "Green Boots is not on any guest or staff list, and no one over the hill has reported anybody missing. I radioed across to the other resorts, and it's all people are talking about, but no one knows anything." Juliette pointed at a printout on the desk, a list of names, which I assumed were all the guests, with small inky ticks next to each one. Accounted for, I guessed. Lucy had already told me this, but it was good to have it confirmed.

I was wondering why she was so interested, oscillating between her wanting to tell me just enough to misdirect me and the fact that nothing much happened up here and she was probably craving a bit of excitement, when I spied, underneath the list of names, a much thicker document with yellow *sign here* sticky tabs poking out. While most of it was obscured, I could see the top corner, which had a logo familiar to me as belonging to a well-known real estate firm. (Some words stand out in crime books, don't they? There's no real way to refer to things of such obvious consequence obliquely, so I may as well put it in bold: **there was a property contract on her desk.**) Maybe she was not so snowed in after all.

Juliette continued. "Which means the dead man came in the middle of the night. So maybe that's him." She pointed at the screen. "I checked, and the car's in the lot now. We could have Crawford run the plates and get us a name?"

Her use of "we" implied some level of sidekickery that I wasn't expecting. Namely, because it seemed out of all of us, including the policeman, Juliette had done the most investigating so far. I was reminded again that I'm only the protagonist by virtue of me writing this down, not because of aptitude. I leaned in. There were two headlights in the driveway. It was easier to tell direction with cars than people, and it was clear the vehicle was headed towards the parking lot. And while the headlights were reflecting off the night-vision filter to overexpose the image, it was obvious that the car was a four-wheel-drive Mercedes.

"That's my stepfather's car," I said. "Marcelo. The one who was doing all the belligerent yelling this morning."

"Oh."

"But he didn't arrive last night. We had lunch in the private dining room. So he must have gone somewhere and come back." I didn't tell her that he'd called off dinner because my mother had been feeling unwell, because my honesty commitment is with you, reader, and not with Juliette the curious resort owner. Still, I was interested in what time he might have left, seeing as he might have lied to do it. Though he could have gone down the mountain to a pharmacy, I suppose. "Go back to late afternoon—you'll see the Mercedes leaving."

Juliette played it in reverse until she found a snapshot of the Mercedes' tail lights, further up the hill but still in the shot, around 7 pm. That was just after he'd called me; I would have been napping at the time.

"Damn," she said, clearly less interested in someone leaving for a couple of hours than in Green Boots arriving. But I was the opposite; my mind flooded with questions. Marcelo had lied to cancel dinner so he could go somewhere. For more than six hours. Doing what? And was my mother oblivious, maybe truly unwell and sleeping it off in the chalet? Or was she complicit? The windows were tinted, so I couldn't tell if anyone was in the passenger seat, let alone who was driving.

Juliette finished my scariest thought. "Maybe he brought someone back with him?"

"Can I watch the rest, through to morning?" I asked. She started the slideshow up again. As it flickered through the three-minute intervals, I was close enough to the monitor to feel the static burr of the ancient bulbous screen on my nose. "If the victim was from anywhere around here, surely someone would have recognized him."

"I didn't see the body, but as I said, everyone here's accounted for, staff and guests. The phone tree's firing with hotels all the way down to the lake, and Crawford's checked with his station in Jindabyne: no one's reported missing. Crawford says he doesn't want to traumatize the guests—there's no point flashing around a photo of a dead guy if he's a nobody anyway. I've gotta say, I agree with him. These are paying customers and, look, comping breakfasts will only paper over so many Tripadvisor ratings." Shamefully, I made a mental note to tell Katherine the breakfast could be comped. "Accidents happen in the mountains—no one's worried about it. Could be a hiker who got lost? The only people calling it a murder are you lot. And you're juicing up that rookie cop while you're at it."

"So why show me this?"

"Because you're asking too many questions not to believe it. And I looked your family up—it's not like you're squeaky clean. If it's a murder . . . that means there's a murder*er*. I have a certain obligation to the safety of our guests."

I was a bit affronted by her allusion to my family history, and I tightened up. "Shouldn't you be sharing this evidence"—that word fell out of my mouth with a clunk; even though I was thinking it was a murder, it was still just a dead man in the snow, and calling it "evidence" seemed to formalize it too much for my liking—"I mean, *information*, with Crawford and not me?"

"I don't know Crawford—he was clearly sent as the errand boy for an accident. Now they know it's serious, Martin—he's the sergeant—will be headed up here with detectives from the city if he needs them. But my money's on them not getting through this storm anytime soon, if he's not stuck already. And, shit, well, fine, I'll just say it: I don't think Crawford knows what the hell he's doing."

"Neither do I," I admitted.

"I'll confess I'm hitching my cart to the best horse. You're the lawyer."

"I'm not a lawyer. I'm a writer."

"Why'd your brother say you were, then?"

"I don't know. I help other people write crime books, so I guess I'm pretty good at guessing the endings? Maybe he thinks I can solve it." I offered this with the kind of upwards inflection that meant even I knew it sounded weak, so I turned my attention back to the video.

The playback had now passed dawn, and the night-vision filter had switched off so the screen was a dull gray instead of green. Crawford's police car was now in frame, time stamp around quarter to seven, heading towards the guesthouse as he arrived. It didn't have tinted windows, so I could see Crawford had one arm stretched across the passenger seat, head tilted in a clear side profile, yawning exuberantly. It must have been an early wake-up to get up here by that time.

"Who found the body?" I asked. There were no blobby shadows between Marcelo's car returning and Crawford arriving: no victim, no killer. "Like, who called it in? It must have been early. No one seems traumatized."

"You'll have to ask Crawford, I'm not sure."

Now that the screen was brighter, the white glancing sharply off the lens made me squint. The photos started filling up with shadows that were more distinctly human in the unfiltered daylight. In the next couple, the shadows grouped together, trailed up the hill like lines of ants. I thought I might have seen Andy and me meeting out the front of my chalet, but couldn't be sure. The morning flickered past: the truck arriving (it *was* stupidly big); the congregation in the entranceway was close enough that you could actually see people's faces; Michael being arrested. The damn photo timing lined up with Erin embracing him, her hand in the back of his jeans. I mean, *come on*.

"You said this was for people to check the conditions before they come up here? Does that mean it's on your website?"

"Yeah, it's a live feed. It's pretty obvious too—the feed's on our homepage."

"So if someone had your website open, they could have timed it, and deliberately moved in the gaps between the photos, to avoid being spotted?"

"It would never work with our reception."

"True. But the timing never changes—it's every three minutes.

If you set your watch to it, you wouldn't even need to watch the feed to move between the frames."

"I guess so."

"And it takes Crawford, let's say, an hour to get up here if he guns it? And yet there's no panic on the screen, no one's rushing up the hill until later, and no one's notified the hotel staff in the full intervening hour. Someone found a dead body, called the cops, and, what, went back to bed?"

"You think the killer called it in? They wanted the police here?"

"Once you eliminate the impossible—"

"—whatever remains, no matter how improbable, must be the truth," she finished. "That's cute. Yeah, I've read pretty much all of Sherlock Holmes too. A holiday lodge is the Lost Sock Portal in the back of your washing machine for moldy paperbacks: no one buys them, no one brings them, yet they're always here. Consider me a bit of an expert. So—am I to assume your entire plan is the elimination method?"

"I mean," I stammered, because that *had* been my entire plan, "I thought it was a fairly widely accepted place to start." I tried not to focus on a particularly long sliver of skin desperate to be plucked from her bottom lip.

"*Widely* accepted." Her tone was incredulous, but playful. "It astounds me that that bloody man created the world's most famous example of rational problem-solving, and we are all supposed to forget he was an absolute crackpot."

"I didn't know that."

"And you write crime novels?" She flung her arms up. "I hate the ones where the main character is a writer anyway."

Dear Reader, while of course I've read Arthur Conan Doyle, he didn't technically classify as what we know as "Golden Age," so, despite me taking a Holmesian approach to my own investigation, I didn't write about him. I explained this to Juliette.

"I'm more interested in people like Ronald Knox. He was part of the establishment of crime writers in the thirties. Anyway, I don't write novels, I write how-to guides. You know: *Ten easy steps to your first mystery*; *How to be an Amazon bestseller*. That kind of thing."

"Oh, I get it. You write books about how to write books that you've never written, bought by people who will never write one."

Honestly, she had it spot on. You'd be surprised how many unfulfilled novelists are willing to shell out a buck ninety-nine for the feeling of progress. My books aren't bad, but my business isn't really helping writers, it's wish fulfillment. I'm not proud of it, but neither am I ashamed.

"It's a living."

"Who's Knox then?" she asked.

"He wrote a set of rules for detective fiction in 1929. In my books I compare them against modern-day murder mysteries. Pretty much all of them are disregarded, shattered into pieces, by current fiction, which tends to like to cheat. He called them his ten commandments. Conan Doyle predates him. Why is he a crackpot?"

"He believed in *fairies*, for Christ's sake. Tried to hunt them down. After the death of his first wife and son, he tried to speak to them by séance. He thought his nanny was a medium. The man was so mad, he tried to convince Houdini, who openly admitted that magic wasn't real, that Houdini himself *was* magic."

"That's one of the commandments," I said, pausing to wonder whether a man who died in a fire and didn't melt any snow qualified as otherworldly. "Number 2, in fact. Nothing supernatural."

"So these rules—that's why you think your brother asked for you and only you? That's a long bow."

"No. I think he asked for me because I'm the least Cunningham of the Cunninghams."

"What's that mean?"

"I'm not one of *our lot*." I meant it to be playful—didn't I?—but it came out laced with acid. I'd missed the mark.

"I didn't mean—" Her thought fizzled halfway through. She shook her head, closed the computer window, and stood up. "Actually, you're right. I should share this with Crawford instead. And let's hope to God there isn't a real murderer out there, or our lives are in the hands of an author. I suppose we can beat them to death with one of your hardbacks."

"Digital only." It came out as a squeak. "I self-publish."

"Well"—she held her belly like it was the funniest thing in the world—"if you're planning to solve whatever the hell is happening up here, I hope you've read a bit more widely than Sherlock Holmes, because even Arthur Conan Doyle believed in ghosts."

CHAPTER 18

Before I talk to my older brother in the Drying Room, there are a few things you should know about my younger brother. The first is that his name is Jeremy. The second is that I'm not one hundred percent confident in my use of tense here: his name still *is* Jeremy, but it also *was* Jeremy. I guess both are right. Please don't mistake my lack of grammatical aptitude for dishonesty. The third is that when he died, I was sitting next to him.

This is difficult to write, and not just because of the cast on my hand.

We never call Jeremy anything but his first name. It's a thing, I've noticed, when someone dies young. Like they haven't lived into the legacy of their surname. Sofia might not think so, that it's not what's in your blood or on your birth certificate that matters, but she still cares which way the names go around the hyphen. It's why you can go from Ernest, as you practice the rigid capital E over and over in bright crayon; to Cunners, on the second-grade football team; to Mr. Cunningham, speaking into the snake's head of a courtroom microphone; to *Ernest James Cunningham* printed inside a wreath, on a pamphlet handed out in the archway of a church.

Because you get your name back when you die—all of it. I've noticed that too. That's legacy. It's why Jeremy never made it past Jeremy.

I'm not saying he's not a Cunningham, because he is, in the truest, deepest sense of the word. But to call him "Jeremy Cunningham," I think, makes him smaller than he is, tethering him to us. As a Cunningham, he is part of those dreams that wake me dry-tongued, gagging. Without our surname to anchor him, he is part of the sky, the wind, the mind.

Names are important in crime novels, too, I reckon. I've read many a denouement in which the detective picks apart an alias, revealing a hidden meaning (for example, Rebus means puzzle, if you didn't know) or perhaps a baffling anagram behind the name. Mystery novels love an anagram. While most of the names in this book are real, I've altered some for legal reasons and others just for fun, so if you laid out the names of everyone in here and tried some deductions, you may well spoil some surprises. I don't mind if you want to do it that way. My name is Ernest, I am truthful: there is no hidden meaning there.

Juliette Henderson (anagram: lederhosen jet unit, make of that what you will) had left me the challenge of orienteering my way to the Drying Room using the painted arrows. I think she was disappointed I hadn't been more enthusiastic at the prospect of us forming a crime-solving duo. Based on the unsigned contract on her desk and her casual mention of Tripadvisor ratings, I'd decided her motivation for looking into the death was more than a curiosity born out of reading too many mystery novels, or even a duty of care to her guests: she wanted to protect the value of her property. Maybe she thought a murder investigation would deter her potential buyer. Especially if a sale was imminent, as it seemed to be.

Crawford—who I've just noticed we've all been referring to intuitively by his surname, as you do with police officers (which makes sense, because if Jeremy is larger than his last name, Crawford, diminutive under his badge, is smaller than his first)—stood as I approached. I shook Crawford's hand; it felt appropriate to the façade of lawyerliness.

"Juliette has some evidence you might be interested in. Video footage of the driveway, if it helps," I said. "It's weird though, no one freaks out until daylight, but someone must have called you—"

"—before dawn," he finished. "Yeah. Took me like an hour to get here. Little under."

"Did they leave a name?"

"I don't know. I was on the radar all night. So I didn't take the call at the station."

"Why you? Juliette said you're not the regular sergeant . . . Sergeant . . ." I'd forgotten the sergeant's name already, spun a few vowels around my tongue.

Crawford didn't help me out, just shrugged. "I was closest."

"And when you got here, were there other people near the body?" I already knew the answer to that one, but I wanted confirmation.

"I was kind of expecting a circus when I got here, but I can't tell you something that didn't happen." I thought again of the three sets of tracks: only enough for one victim, one police officer, and one killer. This supported the theory that no one had found the body at all; the killer must have called it in themselves.

"And we still don't even know who the dead man is." I said it in a dejected way that I thought might compel Crawford to leap in with some information to appease me. "Can I have a copy of the victim's photo?" I paused, before adding, "As the lawyer." I thought it sounded like a plausibly serious request that a lawyer might make.

"I heard that you aren't, though?" Crawford said. "Your dad told me."

"Stepdad," I snapped, aware that it made me sound like a teenager. Marcelo, despite trying to get me on his side, must have told him I wasn't qualified in the hopes of supplanting me. If I was right about Michael wanting to keep people out of a locked room, it didn't escape me that Marcelo was trying awfully hard to get into it. "I'm doing my best. *I* didn't pick me."

"There are kids staying here. I can't risk the photo getting out. You understand?"

I nodded, decided on a compromise. "I may not be a lawyer, but you know you can't keep him in there. Just because he's cooperating doesn't mean he doesn't have rights." I raised my hands in what I hoped was endearing uselessness. "And, look, I don't really know what those rights are supposed to be, but I know it's not this." I pointed at the heavy wooden door, slightly warped from moisture, which had a white plastic sign with a cartoon pair of boots on it.

"He said he was okay with it."

"That's not really my point," I said. "If your suspicion of him is predicated on his being released from jail earlier than he admitted to, well, Erin's alibi is *also* tied to his whereabouts, and I don't see her locked up."

"Are you calling me sexist?"

"I'm calling you blind."

"Well, *she's* not a Cunningham, is she?"

"I see. I'm glad we're clear." Names, it seemed, were important to Crawford too. "Now I'm calling you incompetent. Let me in so I can keep pretending to be a lawyer and you can keep pretending to be a detective."

"You really care about him, don't you? Even though you testified." Crawford cocked his head slightly. I bit my tongue, but I was annoyed he knew so much more about me than he had that morning. Damn Marcelo. The lock on the door was a single slide bolt, no padlock. Crawford flicked it loose with a fingertip—high security—but stepped away from it, inviting me to open it. "I didn't really have brothers growing up, so I can't say I understand it. That's family, I guess."

"If I can confirm where he was last night, and that it wasn't here, you have to let him go—or at least move him to an actual room. Okay?" I meant it, but it also sounded semi-lawyerly and I wanted to have the last word.

Crawford gave a hesitant, nearly imperceptible, dip of the chin.

I thought of one last thing. "Oh, and, um, don't talk to him again without me present. Or whatever lawyers usually say."

I pushed open the door.

If the foyer had the lingering smell of damp expected of a ski lodge, the Drying Room had that of a shipwreck. The room was for people to peel off their sweaty, wet snow gear and dump it overnight to pick up, semi-dried, in the morning, so it was airtight to keep the heat and the smell from escaping: the rubber-lined door had opened with a *phuck* as the seal broke. I needed gills to breathe the dank, thick air. I could almost feel the mold spores in my nose. To say it smelled like feet would be a disservice to feet.

The room was narrow and long. Along both sides there were rectangular footlockers, lids open, filled with dozens of unlaced ski boots. The inner soles of many of the boots had been pulled out, like loose tongues, or removed entirely and leaned against the wall, emitting most of the smell. Above the lockers were racks of ski jackets, raincoats, and more boot innards pegged to coat hangers. In front of a small water heater was a flimsy clothes horse laden with socks. The strangest thing was that the room was carpeted, which soaked up all the moisture. It had a spongy spring to it, a slight ooze as I walked. The room was lit by a glowing red heating element at the far end, above a single unopenable window. A drift of snow pressed against it from outside, blocking any natural light.

Underneath the window sat Michael. He was perched on a footlocker, this one closed, adorned with hastily flung pillows for the pretense of comfort. He had a room service tray with a can of Coke and sandwich crusts on it. His cuffs were off, as was his jacket, and his sleeves were rolled up. The Cunninghams' reputation for civil disobedience somewhat outweighed that of our reedy frames. That is to say, no one had ever mistaken us for a football team. Without his puffy jacket on, Michael broke type.

"You've got shoulders," I said. "Is that a prison thing?"

Michael gestured to the chair in front of him. The orange heat lamp gave off a droning buzz.

"I'd close this"—I propped the door at three quarters—"but I think we both might suffocate." Which was true, but not the only reason I kept it open. I rattled on, hunting for sound to fill the room, still hanging back near the door. If you haven't figured out by now that I use humor as a defense mechanism, I don't really know what to tell you. "You know, Marcelo does this kind of thing for a living. In case you weren't aware."

"Sit down, Ern."

I took a deep breath of soupy air for courage and walked over to the chair. Sat down. Our knees touched. I shuffled the chair back. Michael sized me up. At first I thought his eyes were thoughtful, curious, as they ran over the new lines on my face, looking at what three years did to someone. Then I had a second thought: that he was sizing up a meal.

"I've been thinking about Jeremy," he said. "I know you might be too young to remember exactly. Do you?"

That seemed an obscure place to start, but I figured it was best to go along with it. "Kind of," I said. "I mean . . . well, sometimes I wonder if I actually remember it, or if I've just absorbed enough descriptions that my brain has stitched something together. There's a point where I lose which parts are real and which parts are gaps I've filled in myself." I had been only six, and I knew that I hadn't been awake for most of that day, so a lot of it had to be a construction. "I have dreams, and it's weird, because sometimes it's like I'm dreaming someone else's memories. Sometimes he, well—sometimes he doesn't . . ." I trail off.

"I know what you mean." Michael rubbed his forehead, in a strange mimicry of how he'd rubbed it the night he'd shown up at my house with Alan Holton in his car, that small dent from the steering wheel. "I know Mum's been hard on you. I think you were too young to realize how hard it was. Because it went from the five of us together to three, so quickly. Like that." He clicked his fingers.

I nodded, remembering the foster parents we'd shared when we'd been removed from Audrey's care.

"And when she finally got us back—well, it's not that she didn't want to lose us, it's that she doesn't want us to lose each other. You ever think about that?"

All the time, I didn't say. *You did this*, I didn't say. *A family is not a credit card*, I didn't say.

"I think about Jeremy a lot," I said instead, noncommittal.

"And the three of us—you and Mum and me—in a year, we'd lost a father and a brother. There's a reason she waited so long to have Jeremy's funeral. You remember that, don't you? I thought she just couldn't stomach two funerals back-to-back."

"Seven years is a long time to wait though," I said. I'd been a teenager when we'd had a small ceremony for Jeremy. We did it on his birthday.

"I was glad at the time, I felt I was old enough to understand, to appreciate it. Didn't it, sort of, bring us closer? My point is: *nothing*"—he was speaking to the ground, shaking his head with each word—"not a crowbar, not a war, not a goddamn alien invasion, could split us Cunninghams up. And then"—he lifted his gaze, pointed at my chest—"you did."

I flinched, looking down to break eye contact, and noticed there was a fork on the room service tray but no knife. I had a split second to decide if he hadn't been provided one for safety, or if he'd secreted it and it might suddenly emerge from his sleeve. "If I'm just here so you can tell me that you didn't do it, just get it over with."

"I did kill Alan Holton." His words were slow. Deliberate.

I wanted to put my fingers in my ears and stick out my tongue like a child. My mind was racing through the possibilities. I didn't want to hear how he'd picked a random victim and murdered him in the snow, how he was happy to be locked in the fetid room, just to get me alone. How he'd planned it with Lucy, who'd suggested the Drying Room. I didn't want the last thing I heard to be him gloating that he'd got to me. That he'd slept with my wife. (Okay, so I did care. A little.) I wanted to flick the chair over and bolt for the door, but I had the disadvantage of having to stand up and turn around first; he'd be on me before I took a proper step. And if he had a knife . . .

I would have to try to bargain, I realized. "I have the mone—"

"I did it on purpose." Michael silenced me with a hand in the air. "I put my hands around his neck until he stopped moving. And then you—*you*, my brother—sent me to prison."

Then he lunged, rattlesnake quick.

Suddenly everything I was thinking just became white, like my mind was in a blizzard of its own or I was already dead and didn't know it, and Michael's arms were around my . . .

. . . back.

My back. Not my neck. And there was no knife. He was hugging me. I gingerly reciprocated, holding his shoulders. There was a lot to hang on to.

"Thank you," he murmured into my shoulder. I sat stunned, still not sure if I'd actually died, and trying to decide if responding with "You're welcome" was polite or ridiculous in the circumstances. He sniffed. "I'm sure no one in this family has told you that you did the right thing, and I'm the last one you'd be expecting to hear it from."

"Something like that."

"Lucy thought this place was punishment, but it's perfect," he said, looking around the room. "Because it's safe in here."

"Safe from what?"

"I don't trust a single one of them. You're the only person I can talk to because you're the only one who was willing to stand up in that courtroom and condemn me. That means I know you'll help me do what's right. I know it's hot and airless, but I really think you might want to consider closing the door. Because I already told you I killed Alan on purpose, but now it's time I told you why."

CHAPTER 19

"I've had three years to try to figure out how to tell you this," Michael said, after I'd closed the door. He clearly hadn't, despite the time, rehearsed an opening line. "Prison is good for perspective, it feels like everything stays still while the world spins around you. Lets you look at things. I'd be lying if I said I didn't develop a certain spiritual understanding."

I must have raised my eyebrows, because he went on the defensive.

"I don't want to get too deep into the meaning-of-life crap, but when you've killed someone—sorry, when you've *made the decision* to kill someone—you've got to weigh it up. You know?"

"I don't," I said, because I didn't. Even though, writing this now, I have a somewhat better idea.

"I don't know how to explain how it felt when I hurt Alan. I was in this kind of haze where everything I did was mechanical. Like I wasn't really in control . . ." He put a hand out apologetically. "I know how it sounds, but I'm not making excuses. I'm trying to tell you that I don't know what I would have done next. The damage I might have caused. Who else I might have hurt. I've spent three years in prison with *killers,* Ern. And I thought I was killing for . . . well, something. Something bigger than me. And then I'm in there with people who are congratulating each other over what they've done and, shit, some of the stuff they've killed over is *so damn small*." He shook his head; he was getting lost, making himself upset. He blinked a few times, and breathed, to get himself back on track. "I'm sorry. I'm trying to talk about what a life is worth. You know? Take Sofia's lawsuit. That family is suing the hospital for millions . . . I can't remember the figure Erin mentioned. Point is, they've sat around a table with a bunch of lawyers and shuffled papers until they landed on a figure. They've decided 'Our son is worth this much.' "

"This isn't about Sofia." I surprised myself with how firmly I stuck up for her, seeing as she was hiding *something* worth fifty thousand dollars, after all.

"It's not. But I'm just trying to explain something. I held Alan's life in my hands and I weighed up what it was worth. And what it was worth for me to put an end to it."

"You decided your own life was more important than Alan's." I'd figured out Michael wasn't telling me some big secret, he was only telling me what he'd told himself enough times so he could live with it. He was trying to tell me that Alan's death was *worth* it. There was nothing new here. I made up my mind, shook my head. I gave up. "You can have the money. I brought the bag."

"No. Not, like, money, or anything, but the *cost*. It's a strange feeling to know what a life is worth. That's all I'm saying." He looked pensive for a second, realizing he hadn't won me over. His eyes reflected the glow of the heat lamp in a kind of wicked glint. It sort of sounded like a threat. Like he was telling me he'd weighed one life against the bag of money already, and he'd have no hesitation in valuing my life against it too. I don't know if it was my imagination or not, but the gray wall of snow against the window suddenly felt very oppressive. I pictured the building storm outside, the weight of it pressing harder against the glass, like it might at any moment spew into the room and bury us. Then he said, "It's an even stranger thing to realize that you got it wrong."

I wasn't sure if he was trying to tell me he was unhappy with the price he'd received, or the price he'd paid, and I told him that, though, admittedly, less eloquently than I've made it sound here.

"I'm trying to tell you I've learned from my mistakes, that I'll never choose violence again. And you still think this is about the money?" Michael said.

"Isn't it?"

"The money's not . . . Look, it should have been our money in the first place, okay? We died for it. It's right for them to pay."

Our money. There it was again. But who was the other part of "we"? A Cunningham? I opened my mouth to ask another question, but the roulette wheel in my head stopped spinning on a thought.

Michael had told me it was our money on the night Alan died. I'd thought he meant he had deserved the money, that he'd earned it, by stealing or killing, and that I was welcome to be a part of it. Erin had whispered in my ear only hours before: *It's family money.* I'd thought she meant the same thing: staking a claim, inviting me in. Michael and Erin had been telling me the plain truth the whole time and I'd missed it. They were talking about *literal* ownership.

I could picture the spiderweb-riddled clearing now, Michael hunched over a gasping man. Weighing up his decision. Valuing a life. Everything made sense, including how Michael had known the amount in the bag without counting it: $267,000.

Well, fuck me. I've finally solved something.

"The money's not stolen," I surmised. "It's yours. You didn't blunder into this. You knew Alan. Was he selling you something?"

Michael's eyes lit up as he realized I was ready to hear, if not yet believe, his story. I know eyes lighting up is a cliché, but it's true: though it could have been an electrical surge in the old hotel wiring making the heaters flare. "I guess I should tell you about Alan Holton, then. And how he knew Dad."

That caught me off guard. I was glad I'd closed the door.

"Dad knew Alan?"

Michael nodded sincerely. "What I'm about to tell you is going to sound . . . well, it's going to sound out there. Hear me out, okay?" He took my silence as agreement and continued. "Holton was a cop."

"A cop?" I felt the need to physically lever my eyebrows down from my forehead with my fingertips, but I resisted.

"Former."

"Obviously. He's former everything, isn't he?" I knew my comment was juvenile; it just spurted out while I processed everything. "That doesn't make sense. You can't have only got three years for killing a cop?"

"No. I mean, he wasn't a cop when I . . . that night. He used to be one. Had a"—he twirled his fingers—"shall we say, fall from grace. Landed hard. That's how he wound up bouncing from petty job to petty job and eventually scraping it together selling secondhand trinkets. He was a part-time drug dealer; part-time thief; part-time homeless. And a full-time liability. Marcelo was able to characterize him as a petty criminal because Alan's time in the police . . . it was not a shining example of a noble force. In fact, that's why the prosecution accepted the three-year deal, because if Marcelo had had to pull that history out in court—well, there are some people who would prefer it didn't get aired." That made sense. "Marcelo dangled Alan's past at the judge behind closed doors, and the prosecution took my deal. Three years. Are you following?"

"Sort of. Except for what this has to do with Dad?"

"I'm getting there."

"Snow's melting. I hear I'm allowed to charge every six minutes, seeing as I'm a lawyer now."

"I think I've paid in advance, Ern."

I had nothing to say back to that. Witty repartee is not well serviced by truth.

Michael took a swig of his Coke, grimaced, assumedly at the absorbed foot taste inside the open can, and continued. "So Alan contacts me. Out of the blue, you understand—I wasn't seeking trouble. He says he has something I *want*. That he'll sell it to me. He says he's talked to you as well, actually. That's why I brought him to your door that night. I thought if he'd told you what he told me, you might . . . understand what had happened."

"Maybe he said that to make you believe him." I leaned back in my chair. "But I'm not a part of this. I've never met him."

"Yes and no." Michael shrugged, like my awareness of who I did and didn't know was a matter of opinion. Before I could argue, he kept going. "I figured out he hadn't contacted you, of course I did. Your shock and confusion that morning, not to mention that you didn't change your testimony after you knew his name, gave that away. But you *have* met him."

I went to rebut this, but then he leaned forward and, with a single finger, pressed it into three parts of my body: my belly, my hip and the center of my chest. He did it slowly, rhythmically, each poke a beat. I could hear the cadence of remembered words in my head, matching his movements, without him having to say them.

I'll show you where I shot him. Here, here, and here.

CHAPTER 20

"I spent most of my life trying to forget about Dad," I breathed. I was rapidly trying to put everything Michael was telling me in order and sift through it for the truth at the same time. I'd been willfully ignorant of the circumstances around Dad's death; I never felt he deserved my attention after what he'd done and how he'd died. There's no blaze of glory in dying in a gunfight with police. It wasn't a brave death, a death to be proud of. It was a death to be forgotten. That was why Alan's name hadn't lit up a flashing sign in my brain during Michael's trial. And with Marcelo persuading the court to accept an early plea and therefore suppress Alan's sordid history, I might have never known differently. I pushed at my memory to see the man standing in front of my mother, smearing cream across her dress. Did I see a gold-plated lapel that read HOLTON? Or was that flash of memory constructed by the information Michael had just told me? Was this, as I'd told him earlier, one of those moments where I was losing which parts were real and which parts I was filling in myself? I apologize; that's not something a reliable narrator does. Did police officers even wear nameplates?

I pushed all these thoughts aside and said, to Michael's surprise, "This doesn't change anything. It doesn't mean you get the right to do what you did to Alan. And it doesn't make it right what Alan did to Dad. But"—I was aware that I was choosing a very un-Cunningham side here, sympathizing with the enemy—"Dad was a criminal, he was caught in a robbery and he'd just shot Alan's partner in the neck. If Holton's who you say he is, he was just fighting back."

"I'm not denying that," Michael said. "But think about it. Did we grow up rich? Did Dad drive a flash car? Did Mum wear expensive jewelry? We didn't revel in a life of crime. Dad broke the law to feed us, to care for us. I'm not saying that's right, but he didn't do it to line his own pockets. He wouldn't have."

"That's a very favorable view of our father," I said.

"Just listen to the way Holton told it. And I know it's true because who lies with their last breath?" I could tell Michael was frustrated I hadn't patted him on the back after learning it was Alan who had pulled the trigger on our father. He knew he still had to win me over. He went for his drink, remembered the taste, put the can down un-sipped, and instead worked his jaw around to swallow some saliva, clear his throat. "Dad found himself in with a group. Gang's not quite the right word. Colleagues?" He laughed. "They called themselves the Sabers. As in tooth, you know? That group started to grow a bit, and priorities changed. They moved from robbers who occasionally dealt to dealers who occasionally stole. Harder stuff, too. And with that came more violence, more enforcement. And someone decided ransoms paid better than robberies or drugs. Dad drew a line he wouldn't cross, and when the Sabers started to cross it . . ."

As he said this, something my mother had told me in the library resurfaced: *But a bad person who thinks they're a good one—now, that's what got him into trouble.*

"Dad flipped?" I interrupted. If only we'd been in the library, a much more appropriate setting for grand deductions.

Michael nodded. "He cut a deal to feed along information, and in return they'd go easy on him when the rest of his mates went down. He saw it as a chance to get out. You know how that kind of thing is done—they skip over the worker bees to take care of the queen. Dad was small fry. He was helping them get the ringleaders. But, most of all, they wanted the dirty cops." He paused to let it sink in. "Dad's death wasn't a stick-up gone wrong. They were coming for him."

I remembered Audrey telling me my father wasn't a junkie. Maybe Holton had planted the syringe, to help make the robbery more convincing. A strung-out junkie, after all, is more likely to open fire on a squad car without provocation. If my father had been about to spill the beans on Holton and his partner, it made sense.

"It's a shame no one pegged Holton for something as big as murder, but his dealings caught him eventually. He used to steal cocaine from the evidence locker, take bribes. There're only so many blind eyes one man can ask for." That seemed pointed, but I let him have it. "He served some jail time, and then everything about who he was before then became hush-hush, because it's not a good look for the police force, you understand?"

To be honest, I *was* tempted to believe him. Not because of Dad's vindication, either, but because it seemed to explain a lot about my mother. If this was true, it meant Audrey didn't only mistrust the police because she thought the bad ones had killed her husband. She thought the good ones, the ones who'd promised my father a way out, had got him killed. My betrayal was laid bare: I'd chosen to side with the law, the same as my father, and it had failed to protect us.

Then again, it also sounded like a story where the pieces fit together too neatly. A story that had taken Michael three years to craft especially for me.

"Holton told you all this?" I couldn't keep the skepticism from my voice. It was quite the incriminating confession. "That's a lot of gas for someone who's been shot in the lung."

"He was tight-lipped before he got shot, loose-lipped after. Besides, he didn't tell me all of it. Most of what I know about Alan I found out from others in jail. They all knew him. Half of them had been ripped off by his pawn shop, which was pretty well known for selling stolen goods, by the way—you wanted to move something hot in Sydney, I guarantee it found its way to Alan. And he owed money to the other half. They shook my hand, Ern. Like I'd done them a favor." He grimaced, and it was obvious that this act of solidarity among the other inmates was what haunted him. More, perhaps, than the killing itself.

I closed my eyes, picturing the scene in the bone-white, webbed clearing. *I'll go check on him.* Michael's back to me, his hunched shoulders, outstretched arms disappearing into the webs. *We can bury him now.*

"When Alan woke up in the clearing, and you went to check if he was okay. That was when you made up your mind, wasn't it?"

Michael stayed in the memory, talking as if he were in a trance. "I spent a lot of time blaming him, would you believe it? Because I felt like, in that moment, I was waking up. And maybe if he hadn't said anything, I would have put him in the car. Maybe I would have listened to you. There was blood on his lips, I remember that. It stuck between them as he spoke, little red bridges. I don't know why Holton told me about shooting Dad then. Maybe he wanted one last insult before he died. Maybe he was testing me, to see if I would do *it*. Maybe he *wanted* me to do it." Then he wrinkled his nose. "Sorry. That's what the prison shrink calls 'deferred responsibility.' I shouldn't be doing that."

"So when he told you he shot Dad, you snapped and finished the job?"

Michael nodded solemnly. He was looking at his hands, perhaps imagining them around Alan's neck. "I didn't go there to kill him. I didn't know any of that until the end. He was selling me what Dad died for. Selling someone else out."

I thought again about the money. *We died for it.* "We" was a Cunningham after all: our father, Robert. "But once you found out Dad had died because of Alan, you felt that whatever he had, whatever it was worth, was owed to you. An inheritance. So you shot him and took it. And you took your money back."

"That's not how it happened. It was about the money, yes, but not like that. I brought what I could, but it was less than he wanted. I fucked up. I thought he wouldn't notice." He shook his head sadly, the way people do in hospital waiting rooms. It's a shake that says "if" to the left and "only" to the right. "He pulled the gun on me. I don't own one—I mean, come on. We struggled with it. It went off. He was holding it; I don't really know how. I've never fired a gun before. And then he was sitting down and there was blood pouring from his side. I just . . . well, I left him there. Threw the gun into a storm drain. But by the time I'd got back to my car and calmed down enough to start it up, he'd managed to sort of get moving again. I can't remember if I meant to hit him or if he just kind of jumped in the way, but he went under the bonnet. And then he wasn't moving anymore. That's when I called you."

Two hundred and sixty-seven had always seemed like such an odd number. The fact that it didn't add up suddenly added up.

"Alan wanted three hundred?"

"It was the best I could do. Lucy . . ." He hesitated, embarrassed. "I messed it up, all right? I didn't bring enough."

"How did Lucy not notice?" Something he'd said on that night echoed: *Lucy will know.* I thought he'd been hiding his drinking, but maybe he'd been hiding something bigger.

"Lucy's not . . ." His eyes flickered, happy to be honest about the night in question, but not to plunge too deep into his personal life.

"Lucy's not great with money. Her, um, business, I guess—it became a bit of a problem. A sieve. Katherine told me one of the kindest things you can do to someone is to cut them off. I tried it, but it just made things worse. I thought I could help her."

"Does Lucy know now?"

"I don't think so. You've got the bag. But she *could* know, I guess. If she does, she's keeping mum."

"What could possibly be worth that much money?"

"I told you—information. And it's worth a whole lot more than that, now I've had time to think about it."

"The same information that was worth killing Dad over decades ago? The reason you think you're safer in here than out there? If it's so dangerous, why did you want it?"

"I told you, Lucy got us in a hole. Alan couldn't sell what he had directly, so he wanted someone to do it for him; I got in the middle." I remember wondering to myself if *anyone* in my family was solvent. Michael started to get agitated, rummaging through each of his pockets, muttering as he did. "To be honest I didn't realize I was doing something all that dangerous. All I knew was that Holton got them from Dad. I didn't know that he was, like, *involved*. Then again, I don't think he thought I was much of a risk either, so we all made mistakes."

"What do you mean 'them' plural? And who were you selling to?"

"It's easier if I show you . . ." He rummaged around in his pockets and patted his jeans. He produced a contact lens case (I hadn't known Michael needed glasses, but perhaps with the walls so close in prison, he'd become nearsighted), a few balls of lint, a chocolate wrapper, a pen, and a set of keys. No knife. Whatever he was looking for wasn't there. "Shit. Where's the damn thing?" He couldn't hide his disappointment. "I'll have to show you later."

"You'd been drinking. That night." It had been on my mind, but it just kind of popped out. I said it too quickly. My doubts were too obvious. Michael's head snapped up, and I saw something in his eyes that terrified me. I wondered if that was the last thing Holton had seen.

"Just a bit of courage—I had my wits." He chuckled, but it was sad and slow. "I knew you wouldn't believe me."

"*Believe you*?" I tried to keep my voice level. "I sat in the car because I believed you. I'm an accessory because I believed you."

"Listen—"

"I don't know. These stories about Dad . . . whatever you were buying or stealing from Alan, and you've got nothing to show for it—"

"—listen—"

"—he lied to you about talking to me, whatever he made you think—"

"LISTEN TO ME!" Michael's voice was so loud in the small room I almost toppled off the chair.

I stood. Walked backwards towards the door. Michael registered that I was afraid of him and his eyes changed from furious to baleful, like a chastised dog. He stood too, putting a hand out in an attempt to stop me.

"He must have known what I would do. After the things he said." His voice was calmer, but I could tell it was taking a lot of effort. Each word was like skidding a car in the wet, grappling with the wheel. "Dying men don't lie, Ern, they air their souls. I wish I could show you—" He cut himself off mid-sentence, reconsidered, and then picked up the set of keys he'd drawn from his pocket. "This is getting us nowhere. If you don't believe my words, see for yourself. Then I'll tell you the rest."

He tossed me the keys. I caught them against my chest. *Ask him what's really in the damn truck*. As I was thinking about her words, Sofia's actual voice came through the door. She sounded desperate, though I couldn't make out the words. The door shuddered: it was unnecessarily dramatic knocking for a door we couldn't lock, but maybe she was trying to be polite. Whatever Sofia had to tell me could wait—I wasn't through with Michael. I ignored the knocking.

"Just tell me. Do you know anything about what's going on out there? Do the names Mark and Janine Williams, or Alison Humphreys mean anything to you?"

"Humphreys . . ." He shook his head. "No. But Williams . . . depends if they're from Brisbane." I leaned forward with such interest I almost fell off my chair. Michael relished my attention. "Early on in my sentence I got a letter from someone called M&J Williams, with the return address a PO box in Brisbane. By then I'd realized that what I had, like I said, was worth a bit more than I'd thought it was. A lot of people wanted it. And whoever wrote me that letter—well, they get credit for being the most creative. I guess they were trying to threaten me."

"How?"

"They signed off with a clearly fake name." He said it as a half chuckle. "But, like I said, they were just trying to push my buttons—scare me. I never wrote back. Why?"

"I think Mark and Janine Williams may have been killed by the same person who killed our frozen corpse. It looks like a similar method, but I need to check with Sofia. It's too much of a coincidence for a man to die *this* weekend when we're all here—"

"—and when I'm coming up here with what I've brought. I agree. It has to be connected. Just look in the truck, you'll see."

I stood up. "Where were you last night?" I couldn't leave without asking.

"Open the truck—it'll answer that too."

"There better be something crazy like a spaceship in there," I said.

The knocking shook the door again. I glanced at it. Michael nodded, and I hated myself when I realized I'd paused, waiting for his permission to leave.

"You dropped something." He looked at the floor, next to my chair, where a small square of paper had fallen from my pocket. My cheeks flamed with embarrassment. Michael picked up the paper, read it, and smirked.

"Sofia?" he asked. I nodded. "You've missed one."

Michael picked up his pen, looked at me for a second as if deciding whether he should vandalize the card or not. Then he placed the paper flat on the bench, leaned over it, and made a few dashes. I couldn't see what he was writing, his body blocked my view, but it took a while. He was either writing a lot or thinking hard about very little. I fidgeted, looking back towards the door. I could hear two voices outside now.

When Michael finished, he righted himself and blew on the paper, pressing it with his thumb to check if the ink was dry. I realized what had taken so long: his contacts case was now open on the bench; he must have slid them in to write better. Then he crossed the room (I'm ashamed to admit my pulse thundered in my neck as he did so) and handed me the bingo card. I snatched it out of his hand and examined it. I felt strangely possessive of my bingo boxes, that he'd somehow invaded mine and Sofia's private game, so I wanted to assess the damage. He'd taken so long I was sure he'd have done more, but it was just the one change. He'd crossed through *Someone Dies*.

"Don't lose that. I'm trusting you. I'm not asking you to believe me, I'm just asking you to look closely." I looked at the keys in my other hand, wondering what I'd see in the truck. *Look closely*. Then I realized he was standing near enough now to give in to a husky, intimate confession, the one I wanted most to avoid. He swallowed. "And, listen, with Erin . . ."

"Don't—" I tried to stop him.

He trampled my words. "We didn't plan for it to happen or anything."

Temptation got the better of me. I have a problem with peering into other people's hotel rooms, after all. "Did she tell you we were trying to start a family? Did she tell you about the doctors, the clinics? What it was that broke us? Tell me it's not just about that. I could have given her what she wanted. Tell me it's about more than *that*."

"Ern—"

Sanity arrived. "I've changed my mind. I don't want to know. Besides, I spent quite a bit of your money." (I hadn't spent that much. And I wasn't proud of it. I just wanted to have the last venomous word.) "I guess I didn't plan that either."

On the other side of the door, Crawford and Sofia weren't quite holding water glasses up to the wood, but they were crowded in anxious curiosity around it. I was thankful for the rubber seal, which would have helped the soundproofing, and meant they probably hadn't heard much at all. Except maybe Michael's yelling. Maybe that's why they started knocking.

Sofia made a face that meant *finally* and yanked my arm in the direction of the guesthouse entrance, telling me she'd explain on the way. She took off, expecting me to follow. Crawford slid the bolt back into place and took his seat by the door, clearly unalarmed by or uninformed of Sofia's emergency.

Before I set off after her, I took a second to breathe clean air. Beads of sweat on my neck that had bred in the Drying Room chilled my skin. Michael had said a lot, and I didn't know what to believe of it, but I had started to accept that he might not be the danger. Of course, now I suspected he'd brought the danger with him. But nothing made sense yet. My next step was simple. If, as he promised, whatever was in the back of his truck could clear up his whereabouts last night, he shouldn't have to stay in the Drying

Room too much longer. Now that I'd spent half an hour in there, I was even more keen to rescue him from it. Then we could handle the rest together.

I followed Sofia, folding the bingo card to better hide it in my jacket as I walked. I figured Katherine wouldn't find it so endearing if I accidentally dropped it in front of her next time. Firming the crease, I noticed that there was another scribble. Ink fresh and glistening. Michael had crossed out a word in one of the squares, replacing it with another. My editor will be pleased that he also added punctuation. It now read:

Ernest ~~ruins~~ fixes something.

CHAPTER 21

Looking at Michael's edit to my bingo card, I was filled with a rush of fraternal affection, just as I am now, writing it out. Taken as I am by this feeling, I hope you'll allow me a small diversion to give you a bit more background on our mother. I honestly would have included this earlier, but I thought if one more anecdote delayed my reunion with Michael in the Drying Room, you might have thrown the book at the wall. And fair enough.

To tell it properly, I'm going to need to relate this next part using events I haven't seen and people's perspectives I can only guess at. I'm going to tell you these things as truths. Even if I have to rebuild the color of people's coats or their small talk about the weather (I remember the weather, actually, so I don't need to fictionalize that: it was a baking summer day), it's a worthwhile compromise. My version of events won't be nearly as useful, not least because of patchy childhood memories, but also because I was geographically limited on the day. And I fear that if I just tell my side, you'll be too quick to judge my mother.

So: the Day. It's an important day. There is a death. It is the day my mother shot somebody. It's the day she got the scar above her right eye. The day she earned her Cunningham stripes, so to speak.

It's months after Dad died. But you wouldn't know it.

My mother does not take shit. Not from her children, not from the universe. I mentioned before that I measured my father by the spaces he left. Now he'd left the largest one yet, but we didn't have time to notice. Our mother sought to keep us busy: our extracurriculars tripled as if we were applying to Harvard. Any gap in the schedule was closed. I once got a haircut two days in a row.

We had to join sport teams (in which there was more frolicking with various implements than actual sport, given our ages) as if we were potential prodigies. I swam. Jeremy played tennis. Michael settled on piano instead of sport (and now *he's* the one with shoulders). All three of us would go to the others' practices: sit on the umpire's chair, doodle on the blackboard, dangle our feet in the pool. We moved around town together, eight-armed. This served the dual purpose of saving on babysitting and keeping us busy. Mum was trying to force us to feel normal. We didn't talk about Dad, we never stopped to acknowledge that life might be different, we just powered on. Few friends dared drop by with a casserole or a lasagna after the first attempts were fed to the cat. A boy in my class, Nathan, had had a few weeks off school when his dad died of cancer. I brought it up once and had to join Joey Scouts.

As questionable a parenting technique as forcing your children to repress trauma is, it kind of worked. But I suspect that our mother also found comfort in our new, hectic routine. She'd strap us into the car, our three Disney-Channel-sitcom-perfect car seats side by side, and drop us at school, head to work, then pick us up, click us in, and take us to one of our activities. We were never at home. We were outrunning our grief.

Looking back, having been through trauma again as an adult (*Go wait in the car*), I can see another side to my mother's actions back then. Because now I know that in the months after something so devastating, everything feels like sleepwalking. Life becomes a stuporous fulfillment of routine where even walking to the supermarket feels like you're dragging your limbs through air as heavy as the Drying Room's. Every basic task starts to feel like a decision, and that becomes so draining that you end up unable to make any of them. It's winding up in the kitchen without knowing why you went in there. It's taking us to swim school on a Tuesday instead of tennis. It's getting two haircuts, not because you're busy, but because you forgot we went yesterday. Our routine was intended to keep us busy, sure, but the repetition was a comfort against the burden of decision-making. A burden that, I know now, our mother wore heavily.

Everything is routine on the day in question. Breakfast is an uneventful one. Audrey straps us into the car, makes every green light on the trip, and even arrives at the bank five minutes early, allowing her to make a coffee and have a quick chat with her boss, who, I'll embellish, is wearing a blue coat and a green tie and wants to talk about the weather.

My mother has moved around roles in the banking sector since, retiring from a senior position, but on this day she was a teller. This was the 90s, when banks had a full army of neckerchief-wearing young women behind plexiglass windows instead of one besuited university graduate with an iPad and the audacity to make you do things yourself. The bank was very good to Mum, I've since learned. They were lenient about Dad's infamy; usually it would have meant she couldn't work there, but she was allowed to hang on to the job she had after his death made his actions public. They were also sympathetic about a couple of costly (sleepwalking) errors she made in the months after Dad died. They even offered her additional leave, but I'll let you figure out whether she took it or not. Her first day back at work was three days after Dad's funeral, and the only reason for that gap was because the funeral was on a Friday.

At ten past nine, just when she's getting started, my mother is told that she has a call on the phone in the manager's office, but she's too busy to take it. At nine thirty, the phone rings again, but this time no message is brought to my mother. The phone just keeps on with its shrill echo, usually quite a racket in the hush of the bank and even more so with the manager's door open, the front door locked, and the tellers sitting quietly, cross-legged on the floor with their hands behind their heads.

There are two men. I don't need to invent what they're wearing, because I know it is trench coats, sunglasses, and caps. One is ransacking the tills, while the other stalks down the line of staff, barking at people to be quiet. He carries a bulky black shotgun-looking thing by the barrel instead of the handle, swinging it by his side as he walks. It's the way you'd hold a baseball bat if you weren't actually playing.

There is no alarm. No one managed to get to it. Little League decides to beat access to the safe out of the manager. The phone rings again, and Till Ransacker, swearing, goes into the office and takes it off the hook.

My mother does not take shit from her boys or the universe, and she certainly doesn't take shit from petty crooks. It does not escape me that what happens next could have been rebellion against the crime that robbed her of her husband, the stupidity of the burglary. Or it could have been rebellion against Little League's very existence; behind those sunglasses maybe she saw my dad, and everything he'd left her to deal with, when she pulled the trigger. Or maybe she just thought Little League wasn't holding the shotgun well enough to get off a shot. I can't settle on which is the most likely.

What I can say is that whatever she felt was enough to make her stand up. What I can say is that thirty seconds later, she has a broken nose and a shotgun in her hands. That Little League is on the floor, scurrying backwards. That my mother brings the gun around. That it's very close range for a shotgun, close enough to rip someone in half. That Till Ransacker has put his hands up in the air and is telling her to chill out. That she levels the gun at Little League's chest and—I can't hazard a guess as to whether she hesitates or not, but I imagine the stupor is gone and she's as clearheaded as she's been in a long time—pulls the trigger.

She hits him square in the chest.

A beanbag round is a shotgun cartridge that, instead of exploding with skin-tearing pellets, contains them in a small fabric pillow. These are often used by riot police and are designed to immobilize rather than kill. Technically they are classed as "less lethal" rather than "nonlethal"; they can, for example, break a rib and drive it into the heart, but the most common cause of death from a beanbag gun is, of all things, accidentally loading it with real ammunition.

Don't worry, this isn't one of those books where I describe the velocity in meters per second of every bullet fired, the make and model and factory of commission of the gun in question, and the relative humidity or wind conditions that may affect trajectory. I have a point to make.

The point is, while Little League would still have been plenty scared to have the gun pointed at him, and my mother obliged him with four broken ribs, she didn't kill him.

It has occurred to me that my mother can't have known the gun she was holding was "less lethal" when she made the choice to pull the trigger, but that's for a different time. The point is, my mother's scar is above her right eye, and the bank-heist hopeful had only given her a broken nose. The point is, once the police and the paramedics had cleared the building and stuffed cotton buds in my mother's nostrils, it was mid-afternoon by the time someone finally put the phone back on the hook, where it started ringing immediately. The point is, I remember the temperature of the day: it was baking hot. The point is, the call was from my school, to let my mother know that none of the three Cunningham boys had arrived that morning. The point is, my mother had been, ahead of her usually very tight schedule, five minutes early to work.

The point is, my mother shot someone but didn't kill them.

The point is, there is a death.

The stupor. The sleepwalking. The distracted errors.

Three boys in a rooftop car park on a scorching summer day, forgotten to be dropped off at school, still clicked into their seats. I don't remember the window breaking, the blood pouring off Audrey's forehead as she sliced it on the glass, deep enough to scar. The first thing I know as concrete is the hospital; I was told about the rest later. To this day I wake from nightmares, choking. But, to be honest, I don't really remember the day at all. I have huge black patches.

All I know is that when Jeremy died, I was sitting next to him.

From: <REDACTED>
To: ECunninghamWrites221@gmail.com
Subject: Photos for EIMFHKS

Hi Ernest,

Good to hear from you. I'm afraid that a photographic section at the midpoint would require a gloss-paper insert, not to mention full-color printing, which would need a completely different production process. It's quite costly and is just not within the budget for this book. I'm confident you can get the same result with some well-placed descriptions. I'm sorry but there's just no way we can stretch to it.

How's it going, by the way? Have you managed to iron out a bit of the chattiness? I mean, I know it may be how you process things, but a lot of people died and readers might find it unsympathetic. You'll be pleased to know we've decided to take the bullet holes off the cover—I know you thought they were a bit much. Let me know if you want me to look at any more sections as you get through them.

Best,
REDACTED

P.S. Re: your other question. Yes, it should be no problem to funnel a percentage of royalties to Lucy Sanders' estate. Send me the details and I'll arrange with accounts.

MY STEPFATHER

CHAPTER 22

I caught up to Sofia in the foyer, standing by the entranceway.

"Someone's sniffing around the maintenance shed," she said. She pushed open the double doors, the storm cascading over the threshold, ice spattering my boots. I hesitated, but she herded me outside. The porch was empty. Even the husbands had given up their retrieval missions, choosing to be warm and chastened over shivering and chivalrous. The wind rippled in my ears; it sounded like someone scrunching cellophane beside me. Sofia had to shout to be heard. "I saw a shadow." She hesitated. "From the bar."

"So?" I yelled back. It was all I could get out with the wind barreling into my mouth. It was the type of gale you have to take bites of to breathe.

"Don't the bad guys like to hang around the scene of the crime?"

She was right, but my cowardice activates at quite a low temperature threshold. I was about to suggest that we wait a minute or, better yet, fetch Crawford, but before I could form a word, she'd slung one arm over her brow and powered into the storm.

I gave chase, worried if she got too far her shadow would dissolve. Almost immediately it was impossible to tell what was up and what was down. For all I knew we could have gone the wrong way, downhill, and been traipsing across the frozen lake, about to plunge through the fragile ice to our deaths. I've read that once you hit cold water, your lungs seize up. If it's cold enough, it even affects your blood. You can black out immediately. Everyone knows that going into a frozen lake is dangerous, because once you go through a hole in the ice it's impossible to find it again from the underside, but the old cliché of the drowning person banging their fists against the clear ice isn't real. Everything stops in water that cold. What a disappointment that must be, to be robbed of the fist-bashing. I hope, when I go, I get the chance to rage against my death.

I realized I'd lost Sofia. I tried to look around. Nothing but swirling, endless gray. The howl in my ears was violent, nearly shrieking. The wind sounded like a chainsaw. My eyes stung, so I buried them further in the crook of my elbow, trying to look up only when I had to. I took a few shuffling steps forward. Hulking shapes emerged from the swirling gray. *Bears*. That was my first thought, which was ridiculous, because this was Australia. They were cars, I quickly realized. I was in the car park. Good; I'd been going the right way.

The storm was so vicious the cars were literally rocking on their suspensions. Katherine's Volvo had a broken window, snow caked on the back seat. It was lucky that wasn't Marcelo's car, I thought, where the snow would have soiled the leather seats and short-circuited the fancy electronics. I had an idea, filed it for later.

From where I stood, I thought I could just make out the maintenance shed, further up the hill. It was too far to be a vehicle, too real to be a bear, and it didn't have the triangular peak of the chalets. It was good enough to orientate myself. I went to take a step, but then, to my right, I saw Michael's truck. Despite the blur, it was unmistakable in its size. Both flanks were practically acting as sails in the driving wind, and the whole thing was rocking recklessly on its small wheels, as if it could tip at any moment. I felt the keys in my pocket rub against my leg. Forget the maintenance shed. I took a step towards the truck.

Someone grabbed my arm. Sofia. Her lips against my ear, spit on my neck. "Wrong way, Ern."

Then she was dragging me up the hill, out of the lot. The snow was noticeably deeper already (goodbye, crime-scene footprints) and I punched through it up to my calf with each step. As we got closer to the flat-roofed shadow, I could see huge mounds of snow caked on the roof. We approached from the side, even though the front would have been a better wind buffer, battling the last few steps until our backs were pressed against the corrugated iron. The wind split around the shed and reformed just in front of us, like we were sheltering behind a rock in a river, and the crinkle in our ears reduced to a ghostly moan. I took a few heavy gulps of uninterrupted air and shook an inch of powder from my arms and shoulders. I didn't have gloves on so I shoved my hands in my pockets, clenching and unclenching them to warm them up. Above me, long-fingered icicles hung from the awning. I saw a horror movie once where someone was skewered by a falling icicle, which I knew was impossible, but sucked myself as far back against the wall as I could anyway.

Sofia leaned around the corner, then quickly pulled her head back and elbowed me in the ribs, making eyes at me. *Look*. The shed door was open. The padlock Crawford had used to seal it was lying in the snow. It hadn't been cut; the handle he'd looped it through had been entirely pulled off, screws and all.

"We should get Crawford," I said.

"You go get him then." She made to round the corner.

I put an arm across her, flattening her to the wall. "Stop!"

"I want a closer look at the body, okay? And I'm not going to get a better opportunity. Crawford won't let any of us near it again.

And like he's going to solve it. He may as well be playing dress-up. If this is"—she exploded an imaginary balloon in her hands—"something *bigger*, then we could all be dead by dawn. We have to arm ourselves with knowledge. And here we are and the door's open. The killer's probably been and gone."

"And if they haven't?"

"Well, that's why I brought you. Bodyguard."

"Bad choice."

"How about this? We take a look through the door, just the tiniest glimpse, and if someone's in there, we barricade it, lock them in. There's only one entrance. And then we go get everyone else. Capiche?"

I had a lot of questions. How would we lock them in with a broken handle? How was it possible to barricade the door and run for help at the same time? What if they had a weapon? How do you spell "capiche"?

But I knew I didn't have a choice. If I went back to the guesthouse for help, Sofia wouldn't wait for me to arrive with backup. It was safer together. And, besides, while I hoped that what was in the truck would help clear Michael's name (*Ernest fixes something.*), a proper look at the body might help too. And, look, it's annoying, I know, when people make dumb decisions for this reason—it's the reason icicle-kebab didn't survive that horror flick—but I was, just a bit, curious.

We rounded the corner, edged along the wall, backs pressed for both stealth and icicle safety until we reached the crack in the door. Sofia leaned her head through the gap, then pulled back like she'd been bitten by a snake, her eyes wide. She mouthed, "Someone's there." I pointed at the door, mimed closing it. She shook her head, pointed at my eyes and then the gap in the doorway, and shuffled past me so I was closest to it. She gave me a push. Her intent was clear: *You need to see this*. I bugged my eyes at her in as close to an expression of betrayal as I could figure: *This wasn't the plan.* She gave me another push.

I took a deep breath, resisted the urge to cast one more spiteful look at Sofia, and poked my head through the gap.

Green Boots was where we'd left him, limbs splayed on the too-small stack of pallets, chest thrust up like he was inverted skydiving. The difference now was that someone was hunched over him. I recognized them immediately, even from the back. They were focused on the body, so they hadn't noticed us yet. Ideally, here is when I would have slowly backed away, locked them in, and fetched the real police, as agreed. But I didn't. It was as if some invisible thread was pulling me into the room. I barely felt Sofia's frantic tapping on my arm, her warning hiss swept away in the wind.

My entrance was unnoticed, the rattling of the walls and the groan of the roof, snow still piling up on it, masking my footsteps. It was freezing inside the shed, the cold pushing in from the metal walls and up from the concrete floor. My breath misted. I cleared my throat. The person shot upright, took two steps back from the body, and put their hands in the air. Red-handed.

"Nice things," I said. It's a private joke we have.

CHAPTER 23

The reason I say "Nice things" to Erin so often is, as I told her when we married, if she was ever mad at me, she could always answer the question "How are things with Ernest?" honestly with: "Well, he always says 'nice things.' "

Her shoulders crumpled, her hands came down, and she said, "Oh, thank God," in a huge breath of relief, breaking out into a wider smile than I'd seen her give in a long time. She started to move towards me, but stopped when she heard the steel in my voice.

"What are you doing here, Erin?"

"Have you talked to Michael yet?" Her tone was unexpected, a mixture of confusion and surprise, as if everything should have been, after my cryptic adversarial conversation with my brother, pretty straightforward. "Did he tell you about Alan?"

"He told me about Alan."

"Okay. So . . ." Again, she paused as if she'd filled in enough of the blanks, before realizing she had to really spell it out, putting on her gentle teacher's voice. "How do you feel about it?"

"I don't know what I believe." There was no point lying to Erin; she was always better at it than me. I know, I know—it sounds like a pithy remark to put in a book where she has no right of reply, but it *is* true. Besides, she was the one who had the affair.

"There's a dead man next to us," she said bluntly.

"You know, I'd noticed."

"This wasn't an accident, Ern, like the resort owner wants us to believe. That's just so everyone doesn't panic. But you and I, we *know* that this is a Cunningham problem. Brought here by Cunninghams . . ." She didn't say it, but the rest of the sentence lingered: *committed by Cunninghams*.

I relented slightly. "If I believe Michael, the man who killed my father, Alan, is already dead. That story's finished. What else is there?"

"If?"

"I believe he believes it—that's it for now."

The memory of the webbed clearing chilled me. Perhaps that was part of my refusal to accept what Michael had told me: Alan might seem villainous on paper, but I was the only one there that morning and I didn't want his death, his *murder*, to be justified—no matter who he was or what he'd done.

"It's simple, though. Alan killed your father to cover his arse, sure, but he was killing for *something*." Erin clicked her tongue as she processed everything. "Then he tries to sell that same thing to Michael, and that gets us here."

"Michael told me that already. But why wait so long?"

"Maybe because Alan's career was gone. Maybe he was desperate. All I know is, if it was worth killing over half a lifetime ago, it's worth killing over now." She gestured with a thumb at Green Boots. "Need I, again, point to the aforementioned corpse?"

"Okay then. What was this information Michael was buying from Alan?"

"I don't know." She hesitated. "He wouldn't tell me. Said it wasn't safe."

Rule 9 dictates I must divulge everything as it occurs to me, and here it occurred to me that she was telling the truth, but she wasn't telling me everything.

"But?" I fished.

"We dug something up."

I thought of his prison-filthy hands, as we'd shaken in front of the guesthouse. The dirt under his fingernails. The rest of him had been clean: clean-shaven, dyed hair. Why hadn't he cleaned his nails? "Is it in the back of the truck?"

She nodded.

"Okay. So what is it?" It sounded simple when I put it like that, which made me feel like it might have been true. "Money, I assume, to be worth that much? Something from one of the Sabers' robberies? Jewelry? Drugs?"

"I thought so too. I haven't seen it."

I laughed. It came out a hack, my vocal cords not fully defrosted. "All this over a treasure map?"

"You shouldn't laugh." She folded her arms. "I trust him."

The word "trust" hummed with double meaning. Like it could be taken out of the sentence and replaced with something else.

"Is this because of—"

"Don't do this, Ern. It's not about that."

It wasn't and it was. I'd never confronted her this directly before, even in marriage counseling. My anger was always stoppered by shame and grief. But if I had, we might have got past it; we might have sat down and talked it through, about what starting a family meant to each of us and what the fertility letter, which I'd opened over breakfast, had done to us. To the family we'd been trying to create.

We'd been waiting a long time for the letter. It's strange to put such life-changing news in the post, but I suppose they considered it mundane enough to bypass a phone consult. The letter itself had been slow to come, Erin wringing her hands as she gave me each piece of bad news: the first letter had been a victim of an address mix-up that she'd had to call the clinic to fix and the second, weeks later, a soggy illegible pulp, destroyed in the rain. Erin had taken it hard. Every day she'd been first out to the letterbox in the morning, flicking through the pizza vouchers and real estate introductions as she walked up the drive, shaking her head: another day without the results.

I still have the letter, actually. It's crumpled from my tightened grip that morning, as I'd gazed at my results in disbelief, trying to figure out a way in which they told a different story. When Erin had come into the kitchen, pinning tendrils of loose hair behind her ears, I had the letter smoothed down next to the butter. My arm was dirty, foul liquid on my wrist. I asked her to sit down, and the look on her face when she really looked at me, when she read it . . . I think we both knew it was probably the end of us. We'd cling on for a while, but the flint was gone. If I'd still had it, I would have used it to burn that damn letter.

We'd stayed in each other's orbit for another eighteen months, because we didn't want to go and we didn't want to stay. That's what happens in a marriage, when one of you wants a child and one of you can't give it to them.

Yes, that was my life's third and final eventful breakfast. The one that has to do with sperm.

"So it's real?" I asked. We both knew what I meant. Her and Michael.

She sighed. "It's real. But I'd believe him even if it wasn't. Not all of us get to see our father in a new light. That's a privilege."

I understood then that, through helping Michael understand Robert better, she was vicariously seeking closure about her own abusive father.

"Come on," I begged. "You're smarter than this."

"You always did say such nice things." She smiled grimly. "Have you opened the truck yet?"

I shook my head. "He gave me the keys. But then we followed you up here."

"He told me whatever's in there should convince you."

I wished people would stop telling me that whatever was in the truck was going to change my life. It would, as it turns out, in terms of both what I believed and the function of my right arm, but I still wished they'd stop telling me.

"We're getting nowhere," I said, deciding to defuse things. "Let's try to find some common ground."

"You sound like Doctor Kim."

"We spent all that money on the counseling—who'd have thought it would come in handy." I forced a smile.

"So, what is it then?" She put on our former therapist's languid monotone. "What unites us?"

"Neither of us believe that Michael is responsible for . . ." I gestured to the body. It seemed odd to be having such a casual conversation around it. "And I'm guessing if you're willing to break in and poke around, you don't buy the natural causes explanation either. You think someone's after Michael, after what you both dug up, and I'm just trying to get Michael off the hook and fix something for once in my life. That's our common ground. We're both trying to solve a murder." Once again I am reminded that I am not the main character simply by virtue of being the one who writes this all down. In fact, I remember thinking to myself at the time that more people seemed to have motives to *solve* this damn murder than to actually commit it. "So let's start there. If we can find who did this, we'll also find out if Michael's telling the truth."

"One proves the other," she agreed, then she touched her pointer fingers together, placed them under her chin and furrowed her brow. "I'm feeling there's been some progress in the room today. Wouldn't you say?"

Against my instincts, I laughed. There was a reason we fell in love, no matter what had happened since; it was hard to forget all of that.

"You got a bit of a look before I arrived," I said. "Did you find anything?"

"I mean, I'm no expert, but none of this can be normal." She leaned back over the body. I edged closer.

I hadn't had a good look at Green Boots yet, as I'd been too squeamish when carrying his foot and only glimpsed Crawford's photo of his face. His eyes were closed. The shed was so cold his hair had ice crystals in it. His face was caked in black ash, which I'd first mistaken for frostbite, and around his mouth it had formed a glistening, congealed tar. His neck was ringed with an angry red wound. Sofia had told me about the cut; it had rubbed off on Crawford's sleeves, but it was gorier up close. Whatever had been wrapped around the man had been so tight as to cut through the skin. The bloody laceration had also started to crystallize in the cold.

Erin interrupted my sleuthing. "Looks like someone strangled him. I don't know what the black stuff is. Poison?"

"Ash," I said, repeating what Sofia had told me. "Apparently."

"As in he was on fire? Out here?"

I nodded. "No melted snow though. And if he was, wouldn't he have rolled around? Had burns? Sofia thinks it's a serial killer. The media calls them the Black Tongue. But if you think Michael's caught up in some gangland dealings, same as Dad, it might be some kind of enforcer?"

"Maybe. It seems quite violent, and I suppose people only do that if they either want something to really hurt or to send a message. Backtrack for me, though . . . you're saying this is ash, but the snow wasn't melted. This killer sets them on fire without setting them on fire?"

"It's an ancient torture technique once used by Persian kings, actually," Sofia said from the doorway. "What? I was freezing my arse off."

"Torture?" I raised an eyebrow at Erin. "Fits with sending a message."

"How much does she know?" Erin folded her arms. "Michael told me to only trust you."

"She's okay. She knows about the money."

"It's too bad Ern's already spent"—Sofia shot me a sly glance—"a fair chunk of it. At least fifty kay, right?"

Erin fixed me with a look that I couldn't decipher. It was either annoyance that I'd spent Michael's money, or that I'd become close enough to Sofia to tell her my secrets. I settled on the second, thinking it was a bit rich from someone who'd spent last night with my brother. "You seem to know an awful lot about this serial killer," Erin said, still wary.

If Sofia thought she was being accused, she didn't show it. "We had a victim through one of our hospitals. The Humphreys woman. Someone found her, and everyone thought they'd got her just in time. But her lungs were shot—we had to switch the ventilator off. I found it interesting, listened to a few podcasts. Didn't really think I'd need the information until, well, ever. But here we are."

"Well, close the case. If you listened to a podcast . . ."

"Give her a chance, Erin. She knows more than we do."

"So we're looking for a history buff? With a taste for medieval torture?"

"Kind of." Sofia looked embarrassed. "I didn't make this up, okay? It's called suffocation by ash. Ernie, I told you before that most people who die in house fires don't burn to death, they asphyxiate. That's partly because fire pulls oxygen out of the air, so there's nothing to breathe, but even after the fire is out, if you breathe in too much smoke it can coat your lungs so that you couldn't get oxygen out of the air even if it were there."

"And ancient Persia is known for its house fires?" I asked.

"Very funny. They're the ones who started the torture—they had a specially built tower for it, huge, more than twenty meters high. It was filled with wheels and cogs and things, and at the bottom, a pile of ashes. They would push a blasphemer into it—because that's what got you the death penalty back in those days. Now, being trapped in a room full of dormant ashes is not going to do much to hurt you, so they'd turn the wheels and these giant cogs would start stirring the ash into the air. The criminal would suffocate to death."

"Lucy told me that the first victims were an elderly couple from Brisbane? She looked them up. You're saying *that* happened to them?"

"She's right. And, well, not really. Obviously there's not a three-story torture tower hidden up here somewhere and, anyway, Green Boots seems to have been strangled." Sofia picked up a screwdriver from a nearby bench and used it to push down Green Boots' collar for a better view. "With the density of the ash on his cheeks, and the depth of the wound in his neck, I'd say he had a bag with ash pulled over his head, tied tightly, and then removed postmortem."

"The snow looked like someone had run back and forth in a small area," I said.

"Exactly. Lack of oxygen disorientates you very quickly—he would have been trying to take the bag off, likely panicking. I can picture him frantically running in circles."

"That's not so medieval." Erin realized she'd said it too sharply and raised her hands in apology. "I'm not trying to be sarcastic, sorry—I'm interested. I'm just thinking that anyone can strangle someone, put a bag over their head. Why bother with the ash?"

"I agree. I'm guessing the killer was in a pinch, rushed. Maybe by daylight coming on. Maybe another resort guest interrupted them. With that Brisbane couple, the killer took their time. I told you it wasn't a torture tower, but it was, sort of, a modern incarnation of one. They were found locked in their car, in their garage, their hands zip-tied to the steering wheel. There were indentations on the roof, as if someone had stood on it, and a leaf blower discarded on the floor. The killer would have poured the ash in through the sunroof and stuck the leaf blower down afterwards to stir it up. It was the same with the lady who came through our ER. Zip-tied, in a locked toilet with the window and fan taped shut, except for something to put the blower through. That's the way they like to do it. Slowly. This is all conjecture, obviously."

"From a podcast," Erin affirmed.

"From a podcast."

"It must feel like drowning in the air," I said. I wouldn't wish my dreams of choking on anyone, and I'd been unconscious for most of my time in my mother's car as a child. I'd read of divers drowning within inches of the surface, feeling if they could just break through the water they'd be saved, but it being just, just, out of reach. I couldn't imagine trying to breathe the air in front of you and getting nothing from it. "If you think it's the same killer, you think it's the same equipment, right? It's not just the ash that got you thinking. You think the mark on his neck could be made from a zip tie?"

"I do. It's cut into the flesh cleanly enough to be something plastic, rather than rope, which would tear the skin a bit, and if it was fishing wire, it would be a deeper cut. But here, look . . ." She pointed at the corpse's mouth, which was slightly open, took out her phone (battery: 85%), and shone the flashlight in. It was no mystery why the media had dubbed the killer the Black Tongue; the dead man's mouth was caked with black charcoal, making his tongue a thick black slug behind his smeared teeth. "It's more ornamental, rather than the cause of death. The bag would have done the job of suffocation anyway. This serves no purpose other than to leave a mark."

"Why would he do that?" Erin asked.

"I've seen my share of weird shit in the ER, so I can guess at a few reasons. You know what I'm thinking, Ern, I'll bet. You write this stuff. What's the basic principle of a psycho killer's MO?"

"Well," I said. "I suppose the most common assumption is that psychopaths just *need* to do things a certain way. It's a part of their process—it means something to them. But if it were that important, I don't think they'd put the effort into killing without all their affectations in order, unless they were interrupted. It wouldn't be worth it. And it's not like someone's building bonfires up here. That would be pretty obvious. So I don't know how that helps."

"You don't need fire as much as you might think, actually—the trick is just to get those particles in the air. And you can buy ash in big bags from any garden or hardware store. My point is, they probably brought it with them. They were prepared. So my second theory is, I think, more likely."

My stomach sank as I deduced what she was about to say, and how well it sat with Erin's and Michael's theories, but the sound of wrenching metal distracted us as Crawford flung the door open. He was red-faced, sweating, worked into a state. One hand held the broken door handle, padlock still affixed, while the other clutched a heavy policeman's flashlight. He looked back and forth among the three of us. His mouth tried to form a couple of different words, but it seemed he could choose nothing to best represent his fury, so he just yelled, "Out!"

We filed out like children, heads down, mumbles of "Sorry, Officer" as we went. The storm had died down slightly since we'd arrived, and I could see the guesthouse again, looking more like a gingerbread house than ever: freshly iced.

Crawford tailed us gruffly down the hill. My editor told me it's impossible for someone to walk gruffly, but they've clearly never had Officer Crawford huffing two steps behind them, so I'll stick with the adverb. I held the truck keys up to Erin, who gave an agreeing nod, as we started towards the parking lot. She then turned to Sofia, whispering so Crawford couldn't hear.

"What was your second theory?"

"The Black Tongue is announcing themselves. They want us to know they're here."

CHAPTER 24

The rear of the truck had one of those rippled roller doors that slid into the roof. An empty coffee cup sat on the lip. The key turned easily. I spun the handle ninety degrees. It felt like a big moment, so I paused, looking at the three others who were crowded around. Erin was wringing her hands, anxious to know if this would be enough to win me over, and perhaps for me to tell her what Michael hadn't. Sofia had adopted a smug pout, looking forward to Michael's secrets being exposed. Crawford looked impatient. He'd tried in his best, most authoritative voice to demand we head directly to the guesthouse, but I'd figured that he wouldn't try to stop us with any passion. I'd been right: on being rebuffed, he'd tagged along to make sure we didn't do anything else stupid. Me? I was preparing to be disappointed. Like I'd told Michael, nothing short of a spaceship would blow me away.

I lifted the door a couple of inches. First observation: it didn't explode. (I know that sounds crazy, but a lot of scenarios had run through my head, and the whole thing being rigged to blow was, I'm ashamed to admit, one of the least outlandish ones.) I didn't open it so slowly for suspense: the door was iced in its joints. It took a great heave to open it enough to see even a small slit of the darkness behind it. My gloveless hands felt seared by the icy metal. I went to give it another heave, when a hand on my arm stopped me.

"Maybe this is just for you," Erin said. "At first."

Erin clearly knew *something* about what was in there. She'd helped Michael dig it up, after all. She thought it was money, or valuables at least, which, based on it needing to be transported by truck, meant there was a lot of it. *Michael told me to only trust you.* Michael had said the same thing to me directly, that I was the only one he trusted by virtue of me testifying against him. He'd allowed himself to be sequestered in a putrid sock drawer just to give me the keys in private. Sofia and Crawford weren't supposed to tag along. Erin was right.

"I need a minute to see for myself." I raised my voice above the wind. "Um . . . it might not be safe."

I knew this was thin. Sofia rolled her eyes. I wondered whether she was more annoyed at being excluded or because each time I took Erin's or Michael's side she imagined she was getting further away from a chunk of the money. It occurred to me that it might have been why she'd interrupted us in the maintenance shed when she did: it was conveniently just after Erin and I had found our common ground and started to talk like a team. I expected more resistance from Crawford, for any number of reasons (chain of evidence, witnesses, any semblance of competent police work), but it seemed he'd given up trying to be a cop entirely. Erin shepherded them both around the side of the truck and, with two more frost-cracking heaves, I had the door open.

The air was still so thick with ice and the sky so gray that even open, the inside of the truck wasn't well lit enough to see all the way into. The walls were lined with the usual ropes and straps for moving furniture. But I could see a very specific shape further back. It looked like a . . .

I couldn't be sure; I needed a closer look. I clambered into the cabin. The truck squeaked and rocked on its wheels as I walked over to the object. The air was stale and smelled of, of all things, fresh dirt. *We dug something up.*

My eyes adjusted to the gloom. Out of everything I thought could be in the truck that might speak to both Michael's innocence *and* his whereabouts last night, this hadn't even crossed my mind. I stood stunned for a few seconds, until there was a bash on the flank of the truck. Sofia called, muffled but distinct: "Well, what is it?"

I walked to the entrance and slid the door down, sealing myself in the dark. Erin had been right. This was for me, and me alone.

The coffin still had rivers of dirt caked into the joinery. That explained the smell of fresh earth. I examined it with the glow of my phone's light (battery: 37%). The coffin looked expensive, made of robust wood, perhaps oak, which was well varnished enough not to have degraded too badly, and it had ornate chrome handles on either side. It didn't look new, but it didn't look a hundred years old either. It was hard to tell. Lucy would be pleased: as far as alibis for consummation go, graverobbing was a pretty good one.

My first thought was that this could be Holton's coffin, purely because I couldn't figure out who else my brother would have cause to dig up, and it had a nice circular irony that he was the man my brother had tried to bury in the first place. But this was a coffin designed for showing off, for open caskets, for someone loved and respected. Given Michael had told me Alan owed money to half the prison population, I didn't think anyone would have reached into their pockets to give Holton such a resplendent resting place.

I dragged my fingertips lightly over the wood as I walked the length of it. The truck's axle creaked as I shifted my weight across the thin metal floor. I saw that a row of nails had been pulled up around the rim of the casket so the lid could open. I realized that this might not be a coffin at all, but a storage box masquerading as one, and perhaps Michael had already taken what he wanted from it. People hide things in coffins, right? But if that were the case and he'd emptied it, why did he need me to see it? And if it *was* a person, how was I supposed to identify someone who had been in the ground so long? A pile of bones would mean nothing to me, unrecognizable no matter whose they were. As I was thinking all of this, my fingertips brushed against a rough groove on the otherwise polished wood. A marking. I shone my phone light (battery: 36%) over it.

An infinity symbol, carved into the wood.

I had a sudden memory. Of a state funeral, an event demanding of a plush coffin. Of a Swiss Army knife, scratching a forever bond into the oak. Of hats held against chests and white gloves and gold buttons. I might have doubted my ability to recognize the bones inside, but I *knew* this coffin.

Michael and Erin had dug up Alan Holton's partner: the policeman my father shot.

CHAPTER 25

I knew I had to open it. Pandora be damned.

Lids of coffins are damn heavy: the fancy ones are lead-lined to stop you seeping through the wood as you liquefy and, even without the weight, the joints get warped by moisture and the pressure of six feet of dirt. Rigor mortis of the inanimate. If Michael hadn't previously forced it open, I wouldn't have been able to do it on my own. To get it into the truck, he and Erin must have rigged some kind of pulley system out of the moving straps hanging from the walls.

Since I was on my own, I figured out I could shift the lid by standing on the hinge side, leaning over the coffin, hooking my fingers under the rim, and pulling back with all my weight. It was quite an effort given the cold: inside the four metal walls, on the mountain, the storage van may as well have been an ice truck. My breath puffed in the freezing air with the effort, as the first few centimeters squeaked open, agonizingly slow until inertia overpowered the weight and the lid shot all the way up, nearly knocking me on my arse and flipping the coffin. Luckily, I didn't have to tango with a set of bones: the coffin rocked slightly towards me but found balance.

The truck groaned again, as if begging me to quit moving around so much.

I shone my phone light (battery: 31%) into the coffin.

The coffin wasn't empty, which I'd half suspected, so seeing a body came as more of a relief than a shock, because at least it was what was *supposed* to be there.

Quick science lesson. Thirty-five years is enough, depending on the seal and the coffin's material, to leave a semi-mummified corpse. It's not quite enough time for all of the tissue to liquefy, and the bones don't crumble to dust until nearer the century mark, so the result is a skeleton covered in flaky gray rags of tendon. I didn't know the science at the time—I had to look it up afterwards to write about it—so I wasn't sure what Michael hoped I would forensically or intuitively learn from seeing a half-decomposed body. I shook my head at the pointlessness of it all.

Though there still could be something else hidden in there, I figured. Michael surely would have moved anything truly valuable, though I remembered him trying to show me something, patting himself down and swearing as he couldn't find it. Then again, if it was something small enough to fit in his pocket, why hide it in a large coffin in the first place? And why would Michael bring the whole coffin up here if he'd taken what he needed from it already?

I needed to take a closer look. My phone light (battery: 31%) fell first on the remnants of a human foot, which, in isolation, looked like a small bird: long thin bones that almost formed a cage. I scanned up the legs, waxy in decomposition, trying to remember enough biology from high school to let me know if anything was amiss. It was messier than any model skeleton I'd seen, the rib cage partly crumbled so it looked like there were extra ribs. There was not a shred of clothing left except for a few gold buttons on the tattered-sail remnants of chest strung over the ribs and a belt buckle cradled amid the hollow of the pelvis.

I must admit, even though I was looking at a dead man, a man my father had shot in the neck, I felt nothing. No stirring of guilt, no disgust. It was like looking at the body on the mountain: purely academic. And now, with Michael having told me this corpse belonged to someone crooked, someone who'd tried to kill my father, I felt even less. The body in the coffin was meaningless to me. I'd tried so hard to shield myself with blind ignorance, I didn't know a single thing about the long-dead policeman. I'm not even sure I knew his name.

That said, last time I checked, he hadn't had two heads.

I'd seen inside this coffin before, at the open-casket funeral, and it had definitely been single occupancy. I wondered not only *who* else was in this coffin, but how they'd gotten in there.

The second skull was smaller, though it had the same amount of decomposition. A tight, leathery skin stretched over its scalp. The head was tilted down, jaw facing the formerly white silk cushion, so I could see a jagged hole in the back of the skull, cracks feeding around to the ears. Shot or hit, I wasn't sure, but surely enough damage to have killed whoever this was. Now I was looking closely, I noticed fine, thin bones—a spine—that turned in to the larger skeleton. The ribs had interlocked as the flesh had worn away, which explained the ribs I'd thought were decomposing—they actually belonged to the second corpse.

I followed the spine more carefully, down to the pelvis, the bent knees, feet (small skeletal birds) tucked above the larger skeleton's hip, as if sheltering against it. Clutching. It looked like that famous *Rolling Stone* cover of Yoko Ono and John Lennon. C-grade biology student or not, there was indeed one aspect of the whole scene that was undeniable. The thin circumference of the bones. This was someone small. Young.

Michael had brought this coffin all the way here to show me this: the body of a child curled up against the bones of a policeman.

Now I had to ask him why. I took a half step towards the rear door.

That was when the truck started to move.

The first jolt was only enough to give me a slight wobble, to rock me back on my heels. My stomach did a little bungee jump as my organs tried to match their newfound velocity to my stationary feet. Encased as I was in the dimness, it took a couple of seconds for my brain to be happy I was still balanced. I edged forward on sea legs. It was only a few meters, but I want you to know that everything that happened next happened in seconds. There was a series of urgent thumps on the truck's flank.

"Ernie, get out of the bloody truck!" Female. I couldn't tell if it was Erin or Sofia.

I tried to hurry while keeping my balance. I had a strange feeling of walking uphill, which meant the truck was moving *forward* and I was going against the current to get to the back door. The canvas straps hanging from the walls lilted towards the front cab. The thumping on the flank continued, but the rumble of the now quickening wheels was drowning out the voice that went with it. I knew what they were saying though: *Hurry*. I'd already figured that out. The truck was headed down the hill. And the only place the mountain plateaued was in the middle of a frozen-over lake . . .

A slit of light appeared as the door shuddered up half a meter. Erin poked her head in, puffing, walking to keep up. "Come on, Ernie. Hurry up! The slope just gets steeper."

"What the hell is going on?" I yelled, staggering over to her against the tilt of the floor.

"Handbrake's off. You must have rocked it around a bit and it just started moving. Crawford's trying to break into the driver's side to put the real brakes on. There's some brown shit on the ground, maybe brake fluid, though—so save us all time and just get out in case we can't stop it." She made to grip the underside of the shutter door, but couldn't hold it and jog at the same time. Even in a few seconds she'd gone from a quick step to a jerky wide-legged jog in the shin-deep snow. The truck wasn't going all that fast, but it was difficult to keep up in the slush. I knew it was about a hundred meters or so to the road, and then once we crossed that another couple of hundred to the lake. The slope only really kicked in after crossing the road, but the truck was so heavy, if it got enough speed up, it would be impossible to stop. I knew I had to get out before it started really moving.

"You'll have to go low," she said, reaching out a hand. "The snow's soft enough to fall on so just roll out."

I crouched, one knee down, just as the truck lurched again, harder than the first time. I fell, sliding out of Erin's grasp, reached for a strap, missed it, and landed hard on my arse, sliding backwards until I stopped with a breath-expelling thump, my back against the driver's cab. The truck must have hit a bit of a slope now, because everything was moving: the hanging straps whipped against the walls and my face, a toolbox had fallen somewhere and bolts and spanners ricocheted off the floor and peppered the back wall. I tilted my head just in time for a screwdriver, hurtling tip-first at my eyeline, to clatter off the metal next to my ear.

Then I heard a long, slow screech. A scraping against the floor. The coffin was sliding towards me. Several hundred kilograms of lead, wood, and two skeletons. I tried to move, but gravity and confusion are deadly friends. I've told you already I've been typing this whole thing one-handed: this is why.

There was an explosion of pain in my right wrist, followed by an almost immediate numbness, like I'd sat on it. I went to pry myself off the wall but felt a tugging in my shoulder. My arm wasn't following instructions. It sounds stupid that I had to look at it to figure it out:

the coffin had slammed into the middle of my forearm, pinning it to the wall. I'd just seen a skeleton's hand, so I had a queasy image of the dozens of tiny bones I'd probably broken. But that was the least of my problems. Before, the truck had been ambling down the slope as I unconcernedly tried to stumble out of it. Now, as it continued to pick up speed, I was trapped.

I used my good arm to tug at my immobilized elbow, but it wouldn't budge. I then tried to work my fingers between the coffin and the wall, attempting to relieve even the smallest millimeter of pressure, just a smidge, but it was too heavy. My fingers came away slick and wet. Blood. I couldn't feel it, everything was numb with shock, but I was tearing the skin from my hand as I pulled. A paramedic would tell me later—when I was off the mountain, after three more deaths and an unmasked killer—while threading a curved metal needle through hanging flaps of skin, that the medical term was "degloving." I'm glad I hadn't known that at the time; I would have fainted.

I looked back to the entrance to assess my chances of rescue, which were less than reassuring. Erin was still keeping up, despite the deep snow, but the look on her face gave away her urgency. I could see her reaching into the truck, her head moving in a slight hop as she tried to get purchase and scramble in, but eventually losing her grip and sliding away into the distance, before coming back to try again.

"I'm stuck," I called, not sure if she could see the coffin pancaking my arm. A tinkle of screws and bolts rolled across the floor. "How far to the lake?"

"That's probably a question"—she was panting now; the depth of the fresh snow was tiring her more than the pace, and making it even harder for her to jump into the hip-height truck—"you don't want to know the answer to."

That answered my question as much as not answering it would have. Time was not only borrowed, it was charging interest. I placed my feet against the coffin and tried pushing it sideways instead, pulling back so hard I thought my arm might come loose from my shoulder socket. It didn't give an inch.

"Where's the main road?" I called. "The snowbank that borders it . . ." It was hard to catch my breath. "Might be enough to stop us."

"That was it before, went straight through it," Erin called. Damn. The snowbank must have been the bump that sent me tumbling. Some savior.

I reset my mental geography. If we'd already gone past the road, that meant the slope was about to get a lot steeper very quickly.

"Ern." A new voice, Sofia, arrived. It was hard to see with the slim aspect of light and the acceleration of the truck, but an approximation of her head bobbed into view. "What's happening? You've got about thirty seconds before this gets away from us. Get out already!"

"I'm hurt. I can't move."

"Wait. Is that a coff—?"

"Help me get in there," Erin interrupted.

"Is it safe?"

"Of course it's not. Give me a boost."

Everything was starting to get blurry. The adrenaline must have been fading because the pain was starting to creep into my wrist and radiate up my arm, which was making the edge of my vision fuzzy and unfocused. I tried my best to zone in on Erin and Sofia. They were in the light. They were solid objects. They seemed an infinite distance away. Then a third shadow arrived.

"No luck." A male voice now, Crawford. "I broke the window but it's too high. There's not enough time before . . . Hang on . . ." His next words were muffled, but I caught enough of them. "Did you not get him out?"

"He's stuck," said Sofia.

"Stuck?"

"He's hurt."

"How bad?"

"Not sure."

"Bad enough to not be out here with us," Erin snapped.

"Ow. Watch my toes," Crawford said, as Erin stepped on him. Together the three of them must have heaved the shutter up a bit further, because light flooded in. Crawford spoke again: "Oh my God. Is that a . . . ?"

That was when everything suddenly changed from mild alarm to outright panic. All three were actually running now: we must have hit the steeper slope. I figured the extra light had also revealed more of my injury, adding to the chaos. Erin had started yelling at Crawford to help boost her in. I heard Crawford rebuffing her: it was too dangerous; too risky. Things that would have inflamed her ears, sexism rearing its head under the pretense of heroism.

I waited for Crawford's boots to clang into the truck instead. A strap hit me in the face. I grabbed it with my free hand and yanked with all my strength. Whoever had hung it from the wall hadn't tied it very well; as it came free, the buckle attached to it clattered to the ground. It was like a giant seat belt. I reeled it in, fumbling it one-handed around my waist into a simple knot. The loop was loose but maybe good enough.

"Hurry! Damn it, Ernie, do something!" That was Sofia, a shrill, panicked scream this time. And it was just a little bit further away. I realized I hadn't heard Crawford get into the truck. It dawned on me that he wasn't stopping Erin so he could chivalrously rescue me himself, he was stopping her altogether. I looked up from what I was doing with the strap to see that all three were getting smaller by the second. Then I realized all the straps were back to hanging vertically. Gravity was back to normal. The inertia in my stomach ebbed, indicating that the truck had come to a stop.

That should have been good news. Except I knew the truck hadn't outrun Sofia, Erin, and Crawford. They had stopped chasing it because it wasn't safe to go any further. They'd run out of time.

Which meant that I was now trapped in four tons of metal, in the middle of the frozen lake.

I'll spare you the dishonest suspense of gently creaking ice and spiderweb fractures on the surface: the truck sat for less than five seconds before it dropped several meters with a jolt and settled at a thirty-degree tilt. The cab, to my back, had gone in first. Another lurch, and the whole thing was at forty-five degrees. I knew I had to think of something, and fast.

A kernel of a plan formed. I flung the heavy buckle as hard as I could, but I gave it too much air and it clanged off the still-half-closed door and slid back to me. On my next try, I slid it across the floor; it skittered along before sliding out the gap. I wasn't expecting it to catch on anything that would hold my weight—the lake's surface was barren—but I wanted *something* on the surface. If I went under, my main concern was finding the hole in the ice again. If I didn't pull on the strap, unsecured as it was, I could possibly follow it up to the surface. The walls were groaning from the outside pressure of the water. I could hear dripping, and I could *smell* the cold. I'm not sure, but I may well have been under the water line at this point. I gripped the chrome handle of the coffin with my good hand, ready for what came next. I would only get one shot.

It happened quickly. Another splintering crack of ice and suddenly I was on my back, looking up through the semi-open door at only sky. The truck was at ninety degrees. That was all I needed. Instead of pushing the coffin off me against gravity, like I'd been trying to do, I pulled the chrome handle towards the *roof* of the truck. Before we'd tipped, that would have been like trying to bench-press the thing but now the coffin was basically standing on its end. I only had to tip it over. Ignoring the fact that it was making a mortar and pestle of my forearm, I gave it all I had. And, finally, something went right.

It tipped.

I apologize if I haven't properly conveyed my enthusiasm. *It tipped!*

The coffin slammed into the roof (now the wall), propping diagonally above me and, lid splayed, scattering dust and bones everywhere across the back wall (now the floor), and freeing my hand (now flat) in the process. I rolled to the side just in case it settled back down, clutching my mangled hand, feeling the wetness, but not yet having the willpower to survey the damage. It was either too cold or I was in too much shock to register the pain properly.

I got to my feet and looked up at the sky. The strap I'd thrown still snaked its way up and out above me. I thought I heard yelling—my name, probably. I wasn't sure. I looked around my prison. There was no way I could scale the floor-cum-wall with a brutalized arm. The strap wasn't hooked to anything, so I couldn't climb it. And, of course, the entire truck was still sinking. Water lapped at my ankles, filling from a leak sprung in one of the walls. The Inuit may have a thousand words for snow, but no word can describe how numbingly cold the water was. Years ago when I was waiting for the results from the fertility clinic—after I'd discovered that scrotal heat was apparently a factor in sperm counts, and started swapping briefs for boxers, lugging a bag of convenience-store ice over my shoulder up to our bathtub—I might have been excited by the potential of water this cold. But not now. It was anesthetic. It was heart-stopping. The thought nudged its way into my head that this is how they make caviar; they stun sturgeon fish in cold water before cutting them open.

It wasn't long before water started spouting over the lip of the door. First it was a steady pour from one corner, but then it was half a dozen waterfalls all around the rim. The icy froth swilled to my knees. I kept looking up, hoping the strap would lie unmoving on the ice and not slide into the truck. I checked the knot around my waist with my good hand. My plan was simple: let the water do most of the work raising me as close to the truck's exit as possible, and then, once the truck was filled, all I had to do was swim straight up, as the truck sank away from me. I had to remember to use the floor to guide myself through the gap in the shutter door so I didn't get trapped. And to not pass out due to the shock of the ice water. Or pull on the strap. But even if I did: up, up, up. Simple enough. *Sure.* I felt the strap pull upwards against my waist. It felt like a tug.

The water reached my chest. Nothing left but the roar of water in my ears. I could only see a small patch of sky flecked with spray and foam, ever narrowing. Everything below my neck constricted with the cold. I thought about the sturgeon fish. It was comforting to think that if my heart stopped from the shock, at least I wouldn't have to know I was drowning.

Up, up, up, I chanted in my mind. Then the sky was gone. I took a deep breath. *Up. Up. Up.*

CHAPTER 26

I woke up naked.

My brain tried to piece together whether someone had dragged me across the ice and onto the bank, but, as more of my senses came back, I realized I wasn't cold enough to be outside. I was in a bed. The sheets were tucked up around my neck as if I were a nightmare-prone child, tight enough to be in an asylum. I blinked away the fog.

I wasn't elevated, so I couldn't be in my bed, up in the chalet's loft. I figured I was in one of the guesthouse rooms. There weren't many identifying features; the room was dimly lit and the curtains drawn. That was annoying, because I couldn't tell the time and I didn't want to be one of those clichés whose first questions upon waking were "What time is it?" or "How long was I out?" Two shadows held a murmured conversation across the room, unaware that I'd come to. My right hand had a constant, pulsing ache. I pushed the covers down to inspect the damage and realized I was wearing a floral oven mitt. I tugged at it, wincing as the glove resisted. I put one finger in the opening and felt a sticky membrane; it seemed like my skin had scabbed into the cotton fibers. I'd fused to the damn glove.

Someone put a hand on my shoulder, stopping me pulling. "I wouldn't." I looked up and saw Juliette, the resort owner, shaking her head. Katherine was behind her. "You don't want to see it."

Katherine offered me a pill from a small orange bottle. I took it, inspected it. "Oxycodone, painkiller. It's the serious stuff," she said, by way of explanation. That was enough for me, I popped it in my mouth. She thought for a second, wondering how possessing such pills reflected on her sobriety, I guessed, and added defensively, "For my leg."

I disappointed myself by asking, "How long was I out?"

Katherine walked to the window and pulled the curtains back, revealing the same black forever sky I'd fallen asleep under the night before. It looked like it had stopped snowing, but the wind must have still been high: the window rattled in its frame.

"A few hours," said Juliette. I pulled myself up into a sitting position, which caused a coughing fit and a scramble to maintain my dignity as the sheets moved. Katherine passed me a white hotel robe, flat hand shielding her view. I realized that Marcelo was also in the room, sitting on a small couch, just watching all of us. This was surprising; although he could never be accused of being absent, he also wasn't a sit-by-the-bed type of stepparent.

My coughing kept going, stars bursting across my vision. Too much too early. Juliette pushed me back into the bed, demanding I rest. She held a hand out to Katherine, who shook her head, stingy with the pills. Juliette cleared her throat loudly, and I recognized Katherine's resigned sigh. The next thing I felt was the slim pill wriggling between my lips. Then everything got murky, and I was underwater once again.

Mountain nights bring with them a special kind of blackness. Especially on the dawn side of the peak, the sun sets early and it gets dark fast. Without the glow of a city to interfere, it's easy to mistake any time from late afternoon for that ink-dark pit between midnight and dawn. I woke in this darkness. At least I was wearing a robe this time.

Katherine and Juliette had left, but Marcelo still sat by the window, cast in the light of a lone lamp, reading something pinched from the library. He heard me move, put the book down, and dragged his chair over. I hauled myself upright again, suppressing the urge to cough. I felt lighter, sort of floaty, but in much less pain than before. It must have been the pill. I was thankful to Juliette for scrounging a second dose out of Katherine's tight purse.

"Glad you're all right," Marcelo half grunted, in the way that older men often try to express emotion: by shooting out anything that could be construed as affection as fast as possible, like a sneeze.

"I'll survive," I said without looking at my hand, afraid it might change my answer. "Where's everyone else?"

"You sort of fainted—not sure if you remember—after you woke up the first time. It's only been a blink. Katherine and that resort lady just stepped out to find some food for you."

"How's Michael?"

Marcelo shrugged. "I was hoping you could tell me that. Crawford is still not letting me in."

"I'm surprised you didn't bust in while he was out rescuing me. The Drying Room would have been unguarded that whole time—it's only got the slide bolt on the outside."

"Wish I'd thought of that at the time." Marcelo's tongue darted out from the side of his mouth. It was hard to pinpoint if it was a tell or if he just had dry lips. The air up here did that quickly. I suddenly realized I was parched, my throat scratchy. I hacked a cough, and Marcelo got up and went into the bathroom, calling back, "Besides, we were all a bit tied up with that stunt you pulled down at the lake. Should have charged the other guests for the show—I think you had every set of eyes on you." He retook his seat, handed me a glass of water. "You're right, actually. It would have been the perfect opportunity to sneak in and see Michael."

I drained the glass in a long pull but was still parched when I finished it. Drowning's funny like that. At least I could talk. "So, are you my bedside guardian, or are you just making sure you're the first person I talked to when I woke up?"

"Is it so horrible that I wanted to make sure you were okay?" He shifted in his seat, then tried to laugh it off. "Doesn't mean I don't have questions."

"I think I'll go first, if you don't mind." We both knew I wasn't asking. It was rare to see Marcelo Garcia, impervious to the pressures of court and law, on the back foot. He wanted to know what I knew, which meant that, immobile as I was, I held the power. That small pleasure helped mask the pain in my hand, which, as my body woke up, had started to throb again.

Marcelo gave a deep exhale. It whistled through his teeth. "What did Michael tell you?"

"About Alan."

Marcelo closed his eyes, held still for a beat, and then opened them. I knew that slow blink. It's what people do when they wish they could rewind something just a few seconds. To not see their partner in bed with someone else. To not hear something they know is a lie. To not hear something they know is the truth. With their eyes closed, they rebuild the world unchanged, the way it was before. It's the type of blink done over breakfast tables, that wishes letters unread.

"So you know about the Sabers, then."

"A little. Less than you, I suppose, which I'd quite like to even out."

"It was more a collective than a gang. Your father didn't even like the name, but they needed something to call themselves. They did burglaries, mainly, enough to be noticed by the law but not heavily pursued. Your dad was more of a nuisance than a criminal—he just did enough to get by. That was before it got, well, worse."

I could see him reading me, trying to see how much I'd already been told by Michael, to see where he could cut corners, shave fractions off the truth. I'm terrible at poker, but I figured my firm-set grimace (my mangled hand was demanding attention; all I could do was grind my teeth in an effort to keep focus on Marcelo) could only be dissected as constipation or consternation.

He continued. "I met your father and his friends inadvertently. This was before I got into corporate law—I'd take anyone who came through my door. I was cheap and I was dogged, and I got a few robbery charges downgraded to trespassing, that kind of thing. And then I started getting more calls. I guess I was discreet, did right by someone who knew someone, and one recommendation led to another. I wasn't the Sabers' lawyer per se, and I never broke the law, but I was certainly someone a certain group of people found easy to call over certain matters. I'm not foolish enough to be completely blind to what was going on, but I needed the money. For Sofia."

"For Sofia," I repeated absentmindedly.

I was thinking about something Michael had said to me in the Drying Room: *Dad broke the law to care for us.* Marcelo was saying the same thing, except I didn't believe him. Because Michael's point was that Dad hadn't used his crimes to fund excess, but the same couldn't be said of Marcelo, could it?

"It's true." Marcelo sounded defensive. He'd caught me looking at his Rolex as I turned over Michael's words. He held it up, tapped it. "This wasn't some splurge. Your father left this for Jeremy, actually. In his will. It's a shame we couldn't pass it down."

That caught me off guard. Just as parts of Michael's story were starting to connect, some small dishonesty threw the whole story out again. Michael had been adamant that Dad was the

Robin Hood of criminals, the honorable thief, but if he'd gone around spending his ill-gotten gains on flashy jewelry, maybe he was just in it for greed all along. And if he'd had a high-end watch to give away on his deathbed, he might have had other valuables stashed somewhere else. That's certainly what Erin had expected. Maybe that's what Michael thought he was buying from Alan. Maybe that's what someone else was killing for.

"You know how they market Rolexes?" Marcelo asked.

This seemed an odd question, and I didn't really have time for Marcelo to brag about his successes, but I recalled the pithy advertising campaigns I'd seen, so I answered. "They sell them as a sort of legacy, to be passed down."

"Exactly. We didn't get it for a while after Jeremy—" He cleared his throat, uncomfortable. "So this is yours and Michael's. I'm just the caretaker."

"For a caretaker, you've had it an awfully long time."

"Your mother and I decided one of you would get it when she died—it's got nothing to do with me. It's in her will. You can have it now if you want, though." He went to unfasten the clasp, which may have been a bluff, like offering a friend the last slice of pizza and hoping they declined.

I held up the oven mitt. "I'm not really in the market for a wristwatch."

"This is yours, and Michael's, when you want it. But most of all, this is a watch designed to be handed down through family. I wear it to remind me." He paused, looking at the watch with a sentimentality that I really didn't believe my father had possessed for trinkets. "To look after you both. And your mother."

I covered my scoff with another hacking cough. All I saw was a rich man revering his own possessions, justifying the pursuit of his dead friend's widow as noble. It would have been pure pleasure to point out Marcelo's vanity, more than I'd have gotten from

Katherine's pills (of which, to be honest, I desperately needed more), but we'd strayed too far from the topic and I wanted to get him back on point. "So, your involvement with the Sabers was how you met Dad? They asked you to be his lawyer?"

"That's how we met. And we got to know each other, grew close. I did my best, but your father was on a path and sometimes that can be hard to change. He kept getting strikes, and in the end I couldn't keep him from forty-five days all expenses paid, if you know what I mean. I think you were three, maybe four at the time." I didn't remember Dad's six-week sojourn specifically, but it fit with what I knew of a man I measured by his absences. Marcelo continued, "That was a wake-up call for both of us. He came out ready to start fresh, and by then I was done with taking envelopes of money without knowing where they were from. But the whole thing . . . I don't know how to put it, but your father got caught in the current again. It felt like something had changed. Soon there was more violence on the Sabers' side, less lenience on the law's."

"Michael told me ransoms paid better than robberies," I said.

"Exactly. A real estate agent was shot when he refused to open his safe. He survived, but this was not the type of confrontation the Sabers were known for. They weren't happy with just jewelry scraped from drawers anymore, they wanted into people's safes and, when even that wasn't enough, their bank accounts. This was the late eighties—ransoms were in vogue. The Sabers tried it on, and they liked how it fit them. It pricked the police's ears right back up. By then, everyone involved could be pinned as an accessory on some level. Robert knew if he got another strike, the next time he saw you you'd be shaving."

"So you got him a deal." I had to squeeze the words out. My hand was pulsing with such hot pain that I felt I could vaporize snow if I went outside and lay down in it. "He traded information for immunity?"

Marcelo spun his watch around his wrist. Another slow blink; erasing history he didn't want to face. "I helped set it up. The deal was that he'd sketch out who the major players were. But every time Robert gave one answer to the detective, she asked two more questions. She wanted him in there, still working with the Sabers, which was the catch, because he was only incriminating himself further in an effort to please her, passing along information when he got it. Specifically, she wanted him to find out who was crooked, which officers were on the Sabers' payroll. She wouldn't let him out until she had the smoking gun."

"By which you mean irrefutable evidence against Holton and his partner? Michael told me the night Robert died was a setup, so you're saying these two were the ones Michael needed to incriminate, to have his deal honored? Maybe he finally had something on them."

Marcelo shrugged. "That's always been my guess. Robert never showed me any of the evidence—that was between him and his handler. He used to laugh about what they had him doing, said it was some real spy shit. He thought it was pretty cool that he got to be undercover. At the start, anyway." Marcelo slid back in his seat, rubbed his hands up and down on his knees and stopped talking for a minute. He was in his memory. He missed his friend.

It was strange to think of my father like that, of him being missed. Did that give him legacy over infamy? Marcelo's story filled him out just a little from how I knew him. A man who joked about *spy shit*. A man who had friends. I took Marcelo's introspection as an opportunity to lean my head back against the wall, close my eyes, and try to distance my mind from my throbbing hand.

Undercover. Handler. Spy shit. I turned the words over in my head. I'd written one of my how-to guides on spy novels, so I knew a little tradecraft from Ludlum and le Carré, but it hadn't sold very well.

"That's all I have." Marcelo's voice wormed its way into my meditation.

"Is it?" I kept my eyes shut, hoping that my half-dead appearance was nonthreatening enough to spur a further confession. Marcelo didn't bite, so I applied some extra pressure. I was technically a lawyer now after all; it gave me permission to be ruthless. "You knew about all this during Michael's trial. You used Alan's history to manipulate the prosecution, knowing that they'd rather suppress the information than deal with his sordid history in open court. That's why no one probed Michael's large withdrawal or tried to find the money, why no one pushed the oddness of the gunshot."

"What money?"

That rattled me a little. Surely Marcelo had checked Michael's bank accounts? How did nobody in a murder trial notice such a large amount? Even if Michael had taken it out incrementally, it would have been obvious. I didn't know the specifics of legal discovery. I made a mental note to read more legal thrillers.

"I don't know what you're implying, but I got Michael the best deal I could, using what I had to do so. That's my job."

"You'll bend the rules for Michael but not Sofia." I remembered he was choosing not to act as his daughter's lawyer on her malpractice suit.

"That's . . ." He bristled. There was a rustle of clothes as he sat upright. "That's not entirely true. Believe it or not, I'm doing what's best for her."

"Then what is the truth, Marcelo?" I raised my voice, opening my eyes to put him on the spot. I was aware that they were likely bloodshot, intense, half drowned. Marcelo glanced towards the corridor. I caught this, interpreting his worry that we'd be interrupted as meaning he still felt he needed me alone. Getting worked up was hurting my hand, but it was stressing Marcelo, so I kept it up. "It can't be a coincidence that the truck went renegade down the hill *after* I'd spoken to Michael and I'd started looking at this morning's victim more closely. The truck's handbrake was off. Erin thought there was brake fluid. That has to be deliberate. Someone just tried to cover up something they hoped was buried thirty-five years ago, something that Alan and Michael have brought to the surface. Dad was looking for a smoking gun before he died, and we know Alan sold Michael information about *something*—"

"All right, all right." Marcelo hushed me through gritted teeth. His eyes darted to the door again. "All I know is he was supposed to meet his handler that night, to give her something important. I think Robert witnessed a murder."

There it was.

"A child," I said, matter-of-fact.

He blanched, sturgeon-fish-stunned. "How'd you know that?"

"Hunch."

"That's all I've got too. Hunches and theories." He said it in a way that I didn't entirely believe, as if he was still deciding what to tell and what to withhold. "After Robert's death, I spent some time trying to figure out what could have been big enough to kill him over. Not to mention, something that would scare him enough that he'd start carrying a gun. Trust me—that wasn't normal. I told you the Sabers were becoming more volatile. It wasn't just people getting hurt—you said it yourself, ransoms paid better. That's what your father wouldn't stand for, not when he had kids of his own. But about a week before he died . . . It's an old story, you'll know the beats. A rich kid is taken for ransom. The family fluffs the drop. Even though they can afford it, they try packing a suitcase full of leaflets instead of money. And the girl's never seen again. Nothing was ever proven, but it had Sabers written all over it. Did Michael mention—"

"What was the girl's name?" I stammered.

"McAuley."

"First?" I wanted her to have a real name. A legacy.

"Rebecca."

"How much was the ransom?"

"Three hundred."

My mind was slippery, but something else Michael had said returned. *I brought what I could, but it wasn't what he wanted.*

Alan had sold Michael information about Rebecca McAuley, an unrecovered kidnapping victim from decades ago. Possibly who'd killed her. Definitely where her body could be found: buried forever in the coffin of a policeman. The perfect hiding spot, nestled under six feet of earth in someone else's coffin. With the advantage of a high-speed non-mountain-range internet connection while I type this all out, I've learned that this was a common trick of the Chicago Mafia to disappear people, so of course cops knew about it. It went hand in hand with cement shoes.

It made sense that Alan knew where the body was—he was the one who'd hidden it.

I remembered at the funeral there had been a bit of a row with the family: the policeman, who I now knew was Alan, had wanted the body cremated, maintaining it had been his partner's wish, something they talked about on duty. But the family had deferred to the will and insisted on a burial. Alan had been upset, and rightly so, because burying Rebecca's body wasn't as perfect as reducing it to ash.

And the price? That was the easy part. Alan wanted Michael to pay the debt that he felt he was owed by the family not paying up. A thirty-five-year-old ransom. And Michael was willing to pay up in order to find out who was responsible for our father's death.

I tried to imagine Alan, frantically trying to cover up his misdeeds: the body of a girl and a ransom unpaid. If he knew my father had evidence, it made sense to kill him. When Alan's partner died, opportunity knocked, and he'd been able to bury his secrets.

"Michael found Rebecca's body." I decided to take a leap of faith, both in sharing this with Marcelo and assuming the second skeleton in the truck was Rebecca's (but, seriously, who else's was it going to be?). Marcelo's eyes widened; I pushed on. "It's in the back of his truck. It was the first thing he did when he got out, so if we assume that he's been waiting three years to dig it up, we can also assume Alan told him where it was. The problem is: if my father had evidence on Rebecca's murder, it wasn't where her body was buried."

"Because she was buried *after* he was killed," Marcelo agreed. "So your father was trying to give his handler something else that night. Some other evidence. You think that's what Alan was selling—Robert's final message to his handler?"

"Perhaps. But I can't get my head around why Alan would sell Michael information about a murder he'd committed." It didn't make sense without the answer to this puzzle, and I wasn't sure I'd grasped it yet.

"Unless Alan didn't murder anyone, and was just protecting the person who did. Alan's a policeman, remember—if he was indebted to someone, I'd wager they're a dangerous sort."

This fit what Michael had told me earlier in the Drying Room, that he thought Alan was selling somebody else out. It also brought Michael's sentence into focus, a meager three years because, in his own words, there were some people who would prefer Alan's history not get an airing in open court. Things were clicking together. Reader, it has not escaped me that this scene is the "It Goes All The Way To The Top" one.

Marcelo was watching me digest all of this, trying to figure out if I believed him. "Fast-forward to three years ago. Alan's life is on the skids, he's in and out of jail and barely scraping by. Maybe he thinks that Rebecca McAuley was where it all started going wrong, and he decides he's ready to bring someone down. And so he comes back to where it all started, luring Michael in with promises of revelations about his father."

"I can see why he didn't choose me." I shook my head. "I'm not one for family history. Which is why I'm the only one Michael trusts. I was willing to testify in court against him, which showed that I didn't know enough to be scared, which apparently I should have been. That earned me trust."

Marcelo's jaw tensed, assumedly to trumpet that what he'd done to get Michael a lighter sentence should have earned *him* some trust of his own, but then he seemed to think better of it.

I didn't say it, but Marcelo's age also put him firmly in the suspect category. Now I was looking for someone who'd committed a murder three decades ago *and* a murder this morning. That left Audrey, Marcelo, Andy, and maybe Katherine. Katherine would have been on the young side back then, but she'd had a wild youth; there was no telling what she might have been swept up in. I'd still been wetting the bed, not exactly a prime suspect. Then again, I was assuming that both victims had the same killer—what if the motive was simple revenge? Anger is as much an heirloom as any Rolex. Take age out of it and everyone's a suspect. Hell, maybe Rebecca herself was all grown up and killing people.

"We're forgetting the obvious. In the last twelve hours, more people have told me my father was a good man than the entire rest of my life. What if he wasn't? What if Dad took and killed Rebecca himself?"

Marcelo leaned forward and gave my shoulder a squeeze. "I'm sorry you didn't get the chance to know him better. I know it's not much of a defense, but if you had, you wouldn't believe he was capable of that. To be honest, I'm surprised Alan was."

"So we're still stuck looking for a link. What's Alan's partner's name?"

"Clarke. Brian Clarke. Mean anything?"

If you were hoping for a name that brings everything together—Crawford, Henderson, or Millot (Andy's surname, which Katherine took after they married, and which it's probably time to mention is actually Milton in real life; I told you I changed some of the names for fun and this is one of them)—I'm sorry to disappoint.

"That name doesn't link to anyone I've met so far. Any kids? Him or Holton? It would be a stretch to think anyone would be out to defend their family's criminal legacy to such a point they'd want to target our entire family . . ."

"You're right. Besides, no kids."

Marcelo went quiet at that; it seemed like disappointment. A dead end on Alan's partner. I was struggling to maintain all of the threads and theories now: my head had joined my hand in a metronomic pulse, the pain washing in and out. I didn't know how long Marcelo and I had been talking, but I was exhausted. I must have closed my eyes for a second that morphed into longer in the real world, because a gentle tapping on my cheek brought me back around, Marcelo's face leaning over me.

"I'm sorry. I'll get you another one of those pills when Katherine gets back. But just hear me out. I *am* scared, okay? I'm worried that people who know things, which now, unfortunately"—he lingered with a regretful tone on that word—"includes you, might get hurt. I hadn't heard of the Black Tongue until Sofia brought them up over breakfast. And you asked me to check out the victims. And that set it, in my mind. Everything I've told you I've been thinking about for years—it was only ever a half-cocked idea. I never thought to share it with anyone. But this morning, this Black Tongue thing, that's something I can't ignore. That's one of your rules, right? No coincidences?"

I chuckled. It wasn't one of Knox's rules, but it *was* part of an oath he followed for the Detection Club, so I gave Marcelo credit for being close enough. "You read my books."

"I do care about you, you know." Another verbal sneeze, so quick and quiet I almost missed it. Like a child's apology. "I'm certain someone's cleaning something up. Because there were *three* people involved in the deal that led to your father's death. Not just me and him."

That woke me more than the taps. I remembered Marcelo's hesitation when I'd asked him to look into the Black Tongue's victims; he'd asked me to repeat one of the names.

"The detective—my father's handler. What was her name?"

"You're gonna hate this."

"I'll bet I am."

"Alison Humphreys."

CHAPTER 27

"He's up!" Katherine beamed, shouldering open the door. She was carrying a large, khaki-green plastic case, a red cross haphazardly spray-painted on the side, which I'm pretty sure had once housed fishing tackle. It didn't matter that she'd interrupted my conversation with Marcelo; I was glad to see her. I was so very glad to see her.

"My hand hurts," I said. It wasn't particularly subtle.

"You can't have one for another . . ." Katherine set down the first-aid kit on the coffee table, and then bent over and checked Marcelo's watch. "Actually, it's better if you don't know."

"Please."

She flicked open the clasps and rifled through the contents, then made a satisfied click with her tongue and tossed something at me. A small green packet landed on my covers. "Panadol will have to cut it for now." She must have seen the betrayal in my eyes, because she softened. "I know it hurts, Ern. But after all that's happened, I'm not having you OD. *She* already had to give you CPR." She jerked a thumb at Juliette.

This should come as no surprise: I said you'd read about us

locking lips on the previous page. Just like I told you someone dies in the next three.

"Sorry I had to strip you," Juliette said bashfully. "Hypothermia gets in through the clothes, I'm sure you know." She said it like I might not. (Which, if you'd seen the draft of this manuscript, you'd know I didn't: my editor had crossed out my first go at this sentence and written *Hypo=cold, Hyper=hot* in the margin, in that helpful yet smug voice editors are born with, wishing to both correct you and impart their correctness upon you at the same time.) Juliette continued. "I didn't do much though. If you hadn't tied the cord around your waist, I don't know if Erin would have—"

"Erin?" Realization flashed. The voice on the ice. That tug on the strap, just before I went under. "What do you mean?"

"She saw you throw the rope out the door. Sofia said Crawford couldn't hold her back." Katherine was speaking plainly, far too matter-of-fact for what was running through my head. "She saved your life."

"What did she do? Is she okay?" I stood. Blood surged to my head and I wobbled. Four hands propped me up. Katherine tried to shove me back onto the bed, but I pushed past her to the door. "Where is she?"

"She went out on the ice," Katherine said.

"Erin!" I opened the door, staggering into the corridor. "Erin!"

Then I crashed right into her.

"Jesus, Ernie." Erin reeled backwards, regaining her grip on the tray she was holding, which bore a can of soft drink and two bowls of hot chips. Her forehead crinkled as she said, "You shouldn't be up." She then looked over my shoulder and said, "He shouldn't be up."

I don't remember if I lost my balance or I genuinely dove at her, as I'm not one to throw myself at people, but the next thing I remember is wrapping Erin up as tightly as my oxycodone-limp limbs would allow. Erin returned my warmth, and we stood for a second like we weren't on the mountain at all. Like we'd never changed. Like she didn't have a chapter of her own coming up.

"Been a while since I've had an ice bath," I whispered in her ear. She gripped my shoulders tightly. Her laugh was hitching, a sob mixed into it, and then we were both shaking in each other's arms. I felt wet tears on my neck.

I may as well come out with it. That letter I opened from the fertility clinic over breakfast was supposed to be *good* news. My swimmers were an Olympic team. The ice baths and the boxers and the no-alcohol and the oysters, all those wild experiments to improve my fertility, were for nothing. I'd been confused, trying to figure it out, until I'd called the clinic. They told me my wife had been delighted to hear the news, which they'd passed on seeing as I kept missing their calls. I told them I hadn't missed any calls, and when they'd checked, I realized they had Erin's number, not mine, on their call list. She'd told them that I'd prefer to be mailed the results; they had a note on my file. And they'd had the right address all this time, so they couldn't understand why I kept emailing to request they mail another. Amid that conversation was when I remembered Erin's insistence to be the first to get the mail. Telling me the first letter was lost in the post. The second rain damaged.

All of that had torn through my mind like a cyclone as I read the letter over breakfast that morning. It had been sheer luck that I'd been to the letterbox ahead of Erin. Maybe she'd done it so many times she'd gotten complacent. As I read, the dark, mistrustful thought to check the bins, which were sitting on the front curb, had crept in. I'd come back with foul juice from week-old stir-fry running down one wrist, clutching a small aluminum packet. You know the ones, they're labeled with the days of the week.

Goodbye, flint.

None of that mattered now. She'd saved my life. She was still here.

I could subconsciously feel the three people behind me, pressing in. They were spotting me, in case I fainted again, but it felt oppressive. I was acutely aware that *someone* had tried to send that coffin to the bottom of the lake. Maybe they'd wanted to kill me too, or maybe I'd just got in the way. Michael had sent me there, which was suspicious, but he'd gone to too much effort to bring the coffin up the mountain to simply get rid of it. If he'd wanted to lure me into a trap to kill me, he would have dangled something better in front of my face. Or just attacked me in the Drying Room. Whether I trusted him completely or not, he had let me in on a deadly secret. Now I had to ask him how it all fit together.

Erin helped me limp down the stairs, to the protests of the others, who insisted I keep resting. But my mind was alive, firing on painkillers and adrenaline. There was a cold breeze through the foyer, bright flooding lights; I wasn't sure what they were, glittering through the frosted front windows. The door to the Drying Room gave a familiar *phuck*. Rubber-sealed. Airtight. Which was why, until I opened the door, I couldn't smell that the air inside was strange. Thick with ash.

MY AUNT

CHAPTER 27.5

This is not a spoiler.

The observant reader may have deduced that the section headings here dictate that Marcelo, my stepfather, must have killed Michael, whose corpse I've just discovered in the Drying Room. It makes sense; I've set the expectation that there will be a death in each section and, trust me, there has been.

I've always believed that there are more clues in a mystery novel than just what's on the page. A book is a physical object, after all, which can betray a few secrets the author does not intend: the placement of section breaks; blank pages; chapter headings. Even a cover blurb suggesting there's a big twist can, in revealing a twist is present, ruin an otherwise well-executed one. In a mystery like this one, there are clues in every word—hell, in every piece of punctuation. If you don't know what I'm talking about, think about the book in your hands. If a killer is ever revealed with more than a leaflet of pages remaining against your right thumb, they cannot be the real killer; there is simply too much of the book still to be read. This works to spoil films too: the highest-profile actor with the fewest lines is always the villain, and a sudden wide-shot of a character crossing a road means they are about to be hit by a car. A good author must not only wrong-foot the reader within the narrative, they must do it within the form of the novel itself. There are clues baked into the very object.

I have to be aware that *you're* aware I'm writing this all down, is what I'm trying to say.

Before you get a big head over it, you haven't caught me out. While there is something to be learned from this book's internal logic, it is not that. I may as well come out with it, spoiler and all. Marcelo did not kill Michael. He is not the Black Tongue.

I have not been dishonest, and neither is this a plot hole, although I promised there'd be one. As it happens, that was in the previous section too. If you recall, I said there'd be a hole in the plot you could drive a truck through. I meant it literally.

CHAPTER 28

Flecks of ash swirled in the air. My nose twitched as small particles danced around its tip. The Drying Room was not as gloomy as on my last visit: the orange heat lamp was now complemented by a shaft of natural moonlight pouring in through the back window, which was newly broken, the snowdrift behind it tunneled through in a cylinder. Michael was lying slumped underneath it, a dark shadow even in the relative brightness, as he was coated head to toe in a thin layer of black grime. His wrists were bound to the upright strut of the coat rack nearest him.

I must have been the one who screamed, because Erin couldn't have (she had her hand over her mouth) and Juliette was summoned by the noise, appearing with a worried expression, but I don't remember it. I remember skidding to my knees in front of Michael, ripping the oven mitt off (with quite a bit of skin, but I didn't feel it), and grappling with the zip ties. It was futile with my mangled fingers. Behind me, I recall Erin yelling at Juliette to get scissors or a knife and, if she was in the bar, to bring Sofia back with her.

I gave up on the zip ties and instead started pulling my good palm across Michael's face, smearing the caked-on ash like I was opening a cocoon. The skin underneath was cold. His hair was gray with charcoal dust. I needed to get him flat to try to breathe into him, but Juliette still wasn't back to cut the zip ties. I stood and kicked at the frame, splintering the wooden post into a jagged spear, and sending Michael collapsing to the side. I rolled him over, straddled him, and pounded his chest, one-armed. I swiped more black gunk from his mouth and tried to breathe into him. There was nothing but foul breath and slimy, tarred lips. I sat up. Raised my fist again. Pain shot up my busted arm with every movement. I pressed my mouth over his again, but came away gagging, vomiting on the floor beside his head. It's not pretty, but it is true. I already knew he'd been dead a long time. Still, I wiped my mouth and tried again. And again. Then there was a hand on my shoulder, pulling me away.

On a last look, there were small dots of clear skin against the grime on his cheeks. I realized that was where my tears had fallen.

The family gathered in the bar, dotted around the room in separate clusters. Marcelo sat with Audrey, clasping her hand tightly. Lucy was with them, tucked under Audrey's wing. Like all in-laws, they'd never gotten along perfectly, but they had mutual grief to share. Both of them had loved Michael. Both of them had never doubted him. Now, both of them felt robbed. Katherine was pacing. Andy was lying on his back on the floor.

I was only there because no one would let me back into the Drying Room. I've been told I was, apparently, hysterical. Erin was with me, keeping watch, but also marooned. She'd lost Michael too, but wouldn't be welcome to share in Lucy and Audrey's mourning. With Michael dead, she must have been wondering what her place in the family was. She was keeping a stiff upper lip, both in fortitude and in a literal sense, because she hadn't escaped a few stubborn, snotty tears, which had hardened on her top lip.

Juliette was busying herself behind the bar, I assumed for a distraction. Just prior, she'd draped a blanket over my shoulders and brought me a hot chocolate, both of which had proved surprisingly effective at calming me down. So had her hand, warm and gently lingering on my uninjured one as she handed me the cup. Someone had given me back my oven mitt. I'd seen Katherine walk over and ask Juliette for a warm drink too, to which Juliette had replied, "What's your room number?" and Katherine had stalked off, offended.

The only people absent were Sofia and Crawford, for whom we were waiting to come back with a postmortem report. I'd like to lie here and claim that I was in the Drying Room myself, poking around and making genius deductions, but I was in deep shock. I didn't have the faculty to analyze a crime scene.

If I'd known the answer to the mystery yet, I would have deemed this a suitable place for a grand summation, being that all of us were gathered together. But the room had a very different feel to the parlor or library where the detective usually struts, one hand in their pocket, while they reveal their cleverness. The first difference was that I was still wearing a bathrobe, which meant that I would also risk revealing more than just my cleverness. But the attitude in the room was also wrong. This was not a room of suspects, it was a room of survivors.

Everything had changed. Before, we had the body of an unknown man, brutally murdered but almost comically so. Such was the strangeness of his death in fire and unmelted snow that we could all approach it with, as morbid as it sounds, an intellectual curiosity—or, for those who disagreed with Sofia's serial killer theory, ignore it completely. Green Boots was a puzzle to be solved: an inconvenience, a curiosity. While I'd been strutting about pretending to be a literary detective, had I even bothered to *care*? But this time, the victim had a name. Regretfully, the whole damn thing. Michael Ryan Cunningham.

And me? I'd been trying to figure out what happened to Green Boots so I could free my brother from his improvised prison, feeling partly responsible for the suspicion that he was held in and guilty that I had caused him to be locked in there. Now, it seemed, I'd have to live with having sent him to his tomb. Now all I could think of was Michael, chained to the coat rack, watching the ash fill the air. Of Green Boots, clawing at his neck, splintering his fingernails. I started shaking—the oxycodone was wearing off—so I took a rattling sip of my hot chocolate.

Outside there were lines of people, luggage and children in their arms. The lights I'd seen while heading down the stairs were the headlights of two buses with huge snow tires, parked in the turnaround at the bottom of the steps. The freezing wind was coming from the open foyer doors as people filed out. Tired of fielding complaints, Juliette had jumped on the break in the storm and hired the coaches up from Jindabyne to take guests who wanted to go back down the mountain. It was a limited-time offer; the weather was only having a smoke and would return invigorated. My instinct told me that the weather alone wouldn't have been reason enough for Juliette to organize such an exodus, not to mention the refunds she'd have to give. She'd seemed hesitant about alarming the guests when we'd talked in her office, but somewhere between my *accident* and the discovery of Michael's body, she'd made up her mind and called for the coaches. It had turned out to be a good decision.

At first, take-up of seats had been half-hearted. There was grim weather, sure, but there was a fireplace, board games, and a bar to compensate, which, truth be told, was what most people had had in mind anyway. Of course, there'd been a corpse to factor in. But no one knew who he was, and, remember, us Cunninghams were really the only ones sticking our noses in it. The official story was still that Green Boots had died of exposure. A tragedy, sure, but not one worth cutting a holiday short for. Explaining to the kids on the eight-hour drive back to Sydney why they couldn't go tobogganing: now, that would be the real tragedy. But, in light of a second death, this time more obviously violent, the whispered gossip of "Did you hear?" had rapidly evolved into the panicked rumors of "Haven't you heard?" Those with four-wheel drives had dug them out and made a run for it. The rest were climbing over each other for a seat on the buses, many having to leave their cars for a few days until the storm died down.

Crawford led Sofia into the room. She was wringing her hands; they looked like she'd rubbed them in ink, or at least that's what I told myself. Everyone leaned forward. Even Andy sat up and paid attention, crossing his legs like a child.

"Michael's dead," Sofia said, though she barely needed to. Her diagnosis was etched across her face. She'd looked pale when she'd vomited after carrying Green Boots, fragile as she'd drunk her rattling tea that morning, but now she looked positively gaunt. Maybe it was due to the cold and the stress and the grief, but it was clear to me that her constitution would only hold up to one more corpse. On the plus side, such was the truth in her pained expression that even Katherine didn't bother to object to her medical opinion. "He was murdered, I have no doubt. Tied up and suffocated."

"Jesus." That was Marcelo. Crawford had done his best to hold everyone out of the room once I'd found the body, only yielding to Sofia. And while the whisper that Michael had been killed had worked its way among the group, so no one was shocked by Sofia's first declaration, only Erin and I already knew how he'd died. I could see the terror in Marcelo's face, mingling with the grief. He was going over our last conversation, just like I was.

I'm certain someone's cleaning something up.

"For fuck's sake, Sofia," Erin snapped, skipping the denial stage of grief outright and heading straight for anger. "You were right, okay? Enough with the theatrics."

Sofia scanned the room, perhaps trying to figure out how provocative what she was about to say would be, and if it wasn't too late to snag a seat on the second bus. She sighed, knowing she couldn't lie. It wasn't fair that she'd been tasked with explaining these horrors, that she wasn't allowed to collapse like the rest of us, but she drew a deep breath and channeled as much bedside manner as she could. Any doctor will tell you their special talent is delivering bad news. "Yes, Erin. I think Michael was killed the same way as the man this morning."

"We can't be sure of that," Lucy was quick to object. I was reminded that she hadn't seen Green Boots' body at all, so had no reason to doubt the official story. "This is ridiculous! You're just scaring people. That first guy probably died from exposure."

"You need to be realistic, Lucy. He was murdered too." Sofia challenged the room to object. I could see Lucy was itching to contribute again, but was still figuring out what to say. "Someone tied a bag around Green Boots' head and filled it with ash. He would have died with or without the showmanship, being gagged in plastic and all, but it's sort of the killer's calling card. They did the same thing to Michael, although this time the ash *was* the fatal ingredient. We found"—she gestured to Crawford as if asking him to validate her finding; he just nodded—"sticky residue of tape over the broken window. The snow behind it has a narrow tunnel in it. Remember, the Drying Room is pretty airtight and the door is rubber sealed, which would have helped with sound as well. Not to mention we were all down at the lake anyway. If the killer pushed their circulation system through the snow tunnel and then sealed it into the window with plastic and tape, maybe some packed snow, the room is still airtight. The ash would have been easy to mix up into the air."

Katherine tried to ask a question, but choked on tears. She wiped her eyes with her wrists and kept on pacing.

"I'm sorry." Andy put his hand up. He was the least upset but the most concerned; his eyes kept flicking to the window, to the lines filing into the buses. Even if it was only in the interest of self-preservation, I was glad someone was asking questions, because I was in no state to. "Circulation system?"

"To use ash in this way, you have to move the air around. The snow is gouged into a cylinder, so I'd say someone stuck a leaf blower through the snow."

I dimly recalled thinking the jagged edge of the wind had sounded like a chainsaw as Sofia and I stumbled up to the maintenance shed. I say dimly because it was a faint memory, but also because I think myself rather stupid: I should have registered the sound as unnatural at the time. But wind in your ears sounds like all kinds of things—chainsaws, trains, screams—so I didn't deliberately obfuscate the information, which would breach Rule 8. If the sound I heard was, in fact, the burr of a leaf blower, that meant that Michael had been murdered while I was out playing detective. It also meant, if you're keeping score, that Sofia, who was with me at the time, now had an alibi for both murders.

"How do you know it was a leaf blower?" Lucy had found her objection. I thought it strange she was trying to poke holes in Michael's death, but I supposed her adamant refusal of the facts was a sign that she was struggling to accept it on the whole.

"Well," Sofia admitted, "that part I surmised from the news reports on the Black Tongue. Like I said though, there's a cylindrical tunnel in the snow."

"No. I don't believe you. That bloody fool got himself killed by the weather and then you"—Lucy pointed at Crawford—"locked up *my* Michael and someone . . ." Her voice started hitching, but she pushed it out. "Someone used all this panic that you're making . . . thought it was an opportunity to . . ." She gathered herself. "It wouldn't be that hard to find these fire killings or whatever in the news—to, you know, copy them. I looked them up myself." She was oscillating between explanations. Her head swiveled around the room. It was obvious she was looking for someone else to blame. She proceeded to snipe at everyone individually, growing more angry and frantic with each accusation. Crawford: "You made him a sitting duck." Sofia: "You started all this panic." Katherine: "You brought us all here."

Then she reached Erin. It would be hyperbolic to say a shadow crossed her face, but some kind of feral change settled in her eyes all the same. Something had dawned on her. Something else to cling to. "Like I said, someone with the right motive might have taken the opportunity given to them. He was just clinging to *you* while he was in prison. You were a pastime. A plaything. Because he knew that *I'd* be waiting for him on the outside. Once he was out, he didn't need you anymore. I knew he'd snap out of it once he saw me. If he didn't love me, then why did he fix . . ." A cruel smile blossomed. "He probably told you that? Right? As soon as you got here—that he realized he'd made a mistake? I wonder how you took that?"

Then she buried her glare into me instead. "And *you*." The word festered in her mouth. My heart hammered as, for a second, I thought she was about to reveal she knew about the money. That would give me serious motive. Lucy sneered instead. "Maybe you did it together. Why was Ernest so desperate to get downstairs and see Michael, as soon as he woke up, huh?" she appealed to the room. "Because no one had discovered him yet, and he wanted to be first. That's all I'm saying."

People have a habit of saying "That's all I'm saying" when they're saying an awful lot, I've noticed. I could hear Erin grinding her jaw beside me, her leg bouncing up and down underneath the table.

I decided to stick up for myself. "Why would I hurt Michael?"

"He was fucking your wife, for one thing."

"Lucy!" Audrey hissed, pulling away from her. I don't know who was more shocked, Lucy or me, that my mother was sticking up for me. "You can blame who you want, but only one person here insisted that Michael be put in the only room with a lock on the *outside*."

The room was silent. Audrey was right. And though she'd been quiet up until now, she was seething with rage. Just like everyone else, she'd found someone to blame. She hadn't been defending me, she'd just wanted to drive the knife into Lucy. Lucy *had* been the one to suggest the Drying Room. The only room he couldn't escape. I might have felt that he was in that room because of me, but Lucy had literally put him there. That was why she was slinging accusations around the room: she felt guilty too.

Sofia whispered something to Crawford, who unlocked and passed her his phone. She walked over and crouched in front of Lucy to show her the screen.

"I don't think you've seen this yet," Sofia said, her voice soft and calm. "I know what I'm saying sounds crazy. But if you'd seen . . ." She let the image on the phone finish the explanation for her. "There is a killer here. This man did not die of exposure."

The blood drained from Lucy's face. The hatred had scuttled back to her edges, like a closet full of roaches exposed to the light. When she looked up from the screen, she seemed almost confused, like she didn't remember she was in a room full of us in the first place. An anger hangover, Erin and I used to call them: when you argue over nothing and realize in the cold light of morning that you just look stupid. That's how Lucy looked. Confused and humiliated.

"This is the man you found outside?" Lucy whispered. She could now see what we'd all seen in his blackened face: that Green Boots had died a strange, violent death. And it only further reinforced that Lucy, in suggesting the inescapable Drying Room, had pretty much served Michael up on a platter.

Sofia nodded. I knew she was trying to console Lucy, not persecute her, by showing her the facts. But it wasn't working. All Lucy could see was blame.

"I can't be here anymore." Lucy stood. "I'm sorry, Ernest, Erin, for saying that stuff—everyone. I'm so sorry." She walked out.

No one really tried to stop her leaving. Crawford gave a half-hearted chase out into the foyer, calling to her to come back, but she shrugged him off with something acidic that I only half heard but sounded like "You're the boss," which clearly implied he wasn't. The rest of us peered around the doorframe to make sure she headed away from the Drying Room, where Michael still lay, just in case. She trudged up the stairs, possibly to the library. Possibly to the roof to try to get reception. Not a cigarette. You and I already know she's smoked her last.

CHAPTER 29

"Sofia," Audrey said gently once Lucy had gone. These were the calmest words she'd spoken all weekend, so we hung on them. "My son is dead, and I would like to know why. We're all upset, and we've all got someone we'd like to blame"—I'm not sure if her gaze flickered to me, or if I imagined it—"but the more information we have the better. Because I would like to find whoever did this. And if they're still here, I would like to hurt them." She took a breath, found control. I'd mistaken her tone for calm, but it was, instead, ice. "So, would you mind explaining, for some of us, how a leaf blower and a bag of coal can kill someone?"

"Ash, actually, not coal. It's the flaky stuff," Sofia said, and she couldn't hide a tiny lilt of excitement in her voice, pleased to finally be asked to espouse her theories. "Because there're so many fine particles, it forms a kind of cement in your lungs when you inhale it. You basically suffocate from the inside."

My mother thought for a moment, then twirled a hand, the way someone might waft theirs over a glass of wine, mimicking the imaginary cycle of stirring the ash. "So, you'd have to breathe in quite a bit of this, right? For it to hurt you?"

"Yes," Sofia replied. "A fair bit. Less in a room without fresh air."

"She's asking how long it would take," I added, also interested. It was almost imperceptible, but I noticed a curt nod of acknowledgment from Audrey.

"Oh. Hours."

"Hours?" Audrey asked, aghast, her façade slipping.

"Did it hurt?" Katherine sniffled.

Sofia didn't answer, which effectively answered the question. It would have been agonizing.

"Hours?" Audrey said again, and I realized this time she was addressing Crawford. And she wasn't asking for clarification, she was asking for an explanation. "The doctor here has kindly explained the science. So now you can tell me, copper, how my son took *hours* to die in a room that *you* were guarding."

Crawford cleared his throat. "Ma'am, with respect"—this was a bad start; my mother never took well to either formalities or excuses—"the rubber seal on the door makes the room pretty soundproof."

I made to suggest the storm had been very loud, but I'd learned my lesson from the last time I'd supported a police officer, and zipped it.

"But, honestly, I didn't hear anything because . . ." Crawford trailed off.

"Out with it."

"I wasn't there."

The room suddenly felt very quiet but intensely charged, teetering on the edge of exploding. It could have gone two ways: a lengthy silence or Audrey getting up and ripping Crawford's head clean off. In the end, it was neither, but Audrey was the first to speak. She couldn't summon more than a deep whisper.

"You put my boy in a locked room and then left him there all by himself?"

Marcelo patted her between the shoulder blades, firm but tender.

"Ma—" Crawford made to call her "ma'am" again, this time with an American lilt (*marm*), but caught himself. He looked flustered. He started again, settled on calling her Mrs. Cunningham, hyphen absent, and said, "The room wasn't even locked."

Those of us whose attention had been dwindling, namely Andy, or were about to pass out, namely me and Sofia, who was swaying on the spot with exhaustion, snapped their eyes back to Crawford.

"Juliette had checked the forecast and mentioned to me that she was thinking of taking some people down the mountain when there was a gap in the weather, before it got worse. So we made the decision that, seeing as he'd cooperated so far, we would move Michael into one of the guestrooms. When we went to tell him this—this was after you spoke to him, Ernest, but before I followed you to the shed—he was asleep. Curled up on the bench, with his back to the door. He had pillows and things—he looked comfortable, so we didn't want to wake him. Juliette was there. She can back me up, right?"

"He's right. I was there."

"Then I had to chase these two"—he nodded at Erin and me, neglecting to include Sofia—"from the maintenance shed, and that turned into *Titanic* for a bit for this fella, and then by the time we'd gotten him back here, the buses had arrived, and I was roped into helping usher people on them. And people's cars needed digging out. It was nonstop. But, I swear, I didn't want Michael locked in the room when I wasn't there, in case he woke up and couldn't get out. In case there was a . . ." He stopped short of the word "fire," perhaps figuring out the irony. "I opened the lock before I left. I'm certain of it."

I was desperately trying to remember if I'd slid the bolt back myself before I opened the door, and I didn't think I had. Crawford was right: the door had been unlocked.

"Was the window broken when you last saw him?" I asked.

Crawford appealed to Juliette, who gave a shrug. He shook his head. "I don't know."

"Are you sure he was asleep?"

"I mean, I didn't ask him."

"Was he breathing?" This time I asked Juliette.

"I didn't . . . Look, I didn't check. Nothing seemed suspicious."

"What are you thinking, Ern?" Sofia asked.

"Green Boots had a serrated cut in his neck from the plastic zip ties," I said. "If Michael had struggled against them, they'd have chewed up his wrists. I didn't see any damage to his hands when I found him. Did you, Sofia?"

She thought a second. "No. But there wasn't any blood or bruising on him either, which I'd expect if he'd put up a fight. Then again, there was a lot of ash, so maybe I didn't see it." I could tell she didn't believe that. "A clean hit, maybe, but it meant that whoever hit him he trusted enough to turn his back on."

I thought aloud. "So the window maybe was, maybe wasn't broken. It was pretty obvious when I found him; there was glass on the floor, extra light, and surely you'd have noticed the wind, seeing as the storm was still heavy, so let's assume—" Erin nudged me hard in the ribs with an elbow, but I ignored her. Everyone was watching me piece together the timeline. Analytical as it was, the energy of discovery was helping me work my way out of my shock. I'm sure everyone else would have preferred to scurry back to their rooms and have their own private breakdowns, but we all knew this was important. It could lead us to a killer. "Let's assume the window wasn't broken yet when you saw him. Though he may or may not have been sleeping." Erin nudged me again. "What?" I hissed at her.

"This is all very useful, but it's only reinforcing that you were the last one in the room with him awake," Erin whispered. Everyone heard it.

I turned back to the room. Oh. That was why I had their attention.

"He was alive when I left him," I said. But, with everyone's stern faces, I felt like I was addressing a jury. I knew I shouldn't do it—if you watch any interrogation, only the guilty repeat themselves unbidden—but I couldn't help myself. It came out as begging. "He was alive when I left him."

None of us got on a bus. There was a tacit understanding in the room that whoever wanted to get down the mountain the fastest was probably the fleeing killer, so we all silently bluffed each other into staying. By this point, most of us thought the killer was probably one of us. Some of us, me and Sofia included, wanted to stay and find out who it was. The rest alternated between scared and defiant. Audrey wouldn't leave without Michael's body, which she couldn't very well load into the belly of a coach. Katherine stayed because she was worried about Lucy. Andy stayed because Katherine stayed. Marcelo probably stayed because he'd finally been promised a room in the guesthouse. Crawford never said we could or couldn't go, but knew he couldn't leave us to our own devices or else he might have to explain a massacre when his superiors finally showed up. Juliette joked that she couldn't leave us in case we burned the place down. We would anyway, but she didn't know that at the time.

We stayed in the bar, and our grief, anger, blame, and accusations slowly faded to trading memories quietly through thick throats. Andy mentioned to me Michael's best man speech at my wedding. He'd thought it would be clever to mimic one of my books and had prepared the ten rules to the perfect best man's speech, but then he piled on a bit too much liquid courage and forgot seven of them. It seemed a foolish thing to bring up in present company, but the awkwardness quickly faded into hiccupped, snotty laughter. I'm not glib enough to shrug off Michael's actions as simple mistakes, but there was more to him than just the last three years.

Once we all realized we weren't leaving, someone suggested we should get some sleep and there was an exhausted murmur of acceptance. Crawford locked the Drying Room, not wanting to move Michael's body, and warned us all away from it. Juliette handed out new room keys for the now emptied guesthouse rooms. I declined, preferring my chalet. If someone wanted to murder me, at least I'd see them coming up the loft's ladder. Besides, I needed to go back to my room anyway: I hadn't checked the bag of money since that morning. I wanted to be close to it. Now that I'd learned Marcelo was unaware of the cash, I was grateful no one except Sofia and Erin knew about it, because it gave me motive. Coupled with the fact that I was the last person to talk to Michael, the group, who had mostly dismissed me with a wary suspicion, would have torn me apart if they'd known I had his quarter of a million dollars. *Family* money.

People trotted out, yawning. As Katherine passed me, I tapped her on the elbow, asking if I could have the bottle of painkillers for the night.

"Sorry, Ern, they're too strong. I'm hanging on to them." She gave me a slight grimace of an apology, and then folded a single pill into my oven mitt.

I'd thought it strange when she'd first given me the pills upstairs, but this protectiveness of them was doubly so. There was no doubt she suffered pain down her leg, which must be excruciating at times and would have traditionally been managed with some kind of medication. But she'd chosen natural therapies since the accident. In her words, "alternative medicine." In doctor's parlance, "hogwash." But it didn't matter to Katherine; she was reformed and sober and nothing would break that. Not a Panadol for a headache, not a glass of wine for a bad day at work. When she gave birth to Amy, she'd even declined any painkillers. She was on a wagon and she wasn't getting off for anything.

As I got older, I'd begun to understand how important it was to her. She'd been drunk at the time of the accident that had crippled her leg, so she held anything that impaired her, even for her own good, in contempt. Her faculties were more important to her than her pain: she never wanted to lose her mind again. That was why I'd recommended Sofia ask her about AA if she needed it, because Katherine was staunch, immovable. She was—and I would never say this to her out loud—inspiring.

On top of all that, I'd always felt the pain in her leg, her limp, was somewhat of a penance. A reminder of her passenger that night, her best friend. One she didn't want dulled. One she felt she deserved. If you're wondering if the passenger survived, check the page number.

Maybe I was overthinking it. Maybe the injury had gotten worse with age, and Katherine had finally succumbed to her doctor's advice. Maybe it was excruciating in the cold weather, though Katherine had picked the resort herself; it seemed an odd choice if she was so afflicted. Maybe she had caved to pressure, probably from Andy (though Juliette clearing her throat when I awoke, forcing another pill out of her, sprung to mind), that the pills were essential for my injury, but she could still only bring herself to ration them out in the most conservative doses. If she'd had her way, she probably would have given me some breathing exercises instead. Lucy could have even sold her some essential oils, which I think are next on the list of independent businesses to pursue after Tupperware and cosmetics.

So I decided to be grateful for the slim ration I did get, swallowing the pill with a shot of used-to-be-hot chocolate and placing my mug on the bar on the way out. I was surprised to find Erin waiting for me in the foyer. The front door had been left open, and pebbles of ice skittered across the tiles.

"I don't know how to ask you this . . ." she started, but more words disappeared before she could find them. She looked at her shoes. Wind tousled her hair. Then she looked back at me. Those atoms in the air changed. "I don't want to be alone tonight."

MY WIFE

CHAPTER 30

Erin's whisper of my name floated down from above. The storm had reignited, and the tiny capsule of my chalet groaned as the weather squeezed it on all sides: it felt like we were in a submarine. I was on the couch, having given Erin the loft, and finally out of the bathrobe, into a pair of boxer shorts and a T-shirt from a band I didn't listen to anymore. Erin's request to stay with me had been born out of loneliness and fear, not flirtation, and so there was never any expectation that I would head up the ladder with her. There are no sex scenes in this book.

"I'm awake," I said.

There was a rustle from the loft as she, assumedly, rolled over. Her voice seemed minutely closer when she next spoke. "So, what do you think?"

"I don't know," I said honestly. "I can't get this Black Tongue thing out of my head. This torture, it's so distinctive. It would do well in a mystery novel."

"Almost breaches Rule 4," she said, absentmindedly. "Requires scientific explanation. Not sure if a snow tunnel counts as a secret passage though."

I'd been writing my how-to guides for a long time, so Erin knew Ronald Knox's rules just as well as I did. I wondered if she was spouting them off now in an attempt to make us feel like a team. It seemed strangely possessive from a woman who'd lied so boldly in order to avoid having children with me. And who'd nicked my loft.

"That's exactly the problem," I said. "Those murders are headline grabbing. They're perfect for the front page—they'll be a streaming documentary in a few months. They're statements. Which means they're easy to copy."

"You're saying maybe someone just wants us to think the Black Tongue is up here?"

"What's more believable, that an infamous serial killer followed us up here, or that someone's trying to make it look like they did?"

"Sofia's been trying pretty hard to convince people with all her explanations," Erin observed. "It's almost like she's trying to scare us."

"She *is* a doctor. She treated one of the victims. It's not as if she's said anything that isn't in the news."

"Sounds like you're defending her."

"Gotta trust someone." I decided that was a bit cruel and changed the topic. "Tell me something: how did Michael convince you to go grave robbing with him?"

That caught her off guard. "Well, I didn't know it was grave robbing at first. He kind of sprung that on me."

"How did you get involved in the first place?" The double meaning of the word *involved* ballooned and filled the room.

"Michael and Lucy were having their financial problems. You and I—we'd been struggling since . . . Well, they say a problem shared is a problem halved. It was comfort, Ern. Just comfort." I hadn't meant it that way, but I couldn't bring myself to stop her talking. "It's like snow on this mountain, is the only way I can put it. Lots of little flakes, and then you're knee-deep in it. Or ash on a lung, I guess. Is that too dark? Things seem to only move little by little, but then you look back and they've moved a lot. It was only when you and I had started sleeping in different rooms, but Lucy didn't know."

The revelation that they'd been together longer than I'd thought, before Michael had shown up in my driveway, should have crushed me. I'd had so many parts of me crushed that day, however, that it kind of bounced off.

Something Michael had said that night returned, though. *Lucy will know.* Because a trial for murder, in which every movement is picked over, would almost certainly uncover his affair. Lucy couldn't have known, or she wouldn't have reacted the way she had to the news of them spending *one night* together. Imagine if she did know the whole story? *Lucy will know.* Michael had said it even though he and Erin were already seeing each other. I wonder if Erin knew he was still clinging to his marriage at that point, that he'd only made up his mind much later. It was telling that Lucy was much more devastated over Michael's death than Erin was. I wondered if she knew more about it than I thought.

I put a pin in it. "I meant *involved* with this."

"Michael and I, not that it matters, but we never meant to—"

"I don't need to hear that bit. Tell me what Michael told you. And, more importantly, why you believed him."

"I didn't the first time. I took some convincing. But, well, then I found the bag of money that you were hiding. Michael told me to look for it. I didn't expect there to be anything, but I just couldn't figure out what he had to gain by lying, so I had a poke around. You didn't hide it very well, Ern." She said it like it was my fault. Like she'd tell me, back when we were happy, that she'd eaten chocolate she didn't want purely because I'd left it within her eyeline. "And then I started to think about which other parts of his story made sense. And maybe I wanted it to be true. I was reeling from how we ended, and this was—well, it was insane, but it was redemptive. I bought into it because I thought we could make it up to you. I made Michael promise you'd be in. It was supposed to be our money, Ern—the three of us."

It's family money.

There it was again. Except this time, I finally understood it.

"You're not talking about the bag. You thought you were digging up . . ." *All this for a treasure map?* "Wait, what exactly *did* you think you were digging up?"

"Before he got out, he had me tell everyone the wrong date of his release. And he asked me to hire a truck because he said we had to pick something up, and that we had to do it at night. He said he knew where he was going and he just needed one day after he was out to finish everything off. So, I go along with it, and then we're in a graveyard, and I tell him I don't want to do anything like this, and he tells me it's just dirt and wood and that he needs my help. So we use the straps and the pulleys and the truck's engine to pull this coffin out of the ground. Michael opens it, takes one glance, and says that we have to bring it up here with us. So we put it in the truck, and came up here. I think he was quite pleased with himself. I don't think he thought he was going to die. Your dad did robberies, so I put two and two together and assumed the coffin was just there to house something more valuable. I don't know—diamonds? Obviously I didn't think we were digging up a corpse, in case that wasn't clear. I would have run a mile."

"You told me before that Michael wouldn't tell you what Alan was selling. If you'd gone to the effort of digging up a coffin, why didn't you ask what was in it?"

"I did. He said it was safer if I didn't know."

"You haven't asked me either."

"It seems that everyone who knows what's really in there is

winding up dead, or close to," she reasoned, with a pointed look at my hand. "I figure he was onto something."

"And maybe that's part of it too. Say that Green Boots *is* a nobody. He was killed to make it obvious that the Black Tongue, or whoever is pretending to be the Black Tongue, is here. Or, he was killed because he got in the way. What if Michael was the real target all along?"

"It means anyone who knows what's in that coffin is in danger," she said.

This was the same idea Marcelo had alluded to. Marcelo hadn't known there was a coffin in the truck, and Erin didn't know what was in the coffin. By their logic, I, knowing the most, would be next on the Black Tongue's list.

"If that's the case, you need to tell me something else. We're past lying to each other. We were married for four years, and you still flinched at the thought of kissing in public. But you and Michael . . . It doesn't make sense." I paused, hoping she'd figure it out without me saying it, which would mean admitting to how closely I'd observed them.

"I'm not sure where you're going with this. Is now really the time to explore our intimacy issues?"

"On the front steps, before Crawford took him away, what did you take from Michael's back pocket?"

Erin's embrace of Michael in front of everyone had stood out to me as odd at first, but I'd put it down to my jealousy and her crowing. I'd seen it play out again, Erin's hand in the back pocket of Michael's jeans, on Juliette's weather-cam footage, and it had struck me, once again, as incongruous. Michael, in the Drying Room, had tried to show me something before giving me the keys to the truck, but he hadn't been able to find it. But my envy had masked the reason it had stuck out to me. I knew my wife. She didn't display affection like that.

Above me, Erin made some rustling noises, then something light landed on the cushion next to my head. I fumbled in the dark until my fingers closed around a small plastic object. It was similar in shape to a bottle cap, though slightly larger and deeper. More like a shot glass. I held it above me; there was just enough moonlight coming from behind the clouds that it gradually took shape. One surface gave a wink. Reflective. Clear plastic, maybe even glass.

"You're a clever one, you are," she said.

I had a memory of a shot glass rolling off the dash as Michael backed out of my driveway. I'd been a bit distracted by what was in the back seat at the time, but now I realized this was the same object. And it wasn't a shot glass, but a jeweler's eyepiece. The type where the open end of the cone was placed over your eye, and at the top was a magnifying lens to look through. (My editor has left a helpful note that it is called a loupe, so I'll pretend to be educated and use the proper word from now on.)

It had obviously been innocuous enough that it hadn't been confiscated as evidence, but important enough to Michael that he'd rummaged around to get it from under the seat before he'd been arrested *and* kept it as part of his small envelope of possessions handed back to him on his release from prison.

"Why did you take this?" I asked.

"Use your brain, Ern. I thought we'd dug up something valuable. I don't know, diamonds? Gold bricks? What do you steal and hide in a coffin? Why else would he have this, if not to check something like that? Alan was a secondhand jeweler, wasn't he? I thought it was pretty obvious what they were talking about. And I took it because, well"—she cleared her throat, embarrassed—"because Michael wasn't telling me anything about the coffin, and maybe I wanted to see for myself. Just in case this weekend went a different way than I thought it was going to go. With Lucy."

"You felt you couldn't fully trust him? Once a cheater always a cheater?" I only needled on this point for my personal validation, knowing full well how petty it was. Katherine's pills must have loosened me up. I never would have said that sober.

"Maybe that was part of it," she admitted in that low, shameful voice people use when they admit to things. "It took him so long to tell Lucy about us, and he knew I couldn't tell you before he agreed to tell her. I begged him to pay her debts, so we could have a clean break. When he finally sent her papers, I think it was only because he was still so mad at you. That was the first time I thought maybe he just wanted something of yours. This weekend brought it all up again. I felt on show."

"So you took this from him, knowing he couldn't cut you out of whatever was in the coffin if he couldn't check the value until he got off the mountain."

"It sounds a bit paranoid, when you put it like that," she said. "But then he gave you the keys, not me. And I knew if you didn't go alone into the truck, Crawford and Sofia would see it too, and then everyone would know. I knew, at least, that you wanted to keep the bag of money secret, so I thought you might keep this secret too, whatever it was. That's why I insisted you looked alone." I heard her suck her teeth. It was something she did when she was worried and couldn't sleep. I used to stroke her shoulder, to let her know I was there and everything was okay. I was surprised to see my arm make the same movement towards the empty space beside me on the couch. A muscle memory. "Obviously I was wrong about what was in the coffin"—she paused expectantly, but I didn't take the bait—"so I have a new theory. I think he wanted to check your money."

I thought about that for a second. It made sense. I didn't know a lot about counterfeit bank notes but I assumed there was some microscopic signifier somewhere, a serial number or something. I have since looked this up and I was, indeed, correct.

"This isn't particularly fancy or valuable," I said as I rolled it between my fingertips. I could see it better now my eyes had adjusted. "It looks the same as the ones in my Year 12 science labs. You could get one of these anywhere. But you're right about Alan's job. This was probably his, and Michael took it off him."

"So maybe Alan brought this to check Michael's money and it wasn't up to scratch? And that's why they fought?"

"I've been wondering how Michael got his hands on $267,000 without Lucy finding out about it," I confessed. "It's a lot of money. Even Marcelo didn't know about it. Or you, for that matter, and I wouldn't be surprised if Michael asked you to find it just to see if it was still there."

"But if he already knew the money was fake, why would he need to check it?"

"I don't know."

"What if it's the other way around?" she suggested. "Alan brought the money and Michael wasn't happy."

I let the idea seed. Michael had been clear that he was buying something from Alan. Was that the truth? What would Michael possibly have to sell? "If the money's useless, useless enough to kill over anyway, why keep it?"

"You've spent some," she offered. It wasn't a question.

"A little. I had no problems."

"Just because it's fake doesn't mean it's worthless. Or maybe it's marked—you know, how the police mark bills and all that?"

"Maybe." I was missing something, but I wasn't sure what it was. My intuition told me that one of Erin's theories, something she'd said, was nudging close to the truth. But I didn't know enough to unlock it. Michael had told me the problem was that he didn't have *enough*, so I thought it was unlikely the money was fake.

We ran out of theories and dipped back into silence. The

submarine of our chalet felt like it sank another hundred meters, groaning. It seemed for a time that Erin might have fallen asleep. Then the pale orb of her face appeared above me, leaning over the loft.

"Is it worth me saying I'm sorry?" she asked.

"For which part?"

"All of it, I suppose."

There is some metaphor to be found in her voice, wafting down to me, while I lay on my back and spoke to the stars, but I don't know what it is.

"Okay."

"Just okay?"

"Hmmm." I did my best impression of a sleepy, noncommittal mumble, but I'm sure she could hear my heart beating. It seemed to be vibrating my whole pillow.

"You don't want to know why?"

"Are you talking because you have something to say, or because you can't sleep?" I didn't mean it to sound snappy—there's a certain margin where cruelty bonds with affection in a marriage—but now that we weren't together, even gentle ribbing came across as barbed.

"Can it be both?" The appeal in her voice was clear.

"Sure." I softened. "But if I lose a footrace to a serial killer tomorrow because I've under-slept, I'm blaming you."

Her teeth flashed white in the dark. A grin. "There he is."

"You don't have to apologize to me, Erin. I shouldn't have put that pressure on you. I thought you were happy, I thought we'd made the decision to have kids together, but I mustn't have seen how much I was pushing you into it. I was mad for a long time, but what right do I have over your choices? You shouldn't have lied, and I wish it was anyone but Michael—I'll never be past that—but I've asked enough of you. I don't need an apology."

This was only half true. The real truth was that I didn't want to have to lie there and listen to her spout excuses. I'd heard them before—in therapy, at home, whispered and yelled, texted and emailed, tear-splattered and hate-fueled. I thought I'd heard every excuse in every form.

Then she surprised me by saying, "I killed my mother."

CHAPTER 31

The words were like a bomb in the small room. I didn't know what to say to her confession. I knew her dad had raised her—it was one of the reasons we'd understood each other when we started dating—but Erin had told me her mother's death had been from an illness when she was young.

"She died giving birth to me." Her voice was barely above a whisper. "You're about to tell me it's not my fault, but it doesn't matter. It's what my father told me, and I believed it. Still do. I killed her. I know, it happens. I know it's not my fault. That's why I started telling people it was cancer, because people just say, 'Oh, I'm so sorry,' instead of all that other stuff. But my father told me every day growing up, right up until he died, that it *was* my fault. I always knew he would have traded me for her."

I'd known her father was abusive, but I'd never known it had been so targeted, filled with such blame and hatred. "That's a horrible thing to say to a child," I said. "I didn't know."

"Please believe me when I say that I didn't mean to hurt you. I just, well . . . After we talked about trying for a baby . . ." She caught herself in a sob and took a second to compose herself. "You were so excited, Ern. I couldn't believe how happy it made you, just talking about it. You were in love with the idea before we even started trying. I wanted to be what you wanted me to be. And you were so happy when I agreed. But then . . . I'm not saying it was your fault—I'm trying to explain. I was scared. I just needed a bit more time.

"I was only supposed to keep taking the pill for a few weeks," she continued, "until I got used to the idea of getting pregnant. And, God, I loved those first few weeks. It was the happiest we'd ever been, I think. You had a light in your eyes that I couldn't bring myself to snuff. But then a few weeks turned into a few months, which turned into a year, and suddenly you wanted to figure out what was going on and we're driving to clinics and doctors, and you have that little plastic cup and I realized I'd trapped myself into never telling you, so I just had to go along with it, knowing that the only solution was to stop taking the pills and reveal a miracle pregnancy before someone else told you first. And I just couldn't bring myself to do it. It was like feeding fivers into a slot machine. I kept putting off the clinic. I kept thinking that I just needed to get rid of one more letter, I just needed to shrug off one more phone call, and then I'd be ready. Every prescription was my last, and then I'd find myself in the chemist waiting for another one."

I was crying too now. "I wanted just you—just you as you were. I didn't want a vessel. I was only excited because I thought we were doing it together. I would have listened."

"But if I'd have told you, you would have pushed. You wouldn't have known what you were pushing against, and you would have done it in your funny charming way, and maybe you'd have dropped it for a year or two, but you would have pushed. I couldn't tell you about Mum. I haven't told anyone since I was a teenager, when I realized it was easier to tell people she was sick. I couldn't face the judgment. I thought, with enough time, I could give you what you wanted. I really tried.

"I'm not asking for pity. I'm trying to tell you why I was scared. Scared of being physically hurt, yes—of dying, like her. But mostly I was scared that if something *did* happen to me, you'd look at the child, the baby you'd wanted so badly, with the same eyes my father used on me."

"I wanted a family so badly—"

"Oh, Ernie. I know."

"—maybe I forgot I already had one." I sighed. "I'm sorry."

"*I'm* apologizing to *you*, you prick." She gave a choked laugh. "I'm sorry I lied to you. I didn't want to be the one who couldn't give you what you wanted."

"I would have loved you just the same." I still did, but I didn't say that. It was too painful, even with the oxycodone, to confess. Maybe I should have said something. Maybe that's part of the reason I'm writing this all down. A book is a physical object, remember. It is written to be read.

After a pause, her voice floated down again. "Do you want to come up the ladder?"

I knew she was only hunting intimacy as a reaction to Michael's death. I knew it would be false and hollow, and would only make everything hurt afresh tomorrow. I knew all of this, but still I lay there, unsure how to answer her.

"More than anything," I said at last. "But I don't think I will."

CHAPTER 32

I dreamt of my wedding day, though it was more of a memory than a dream. Michael was leaning on the lectern like it was the only thing keeping him upright, slurring his words as he tried to get his third rule of best man speeches out, the guests laughing along with his struggles. Even Audrey was smiling. He took a swig of his beer and held a finger up—*Wait a sec, I've got this*—hiccupped, wiped his mouth with his sleeve, and tried once again to get his tongue to form the words "happy wife, happy life." The room roared with laughter, and he grinned, believing he was earning those laughs through talent and not buffoonery. He hiccupped again. But this one sounded different, a little more like a . . . Another hiccup, but this was definitely more of a gag, and then he was clutching at his throat, eyes bulging, as his hiccups turned into a full-blown choking. And the room kept on laughing, riotous, as black, bubbling tar seeped from his lips.

The morning was gray-skied, dim, the storm back with renewed fury. The snow had dumped so heavily that the door needed a shoulder charge to carve an opening. Outside, we were wet-shinned and shivering within thirty seconds. Flakes of swirling ice bit my skin like sand flies. The cars remaining wore white toupees, and drifts sloped against the walls of the guesthouse like suspended waves.

Erin and I had dressed and left the chalet without talking much; the space between us had the awkward air of long-time friends who'd slept together. After last night's confessions and her invitation, we weren't sure what to say. I'd slept in the oven mitt, and now it was half bio-material. I couldn't take it off if I wanted to. I'd had to force it, seams straining, through my thermals. Seeing my one-handed struggle, Erin had helped me pull a beanie down over my ears. Yesterday I'd seemed to find myself in the cold more often than my crackling-fireplace wardrobe allowed for, so I was determined to be prepared. I chewed a single glove down my good wrist until it slid over my fingers. As we left, I grabbed an iron from one of the chalet's back cupboards. Erin had raised an eyebrow when I'd picked it up, but I saw her question rise in her chest and give up halfway, no doubt deciding she didn't care to know.

I had the loupe in my pocket. I'd woken before Erin and had examined it in the morning light. It had *50x* written on the side, which I assumed was the magnification. I'd fetched a fifty-dollar note from the stash and held it aloft, looking through the eyepiece for anything interesting.

There was one thing I knew about Australian fifty-dollar bills, and that was thanks to an old party trick that comes in handy for writers. In 2018, the yellow fifty-dollar banknote was redesigned to include a miniature reprinting of Edith Cowan's inaugural speech to parliament underneath her portrait. Unfortunately, it featured a misspelling of the word "responsibility," which had gone unnoticed for six months, after millions of bills were already in circulation. It was an easy dinner party anecdote: I'd ask around for fifties and, upon spotting one of the misspelled ones, launch into the story, climaxing with the glass-chinking exclamation that "It's proof they don't pay us writers enough—we would have found the error much faster if we'd seen a few more of these!" Cue raucous laughter. But that was the extent of my knowledge of currency. Examining the bill, I could see it *did* have the typo in it, which suggested the money was more likely real than fake in any case.

There was indeed a serial number, as I'd guessed, as well as intersecting dashes of color and a small hologram on the bottom left. But all of those features, including the typo, were visible to the naked eye. The loupe wasn't necessary. The 50x magnification was strong enough to show me the very seam of the plastic, the bleed of the different colors of ink. The loupe was to see something else. I gave up. Looking was pointless if I didn't know what I was looking for.

As we passed the cars, I patted Erin gently on the elbow to get her attention. In the howling storm there wasn't much point talking, so I simply raised the iron and nodded towards Marcelo's Mercedes. We slushed over to it. I thrust the iron, the heaviest removeable object I could find in the chalet, at the glass, which cracked but didn't shatter, bending around a crater in the middle instead. The tinted window was marked with long, white streaks.

The idea had festered since yesterday, when I'd seen the glass around Katherine's car, but I'd been a touch too busy being half-dead to try. I'd figured, seeing as Katherine's Volvo had suffered similarly in the storm, that another broken window wouldn't raise an eyebrow. But I hadn't accounted for the alarm, which started shrieking into the wind as soon as I hit the window. The storm was loud, but I wasn't sure if it was loud enough to cover the wail, and the wind's direction was working against me, ferrying the sound towards the guesthouse. The hazard lights were blinking like a beacon too. Erin was keeping watch in case someone decided to investigate, but it was completely futile; her visibility was only a few meters. I had to hurry.

I hit the window again and it bent further, air now breaching as it flexed like an eggshell, but still the glass held. I only had to hit it once more before my whole hand exploded through it. I used the oven mitt (coming in handy now) to push the remnants of glass through the frame and leaned through. Erin was bouncing slightly, agitated and ready to leave, but I knew what I wanted. I yanked at it, ripping a cascade of cords from their sockets, and had just stood back up and turned to yell to Erin that we could go when a fist slammed into the side of my jaw.

Morning powder is quite good at catching a fall, but I didn't make it to the ground. Erin caught me under both arms like a boxing coach.

"Jesus, Ernest." Marcelo was shaking out his hand, surprised to see me.

I gingerly stood back up, probing the side of my jaw. He'd hit me with his right hand, so I was thankful his reconstructed shoulder had weakened his punch, because that was the wrist he wore his Rolex on. It should have felt like being socked by a dumbbell. I was surprised I still had teeth.

"I'm so sorry," Marcelo said. "I was checking Lucy's car and I heard the alarm. With everything that's going on, I thought someone was . . . Hang on . . . What were you doing here?"

He looked at his car, clearly thinking about the broken window. I realized I'd dropped the iron just below the door. It was half dusted in snow by now, but still visible. I used my foot to nudge it under the car. Marcelo stepped closer to the window. If he peered in, he'd see the cables strewn across his dash and know that something was wrong.

"I saw the window was broken from the storm." I said it too loudly, but it worked, making him turn back to me. "Those nice leather seats and all. Thought it would be a shame if those were ruined. I was hoping to find something to cover them with inside."

"Good man," he said, slinging an arm around me and steering me away from the car. "Forget the leather, let's get you inside.

Hang on . . ." He paused, dropping a knee into the snow. My stomach, which had had far too many opportunities to gravitate already, found another one. Marcelo groaned in standing, hand outstretched, holding something for me to see. But it wasn't the iron. "You dropped your phone." He handed me the device.

Look, this is a borderline breach of Rule 6—a fortunate accident—but every detective needs a bit of luck. Narrative suspense is built by stacking the odds against the gumshoe, but every now and then, just like in real life, the dominoes topple in their favor. And, honestly, I don't know why Marcelo didn't see it. Maybe he was distracted, calculating how much his window would cost to replace, or maybe the cold had fogged his vision. Maybe his hand hurt from socking me in the jaw. It was a similar device to a phone, of course—small, rectangular, and electronic, with an LCD screen—but he really should have noticed. But I wasn't about to question it. I figured, after yesterday, I was owed some good fortune.

So I snatched the portable GPS device, freshly wrenched from its windshield mount, and burrowed it into my pocket before he got a better look.

There was an abomination of a vehicle parked outside the front of the guesthouse. A bright-yellow windowed cube sitting hip-high atop garish mechanical treads, it looked like the offspring of a military tank and a school bus. Steam was hissing out from underneath it, the engine on and hot.

A small group huddled by it: Sofia, Andy, Crawford, Juliette, and a man I didn't know, whom I allowed to momentarily lift my hopes—perhaps he was a detective. But, as I joined the group, I saw he was zipped into a sleek plastic raincoat with *SuperShred Resort* embroidered on the breast. Everything he wore had a logo on it—from his blue-and-gold holographic Oakleys, to his Skullcandy bandana tied over his chin (skull and crossbones over his mouth), to his puffy plastic pants with *Quiksilver* emblazoned all the way down one leg. He looked like a well-stickered beer fridge. I pegged him as a snowboarder: the only part of his face showing, his nose, looked often broken. As I got closer, I saw the *SuperShred* insignia was similarly printed on the flank of the bus-tank. He must have been from over the ridge, the resort in the adjoining valley.

I nudged my way between Andy and Sofia. Sofia was shivering intensely, winter pale. I could tell she wasn't focusing on what was going on, rather counting down the seconds until she could go back inside. I expected at least one raised eyebrow at Erin and I arriving together, Erin in the same clothes as yesterday, but nobody seemed to have the energy for schoolyard gossip. Everyone was too focused on Marcelo, returning with us, to pay us any mind.

"Are we leaving?" I asked. The vehicle could only be designed to travel through thick snow, and it wasn't here for joyrides.

"Well?" Juliette spoke over the top of me, to Marcelo.

"Chalet's empty. Her car's still there."

"Shit."

"I can take you up the ridge." The Walking Billboard's voice was no exception to his outfit, his accent sponsored by Monster Energy drink. If he hadn't been talking about a missing woman, I'm sure he would have used "dog" and "bro" as punctuation. There was a slight Canadian lilt, which I took to mean he was one of the snow-chasers who spent six months in the Northern Hemisphere and six months in the south. "But we're not going to find someone in this unless we run over them."

"What's happening?" I tried again.

"Lucy's gone." Marcelo finally addressed me, albeit with the distracted air of someone who's just been asked "What did I miss?" during a film. "No one's seen her since last night."

It made sense. Marcelo had sprung me looting his car because he was already there, checking to see if Lucy had driven out overnight. I assumed that's why Katherine and Audrey weren't with the group: they'd split off to search the house.

The Walking Billboard swiveled his head across our group. "Excuse me for asking, but what the fuck happened to you lot? Jules, I should take you all back to Jindabyne right now."

"This is Gavin." Juliette put a hand on his arm. They seemed to know each other well; I assumed there were quickly forged friendships between seasonal workers. Not well enough for her to tell him about Michael's murder, though, or he wouldn't have been asking. "The weather's getting worse, and the Oversnow"—she patted the side of the bus-tank, which gave a hollow *thunk*—"is our only option down the mountain. Gavin's offered to take us."

"But we have to go now," Gavin added, looking nervously at the sky.

"Without Lucy?" Erin asked.

"This is our window." He shrugged. "You've got all the cops. I'm on my own. Which means I've got my own staff to worry about."

"We've got one cop," Marcelo corrected. "And barely that. Listen, it's all of us or none of us. We're family."

It struck me as a strange thing for him to say, Lucy being his ex-stepdaughter-in-law, but I knew that the Garcias' policy on hyphens was different to my own. Besides, if clashing with the law was a Cunningham trait, Lucy had copped that speeding fine on the way up, so I guess she was one of us after all.

"I appreciate you coming over," Juliette said. "But we can't leave her. Take us on one loop. I'll owe you."

"Shots?"

"Shots. Just like Whistler."

The memory of an assumedly wild night perked him up so much his sunnies changed color. "Right, who's coming with me then?"

"I'll come." I suspected Andy volunteered because the unwashed pheromones of a gap year were mingling with his middle-aged regrets, and he associated movement with usefulness, or perhaps he just wanted a ride in the big clanky thing.

I felt Erin bump me. *One of us should go*. "Me too," I said.

Gavin seemed to notice me for the first time and held out a North Face glove in greeting. I raised my oven mitt, apologetically declining.

"Nice glove, dude," he said.

Crawford moved to follow the volunteers, but Juliette stepped in front of him. "You should stay here and keep control of things. Erin, Marcelo—help Katherine and Audrey search the rest of this place. Sofia"—she looked her up and down—"to be honest, you look like you need a lie-down." Sofia nodded gratefully. "Gav, I'll come too and look at those papers. I *know*." She must have seen his eyes light up. "Don't push it. Just a look. Ernest and Andrew, hop in."

I was impressed that she knew all of our names, and told her as much. She shrugged and said that if the roll call kept getting shorter, she'd have no trouble at all. That got a grin out of me, dark as it was. I realized I was glad she was coming with us.

Gavin walked around to the rear of the beastly machine and pulled open the door. We clambered up a three-rung ladder while he made his way to the driver's seat. It was barely a vehicle; instead of seats in the back it had long steel benches down either side. It was as cold as a fridge inside a freezer, the temperature wrapping me up in a rib-cracking squeeze. Everything smelled of fuel. The floor rumbled with the engine's throaty growl as Gavin maneuvered a gearstick the size of a tree branch.

We started at a slow crawl between the buildings, but then Gavin roared the throttle up the hill and started bouncing the three of us around. I held on to a steel bar above one of the windows and tried to peer out the frosted glass. Gavin was right—we would hit Lucy before we saw her. Given the giant tank wheels, I doubted we'd even feel it. The snow had dumped too heavily to leave tracks.

While we drove, I took Marcelo's GPS from my pocket. It was solar powered, but still had some battery left, so it turned on easily in my hand. I searched the menu for recent trips. A rudimentary map loaded. Sky Lodge wasn't even marked; it was just a small arrow icon in the middle of a blank area. I zoomed out until I could see the nearest road. The green line started near the BEER! sign that felt a thousand kilometers and years away, and then continued down towards Jindabyne, and then—I scratched my jaw in confusion—back up the hill on the other side of the valley. The trip was a perfect U shape, estimated at fifty minutes one way. I knew from Juliette's snow cam that he'd been gone six hours. Which begged the question: what had he been doing at SuperShred Resort for the other four?

"This is pointless," Andy yelled after fifteen minutes. We were probably halfway up the slope. I could see a small halo of light, which I knew was the floodlight at the top of the chairlift, but nothing else. There weren't even trees or rocks this far up. No one replied, so he tapped Juliette on the shoulder and repeated himself. "I said, 'This is *pointless*.' The snow's so heavy there's no trace of her. She'd have to be mad to go out in this."

"We have to try," Juliette yelled back. It was like talking in the cargo hold of an airplane. "The chairlift looks closer from the bottom of the valley than it is, the mountain less steep too. Maybe when she couldn't move her car, she thought she'd walk up there. She wouldn't have known she was in trouble until she was halfway up."

"Or she's gone to the road and is trying to hitch," I added.

"Exactly."

"But why would she have gone . . ." A particularly rough bounce dislodged Andy's words, and he fumbled them back: ". . . gone into the storm at all?"

"Maybe she was scared," I suggested.

Andy nodded. "She looked pretty unsettled when Sofia showed her that photo."

I'd thought she had just felt confronted by death, but Andy was right. She had been upset, leaving the room straight after. What if it had been a threat from Sofia? In front of all of us, that would have been a confident move, but I already knew confidence was not something the Black Tongue lacked. But what would the threat have been? Was it *I know about you* or *I'm coming for you*?

Andy was thinking the same thing. "Even if something scared her, why come out here?"

"She thought she could make it." There was a dark edge to Juliette's voice; it was obvious she didn't believe her own words. But then why were we out here?

"In this weather?" Andy shook his head. "That would be suicide!"

At that, Juliette's eyes met mine for the slightest flicker and then shot to the floor. I realized what she was thinking, why she thought Lucy might have taken herself out into a lethal storm. I thought about the way Lucy had canvassed the guilt in the bar, before she'd been shown the photo of Green Boots and left in a hurry. Maybe Sofia *had* scared her. After all, the only thing linking the deaths so far was the method, and Erin had rightly pointed out that the Black Tongue's MO was easily researched. I knew for a fact that Lucy had googled it; she was the one who told me about the first victims. And she had more grievances against Michael than many of us. Maybe seeing him arrive with Erin was the final straw.

I looked back at Juliette, her eyes fixed grimly out the frosted window.

We weren't out looking for Lucy, we were chasing after her.

MY SISTER-IN-LAW (former)

CHAPTER 33

Gavin took us up to the top of the chairlift, high on the ridge. A giant, hulking column raised thick black wires into the sky, dotted with three-seater benches hanging underneath, which dropped away from my window into the churning clouds. Out Andy's side of the vehicle, the wires fed uphill into a corrugated metal shed. Gavin stopped to allow Juliette to jump out and check inside, thinking perhaps Lucy had stumbled into it for shelter, but she came back quickly, shaking her head.

Gavin set off again, following the path of the wires down the hill. I thought it was a good idea; the pillars of the lift stood out among the maelstrom as looming shadows and, if I were stuck out there, I would have followed them too. That was, of course, assuming Lucy was trying to get anywhere. The chairs swung above us in the wind, turning almost ninety degrees. I was glad I wasn't on one. Gavin slalomed around the pillars as he came to them, crunching the gearstick with a gusto that could have given him tennis elbow. In the back, we iced our brows against the glass, pitching forward with the steepness of the slope and squinting into the whiteout. But no Lucy.

As the ground leveled out, we passed another tin shed fed by the descending wire. Juliette ran out again and returned just as quickly. Our thin ration of hope was siphoning out. The further we went, the less likely it was that she'd have made it this far.

A few more minutes and a collection of buildings came into view; we'd made it to the resort.

"Damn it," Andy muttered, jabbing at his phone. "Piece of junk."

"Reception any better here?" I asked.

"Nah, battery's had it. You?"

"Phone took a dive in the lake, remember."

SuperShred Resort looked more like a military base than a holiday retreat, populated by giant square sheds that, I assumed, consisted of dorms a tenth the price of Sky Lodge's chalets and, as a consequence, had ten times the occupancy. It was deserted, with the creepy air of an abandoned amusement park. (I guessed people were huddled inside; the weather was grim but not apocalyptic, so unless they had corpses of their own to deal with there'd be no reason to leave.) I could almost feel the ghosts of activity in the flutter of the fluorescent triangular flags set out to guide crowds, the well-trampled thoroughfare that, even with a heavy dumping of fresh snow, was packed down underfoot. The signs heralding HIRE or FOOD seemed rueful in the emptiness, a promise of a different place. We glided through it on our rumbling beast the way you would dive through a shipwreck. It was quiet, eerie: alive and dead at the same time.

It was the opposite of Sky Lodge, designed to excite instead of rejuvenate, with the money scrounged on sleeping arrangements poured into lift tickets and gear hire. Shared bathrooms and tinea were part of the package, and I'm sure they would have gotten away with removing the beds entirely if people didn't need somewhere to put themselves between 3 am when the bar closed and 6 am when the lifts opened.

Gavin brought us to a stop next to a gigantic map, where underneath a layer of ice I could see lines of varied colors tracing their way down the mountain. The right side of the map was all iced, except for a series of glowing red lights that I knew were next to the names of the chairlifts. It meant *all lifts closed*.

"Sorry, folks." He swiveled in his chair like a bus driver. "I'll take you back around, but why don't you grab a warm drink first? Jules and I have some business to discuss." He swung open his door.

"Really, Gav?" Juliette stayed put.

"If she's here, she'll be inside," Gavin said. "Your mate can check the room list, too, though everyone's accounted for."

"It might be useful," I wondered aloud. "I might recognize a name you've missed."

"I'll take a coffee. Irish, if it's going. And a phone charger." Andy lifted himself off the steel bench, standing hunched in the back and rubbing his hands over his backside. "If I don't get a break, I'm a shoo-in for hemorrhoids." He caught Juliette's impatient scowl. "What? She could have made it up here."

He pushed open the back door and jumped into the snow with a crunch. I followed, figuring that he had a point: even if Lucy was unlikely to be here, we may as well ask a few questions. Someone might know who Green Boots was. Not to mention, Marcelo had been up here the night before this all started. Juliette, resigned to our visit, hopped out and followed Gavin to the largest shed, which looked like an aircraft hangar.

The storm wasn't any lighter on this side of the mountain. I could hear the wires of the chairlifts creaking under the battering wind. Cars turned into huge white termite mounds lined the road. Skis and boards were stabbed into snowdrifts, I assumed once neatly, but now splayed or knocked over like bad teeth. Gloves had been slotted on top of ski poles, evidence that many who had retreated indoors were hopeful of getting back on the slopes quickly, but they were now frozen through. It was like an avalanche-struck version of Chernobyl.

"This is some seriously creepy shit." Andy spoke low beside me as we approached the building, a throbbing orange glow in one of the windows the only sign of life. My cheeks were so cold they tingled with his hot breath. "It's like a ghost ship. Is anybody even at this resort?"

As Gavin led us closer, I thought I heard, from deep inside, the blaring klaxon of an air-raid siren or a fire alarm, as well as a series of distant thuds, loud enough to make the ground vibrate underfoot. Unease festered in my stomach. I started to dissect things. Gavin had certainly seemed more concerned with getting us, or at least Juliette, up here than finding Lucy. And, while Lucy was missing and we were worried, she *wasn't* dead. In books like this, you should never believe someone is dead until you've actually seen a body. They tend to show up. We've all read *And Then There Were None*.

On the other hand, suspicious as I was of Gavin, it's simply unfair to introduce the killer this far past the midpoint. Knox would have me drawn and quartered—that's his first rule. And, reader, your right thumb should tell you there is just too much to go.

Regardless, there should have been hundreds of people around: it was peak season and this was a resort for hardcore thrill-seekers, unlikely to be scared off by some wind and ice. Where were they?

My question was answered when Gavin opened the door.

The roar of the storm was nothing compared to the roar that greeted us as we stepped over the threshold. Electronic music was blaring, flashing colors assaulted my eyes, and the bass rumbled the walls in deep, repetitive thuds. Rotating spotlights illuminated writhing bodies, glowsticks hanging off their necks and wrists. A man on a platform surrounded by green lasers bounced one arm in the air. Chairs and tables were pushed alongside the walls, cleared from the dining hall to make way for the dance floor. We'd walked straight into the middle of a rave.

Gavin plucked his way through the crowd and we tried to stay as close as we could. It was hot, hotter than I'd felt in days, the air laden with sweat. People feasted on each other's faces. Andy was in awe, transfixed by flesh and fantasy. People wore ski goggles with underwear, boardshorts with snow jackets, towels as capes, helmets, gloves, and T-shirts tied around heads. One woman wore a Hawaiian lei, a balaclava, a bikini, and a huge multicolored sombrero. My oven mitt fit right in.

I was nearly decapitated by a line of shirtless men drinking from a horizontal ski, six shot glasses screwed into the wood. The crowd was thickest by the bar, where the menu had prices hastily crossed out and rewritten, enormously inflated, in thick black marker alongside a large CASH ONLY sign. Gavin reached another door and held it open for us. We filtered into the corridor. I had to yank Andy the last few steps.

"Jesus Christ, Gav," Juliette gasped, leaning with relief against the wall. The floor still shook with the bass, but at least the air was breathable. "That's out of control."

"That was insane!" Andy's eyes lit up with repressed youth. "We picked the wrong resort!" I thought it was a pity Katherine wasn't here to react to that.

"It started small. Some guy said he'd brought his DJ kit and asked if he could set it up—we've had bands and stuff before, so I said sure. I thought it would be a bit of fun while the storm passed. But as the weather got wilder outside, it got wilder inside, and it's turned into a bit of a bender." He shrugged. "Everyone's having fun. No harm in it."

"We can't even get help to Sky Lodge," Juliette cautioned. "If something goes wrong, who will come to help you?"

"You've got two dead and one missing, and how many parties did you throw?" Gavin shot back as he guided us further down the corridor. "Look, I can't shut it down. It's too far gone. I cut the power and they'll have a sing-along. I cut off the bar and then I'm going to get my fridges smashed and ransacked. Once the storm passes and they can get back out there, they'll filter out on their own. I've just got to let them wear themselves out." He chuckled. "Gosh, I do feel sorry for the old couple though. Bet they wish they'd booked over the ridge."

"I bet the markup on the bar doesn't hurt your end."

"You wouldn't have me starve?" He smiled.

We threaded our way through the bowels of the hotel. As predicted, it was the polar opposite of Sky Lodge: closer to a university dormitory than a hotel, with breakout spaces such as communal kitchens instead of libraries, and flat-screen TVs in place of log fires. Stainless steel was abundant. Gavin's office was not that much more sophisticated: he had a pool table with a scar ripped through the felt and bottle rings on the oak perimeter, a standing desk adorned with a much more expensive computer than Juliette's and two monitors, and a corkboard with an A3 map of the whole mountain, Sky Lodge included, and various weather and satellite images. Gavin walked around his desk to what I at first thought was a small black safe, but instead turned out to be a fridge. He plucked out a few Corona beers, hanging them between his fingers, and offered them as if he were Edward Scissorhands. Andy grabbed one quickly, but I shook my head.

"We're in a hurry, Gavin." Juliette waved a bottle away. Andy, on realizing we'd both declined, held his bottle awkwardly, figuring it too treacherous to drink.

Gavin held out surrendering hands. "I know, I know." He tapped a few keys on his computer and the monitor came to life. The screen had a thick coating of dust over it. He clicked a few things and gestured to Andy and me to look. He'd brought up an Excel spreadsheet. For a second I thought Aunt Katherine had invited him to the reunion, but I'll chalk that up to PTSD: Post-Traumatic Spreadsheet Disorder. "There's the room list," he said to me. "You've got internet too. Five minutes?" This last part was appealed back to Juliette; he wanted her attention. He was offering Andy and me his computer to occupy us the same way you'd give a video game to a child. "It's worth your time."

"I already told you. It's not about the money." Juliette marched to the door, held it open. "Let's talk out here."

Gavin's grin exploded. Andy surrendered and took a guilty sip of his beer.

I turned to the computer screen. The Excel spreadsheet was, in contrast to the rest of SuperShred, quite organized. There was one tab labeled *Room List* and another labeled *Room Check*. I was keen to read through it, but the ability to use the internet indoors for once was too tempting, so I opened a browser.

If Ronald Knox had been born one hundred years later, I'm sure his eleventh commandment would have forbade any Google searching. But what can I say: he's long dead and I was trying not to join him. The more information I had the better.

I understand googling news articles is not quite the high drama one reads books for. I'll save you the scene of me clicking and scrolling as I googled "the Black Tongue" and "the Black Tongue victims," and I hate it when news articles are reprinted verbatim in books. And, look, it's the twenty-first century and I hadn't had internet for two days, so forgive a bit of extra surfing. Here is what I learned:

- I confirmed what I knew secondhand from Lucy and Sofia. Ash; suffocation; ancient Persian torture. As Lucy had said, the information was readily available. Anyone could have copied it.

- In fact, when I typed "the Bl . . ." Google autofilled "the Black Tongue" from its own history. Gavin had been searching too, so word had spread a little further than I'd thought.
- The reported murders were actually very spread out, with the first occurring three years ago (after Alan's death), and the second eighteen months later.
- Andy asked me to take a quick look at cryptocurrency values.
- The first victims, Mark and Janine Williams, were from Brisbane. Mark was sixty-seven and Janine was seventy-one. They had been retired after having run a fish and chip shop in Brisbane for thirty years. The article took the "Life's unfair" angle, describing them as pillars of the community—volunteers, board members, fostering countless children because they were unable to have their own—which made their deaths all the more depressing. One article included a photo of their funeral, lines out the door. They'd been much loved. Not really A-grade gang member material, is my point. Sofia's description of their deaths was accurate: they'd been zip-tied to the steering wheel of their car in their own garage, with ash circulated by the killer standing over the sunroof with a leaf blower.
- The second victim, Alison Humphreys, was found still alive in her Sydney apartment, in a bathroom with the window taped shut, ash poured through the ceiling fan. She'd died after five days in the hospital where Sofia worked (I noted this matched her information from the maintenance shed), when the decision had been made to turn off Alison's life support systems. People had linked her death to Mark and Janine's, and suddenly the task of naming a serial killer had fallen on a sub-editor, and the Black Tongue was born.
- I checked my Facebook quickly.
- According to Alison's LinkedIn (there is nothing sadder than a posthumous LinkedIn account: *employed 2010–present*), she

was a former detective turned "consultant." On what she had been consulting was unclear.

- The listing price of Sky Lodge (I'd remembered the name of the real estate company I'd seen on the contracts) was by inquiry only. Tripadvisor gave the resort a 3.4, which I thought, corpses excepted, was a bit harsh.
- I opened Lucy's Instagram account, figuring if she'd gotten all the way up to the roof last night, the temptation of phone reception and social media would have been too high for her to resist. Sure enough, there was a new post: a screenshot of a deposit to her bank account, a few thousand and change, with the rest of the identifying details blurred out. The caption read: *It's hard work but it's worth it in the end—contact me if you want to learn about financial independence. Swipe to see what this amazing company has provided for me #dailygrind #earningandlearning #corporateretreat #bossbabe*. Swiping showed a second photo—a gorgeous mountain vista, taken from the rooftop—and a third—a photo of everyone (except me, running late) around the lunch table from the first day. I didn't even have it in me to mock how she was pretending our reunion was a company retreat (*#fakeittillyoumakeit* would have been a better hashtag); I was too disappointed by the bright, sunny sky above the rocky peak. The photos had been posted the afternoon before the storm. It gave me no new information.

I opened the Sky Lodge homepage on the second monitor and clicked on the snow cam. It was almost a complete whiteout, but Juliette and Gavin returned, so I returned my attention to the room spreadsheets. Looking through the names of the guests was as fruitless as I'd expected. They were all generic names that blurred together and, even if there was something to jump out, the odds of me simply scrolling past it were high. I searched, on a whim, for Williams and

Humphreys, Holton and Clarke. Nothing. My only real thought was that were too many people named Dylan. Snowboarders. Eventually I swapped to the *Room Check* tab. There was a column for room numbers, a column for the number of beds booked, and a column titled *Accounted For* filled with a corresponding Y/N, seemingly in an attempt to verify who was present and identify any potentially missing person. I scanned the columns. They were all Y, everyone ticked off.

Juliette busied herself looking at the map of the mountain on the corkboard, but I could tell she was impatient, anxious to leave. Lucy was still missing, after all. "Anything?" she said eventually, deciding I'd had enough time. She leaned over my shoulder. "I had a friend in one of those schemes." I realized she was looking at Lucy's Instagram account on the other monitor; I'd left it showing the screenshot of her bank account. "It's all fake. They encourage people to photoshop these and post them so they look like they're making money. Even if the money's real, it never shows you how much they spend to get it. It's almost all their own coin, just coming back to them at a loss."

Erin had said that Michael shared Lucy's financial problems with her, that it was part of what had brought them closer. Then again, he'd summoned $267,000 from somewhere. Maybe they were both keeping their debts secret from each other.

I had one final scroll through the room list, hoping I'd land on something that would set off a spark. Dylans abounded. I reminded myself again that this was the party resort, the opposite to Sky Lodge. It was futile hunting for anyone associated with an historic crime from thirty-five years ago: no one over forty would dare set foot in this resort. It would be like taking a retirement cruise to Cancún.

Except . . .

"Gavin." Now I was hurriedly scrolling through the room spreadsheet. "You said there was an older couple here?"

"Yeah. They've holed up in their room. I think they booked the wrong resort, because, honestly, we get all sorts, but they're not really our clientele. We've been doing them room service, which we don't usually do, because I feel a bit bad, you know?"

"And I'll bet they tip," said Juliette.

"Like I said, not *really* our clientele."

"Room 1214?" I asked, already striding out of the office. "Can you show me?"

"Yeah, that's right actually," Gavin puffed, catching up both physically and mentally. Juliette and Andy followed. "Do you know them or something?"

I doubted the name on the spreadsheet meant anything to any of them. Twelve hours ago, it would have meant nothing to me too. But there are no coincidences, and it was written in the spreadsheet, plain as day.

We arrived at the door. To think, a spreadsheet had started this whole thing and now one was about to crack it wide open.

Room 1214, McAuley.

"Not yet," I said, knocking.

CHAPTER 34

Edgar and Siobhan McAuley were all too eager to invite me in when I introduced myself as a Cunningham. They were older than my mother but appeared more sprightly. Edgar had a bulbous whiskey drinker's nose and was wearing a lime-green polo shirt tucked into belted brown slacks. Siobhan was short, with a gleaming silver pixie cut and thin arms that reminded me of the frost-stripped tree branches on my drive up. She was wrapped in a Burberry scarf. Not Gavin's usual clientele indeed.

The room was narrow: one set of bunk beds on the left and a clothes rack (there was no room for a wardrobe) on the right, next to a lone chair, no desk. A suitcase, placed on top of a stack of books between the chair and the lower bunk bed, acted as a table, playing cards scattered on it. Nearer the entrance, there was a closet-sized bathroom. This resort had been built like a cruise ship: maximum occupancy in minimal space. The room smelled like everything else here: wet and damp. No ash in the air, as far as I could tell.

They fussed over us as we got settled, Edgar chattering about the storm, Siobhan clattering around with an electric kettle, apologizing that they only had two cups and so one of us would have to go without. Andy, who still had his beer bottle hanging from his fingertips, had raised it slightly to decline her offer. Juliette, Andy, and I took an awkward seat on the sagging bottom bunk, our knees near our chests. Gavin stood in the doorway.

Edgar took the solitary chair and leaned forward, his elbows on his knees. "We weren't sure we'd see anyone, with the storm and everything, so I can't tell you how thankful we are that you made it up here." His accent seemed like it was British trying to chase away Australian. Upper class, but trained to be so. "We hadn't heard from Michael—we thought you might be as stuck as we were, so we've just been waiting. Not our usual accommodation, obviously, but it's been a thrill, actually. Isn't that right, sweetie?" he called.

"Oh yes, love." She poked her head out of the bathroom, glasses fogged with steam from the kettle. "Sky Lodge's main house was booked out, and I'm getting on a bit to trudge through the snow from those lovely chalets. Michael thought it would be better if we stayed over here anyway, though it's been a while since I slept in a bunk bed. But why not? I suppose with what we're doing and everything, that makes it feel like more of an adventure."

I was thrown by the fact they were expecting Michael, and even more so by their attitude. I was expecting hostility, or even fear, but not . . . *excitement*? No one else in this room knew who the McAuleys were, so it was up to me to keep the conversation going, but I didn't know how. I could hardly come out with the fact the body of their long-dead daughter was just over the ridge.

"Well"—Edgar did it for me—"did you find her?"

That was enough for me to form a pretty good idea of what was going on. I thought I'd try to play along as best I could and see if my guesswork was correct. "Yes, we found her," I said, ignoring Andy's bulging eyes beside me. I could tell what he was thinking: *Who was she?* "There have been some complications, though."

"He wants more money again," Siobhan announced, emerging from the bathroom with two cups of scalding tea. But she didn't seem put off or offended at all, calmly handing us the mugs. "It's okay, love, we thought Michael might. We brought extra." She nudged their makeshift table-suitcase.

"Can you just . . ." I hesitated, not sure what to tell them. They seemed to not know Michael was dead. In fact, they thought I was here on his behalf. Then again, it could have been an act, in which case it would serve me better to keep some cards close to my chest and try to catch them in a lie. "Would you mind just helping me out with a few of the details first?" They looked confused at that, so I hurried an explanation, making my smile as relaxed and welcoming as I could, laughing it off. "It's just . . . family, you know? My brother gets me into stuff. Sends me up here without telling me much. I'm just trying to see that the price is fair. Not"—I waved my hand towards the suitcase, hoping to make them feel comfortable that I wasn't extorting them—"from you. Just family stuff, you know?" They still didn't look convinced, swapping side eyes at each other, so I threw in, "Like I said, we *have* found her."

That seemed to be a carrot well enough dangled, because Edgar said, "What do you want to know?"

I gambled. "How much have you given him so far?"

"Half," said Edgar.

I wanted to start with questions I thought I'd already guessed the answers to. Michael had clearly been the middleman between the McAuleys and Alan Holton—I'd figured that much out. It would have been the McAuleys' money in the bag, which was the reason no one—Lucy, Marcelo, the cops—had noticed it missing from Michael's accounts. I also suspected Michael was selling the McAuleys something he didn't have: he was going to use their down payment to pay Alan, get what he needed to sell on, and then collect the second half as his profit. But he'd gone to jail after the buy, and so hadn't been able to complete the deal until now. That was why he'd brought the bodies up the mountain. It was a trade.

There were still questions. I'd assumed Alan had been selling my father's final message, some incriminating evidence of Rebecca's kidnap and murder that Dad had died trying to pass to his handler, Alison Humphreys. It made sense that the McAuleys would want that, and would pay handsomely for it, but my father's message couldn't be the location of Rebecca's body, as my father had died before she'd been buried.

"Well, there's four hundred in there," Siobhan said unprompted, pointing to the suitcase and removing the need for me to ask for specifics. She gave Edgar an apologetic grimace, clearly not great at negotiating, and too impatient to hear about their daughter. "We added a hundred. For the photos."

The amounts added up. If the three hundred in the suitcase was the second half of the payment, it matched what I'd expected Alan's price would have been: the original ransom amount of $300,000. But my thoughts ran on with more questions: If Michael had gotten the money from the McAuleys, why had he been short? If they were able to offer an extra hundred grand for the photos, they'd have no incentive to stiff . . . Hang on . . . what photos?

"Hang on," I said. "What photos?"

Siobhan stuttered. "Michael said—"

"I'm sorry." Edgar leaned forward and dragged the suitcase towards him, the playing cards cascading off it. He kept one hand on it protectively, but I could see in his eyes a sliver of fear. He knew that if we wanted to take it, we would. And his wife had just told us how much was in it. They weren't used to dealing with criminals. Or Cunninghams. "Who did you say you were again?"

Siobhan straightened her back, to prove she wasn't intimidated. "Who are these people with you? And where's Michael?"

"Michael's dead."

That shocked them into silence.

"But he did find your daughter's body. I'll tell you where she is."

"Oh, thank God." Siobhan's relief was so physical that she gripped the side of the clothes rack to steady herself. "I'm sorry. I didn't mean to . . ."

"It's fine. You can even keep the money"—I felt Andy nudge me as I said this: *Are you sure, man?*—"but Michael's dead because of what he found. Whatever he dug up . . . someone else is trying to bury it. What you can do for me is help me fill in the blanks. Because whoever knows too much about your daughter seems to be in danger, and that includes me and my family. And now you, I suppose."

"Tell us how we can help," Edgar said. Siobhan nodded behind him. I could tell she didn't care about the risk, she just wanted to know about her daughter.

I desperately wanted to ask about the photographs, but knew I should start at the most logical place. "How did you meet Michael?"

"He came to us, actually," Edgar said. "He had some big story he was spinning and, honestly, it was nothing we hadn't seen before. For years we tried some private investigators, a few different ones with varying levels of legality, but they all got the same results: useless. We tried offering rewards, too, and, believe me, our phone rang then, so we know a con when we see one."

"But we haven't done that for twenty-eight years," Siobhan added. It struck me as a very specific number. "Now it's mostly people who want to make a movie, or a podcast, or write a book."

Edgar took over from his wife. "Michael was different, though. We knew that immediately. He told us some things about a policeman who worked on the original money drop, the one that went wrong. A guy named Alan Holton. Your brother said he knew where Rebecca was buried, and not only that, he had proof of who killed her."

"Photographs," I whispered, half to myself. Marcelo had thought my father had witnessed a murder, but, I realized now, he'd also recorded it. No wonder someone wanted the photos covered up.

"Of the murder. That's what he told us, anyway. He was supposed to bring them. Have you seen them?"

"Go back a bit. Alan Holton worked on your daughter's kidnapping?"

Siobhan nodded. "There were around fifty police officers. Plus the detective. I don't mean to be condescending, but this wasn't just any kidnapping."

I knew what she meant by that. Rich kids make the news.

"Did Michael show you the photos?" Edgar repeated himself, annoyed that I'd skipped his question the first time.

"No. I haven't seen them. But I think Michael has them, or had them, I guess. He was a careful man, my brother. He'll have put them somewhere safe—I just don't know where that is yet." I turned back to Siobhan. "Why now? You're willing to lay out seven hundred thousand dollars for this, so why not just pay the three hundred at the time? She might still be alive."

"He doesn't mean to be brash—we're short on time," Juliette chipped in apologetically.

"It's all right," Edgar said over his wife, frowning. "Time helps you value things differently. It's easy to see now that we made a mistake. Back then, we trusted the detective when she said that withholding payment was the right thing to do. And we—well, it seemed like a lot of money at the time. The thing is, we could have paid it. *Should have* paid it. We'd pay anything now."

"The detective, this was Alison Humphreys?"

Edgar and Siobhan both nodded. Andy tried to take a subtle sip of his beer, but missed his mouth and dribbled it down his front. He glowed red with embarrassment.

"Why didn't Alan just sell you the information directly?"

"We didn't know Michael had anything to do with Alan. He just told us Alan had screwed it up from the inside. We were buying what *Michael* knew."

"We didn't pay him to kill Alan, if that's what you mean," Siobhan cut in. "We read about that in the news. We're not like that."

"We guessed they were partners or something," Edgar explained. "Alan knew we were vulnerable, and he gave Michael enough information about our daughter to appeal to our sentimentality, which worked. But they had a falling-out over the money, as people tend to do. We figured our investment was probably down the drain." The word "investment" was a strange choice, but then so was a green polo shirt in the snow, so I thought it fit Edgar well enough.

"Until Michael wrote to us from prison," Siobhan said. "He said he had the photographs and, by the time he got up here, he'd have the body too. And so we're here."

"Honoring our end," Edgar said, the gravitas in his voice making it clear that he wanted me to respect this.

Credit to Michael; it seemed like pretty easy money. The only problem was, he had showed up to meet Alan thirty-three thousand dollars light. He'd told me it was the reason that Alan pulled a gun. I thought I might just understand that part, and it didn't involve the McAuleys. I tucked the thought away to examine later and turned my mind to the other players.

Detective Humphreys, for her part, had led an operation that had resulted in Rebecca's death, a high-profile case. She must have been clutching at straws to keep her job, that's why she'd pushed Robert Cunningham so hard, reneging on the original deal and asking, as Marcelo put it, two more questions for every answer. Alison was desperate to find out which officer had been double-crossing her team. The answer was Alan Holton and his partner Brian

Clarke. My father had found that out the hard way. Maybe Alison had opened up the cold case, eighteen months ago. Maybe that was why she'd been attacked?

There were still gaps in my narrative—Alan and Brian were dead, so they couldn't be killing anyone over the photographs—but something was emerging, like a chairlift pillar through the fog.

"Michael was the second death at Sky Lodge," I said, returning from my thoughts to see Edgar and Siobhan gazing expectantly at me. "Maybe, if they're linked, you'll recognize the first victim too. Perhaps someone else who helped with the kidnapping negotiations. Juliette, would you mind showing them the photo?"

"I don't have the photo," Juliette apologized. "I haven't even seen it—after I checked everyone off my guest list, there wasn't any need, as none of our staff or guests were missing. Crawford was only showing select guests who'd cause the least panic. I was not on that list, apparently."

I turned back to the McAuleys. "Did you have anyone up here with you? Friends? Hired security?"

"Just us," Edgar said.

"That's enough. *Where's our daughter?*" Siobhan finally let it all out in a wail, unable to wait any longer for me to answer. "Take it. Take it!" She thrust the suitcase at me, but I pushed it back a little too hard and she stumbled backwards. She didn't fall (the room was too small for that), but she bounced lightly off the wall and then cradled the case to her chest, deflated. "That's all we know, we swear. We just want to put her to rest. Even if we never find who did this to her, we just want to bury her. Please."

"She was buried in a policeman's coffin—that's how they hid her. They must have paid off the coroner." I knew this was hard for them to hear, so I let them have a moment to digest it, and for me to build up the courage to tell them the bad news. "Unfortunately, that coffin is now at the bottom of Sky Lodge lake."

Siobhan gasped, tears brimming.

"We can hire divers, honey," Edgar consoled her.

"Pretty morbid, buying your daughter's corpse," Juliette said, unprompted.

"Pretty morbid selling it," Edgar replied.

I gestured for Andy and Juliette to stand up. We hauled ourselves off the bunk bed. Edgar and Siobhan had collapsed into a hug. I was loath to interrupt them, and after Juliette's comment they'd surely want us out, but there was still something I needed to know. "I'm sorry to put you through this, but I have one more question for you. Did my stepfather come to visit you, two nights ago? A heavyset South American man? His name's Marcelo."

"No." Edgar shook his head. "But a woman named Audrey did."

CHAPTER 35

Andy took the front seat as we bounced back over the ridge. Juliette sat across from me in the back, like we'd been arrested. Gavin was driving for speed this time, which made it a teeth-rattling ride. None of us bothered to look out the windows.

"So your mother knows more than she's saying," Juliette surmised.

Before we left, I'd asked Gavin if I could check the security cameras in case there was anything in the footage. He'd said, "Mate, my bar's cash only," as if it explained the lack of technology, and left it at that.

"I don't understand it," I replied.

"Add it to the list." She tapped a finger to her lips. "I downloaded your book last night. Your mum got a twin?"

Was she trying to impress me? That was Rule 10: identical twins must be duly prepared for. "Knox would kill me."

Juliette laughed, then rested her forehead against the window, her eyes darting across the blinding snow. Her breath was foggy in front of her. "We should leave."

I knew what she was really saying. If Lucy was out in the storm, she was already dead. People die in horror movies by splitting up, but that's not how people die on mountains: they die by going back for each other. We were at the point where we had to save ourselves.

I leaned forward. I didn't have to keep my voice that low—the roar of the Oversnow would drown me out unless I deliberately shouted at the driver, but I wanted the physical hint of secrecy. "Is Gavin trying to buy Sky Lodge?"

Juliette frowned. "How did you know that?"

"I saw a real estate agreement on your desk, but it's unsigned. Gavin has a map of your resort pinned to his corkboard. No one's hiding it. But if you'll excuse the guesswork, I figure you guys have, let's say, *different* business ideals, judging by the dust on his expensive computer and the look on your face walking through the party. It seems to me that he works less hard but makes more money. That pisses you off, so you're holding out on the sale."

I'd overplayed my hand to show off my deductions. Maybe I was trying to impress her too.

"He doesn't want Sky Lodge," she said. "He just wants the land. He'll knock it down just to put another SuperShred on this side of the ridge. That way he has both valleys. It sounds stupid when we're talking about mill— well, a lot of money, but it's got no charm." She looked out the window again.

The lights of the guesthouse were coming into view. I weighed up how I felt returning to this advent calendar house versus driving through the collection of airport hangars that made up SuperShred. It didn't sound so stupid after all.

She was clearly thinking the same thing. "I told you I came back after my family died, and I wound up getting stuck here. That happens in this life, you know? The mountain kind of holds on. And business was booming, but then we had a couple of warm winters—everyone's saying we're going to have more than a couple more." She paused. "I can't afford to put in those big ice blasters Gav has.

So when he made an offer, a good offer, I was glad of it. Gav and I go way back. We're both kids of resort families."

"Whistler?"

"Whistler." She smiled in memory. "He's a good guy, you know? And he was offering me a lifeline." She read my thoughts and raised an eyebrow. "He wants my land, but it's not like he'd do anything to get it."

Money is, of course, all too common a motive. I hadn't focused too hard on Sofia, as fifty thousand seemed a small amount to kill over, but if this land was worth millions . . .

"So I agreed," she continued. "Back when I thought he'd just keep running the hotel. It was exciting—I was free of this . . . legacy, I guess. But when it came time to sign and I learned that he wanted to knock it all down, well, legacy is the right word after all, isn't it?" Her breath plumed as she sighed. "That building is a lot of history to walk away from. My family's in those walls."

I considered why Gavin had been so keen to get Juliette to his office. Him telling her it would be *worth her while*. "He's upped his offer? Just now?"

She nodded. "He's got a new investor."

"I'll bet he does," I said. "You're considering it?"

"After this weekend . . ." She looked out the window again and the sentence finished itself in her silence.

"Holy shit," Andy piped up from the front. He was rubbing his forearm against the fog on the front windshield. Through the whorl, I could see a large smudge, the size of which could only be Marcelo, waving his arms above his head like he was landing a plane. Behind him shimmered a bright red flare, lodged into the snow around the side of the building. There were more shadows huddled around it. One crouching. "I think they've found her."

*

Lucy must have been there all night, given several feet of snow had banked up on top of her. I could only see her hand, pale white and cold, reaching out from the mound.

No one had tried to dig her out. There was a small excavation above her torso, a hole just big enough to look into, reach in and check a pulse. That showed how quickly the dig was abandoned. If there'd have been any hope at all, the hole would have been bigger.

The flicker of the red flare blooded the snow around us. I leaned forward, saw a quick glimpse of Lucy, and pulled away. Her fluorescent lipstick was even brighter against her blood-drained face. She was still wearing the yellow turtleneck she'd worn yesterday. Nothing that would keep her warm outside. There was a crown of crimson-stained ice behind and above her head. Crucially, there was no ash on her face. I felt sick. Did anyone tell her the Drying Room wasn't locked?

"I only found her because I stood on her hand . . ." Katherine started. It was her, Sofia, and Crawford standing around the body. Audrey was keeping warm inside and, after Marcelo had flagged us down, he had gone to join her. I wasn't sure where Erin was.

"Fill in the hole," Juliette said.

Everyone looked at her strangely; it seemed such a callous thing to say.

"We have to leave. We can't take the bodies with us—we can come back when the snow's cleared. So we should cover her up, to protect her from animals." She leaned over and scooped a mound of snow into Lucy's impromptu grave with her forearm. I helped cascade in more. "Gavin, how long until we can leave?"

It was unfair of her to ask him to take us all down the mountain, but I knew Gavin was obliged to do Juliette a couple of favors if he wanted her to consider his offer on her hotel.

"I'll need to refuel. Will take a few," he said.

"Are you saying—" Andy began.

"Everyone start packing your stuff. We're leaving."

I was grateful for Juliette's firmness. Searching for Lucy had been the only thing stopping us leaving. We weren't really trapped by the storm, as happens so frequently in these types of novels. We weren't *trapped* at all. But we were chained by our own egos, our regrets, our shame, and our stubbornness. It was time to swallow that. This is about the right time for an exodus anyway, I figure, being six chapters from the end.

I patted down another armful of snow. That would be enough to shield Lucy from the elements. She hadn't deserved this. She'd only come on this trip to try to win Michael back. She'd *wanted* to be a Cunningham. That was why she was here. Divorce or not, she was family, but we hadn't treated her like it. We'd ignored her for the first half of the weekend. Then Audrey had let her take the blame for Michael's death, loaded the guilt on her. And none of us had followed her to the roof. She had died alone. Some family. It's hard to cry when tears freeze on your face.

Lucy's hand stretched out from the snowdrift, palm to the sky, and I realized she was still wearing her wedding ring. I couldn't decide whether it was more respectful to take it off and keep it, or to leave it on her. I decided I didn't want to grapple with her frozen fingers, so I scooped a mound of snow over her hand. Then I took off my beanie, bracing against the chill that scraped my scalp, and stole an abandoned ski pole leaning against the side of the lodge. I staked it on top of the snow, the beanie on top, so that we could find her again when the storm had passed.

"We'll come back and get you," I said to the mound. Someone put an arm around me, but in the wind, I didn't even see who it was.

We all headed inside. I knew I'd have to go and get the bag of money from my chalet before we left, and I should have been thinking about how to get my mother alone to question her about the McAuleys, but at that moment I didn't really care: I just wanted to leave. I needed to warm up, find another painkiller somewhere.

I finally understood what it was like to be an addict; I would have given the whole bag of cash for something to dull my thoughts and my hand. I trudged after everyone else into the restaurant.

Erin, it turned out, had been inside the whole time, replacing the staff Juliette had sent home. She'd cooked us all lunch. I took a bowl of chicken and corn soup with desperate gratitude and sat down next to Sofia at an empty table. Someone had gone to find my mother, to convince her we were leaving. Before eating, I held my face over the soup, thawing myself in the steam until the tip of my nose singed.

"There's no ash," I said to Sofia after a few mouthfuls, shaking my head. "Not like the others."

Sofia grimaced, understanding my question even though I hadn't asked it. She explained simply: "She would've broken a lot of bones."

Sofia looked out the restaurant doors into the foyer, and I saw her eyes trail up the staircase. I'd been wrong about Juliette's dark suspicion in the rattling Oversnow. Andy had said, "In this weather . . . that would be suicide." The photo of Green Boots that Sofia had shown Lucy was a detailed depiction of what had happened to Michael, and Lucy had already been struggling with the knowledge that she had put him in a room he couldn't get out of. Crucially, Lucy had stormed out of the bar *before* Audrey had interrogated Crawford on specifics. The last time anyone had seen Lucy, she was climbing the stairs, guilt-ridden. To the roof. Juliette had meant that we needed to catch her before she hurt herself in the storm. But Lucy hadn't needed a storm. The guesthouse roof was high enough.

Sofia and I let the sad understanding settle over us: no one had told Lucy that Michael's room wasn't locked. That it wasn't her fault.

The title of this book is true: everyone in my family *has* killed someone.

It's just that not all of them killed other people.

CHAPTER 36

I assume my mother was quite the thorn in many a bulldozer's side in the 1970s, if the gusto with which she chained herself to her bedpost was anything to go by. Marcelo had come into the restaurant, where we'd all spent the last hour piling our bags in the center of the room (I had braved the storm once more, and folded the sports bag inside my wheelie case), and shaken his head. Katherine and I, volunteered by virtue of being the closest remaining relatives, had trudged up to the third floor to find Audrey propped up on pillows, one arm chained to the bedpost. I say chained: she'd lifted the gormless Crawford's handcuffs from his hip. It looked a very comfortable protest.

It was an unspoken agreement that Katherine, being the less hated, would take the lead. She held out a hand. "Don't be ridiculous, Audrey. Where's the key?"

My mother shrugged.

"The guy with the snow-truck can take us now or not at all. You're putting all of us in danger."

"So go."

"You know that's not fair. We can't leave you here. What if the storm gets worse? Your family's in danger. *People are dying.*"

"It sounds to me like you'll be taking the killer down the mountain with you. I'm not leaving Michael here to rot."

"We'll come back and get him when we're safe, when the weather's settled."

Marcelo hovered behind us, assumedly having already tried most of Katherine's arguments himself. Katherine was getting more frustrated, her voice rising in pitch, leaving behind the rational arguments and pulling out words like "selfish" and "difficult" and "silly woman" while yanking at the bedpost to see if it came apart at the joints. In normal circumstances, calling my mother a "right bitch" would have been cataclysmic, but Audrey simply turned her head. From the grimace on Marcelo's face, he'd tried that approach too.

"I need a screwdriver or, hang on"—she squinted at the frame—"an Allen wrench," Katherine said to Marcelo, turning from the bedpost, disgusted. "Four hundred bucks a night and it's IKEA." Then to Audrey, a threat: "We'll carry you out of here."

Marcelo, glad of the escape, left to find the tool.

"My son is dead," was all Audrey said. "I won't leave him."

That it was the same thing she'd said in the bar, when Sofia and Crawford had been explaining the murder, made me snap. I'd begged to be considered a real Cunningham since we'd got here. I'd cared more about that than Green Boots, than Michael even. Finding the killer was not about justice: it was a chance to prove myself, a sycophantic appeal to my mother that I was worthy of my own name. But my mother, in her oft-repeated distress over Michael's death, didn't even consider that there was a woman, dead in the snow outside, who was a part of this family too. Regardless of names or divorce contracts, Marcelo had acknowledged that: *It's all of us or none of us*. My mother, for all her insistence, didn't know what family meant.

"Your son?" I shocked Audrey and Katherine by yelling. Marcelo told me later he'd heard me down the hall. My anger was more pent up than I'd realized. "Your son? How about my sister—your *daughter.* 'In-law' is just a word. You know Lucy's outside in the snow? You know that she died because of how *you* made her feel. Because of how you loaded her up with guilt over Michael's death. She's dead the same as he is, and all you can say is *your son.*"

"Ern." Katherine tried to step in front of me, but I was advancing on my mother, incensed. My mother, for her part, didn't flinch.

"No, Katherine. We've indulged this for too long." I turned to my mother. "You put your hurt above everyone else's. You raised us in pain because *your* husband died. You cast me aside because of what I did to *your* family. Well, it's my family too." I softened, because despite my anger, I had come to understand her better. I sat on the bed. "I know it was hard. After you lost Dad, you had to do it all on your own. And I know you started to define yourself because of your name, because of what people thought of Dad, and I know that the only way to deal with that was to turn inwards, to make that name your own. But in doing so, you started to live up to the label that other people made for you. Cunningham doesn't mean what you think it does. I know"—I surprised myself by picking up her hand; she let me take it, limp—"what Dad was trying to do when he died."

My mother's eyes were glassy, but her jaw was firm. It was hard to tell whether she felt threatened or understood. I held her gaze, refusing to break first. "You do?" she said.

"I know about Rebecca McAuley. I know Dad had photographs implicating someone in her kidnapping, and probably her murder. I know Alan Holton was crooked. I know why you were so hurt that I took the law's side over Michael's. It took me a long time to see it through your eyes, but now I can. I know you went to visit Rebecca's parents, two nights ago, when you canceled dinner claiming to be sick. You told them to go home." I recited everything the McAuleys had told me, about my mother appearing at their door two nights ago. "You threatened them, Audrey. You asked if they had more children, if those children had grandchildren. Those people *lost a child*. How dare you use what happened to Rebecca as a threat. *How dare you*."

"I didn't threaten them," Audrey said quietly. "I *explained* what the risks were."

"They know the risks. They lost a daughter." I took a deep breath, and then took the plunge with something I thought I'd figured out. "Just like you lost Jeremy."

"You don't know what you're talking about," she said through gritted teeth.

"It was something Siobhan McAuley said," I plowed on. "That they hadn't hired private investigators for the last twenty-eight years. That struck me as a very specific number. Rebecca was kidnapped thirty-five years ago, which means the difference is seven years. That's the same amount of time you waited to have Jeremy's funeral. Seven years. There are no coincidences—those timings are the same for a reason. That's how long it takes to declare a person legally dead, isn't it?"

"What are you saying, Ern?" Katherine said over my shoulder.

Audrey stared at me, jaw trembling, but stayed silent.

"You let something else slip too, when we last talked in the library." I ignored Katherine and held my mother's gaze. "You said our family had to pay the price for Dad's actions. But you also said that he'd left us without a weapon to fight with. Your exact words were 'nothing in the bank.' I thought you meant money, but you didn't, did you? You know about the photographs—that was the weapon you were talking about. If the Sabers, or whoever the Sabers were protecting, didn't get them from Dad the night he died, it makes sense that they might assume that you had them. That they might target, say, the bank you worked at, where it was likely Dad kept a safety box."

"You don't understand. They will do *anything* to keep this quiet. Robert's photographs—*no one* ever found them. I wish they'd found what they were looking for, some yellow envelope stamped with *In the event of my death please send to the media*, some kind of clue. Anything. I wanted them to find it. I really did. I searched *everywhere* for those goddamn photos."

"But the Sabers didn't come up empty from the bank, did they? They might not have found the photographs, but as they escaped from the rooftop car park, I think they found the next best thing: sitting in a car. They decided there was only one way to be sure you didn't have the photographs. Leverage. A guarantee that, if you had the photos, you'd give them up in a heartbeat. And we all knew they had no problem taking children—Rebecca is proof of that. Seven years, Audrey."

My mother hung her head. Gave up.

"They took Jeremy from the car," she whispered. I heard Katherine inhale sharply behind me. I let the quiet expand until my mother was ready to continue. She spoke into her lap. "Alan was their messenger. All they wanted was the photographs, he said, not money. And I couldn't tell the police, because that Humphreys woman had gotten Robert *and* Rebecca killed already, hadn't she? And Alan was clearly playing both sides—who knew who else was? I had to protect you and Michael."

"There must have been an investigation, though?" I prompted gently, worried that even the slightest rise in volume might break my mother's confessional trance. Nobody was moving. Katherine had stopped looking for the handcuff key.

"Of course. They treated it as a missing person. Whether it was because they were in on it, I don't know, but it looked like Jeremy had gotten out of the car to go and get help for you and Michael. I had to play along with it. I cut my forehead on the glass but the window was already broken. A five-year-old wouldn't get far, they kept saying. And then, as more days passed, I could tell they'd changed their thinking from *not getting far* to *not lasting long* and they're running a search that I know is a dead end. Meanwhile Alan keeps on asking me for the photographs, and I tell him I don't have them, that I can't find them. And he says he believes me . . ." She looked up at me, and her eyes were red rimmed. "He says *he* believes me, but there's only one way to be sure I wasn't keeping the photos to myself. They had to know for sure . . ."

She trailed off, but her meaning was clear. The only way to be sure Audrey wasn't hiding the photos was to carry through on their threat, and to leave the threat lingering for her two remaining children. I felt sick at the thought of Jeremy buried in another policeman's coffin. It occurred to me that I didn't know for sure the child's body I'd found was Rebecca's.

"I never meant to take sides, Mum." I reflected on her telling me I'd been making the same mistakes my father had, and I understood her a little better now. I felt her hand, until now only resting on mine, clasp tightly. "I was trying to do what was right. But there's *right* and then there's right for us. I didn't know you'd had to pay so high a price."

It's all well and good for the heroes to play cops and robbers in novels and on TV, but in real life it's the side characters, the Cunninghams, who take the blows, who bear the pain, so someone else can raise their arms aloft in victory. My father had tried to do the "right thing." And it had cost him. It hadn't cost the rich couple grieving their stolen child. It hadn't cost the detective, pushing her informant with a promotion in mind. And so, for Audrey, there was no longer right or wrong. There was family, and there was everything else. Maybe she did know what it meant after all. I squeezed her hand back.

"Marcelo knows?" I asked.

"Only later."

"You never told me," Katherine said. It was hard to tell if she was offended at being left out or trying to defend herself from an interrogation.

"I don't remember much of that morning." I kept my attention on Audrey.

"You were too young. There was something in there, all scrambled up, but you'd listen to what I told you. And I told everyone, including you, Katherine, that Jeremy died in the car because it was easiest, and because I worried if there were too many questions Alan would come back for you or Michael. I'll be honest—I didn't mind the blame. Ironically, if the Sabers hadn't broken the window to take Jeremy, all three of you might have died. So it felt like I deserved it."

"And then seven years later, Marcelo helped you privately take care of the legal side of things. When you had the funeral. You let him in on the secret. Is that right?"

"Yes. He sorted that out, helped finalize Robert's will, all that stuff. I have some more things I need to tell you, I suspect. But not here. I can't think straight. Let's get off this mountain. The key's in the bible."

Katherine rummaged in the bedside table for the bible, flicking open the pages until a small silver key fell out. She unlocked my mother from the bedframe and was helping her up off the bed, when Audrey shooed her away and instead reached out for my assistance. I leaned in, offering my shoulder as she stood, her weight pressing down on me.

"I just wanted to warn the McAuleys," she said. "These people have no problem killing kids. It doesn't matter if they want ransom or leverage. I'm sorry they took it as a threat."

I didn't reply, just gave her a hug that I hoped conveyed my understanding. I was glad we could now leave, and once we were down the mountain, we could begin to heal. Apart from the murders, it had been a successful reunion after all.

Illuminating as hearing Audrey's side of the story was, I was still plagued by niggling questions.

If Rebecca McAuley wasn't the Sabers' only victim, how could I be sure it was her body in the coffin? And how the hell did Alan Holton get a hold of something my mother couldn't find for him thirty-five years ago?

I told Katherine I'd meet them downstairs after she helped Audrey pack, and headed after Marcelo, questions brewing. I was distracted passing the library on the first floor. The fire still sizzled in the hearth at the back of the room, the warmth bracing my cheeks, beading sweat on my brow. Or maybe the heat was coming from my stomach, crawling up my neck. Because intuition was telling me that little pieces of the mystery were coming together, but not yet into a whole. I browsed the shelves of Golden Age mysteries. Audrey had put Mary Westmacott in the wrong spot, hiding under a different name in the Ws, so I moved her back to the Cs. I ran my thumb over the spines, perhaps seeking inspiration for a denouement. Knox didn't have a rule against it, but in all the books in front of me, it was implied that the detective didn't simply give up and head down the mountain at the end.

But those detectives were smarter than I was. I had no author pulling my marionette strings, no gifts bestowed upon me. I would not qualify for the Detection Club. I remember thinking the only thing I was sure of was that I was missing something. Something small. That there's always one thing in these books that unlocks everything else, and it is so often the smallest of things. There was something I couldn't see. Not without a good old-fashioned Holmesian magnifying glass, anyway. Or a loupe.

And then I solved it.

In these kinds of books, there's often some impressive

metaphorical illustration of the deductive moment. The detective will be sitting and thinking, and maybe the jigsaw in their head slowly locks into place, or maybe it's fireworks, or dominoes; maybe they're stumbling down a dark corridor and they finally find the switch. Either way, the information collides in a fascinating waterfall of discovery that compels them to the Eureka moment. I promise you it is not so dramatic in reality. One second I didn't know the answer, and the next I did. I checked my suspicion by walking to the mantel, and then I was sure.

To keep Ronald Knox happy—since all clues lighted upon must be presented to the reader—here are the clues I used to put it together: Mary Westmacott; fifty-thousand dollars; my jaw; my hand; Sky Lodge's snow cams; Sofia's malpractice suit; a Brisbane PO box; Lucy cocking an imaginary gun against her head; a double-occupancy coffin; vomit; a speeding fine; a handbrake; a loupe; physiotherapy; an unsolved assault; a chivalrous and shivering husband; "the boss"; a jacket; footprints; Lucy's nervous wait; a pyramid scheme; sore toes; my chalet's phone; my dreams of choking; Michael's newfound pacifism; and F-287: a dead pigeon with a medal for bravery.

Katherine announced her arrival with the multiple thunks of a suitcase being dragged down stairs. She noticed me and stopped, suitcase and my mother tailing her, either to ask for a hand or to tell me to stop lollygagging, but I never found out because I cut her off.

"Will you gather everyone?" I asked. "I need to tell them something. I need everyone, because I still have questions for some of them. And so no one runs."

Katherine nodded, picking up on my tone. "Where?"

I looked around at the bookshelves, the crackling fire, and the plush red leather chairs. "If we get out of here alive enough to sell our story, I'd say Hollywood would be pretty pissed if we didn't use the library, don't you think?"

CHAPTER 37

Marcelo and Audrey took the leather chairs, like royalty in thrones. Crawford and Juliette stood at the back, either side of the fireplace, having learned, from spending a weekend amid Cunningham family affairs, the meaning of the phrase "safe distance." Katherine stood, leaning her arm against the back of Audrey's chair. Andy sat on a side table, though he seemed to lack structural confidence in it, keeping his knees high and holding most of his weight on the balls of his feet. Sofia sat on the floor. It was like another wedding tableau, similar to yesterday morning on the steps outside, except later in the night when the party has thinned out, everyone's nose is booze-red, their clothes a little tattered, their hands smashed and stuffed into oven mitts. Gavin had been excused, innocent by virtue of Rule 1, and was loading our bags into the Oversnow. I made sure to block the doorway, because the killer always tries to make a break for it once they've been revealed.

The rush of discovery had faded somewhat, and now I had to figure out how best to present my accusations so that they made logical sense. It was hard to find a place to start: there were plenty of killers in the room, but only one murderer.

"Well?" Marcelo spoke first, his impatience betraying his curiosity. That gave him the short straw. I'd start with him.

"It's time we all came clean about why we're here," I said. I took the GPS out of my pocket and tossed it to Marcelo.

It took him a moment to realize what it was. I could tell he was about to ask me where I got it, but then he remembered meeting me out in the snow, handing me the device in front of his broken window.

"You're Gavin's new investor for buying this place. Of course you are—you're the only one here with enough money, and how else could Katherine convince you to come and spend a weekend here? You hate the cold more than Sofia does; you've been grumbling about it the whole time. That's part of the reason you were so annoyed at Katherine putting us all up in the chalets: you knew Gavin wanted to knock down the guesthouse, but you wanted to see what the rooms were like, to figure out if it was worth keeping."

"I am working on a business relationship while I'm here, sure. I noticed the place was for sale when Katherine booked it in. Does it matter?" Marcelo barked his defense, so accustomed to doing the accusing instead of being the accused. He was staunch, chest puffed in outrage.

"It doesn't. But your first lie was that Audrey was ill for dinner two nights ago," I said. "Did it seem strange that she asked you to lie about it and then asked to come with you for your meeting with Gavin?" I already knew it was because Audrey wanted an alibi to give to Michael, after she'd, hopefully, convinced the McAuleys to flee. Marcelo would back up her claims of being sick, and she would be able to skip away from dinner. I could see the doubt in Marcelo's eyes as he looked at his wife.

Eventually he cleared his throat and said, "I haven't killed anybody."

"Well, that's another lie, isn't it?"

"I never touched Michael. Or Lucy. Or that bloke in the snow."

"That's not what I said."

"Enlighten me then. Who am I supposed to have killed?"

"Me."

MY STEPFATHER (again)

CHAPTER 38

The water had been heart-stoppingly cold when I went into the lake, remember? Juliette had to resuscitate me with CPR. It's a technicality, sure, but an honest one.

"Let's think about what we know," I said. "We all know that Michael killed a man named Alan Holton. *Some* of us know that Alan Holton is the man who shot my father, Robert. *Very few* of us know that the reason my father was killed was because he was working undercover for the police. His last snitch, his final message to deliver to Detective Humphreys—"

"Did you say Humph—" Erin started, quick to assemble the pieces I was laying out, the name ringing a bell as one of the Black Tongue's victims.

"I did. Try not to get ahead of me." I smiled. "Robert's last message was incriminating photographs of a murder, which we'll get to. They were never found, despite both Alan's and Audrey's best efforts. And then three years ago Alan suddenly has them, and they're for sale. Marcelo, you're the one who tried to stop me finding out about it."

Marcelo's fingers squeaked against the leather arm of the chair as his grip tightened. He didn't speak. He was letting me get it all out, seeing how much I knew. He didn't want to come in early and fill in any blanks for me, in case he needed to call my bluff. It didn't matter, I knew I was right.

"Marcelo, you're the one who set up Robert's deal with Detective Humphreys, and you saw firsthand how that went wrong. Audrey had also told you about what the Sabers did to Jeremy when you helped finalize the legal side of his death. This meant you knew just how dangerous whatever Michael had could be for whoever had it." Most of the room didn't know what I was referring to, but I was focused on speaking only to Marcelo. "When you saw Michael's filthy hands, his ridiculous choice of vehicle, you suspected he'd dug something up. And you'd always suspected this had something to do with Rebecca McAuley. You didn't know what Michael had, but you were worried that people were about to start dying for the same reason Robert did all those years ago. You wanted to get rid of whatever he had." I let that sink in. "But . . . you didn't do it to cover your own tracks. You did it to protect Michael, didn't you?"

Marcelo sank deeper into his chair. "I didn't mean to hurt you. I just wanted it to roll down the hill. I thought it would look like an accident," he admitted. "It was an old model, so I could get in with a coat hanger through the window and lift the handbrake, but I didn't have the keys to start the engine, so I poured some hot coffee under the wheels to melt the snow. I was interrupted by Crawford running up to get you lot out of the maintenance shed, so I had to leave it before I could push it down the slope."

I heard Erin's voice in my head—*There's some brown shit on the ground, maybe brake fluid*—and remembered the empty coffee cup sitting on the lip of the rear door. "I didn't think anyone would get in the back and jump around. I'm sorry about your hand. I swear, I was just trying to stop you from knowing what was really in there. Hell, I didn't even know what it was! I was scared by the body on the slope that morning, and when you asked me about Humphreys,

I knew something was coming. I wanted to be able to wash our hands of it, for whoever this was to feel their secret was hidden and safe. I just wanted it to end. I swear on my life."

"Or mine, as it would happen."

"I sat with you until you woke up," Marcelo said, looking more embarrassed at having his kindness revealed than when I was accusing him of covering up a murder. "I don't know what I would have done if you hadn't. I'm sorry."

"Who's Rebecca McAuley again?" Andy actually put his hand up. "Is this something to do with that old couple with all the cash?" He looked around sheepishly. "What? I'm confused!"

"I'm getting ahead of myself." I decided to leave Marcelo alone. "Again, let's ask ourselves why we're here. A reunion, sure. One big happy family." The sarcasm dripped through my teeth. "But we're *here* because one of us picked it. Isn't that right, Katherine?" I turned to her. "You deliberately chose the most isolated place you could find. No getting out of here easily. And you've been outspoken that we should stay—sure, we all know how you feel about non-refundable deposits, but there's more to it than that, isn't there?"

"Not in front of everyone, Ern," Katherine said, but her tone wasn't guilty or threatening; it sounded compassionate—embarrassed even—on behalf of someone else. "Come on."

"Katherine, if this doesn't make sense, nothing does. It's time to put everything on the table. And that includes you. Because *you* broke into Sofia's chalet the night that Green Boots died. You or Andy. It doesn't matter who, but let's just say it was you for the sake of reason. I initially thought it very good luck that the snow cam didn't catch whoever broke into Sofia's chalet. That camera takes a photo every three minutes, so it would require a conscious effort, and good timing, to avoid it. Of course, you're the type of person who checks the weather for the weekend. You're the most organized here, you would have looked at that website fifty times before leaving home. Which means that you knew there was a snow cam, and you knew to time your movements around it so you didn't get caught."

Katherine swapped a guilty look with Andy.

"So why break in? You were looking for something in Sofia's chalet. And when you found it, you dialed Andy to tell him you had it, or perhaps so he could tell you the time, so you'd know when the snow cam refreshed and you could make a break for it. But you forgot we'd switched cabins, so you called the wrong room. So the question is, what were you looking for?" I held up my oven mitt. "Those pills are dynamite, by the way. Oxycodone, was it?"

Katherine shot an apologetic look over to Sofia.

"You don't take painkillers, Katherine—you never have since your car crash. Your personal pain is a penance for the hurt you've caused, and you wouldn't fall off the wagon so easily. So why do you have a bottle of powerful painkillers? I'm thankful for them, by the way, but they're not yours. Oxy is the drug most doctors get hooked on, right? It's powerful and it's not too hard to get in a hospital." I shook the bottle and the pills clattered accusingly.

"I took them from Sofia's chalet," Katherine said. "I don't give a rat's about refunds. We couldn't leave early because Sofia *needs* to be here. And she needs all four days. She's detoxing."

Everyone turned to look at Sofia, pale and tired. She simply hung her head in shame.

"Her health has been deteriorating the longer she's gone without the pills. Her hands have been shaking, for one thing," I said, recalling her rattling coffee cup in the bar. "She's been vomiting, pale, and sweaty since yesterday morning."

I'll interrupt myself here to head off a possible complaint. I'll clarify that I never said you *shouldn't* pay attention to Sofia's vomiting in Chapter 7. I just told you it didn't mean she was pregnant. I will not be accused of hoodwinking.

"I'm guessing, Sofia, that you're a high-functioning addict. After all, you continued to work, even operate. And you told me yourself they don't test doctors like they test athletes, that even after a death it's not mandatory. But you got scared after that surgery went wrong. And you were flagged—for the wrong reason, a glass of wine at a bar, but flagged all the same. Because what the coroner does look for is patterns. Maybe there are other incidents, smaller, everyday ones that can't be helped, around you. Maybe, like each individual fleck of snow that falls on this mountain, they are not so damning on their own, but together, a picture starts to build. So Sofia approached you, Katherine, because her addiction was spiraling, and she knew she was under a closer watch and that she'd fail a drug test if the coroner called for one," I continued. "If she shows up to court next week with oxy in her system, she'll stand no chance." Sofia had jokingly asked me if I was free next week, when I was planning out how to be Michael's faux-lawyer, inadvertently revealing the timing. "So this weekend is her last chance to get clean. That's why you've been so snappy with her. That first breakfast you went out of your way to enforce that she wasn't a doctor, because by then you'd already searched her room and found the pills. You were upset that she'd hidden them from you, but you were also trying to scare her into understanding what's on the line: her whole career, her whole identity. You asked Marcelo to cut her off too—that's why he's refusing to help her. Though he will if he has to, we all know that. But for this weekend, you needed to scare her straight. You tried to get me to doubt her too. She had to feel like she was on her own."

Marcelo gave a gentle, apologetic nod to Sofia. I'd figured that one out because of what he'd admitted when I'd accused him of playing favorites between Michael and Sofia. He'd stammered out: *That's not entirely true*. Michael had told me that Robert and Audrey had used the same tactic on Katherine all those years ago:

cutting her off. It was also the advice Katherine had given Michael to try on Lucy's financial issues. A last resort.

"Back to the pills, Katherine. You locked them in your car to keep them safe. But Sofia"—she was still looking down at her lap, shoulders shuddering with silent tears—"wasn't done. She tried to get the pills back. Sofia, when you told me you saw someone at the maintenance shed, you *couldn't* have seen them from the bar. That storm was a whiteout: I'd been sitting by the window myself and couldn't see into the car park. Which means you had to be *in* the parking lot to see Erin go into the maintenance shed. Katherine's window wasn't broken by the storm, it was broken by you, desperately trying to get the pill bottle you thought she'd locked in her car. But Katherine had sent Andy out into the storm to get her bag earlier. She suspected you'd try something like that, so she changed her mind and wanted them on her at all times. Which is also why she wouldn't let me keep the bottle overnight."

I knelt in front of Sofia and put a hand on her shoulder, squeezing gently. "I'm not saying all this for no reason, Sofia. We will help you through this. But I need you to be honest with me with this next question."

She looked up at me, eyes bloodshot, and dragged her forearm under her nose. "I swear. I did that surgery the same way I would have done any other. It's like the story of the drunk pilot who lands the plane, you know? I didn't"—she hiccupped—"I don't know what happened. It just went wrong. Since then, Katherine's been helping me. I want to get better."

"I know." I gave her a hug and whispered in her ear. "You're a good surgeon. You let your addiction get out of control, but we can fix things. I just need you to be honest here, and help me find the real killer. For Michael and Lucy. You're strong enough to give this up and you're strong enough to help me, even if you might be embarrassed at first." I felt her nose brush against my neck, up and down. A nod. I stood. It wasn't fair that I was hanging everyone else's laundry out to dry and not my own. It was my turn.

"Sofia asked me for fifty thousand dollars two nights ago. Here's my confession: I have much more than that in cash on me. About two hundred and fifty—well, forty-five. It was the money Michael was supposed to pay Alan Holton with. He asked me to look after it after everything went south, and I didn't tell the police. Partly because it never came up, and partly because . . . well . . . I didn't want to. I'll admit it"—I put my hands up, hoping it made me look just as fallible as the rest of them, seeing as I was going around the room pointing fingers—"I brought the money with me in case Michael wanted it back. I told Sofia what I was doing, and she asked me for some, saying it would help her out." I changed tone to address Sofia sympathetically. "And now that I know you're here to try to overcome your addiction, I understand that a little better. Because money troubles are common for addicts, but when you asked me, it didn't seem desperate, your life didn't depend on it. You asked me because it was easy, because the money was untraceable, and because it was in front of you. A fifty grand debt wasn't going to ruin your life—you have a house, if it really got down to it—but it's true that you were spending too much money on oxycodone, and that, seeing as what you were doing could end your career more easily than if you were, say, an accountant, untraceable cash was important. Money problems are common for addicts, and so is stealing. You stole something from one of us to get some fast cash, didn't you?"

Sofia gave a sniffling nod.

"I'm a fan of rules—some of you know this. And Step 9 in AA is to make amends." I looked over at Katherine, who nodded confirmation, and turned back to Sofia. "You brought the pills, yes, but just as a safety net. You fully intended to follow the program this weekend. That's why you asked me for cash. It wasn't a debt, but it was something you felt you needed to repay, even if no one else knew."

"I think someone might have noticed if Sofia had stolen fifty grand." Marcelo raised his voice. "She's admitted it. You need to lay off."

"Sofia can stop me if I'm wrong."

"If it's important to Michael and Lucy . . ." Sofia took a deep breath. "I needed the money to buy back what I stole: a fifty-thousand-dollar platinum Presidential Rolex watch."

Marcelo's jaw dropped in horror. He checked his watch, tapped it a few times, then eventually managed to close his mouth.

Sofia looked exhausted by the confession, so I picked up the thread again. "Marcelo never takes his watch off, we all know this. *Except* when he underwent a shoulder reconstruction. A surgery that Sofia conducted. She used the surgery as an excuse to swap his watch with a fake. I noticed because Marcelo punched me in the jaw earlier and I still have all my teeth. That model of Rolex, with the platinum chain, is supposed to weigh just shy of half a kilogram. A punch, even from an old man—no offense—should have floored me like he was wearing knuckle dusters."

"He would have noticed the difference," Juliette scoffed. "Surely. If the fake was so light."

"You're right. But Marcelo was recovering from surgery. Anything would have felt like a brick on his wrist at first, and so he grew accustomed to the lighter weight, thinking his arm was growing stronger in recovery instead." I saw Marcelo lift some invisible weights with his right arm, testing the heft, confusion plastered across his face. "But the problem was, it wasn't any old wristwatch. I'll admit, I've always been a little bit jealous of the thing. I've googled how much it was worth on occasion, so imagine my surprise when Marcelo tells me the watch belonged to my father. He was a criminal, sure, but not a showy one. He never bought flashy jewelry or souped-up cars. That seemed strange to me. I assume it was stolen in the first place, but even so, Dad wouldn't have been the guy to take it from a haul. And then I learned about the photographs. Which everyone wanted and no one ever found, even though the gang's thugs turned over the very bank his wife worked at to get to his safety-deposit box."

"Robert left the watch to Jeremy," my mother muttered.

"Rolexes are designed to last—their whole marketing campaign is based on them being handed down through generations. In particular, a platinum Rolex is so heavy because it's so robust: it's even got bulletproof glass." *SAFE AS A BANK VAULT* shouted one of the ads that had peppered my social media feed. "So, it's going to last a long time *and* be protected. There's no better place to keep something vital. Provided it's small enough to fit under the glass, right?" I took the loupe out of my pocket and held it up. "Juliette, toss me Frank's medal, will you?"

Juliette frowned in confusion, but obliged and tossed the glass case in a careful, underarm lob.

I caught it. I'd already checked; it was the one thing I'd done to confirm my suspicions, and so I knew how important it was. As I said on page 116, I didn't spend eighty words describing the damn thing for nothing.

"Juliette told me that F-287, or Frank—that's the dead bird above the fireplace—carried a map, infantry locations, coordinates, and other vital information across enemy lines. But, even in code, the map alone would be enough to weigh down a bird. I didn't realize that your father had framed the actual life-saving message too, Juliette." I held the loupe underneath the medal, where the small slip of paper with the meaningless dots on it had been mounted. It was obvious, even without peering into the lens itself, that it was magnifying out of the tiny dot a detailed map. We're moving into le Carré over Christie here—"spy shit" as my father called it—but stick with me. Though my how-to book on it hadn't sold very many copies, it was about to pay dividends. "They're called microdots. It's a technique used to shrink information. An entire A4 sheet of paper, or an image, like a map, for example, can fit on a dot the size of a full stop. Spies were quite fond of these in the Second World War—they'd put them on the back of postage stamps. This"—I held up the loupe again—"was rattling around in Michael's car when he buried Alan. He also brought it with him here. Erin took it when Crawford arrested him. It's a jeweler's magnifying thingy." (Remember, I only learned the word "loupe" while writing this book, so it would be disingenuous to fake my dialogue.) "Marcelo, your watch, *the real one*, had a microdot under the glass. Robert never used drugs. The needle they found on his body, which led to the conclusion that he was high and trying to stick up a petrol station, wasn't for injecting. Microdots are so small that I assume you need something fine like a syringe or the tip of a pen to apply them to a surface."

I held up the loupe.

"But every pawnbroker has one of these, or something better. Anyone would have seen the dot right away when inspecting the quality. Sofia thought she was just selling a watch, but she was selling much more. I doubt Sofia had the bad luck to sell it to him directly, but Michael told me that stolen goods in Sydney tend to make their way through Alan's shop. Sofia would have had to go someplace dodgy. Maybe your oxy dealer pointed you in the right direction, or maybe you traded it for drugs and they sold it on. I'm not ignoring that Alan might even be in the photographs himself and someone tipped him off. I have no idea. Either way, this is the butterfly that flaps its wings in Turkey and causes a tornado in Brazil. The short version is that the wrong watch landed with the wrong person. Alan knew the value of what he had, and, more importantly, he knew who would want it. That's why Michael met him that night, a bag of cash in tow. He was trying to buy the microdot."

I had everyone's rapt attention. "Does anyone care to fill in some gaps here, or should I keep going?"

You call something like a microdot in a book like this one a MacGuffin. It doesn't matter exactly what it is, it just matters that people will kill over it. You know, the thing that James Bond is always chasing after: a USB with a world-destroying virus; bank account passwords; nuclear launch codes. Or, in our case, photographs.

"I have a question," Audrey offered, putting her hands out in a *don't shoot* gesture. "Ernest, everything you're telling us is about how *small* what we're chasing is. Michael brought a furniture truck. For a tiny photograph?"

I realized that everyone in the room except for Audrey and Katherine knew there was a coffin in the truck—Erin from digging it up; Sofia and Crawford from chasing after it; Andy and Juliette from our conversation with the McAuleys; and Marcelo because I'd told him.

"Michael needed the truck to bring Brian Clarke's coffin with him, which he and Erin had dug up the night before. Brian is the policeman my father shot the night he died, Alan Holton's partner. Marcelo didn't know what he was getting rid of in the truck, but I saw what Michael wanted me to see. Brian's coffin had two bodies in it: one of them a child." This, I'm pleased to report, drew my first unanimous gasp. "Andy, if it helps, *this* is Rebecca McAuley. She was kidnapped thirty-five years ago. Her parents tried to deceive the kidnappers to save a few bucks and it backfired: they never saw their daughter again."

"And Robert had photos of it," Erin said. "That's what you think is on the microdot. Evidence of her murder?"

"Exactly. Alan was delighted to have the watch fall into his hands, because he knew the McAuleys would pay handsomely for the evidence it contained. This next part is guesswork, but I'm ruling out Alan as Rebecca's killer, because Marcelo told me he was too soft, and because otherwise he would have destroyed the photos instead of selling them. And because he's selling them, I figure that thirty-five years is long enough and Alan has burned enough bridges that he figures it's no longer worth protecting whoever he was protecting back then."

I took a second to see if most of the room agreed this was reasonable. Some were nodding along. Sofia looked like she was about to vomit. Andy looked befuddled, as if I were explaining quantum physics. Good enough.

"But Alan's got a problem. He might not have killed Rebecca, but he's not innocent: he was working for the Sabers. He targeted Robert and helped hide Rebecca's body, at the very least, and it's likely he interfered with the ransom drop too. So he can't just show up on the McAuleys' doorstep. They'd hold him just as responsible. So he needs a middleman."

"Why Michael?" Katherine asked.

"It took me a while to figure this out. I think that Alan wanted someone else with something to gain, to be sure that he could trust them to deliver such a large amount of money. A Cunningham had plenty to gain from the photographs, and from what else Alan knew from his involvement. The most obvious is learning the truth about Robert, of course. I suspect that's only half of it, but we're getting there. Michael seems like the right choice—Marcelo, you were Robert's lawyer; Katherine, you're straight as an ice skate; Audrey, your age puts the odds against you here, no offense. But this was Alan's mistake. The personal connection he thought would guarantee the deal turned out to be the reason Michael killed him.

"And the deal itself is the simple part. Alan's price tag is the original ransom amount: three hundred thousand dollars. So Alan gives Michael enough information to rope him and the McAuleys in, Michael gets the money from the McAuleys to buy the microdot from Alan, Alan gives him a cut, and then Michael delivers the photographs back. It's all so simple. Except, of course, Michael ends up killing Alan and keeping the cash."

"Because Michael didn't have three hundred thousand dollars," Sofia slurred, surprising me with her attention. "You told me he gave you two sixty-seven."

"Bingo," I said. "Michael took out some of the money before he gave it to Alan. The reason he did this?" If I'm honest, I really had nothing to back this up except gut feel, but I was pretty confident. And I was on a roll, so wasn't keen to slow down. "Lucy was having trouble with her business. She was losing money and she was stuck with a car she couldn't afford under the brutal lease conditions. When she told you it was paid off over breakfast, Marcelo, most of us thought it was her usual indignant defensiveness. But it turns out she wasn't lying. Michael used the money to pay off her debts, including her car, before he went to meet Alan. He probably did this to make sure she'd be okay if something went wrong." And because he needed a clean break to leave her for Erin. I was glad Lucy wasn't there to hear that part. "But he didn't realize the effect that skimming off the top would have. Alan's not stupid—he counts the money, finds it under, so he pulls a gun. They fight over it . . . and you know the rest."

"This is all very entertaining." Andy couldn't contain himself. "But what about the Black Tongue?"

"I haven't got through everyone else yet. Erin, Sofia, Marcelo, you don't know that Rebecca McAuley's parents are here—they're staying in the resort over the ridge. Seeing as Michael's now got the microdot and knows where the body is buried, he writes to the McAuleys from prison, asking for them to double the payment." Siobhan McAuley had revealed this to me at SuperShred when she'd said, "He wants more money *again*." Michael had told me in the Drying Room that what he had was "worth a whole lot more" than the three hundred grand Alan had originally priced it at. "Michael was planning to meet the McAuleys over the ridge to sell them both the photos and their daughter's body—that's why he brought it up here. He told you this was his plan, didn't he, Audrey?"

"I warned him against it," Audrey confirmed. "And when he insisted, I went up there to warn them myself."

"I'm sorry"—it was Andy again, showing no respect for the building of suspense—"but Ernest, all this gangland kidnapping stuff is from thirty-five years ago. What does this have to do with the damn ash?"

"All right." I put up a hand. "I get the message. Let's go back to Green Boots. Our unidentified victim, or at least unidentified to most of us. Lucy actually solved it first."

"If you're suggesting she was killed because she figured it all out . . ." Sofia used her palm to lift her head, gave a small shake. "We know she fell—there wasn't any ash on her and she had several broken bones. There was no sign of a struggle."

"No. She did jump," I agreed, recalling Lucy's finger gun when we were talking on the roof: *I'd rather . . .* "But she told me yesterday that she'd rather kill herself than choke to death under the Black Tongue's torture. She threw herself off the roof, but only as an escape from what was about to happen. I think she went up to google something, to double-check her suspicions. Our killer got scared and confronted her up there, after we'd all left the bar. Remember the fear in her face when she looked at the photo of Green Boots? I thought she was just horrified at seeing what had really happened to Michael, especially since she thought it had been partly her fault. But I was wrong. She was scared because she recognized him."

"None of us have ever seen him before. How the hell does Lucy know the dead guy?" That was Andy. He was still the most confused. Everyone else looked like they understood parts, but had brows furrowed, still working to understand the whole. Only one person had their jaw set, poker face on. With every statement, it was like I was cranking a winch, tightening the muscles in that person's neck.

"I didn't say she knew him," I said. "I said she *recognized* him. She'd only met him once—he gave her a speeding ticket on the way up here."

I let it sink in. People swiveled to look behind them, everyone's gaze settling on someone standing at the back of the room.

"Crawford, those stripes of blood on the inside of your uniform's cuffs, they aren't from carrying the body down the mountain. They're on the inside of the wrists. Whoever made those stains got them from clutching at their own throat." I mimicked clawing at an imaginary zip tie around my neck. "You're wearing a dead man's coat."

"What the hell is that supposed to mean?" Crawford asked.

I gave Juliette a knowing smile ahead of what I was about to say, which I'm proud I haven't embellished in the slightest here, before turning my attention back to Crawford. "I'm saying that even Arthur Conan Doyle believed in ghosts. Isn't that right, Jeremy?"

MY BROTHER

CHAPTER 39

Jeremy Cunningham, now looking very silly (costumed, even) in a policeman's coat that was stained with someone else's blood, gave a feeble smile and a weak shake of his head. He tried to say something—*That's ridiculous*, perhaps—but it came out, well, choked.

Audrey looked as surprised as everyone else: she clearly thought the Sabers had followed through on their threats to kill her son. Jeremy had, like the Agatha Christie on the shelf, been hiding under a different name: Darius Crawford, the name he'd given himself as he acted out a bumbling local cop. His other alias, the one the media had given him, the Black Tongue, was the opposite of bumbling. He had chalked up five murders and one coerced suicide. Like I said, some of us are high achievers.

It's not one of Knox's rules, but you should never believe someone is dead until you've actually seen a body.

I addressed Jeremy directly now. The parlor show was over. "Green Boots *had* to be a local. It's why you only showed the photo to our family, but kept it from everyone else, even Juliette, under the guise of preventing panic, because any local would have recognized him. All the staff are up here on the mountain for the season—they've been here for months. It might not be suspicious that there's a new cop from town they hadn't met, but they would recognize the sergeant immediately. That's why you wanted him out of sight so quickly, locked away in the shed. And you took his coat, but you didn't take his shoes: steel caps are a usual part of a policeman's uniform, and the body was wearing them, but Erin stepped on your toe while chasing the truck, and it hurt, which means that you are not. You could have pretended to be anyone, really, but I think you wanted to be someone with the power to separate us. That's also the reason you made the sergeant's death such a public statement, so you could split Michael off. But you were nervous, too nervous, and every step you took that looked like legitimate police work—identifying the body, controlling panic—was instead to make sure your disguise held up. So, when a Cunningham asked, you showed us the photo. It looked like you were doing the right thing. You were really making sure we didn't know the corpse's true identity. That's why you were nervous when we were around the body. I just thought you were squeamish.

"But what you weren't expecting was Lucy's reaction, for her to recognize the victim as the policeman who'd given her a speeding ticket on the way up. When she stormed out, I thought she said, 'You're the boss.' But she actually said, '*It's your* boss.' She hadn't thought to accuse you yet—she was thinking aloud—but she knew something was off. She didn't put it together until she got up to the roof and googled the Jindabyne police department. But by then we'd filtered off to bed and you'd followed her up there, and she didn't want to die like Michael, so she jumped.

"You lied about how you got here so fast too. You said you'd been on the speed radar all night catching tourists, but that can't have been true because Lucy, at some point, would have surely spat on you over the ticket she got. More police were never arriving—you told us they were caught dealing with the roads, but how do two passenger coaches get up here and one police car can't find its way when there have been two murders? Of course, none of this twigged at first. You seemed reliable. There were three sets of footprints to the body and only one back: enough for one victim, one arriving policeman, and one killer who'd left. I thought this meant the killer had called in the body themselves, before"—I used air quotes here—"*Officer Crawford* had arrived, being the third set. I was right that the killer *did* call it in, or at least pretended to. Because no one else discovered the body, you discovered it yourself—it was part of your act. You went up there twice. First, with the sergeant, when you tied the bag around his head, walked him up there to die, and then took his coat, and then again in the morning."

"He's on camera arriving much later." Juliette sounded unsure of my conclusions. "We both saw that."

"I think you'd been checking out the resort when you were planning to follow us up here. And the snow cam is on their homepage, so you knew the driveway was, in a way, monitored. I assume you attacked the sergeant on the road, where he'd have parked his patrol car to set up the speed gun. At the top of the hill you would have had mobile reception to check the website. I'd thought myself that if you really floored it, a car could skip the three-minute window where the camera refreshed. Then you just needed to go back later and make sure you were captured arriving at the correct time. It looks like you're traveling towards the car park in the photo, sure, but your arm is over the back of the headrest. You're reversing."

"Jeremy? It can't be." Katherine was peering at him like he'd come home from a desert island. Then she turned to Audrey. "How could you not know?"

"The Sabers took him, Katherine. But there was no ransom—they wanted the photographs. The ones Ernest has been talking about. I didn't know about the watch or anything . . . and Jeremy, if that is you, I *tried*—I tried to find them. They said they had to be sure I wasn't hiding them. So they told me they had to"—she choked on the word—"to be sure I was telling the truth." Marcelo moved towards Crawford/Cunningham (what's in a name?), but Audrey took his hand. I saw her give it a squeeze and he let his arm trail behind him, like a pit bull restrained by a leash. "I couldn't tell the police, not only because Alan *was* a policeman at the time, but also because I was worried they'd come back for Michael and Ernest. Our family had lost so much over these silly photos, I just wanted it finished. So I pretended. If it's really you, Jeremy, I'm sorry. Are you sure, Ernest? Are you really sure?"

"Michael told me Alan had tried to contact me first," I said. "I'd told Michael it wasn't true, convinced it was a lie Alan had spun to build trust with him. But then I thought about it. Alan had said he'd contacted *Michael's brother*. You didn't know you were adopted until he approached you, did you, Jeremy?"

Jeremy swallowed hard. Chewed his lip. Said nothing.

"But of course, Alan knew you were alive. Marcelo told me he didn't have the stomach for killing—maybe he was the one who let you go? But you don't remember any of that, so here comes a man you don't know, talking about a family you never knew you were a part of. Mark and Janine Williams, they were heralded for their foster caring, and I'm thinking they took you in, but maybe you never knew you weren't theirs. And I'm thinking you weren't too understanding when you discovered they hadn't told you everything. You wrote a letter to Michael in prison, trying to explain what had happened, who you thought you were, as you were piecing things together. But Michael took the name Jeremy Cunningham in the letter as some kind of threat." I'd asked Michael if there'd been a name on the letter, to which he'd replied, almost with a laugh, *Oh, there was a name . . . they were just trying to push my buttons.* "It makes sense he'd think that, especially if Alan had told him anything about what the Sabers had done to our mother. He didn't believe it, and I'm in the press as a family traitor anyway, so who else could you turn to? Someone close to him. Lucy.

"Lucy was waiting for you to arrive, and when you hadn't yet, she was worried that you might be Green Boots. Trapped outside in a terrible accident. I thought she was worried about the general police presence an unsolved murder would bring, which would be hard for Michael. But she was worried that, if you'd frozen overnight, it would ruin her plans to not only reunite you with Michael, but also take the credit for it. She'd tried to identify the body: she'd checked the guest lists before I did. She asked me if the body looked like Michael. Not if it *was* Michael. She was asking about a family resemblance. She was on the roof trying to get a text through to you to check where you were." She'd told me this weekend was her chance to give Michael his family back. She hadn't been talking about herself. "Another reason why she was so devastated when she realized who you might really be, and what you might have done: she'd invited you up here."

"It's just the way you planned it, Katherine." Trust Andy to steal my thunder. "It's a goddamn family reunion."

There was only the shriek of the wind while everyone digested.

Finally, Jeremy spoke. "This is not what I expected, being in a room with you all."

His hand was gripping the mantel, clawing flecks of paint from it, as his eyes darted among us. There were too many of us between him and the door to escape, and there was a liberally iced window behind him. He could possibly go through that, depending on the softness of the snow below, but I felt confident one of us could grab him if he tried.

"I . . ." He hesitated. "I waited so long to meet you. I thought it would be different." He had the same wistful tone he'd used when letting me in to see Michael in the Drying Room. *You really care about him, don't you? . . . I didn't really have brothers growing up.*

"I was always different when I was young. I never fit in. Got into fights. And then Mu—" He cut himself off and I could see anger in the flare of his nostrils. "I thought Alan was a liar at first. I'd always called them my parents. I asked them, and they just . . ." I could tell he was struggling with the memory. "They just *admitted* it. And these people, who I'd thought my whole life were my family, they looked so *happy* about it. They couldn't tell me who I was. I'd had foster brothers and sisters, but the Williamses always told me I was theirs. They said they didn't know anything more, that they'd taken me in without a name, when I was seven years old."

"*Seven?*" Audrey gasped. "No wonder no one knew who you were. What happened to you in those two years?"

"I don't . . . remember." Jeremy looked like he was fishing for something that wasn't there. Too young, too beaten, too abused, perhaps; those memories all repressed. The Sabers had been so scared Audrey would bleed their secrets that they'd told her they'd killed her son to be sure she wouldn't double-cross them, but then they hadn't had the gumption to do it themselves; they'd simply left him on the street to die. How long they kept him and how long he lived on his own is something I'll never know. But how that experience might transform a young mind—well, I didn't have to look far to understand. DNA testing wasn't widely used thirty-plus years ago, and neither were missing persons reports spread across the infant internet. Hair analysis could match family lineage, but it never held up in court—just ask the Queensland detective who'd driven across state lines to accuse a Cunningham. *Got into fights.* Across state lines, Jeremy was a nameless child in a city he didn't know.

"But Alan said he knew who I was," Jeremy continued. "He said he'd kept an eye on me, that he'd looked after me when I was younger. He said he was supposed to kill me, but instead he let me go and I should be grateful for that. He knew the Williamses had money, and he wanted it for the photos that he said would help me find peace. But I told him to get lost, and the next thing I saw he's on the news. Murdered."

"So you confronted the Williamses?" I prompted.

"These people that *dared* to say they were my family, they kept lying. They just kept lying, saying that they didn't know who I was! I got angry and . . . I didn't mean to . . . I found a way to make them feel what I felt"—he pulled at his collar, at his neck—"and I just can't breathe when I'm upset."

"And Alison? You tracked her down because of her involvement in the McAuleys' case. How did you know about that?"

"No. I tracked her down because I wanted to ask her some questions, to find out more about Alan. I understood she'd been his superior." The collar was getting a workout now. "I didn't realize this was all her fault. *She* made my father, my *real* father, keep doing something that would get him killed, just to cover her own arse. I just wanted to ask her some questions. Honestly." He rubbed his forehead, ran his tongue around his teeth.

I could tell it was taking a conscious effort to disassociate himself from his actions, but that he believed his hand had been forced. It can't have been *that* forced, seeing as he'd brought all the gear along with him to reconstruct an ancient torture technique, but I wasn't going to correct him.

"You all understand that, right?" There was something sinister underneath his words, like he was appealing to us as equals.

"If you're desperate to belong, we're all here." I spread my arms. "Why kill Michael?"

"Michael was supposed to be like me." He said it mournfully. "I mean, one day there's a man I don't know telling me I'm a Cunningham, and then I'm seeing in the news that a Cunningham has killed him. Then I start researching Robert, and he killed that Brian Clarke, and I started to think that maybe I wasn't so alone after all, that I wasn't the only one who felt . . . *different*."

"That was when you reached out to Michael?"

"He didn't reply to my letter. I could understand why he didn't believe me. So I needed another way in. His wife was much more willing. She told me when he was being released. About your weekend here. I couldn't wait: not only would I meet Michael, but the rest of you as well." He was, strangely, smiling, reliving the excitement of planning out his first time meeting us: his real family. "But I wanted to do it right—I wanted the first time I met him to be just us, and I wanted to prove myself worthy of this family. When I went to the prison a day early, he wasn't there. I rushed up here. The local policeman, he was parked on the wrong shoulder at the wrong time, and his sacrifice gave me the opportunity to show you who I was."

Juliette and I swapped a worried look over the word "sacrifice." Jeremy was talking exuberantly now, caught up in his own self-mythologizing.

"It also gave me the opportunity to get Michael on his own. And I could make my reasoning convincing because I knew he'd lied to you all about when he was released. I wanted to tell him right away, but everyone was fawning over him and I knew that it was the only way we'd be alone all weekend. Then everyone started yelling and maybe my choice of clothing wasn't as clever as I thought it was, because suddenly I had to help with everything, and Juliette was stuck to me like glue, or people would start asking questions. I couldn't break off to get to Michael. It was only after you'd spoken to him, Ernest, that I could show him . . . to show him I belonged. To show him I was like him."

Sofia's theory held: *The Black Tongue is announcing themselves. They want us to know they're here.*

Jeremy thought he'd found his place in a family of killers. The sergeant's death was no more than a dead bird brought to a door by a feral cat. An offering.

"But Michael wasn't welcoming, was he?" I countered. "He was horrified. It was clear when I spoke to him that he'd spent the last three years learning to live with the life he'd taken, and he'd come out the other side wanting to do better. To *be* better. But that's not what you expected, was it? Did he make you feel like an outsider, all over again?"

"He was supposed to be like me. *You're* supposed to be like me! I tried to reason with him. I knew he'd tell you the first chance he got. And he knew—he had those photos Alan tried to sell me first and he knew who hurt me, hurt *us*, when I was a child and he refused to tell me. He said I'd just kill them, that he'd learned it wasn't the way forward, and I realized he wasn't like me at all. He made me feel *alone*, just like my fake parents did. Sometimes . . . I *can't breathe* when people . . ." He was pulling at his collar again. "The things he was saying. I couldn't breathe . . . And then the woman . . ."

"Lucy." I was surprised, and a little impressed, to hear Audrey correcting him.

"I tried to figure out how to leave, but how could I when you were all refusing to go and I'm stuck playing the role of the police officer? And she figured it out. She'd been waiting for me, and I hadn't shown up. Once she knew the first body was a cop, I was revealed. I begged her to keep quiet. I gave her a choice, you understand? She chose to jump." His voice had turned pitiful, begging. He really had believed we would all be like him, and he was shocked that we weren't.

"Why?" That was Katherine, disgust on her tongue summing up the feeling of the room. "Why would anyone think *our* family was a place to fit in?"

"Michael had no right!" Jeremy was shouting now. "He had no right to tell me where I belonged. To tell me that what I'd done was wrong. The hypocrite!" He spat the next words. "Look at yourselves. Cunninghams. You're all killers, aren't you?"

We all looked at each other. Andy went to raise his hand, presumably to suggest that he hadn't killed anyone, but thought better of it.

I pictured Jeremy, sitting against the wall of Alison Humphrey's thick-aired apartment, toilet door closed, looking at his trembling, ashen hands, having just learned about his real family. We were easy to research online. Everyone knew what type of family we were. Michael, Robert, Katherine—and later Sofia—theirs were all public incidents, after which they were reported as having blood on their hands. We were infamous, in the media and police circles. Jeremy had found us, steadied his hands and thought, *I'm not so different after all.*

There was a flurry of footsteps behind us. We turned to see Gavin, who looked surprised to see everyone so agitated. "Bags are ready," he said. Then did a double take. "Who died?"

This was enough of a distraction for Jeremy to move. We spun back to see that he'd knocked the grate of the fireplace over with a clatter and armed himself with the poker. Juliette moved towards him, but he swung it in an arc and she pulled back. He still had nowhere to go, but he was swishing the cast-iron weapon through the air with abandon.

"I could have just left you here," he hissed. "Up until now, I might have. After Lucy, I thought I'd done enough to disappear. But now that I know that I was *left* to fight on my own. That I was abandoned, discarded. By *you*." He was talking to all of us, but glaring at Audrey. "At least we'll burn together."

He lunged with the poker, and everyone flinched, but he was plunging it into the fire. Using the rod as a lever, he flicked a giant, flaming log onto the carpet. It landed on the floor with a thud, sending fireflies of sparks into the air. We all held our breath. Juliette had told me her father built the guesthouse in the late forties, which meant it was held up by timber, shortcuts, and asbestos: the walls may as well have been matches. Some of the carpet fizzed, browned, but it was too damp to catch; the log just sat there smoking. We all went quiet, Jeremy looking forlorn, the rest of us marveling at how uninspired his getaway plan was.

Then, seemingly out of nowhere, one of the books on the wall exploded. A single spark had carried, lighting the crisp leaf-dry pages.

It figured. These books were perhaps the only things in the resort, me included, that weren't damp to their bones. I wish I could tell you the book that exploded was *Jane Eyre* (it would be fitting, considering what's about to happen) but it just wouldn't be true.

Once the first book went up, the rest went too, one by one, like popcorn in a microwave, jolting into flames as sparks leapt. Some, I suspected, seeing as it was almost spontaneous, merely caved to the peer pressure of the books around them. And then the walls were blazing. The floor steamed, drying out, and then glowing spots formed in the dry patches.

We all darted towards the door. Erin was first out. I hauled Sofia to her feet, draping her over my shoulder with my good arm. Marcelo was dragging Audrey, who was stunned and crying; they'd knocked one of the red thrones over, which had started a small bonfire in the middle of the room. Juliette was yelling, waving her arms. The flames had started in earnest now. Jeremy dropped the poker and slammed his elbow into the window behind him, shattering it. The air entered, feeding the blaze, flames tripling in size with a *whoosh*. F-287 was a blackened husk. Sofia and I weren't leaving until Marcelo and Audrey got past, so I'd know they were safe. I'd lost sight of my aunt and uncle, but then I caught a glimpse of Katherine, moving in the wrong direction.

"Katherine, just go!" I yelled, but flames *roar* in a way I could have never imagined. Everything was drowned out by the consuming growl. I winced with the heat, knowing we were running out of time. Behind me the doorway was literally hissing with steam.

Once the frame dried, it too would go up. And then the same for the carpet in the hallway, the banister, the stairs, and soon the whole building.

Marcelo was moving past me, Audrey now on her own. I ladled Sofia onto him and ran towards the window, sidestepping the firepit of the red chair. As I passed it, the bonfire dropped away entirely. It had burned through the floor, crashing into the level below us. If we didn't move fast, that would catch too, race into the foyer and block us from the main door.

Katherine had reached Jeremy, who had one foot out the window. He'd knocked the sharpest shards from the sill and was getting ready to jump. Katherine reached out and grabbed him by the shoulder, but Jeremy sensed her movement, spun, and clutched her by the throat. She gagged, and he thrust her into the mantel, her head bouncing off the sharp corner with a *crack*. He squeezed harder. Katherine's eyes bulged. I yelled again, but my voice dissolved as a surge of flame, fed by the wind, flashed and singed the side of my face. I smelled burned hair. I was too far away. Jeremy saw me, then looked back at Katherine. There was blood on the corner of the mantel. Jeremy's eyes were merely reflecting the fire, but there was something ablaze in them all the same. He pulled Katherine's head back, and thrust her again towards—

Andy's war cry was so loud it conquered the howl of the fire. He'd picked up the poker and was at a run. Jeremy's eyes widened. Andy pulled back his arm to swing—a long, wide arc, in a loose-hipped stance like he was teeing off the golf balls he'd never got to hit from the roof—and unleashed. The poker slammed into

MY UNCLE

the side of Jeremy's face with a *crack*. It hit him under the ear, across the cheek. His jaw seemed to dislodge from his face, giving him a wide-open look of surprise. Then the blood started pouring from his mouth. He dropped Katherine, who scrambled to Andy's outstretched arm. Jeremy took two steps (pendulum jaw swinging) towards me.

He never reached me. He might have been surprised when the floor gave way beneath him, but his jaw couldn't drop any further. He was gone, into the now fierce flames on the first floor.

Andy, Katherine, and I literally hotfooted it out of the room. Katherine was between us, her legs pinwheeling the ground as we hauled her down the stairs. Erin stood by the entrance, waving for us to hurry up. Spot fires danced across the foyer, not yet an obstacle, but the paint on the ceiling was bubbling, fire crawling across the beams. The chandelier came down with an almighty crash just as we reached the door.

I collapsed at the bottom of the front steps. Crawling in the snow without gloves is like dashing across hot sand—it sears and bites the skin. Then I was lifted, and realized it was Erin holding me up, dragging me through the snow until eventually we plopped down in watery divots and watched the inferno, eyes glazed, coughing, astounded we were alive. There was my crackling fire from the brochure, at last.

The storm hadn't ebbed. The wind was bracing and snowflakes still stung our eyelids and cheeks and for once I didn't mind at all.

CHAPTER 40

It didn't take long for the roof to collapse. The walls quickly followed, imploding inwards and sending a shower of sparks into the night with a hiss that, if this was a different hotel and this book a different genre, could have been a freeing of spirits.

Juliette turned to Gavin and said, "I think I'm ready to sell. Seeing as I've done the demolition for you."

Some of us, those with energy left, laughed. People put arms around each other. Andy, for all my pithy remarks to this point, held Katherine like she was the only thing in the world. Marcelo and Audrey tucked Sofia between them. Juliette patted Gavin on the back in camaraderie. Erin and I didn't do anything so clichéd, but we were near each other. I knew the fire was too far away to stand in for our flint, to reignite us, and that was okay.

"What's that?" Katherine asked, pointing at the rubble.

There was a dark shadow moving across the white snow, backlit by the glowing embers. It made it maybe fifty meters from the blaze, then collapsed in the snow.

"Let's get out of here," Andy said.

"Is he moving?" I can't remember who said that.

"If he's hurt, it doesn't matter who he is or what he's done," Juliette reasoned. "We can't just leave him here like this."

"I'll go check on him." I was surprised to hear myself volunteer. There was a murmur of half-hearted dissent that didn't overpower the relief that none of them had to go, so I hauled myself to my feet and staggered towards the shape. I had a vivid memory of another black shadow in a field of white, but I shut it out.

I reached the body. It was Jeremy. He was lying on his back, his eyes shut. His hair was burned, his cheeks cooked in places and ash-streaked in others. His chest was moving up and down, very slowly. I sat down beside him, because there was nothing else to do.

"Who is it?" Jeremy spoke slowly, with a lisp as his broken jaw slipped, his tongue slicked black with blood.

"Ernest . . . your brother."

It was quiet for a while.

"Do you dream of choking?" he asked.

"Sometimes," I admitted. I understood the ash, the choking, the torture, now. That repressed trauma leaking through, of being trapped in that car. The things that he couldn't remember but bubbled up to haunt him. *I can't breathe when I get angry.*

"Okay." He sounded pleased. That I was like him, perhaps. That was all he wanted to know.

He wheezed out a long time. His chest stopped moving.

Then, just when I was about to leave, it started again.

I looked from my brother back to Gavin's big yellow tank. There stood a collection of people, only a few of whom had my blood and even fewer my surname, waiting for me. They were a collection of hyphens and prefixes and married names and ex-this and step-that. And there was one more Cunningham lying next to me, struggling to breathe.

I'd been so desperate to make a family, to force Erin to make me one, that I'd forgotten the one that had formed around me. Family is gravity. I realized then what Sofia had told me back at the very start of all this. Family is not whose blood runs in your veins, it's who you'd spill it for.

ME

CHAPTER 41

"We can go," I said, hauling myself up the high step and into the Oversnow.

They'd all piled into the contraption by the time I got back. Gavin punched the engine, which spliced the night air with its waking cough.

"What happened?" Katherine asked as I sat down next to her.

"I got there and he just stopped breathing."

"He just stopped breathing?"

"He just stopped."

"He's dead?" Audrey asked. There was hope in her voice, but whether it was that he was dead or alive, I couldn't be sure.

"Yes."

"You're sure?"

"Yes."

"How?"

"He just stopped breathing. Let's go home."

EPILOGUE

The FOR SALE sign was staked into the ground with the lopsided laziness that comes from a sure commission. Juliette had come to help pack up the last of my things. Erin and I had decided that the best way forward, if we were trying to move ahead with a clean slate, was to sell the place and leave all memories and actions behind us. I'd met Juliette at the house, having just come from breakfast, which had been fantastically uneventful.

Juliette unlocked the door. The house was stripped, ghosts of furniture leaving dark shadows across the otherwise sun-paled wood floors. The last of my boxes were in the attic. She pulled the ladder down and climbed up; my position below was trash-catcher. She passed me a few boxes and then a small suitcase, one with wheels on it, good for airports but bad for snow resorts. When I'd finally gotten home—after police stations, hospitals, and media galore—I hadn't had the heart to unpack it.

Of course, I'd taken the sports bag out of the top. The McAuleys wouldn't take it back. They'd accepted the photos were gone forever, but had still sent divers into the lake to retrieve the coffin. I hoped they'd had the funeral for their daughter they'd always wanted.

I'd told everyone about the money, and we'd agreed what to do with it together, as a family. We'd given half to Lucy's parents, brothers, and sisters, and we'd also paid for her funeral. Then we'd agreed to split the rest. I'd forfeited my share, figuring that I'd already spent it.

Michael's funeral was short, cold, and depressing. It wasn't his fault; the weather did him no favors. I checked the coffin before it went in the ground. Lucy's funeral was organized by her family. It was tragic, sad, and beautiful. The church was packed, and it took me a while to figure out why, but the mystery solved itself: I've never been pitched so many business opportunities at a wake. Even though Lucy's not with us anymore, I'm pretty sure last week she got promoted to Associate Vice President, Oceania.

Andy and Katherine have never been more affectionate, and Katherine never more relaxed. It's a bit much. Andy is still the type of guy whose shoulder you look over in a bar to find someone more interesting, but now I've seen him knock the jaw off someone, I'm open to enduring at least fifteen minutes of mundane conversation.

As it turns out, Sofia was one of the most badly burned in the fire, which did her a favor in the end, because guess what they dosed her with for the pain? Oxycodone. Her bloodstream's alibi secure, the coroner had nothing to gain from testing her, as no pattern could be proven. She was found to have acted as she could have reasonably been expected to. Katherine's keeping an eye on her, and she's doing better. They are almost friends.

Marcelo, Audrey, and I have dinner once a week. Audrey stands up far less often, which is nice. I'll invite Erin soon; she'll always be family, flint or not. Divorce is a word that's scary and formal, but we're working towards it, ironically enough, as a team. Juliette and I got to know each other better on publicity tours, since she's also signed a book deal for this story. Hers is called something like

Hotel of Horror. My publishers are trying to squeeze mine out a month before hers.

What else?

There are some technicalities to go through, I suppose.

You might think that my mother didn't kill anybody. You'd have a point. I'll argue that I told you I'd tell you the truth as I knew it to be at the time that I thought I knew it. I also told you that my use of grammar was not deliberately dishonest. Perhaps I could make the argument that a locked car on a baking summer's day was the end of Jeremy Cunningham. That my mother was responsible for ending that life and birthing another: one who dreamed of choking. Where Jeremy ends and the Black Tongue begins is up to you. Or at least that's my excuse. We can debate the literary merits of this reasoning later. Email my agent.

And Andy and I both having our own sections? I don't know what to tell you there. Andy struck Jeremy. I'd say it was a mortal strike. Jeremy was burned and bloodied and was surely dying in the snow from his injuries when I got to him. And me? My lawyer tells me to tread carefully here. All I've told you is the truth: that when my brother died, I was sitting next to him. You can make up your own mind.

Katherine Millot is an anagram of *I Am Not The Killer*, by the way. Darius derives from a Persian king, Persia being where the suffocation by ash torture began. I didn't change that for the book though; it really was the moniker Jeremy gave himself. Too bad he didn't target a group of history professors; they would have solved it straightaway.

Juliette's phone dinged, loud enough to echo in the attic. Her laugh barked out of the hole I was standing below. Her face appeared above me. "Katherine's planning the next reunion," she said. She was on the family WhatsApp chat: I know, big steps. "Wants suggestions."

"Somewhere warm."

She laughed again and clunked off to toss around more boxes. I turned back to my bag, pulling out a crumpled, moldy jacket. It had still been damp when I'd shoved it in, hurrying to leave. The smell was foul. That decided it; I'd toss the whole bag. There was nothing in there I needed and I didn't have the stamina to sift through it. I checked the pockets just to be sure, and pulled out a folded piece of paper. Sofia's bingo card.

I looked at Michael's edit: *Ernest ~~ruins~~ **fixes** something.*

And I had. Despite everything that it represented, I still felt a warmth as I took out a pen and crossed through the square. It wasn't enough for a bingo, but it was pretty damn satisfying.

That was when I realized I hadn't been taking my own advice.

I took out my new phone (battery: 4%; I'm ashamed it was lower here than during a mountaintop snowstorm). I downloaded a magnifying app, which wasn't as good as a loupe, but I figured it would be enough.

I remembered Michael had taken a moment of thought before writing on the card. Or maybe he'd spent those few quick seconds, his contact lens case beside him (I knew he hadn't worn contacts!), fiddling with something else. Something small enough that my father had to use a needle to handle . . . but I supposed the tip of a pen would do. *Don't lose that*, he'd said, holding his thumb down firmly as he handed the bingo card back to me, as if pressing the ink in. *I'm trusting you*. He'd written some words, but he'd also added the full stop. I told you: in a mystery, there are clues in every word—hell, in every piece of punctuation . . .

My heart pounded in my throat with the sense of discovery. I scanned my phone camera (battery: 2%), magnifying app running, over Michael's added full stop. Photos. Sixteen of them, in a 4x4 grid.

The photographer was at the bottom of a sprawling driveway, looking up at a palatial estate, the rigid lines of a security fence imposed on the images. There is a sedan, trunk open, by the pillared entryway. The setting remains static through all sixteen photos, but there are two people in the frame, faces hidden, that move from image to image. In the fifth picture, the figures disappear, but the front door is a black hole: open. The figures return in the eighth picture, except they are carrying something—it looks like a sleeping bag. The figures are each holding an end. In the ninth, they are halfway to the car, and I could see what appeared to be long tendrils of hair hanging from one end of the bag. In the tenth, the sleeping bag is gone, and the car's trunk is closed. In the sixteenth photo, the car's position has changed. One of the figures is still on the porch, watching it leave. Finally, a face.

It might be disappointing that I can't give you the typical catharsis of the bad guys getting their full comeuppance, but my editor tells me we have to go to print and it's all still before the courts, so I don't really have the details. It will have to be enough to know that I zoomed in as close as I could on Edgar McAuley's face, revealed in the porchlight of his mansion, and that if his name is not redacted here, it's safe to assume he's gone to prison for a very long time.

Did Michael show you the photos?

Edgar McAuley had asked me that question twice. The second time he'd been insistent, I remembered. I'd thought he was annoyed, but I realized now that his tone was not impatience, but desperation. He wanted to know if I'd seen the photos, if I'd seen him in them. I remembered Siobhan's dismay at the body being lost and his calm words to her: *We can get divers.*

The McAuleys had been unwilling to pay half as much for their daughter's safe return as they were for her dead body and the photographs of her killer. Alan wasn't selling them closure, it was just good old-fashioned blackmail. He'd gone to Jeremy first, in the hope he'd be able to swindle money from the Williamses without having to put himself at as much risk as selling to the McAuleys. When he'd struck out there, he'd had to take the more dangerous path. He'd needed someone as a shield to go in between him and Edgar, but a Cunningham also gave his threat legitimacy, which was why he'd then approached Michael. And then Michael, when he'd been released from prison and had seen who was in the photos, had decided that the McAuleys owed him as well. What had he told me in the Drying Room? *It's right for them to pay.* Them.

A false kidnapping to cover up a murder. It was clever. Hire a well-known gang to put on the front, create motive in the fluffed ransom, and come out the other end a victim rather than a suspect. Just like Marcelo had told me, it was an old story in which I'd know all the beats: easy to understand and easier to accept. As everyone had at the time. Rebecca was already dead before the first demand was ever made.

I called the police. A detective said they'd come past that afternoon to pick up the evidence, and then my phone ran out of battery.

"Hey, Ern." Juliette's face appeared again. She held up a dusty bottle of wine. "This has either aged well or terribly. Wanna come up?"

I promised certain things wouldn't happen in this book, so I'd best end it here lest this chapter make me a liar.

I followed her up the ladder.

Ernest Cunningham's *10 Easy Steps to Write Crime Like You Lived in the 1930s* and *Golden Age to Your Golden Page: How to Write a Mystery* are available for $1.99 online.

ACKNOWLEDGMENTS

The tone of every good acknowledgments section should be: *thanks for putting up with me*. A *lot* of people have put up with me during the writing of this novel, and I am grateful for their passion, patience, and help at every stage.

Beverley Cousins, my publisher. Thank you for simultaneously letting me swing for the fences and patiently reeling me back in when my ambition outweighed my sensibility. Thank you for never being scared of an idea, for reading countless drafts that just weren't quite working, and for having faith in me to find my voice and the story I wanted to tell. I feel both proud and fortunate to be one of your authors—thank you.

Amanda Martin, my editor. Thank you for your sharp editorial eye, sympathetic edits, and astute problem solving. Editing a mystery novel is like building a house of cards: one piece tumbles and the whole thing comes down. Editors are the glue that keeps the tower upright. I'm sorry about the joke about editors in Chapter 27. I wrote the chapter number here and not a page number just in case you have PTSD from the page numbers. While we're on the topic, I'm also sorry about the page numbers.

Nerrilee Weir and Alice Richardson have done an incredible job of finding opportunities for this book to reach readers all around the world. I am in awe to think that I'm able to tell my story to so many people, and I am grateful for all the hard work, late nights/early mornings, and Zoom meetings. To Katherine Nintzel and the team at Mariner Books, thank you for the amazing support and for your faith that my rogue Australian humor would match American sensibilities. Ernest would be thrilled to be published by you, and I am too. Tavia Kowalchuk and Jessica Lyons in marketing and publicity, respectively, thank you for being such loud and enthusiastic voices for this book—any author would be lucky to have such champions of their work in their corner.

Pippa Masson, my agent, ably supported by Caitlan Cooper-Trent—thank you both for the encouragement and guidance, and for believing that I could get this book to the next level at every step. I couldn't do any of this without you in my corner. Life-changing would be an understatement for your help in guiding my career. Jerry Kalajian, thank you for your enthusiastic championing of screen rights. I'd also like to say that agents, being equal parts counselor and therapist, should really be eligible for Medicare rebates.

Rebecca McAuley generously donated to the RFS to aid in Australia's bushfire recovery in return for a character name—thank you.

Thank you to my parents, Peter and Judy, my siblings, James and Emily, and the Paz family, Gabriel, Elizabeth, and Adrian, for their support of all of my creative endeavors. James, sorry I keep killing the brother off. I swear I don't mean anything by it. Also, no one in my family has actually killed anyone. To my knowledge, anyway.

And to Aleesha Paz. I promised you long ago my third book would be dedicated to you. Funnily enough, without you I don't think I would have ever finished it. So this one's yours. Who am I kidding—they're all for you.

Thank you to all the authors who generously provided blurbs or social media support for my work. I won't list names, but I will say to readers: go out and read as much Aussie crime fiction as you can. It's the best in the world. I believe that in a hundred years we're going to look back and think we went through our own Golden Age, and then some smart-arse author will probably write some kind of piss-take about it. So get in on the ground floor is all I'm saying.

And lastly—thank *you* for reading. There are so many books out there and you chose mine, and that's truly special. I hope you had fun.